Claiming The

Mated To The Night: Book 3

Lindsey Devin

© 2023

Disclaimer

This is a work of fiction. Names, places, characters, and events are all fictitious for the reader's pleasure. Any similarities to real people, places, events, living or dead are all coincidental.

This book contains sexually explicit content that is intended for ADULTS ONLY (+18).

Contents

Chapter 1 - Bryn

Prisoners shouted to be let free as the four of us marched up to the holding cell that was supposed to house Troy Redwolf.

The man had spent so much of his time making me miserable. Less than a month before, he had been the alpha of the Kings. One of his first acts as alpha had been kidnapping and hurting Tavi and me. Mere minutes ago, we'd figured out that he might be behind the feral wolf attack that had devastated the Kings Pack. *My* pack.

Night—though he was still recovering from the injuries he'd sustained from the silver bullet shot by Evan, *the wolf I'd killed*—led the way to Troy's cell. He grabbed the door handle and yanked it open.

A soft gasp slipped past Tavi's lips.

"Fuck," I muttered under my breath.

The cell was empty, and the only indication that it had been used was Troy's lingering stench. I clenched my fists at my sides, and my wolf began to snarl inside me.

"The attack must have been a distraction," Dom said, his voice little more than a growl.

"He sacrificed so many lives just so he could escape." Tavi's voice was a whisper but was just as angry and alarmed as Dom's. I couldn't say anything more.

Of course I was afraid. Of course I was shocked. Of course I was angry. But a fourth emotion coursed just as powerfully through my body: guilt. I was the alpha of the Kings, and yet I'd allowed the greatest threat to them escape while under my watch. I should have seen this coming. I should have done more. I had failed my people.

As these emotions boiled inside me, four pairs of footsteps came rushing toward us down the path. These men were meant to be guarding the cells. The moment they neared, Dom grabbed one of them by the collar and lifted him off the ground.

"You," he growled, his eyes glowing like amber in the dark. "*You* let this happen."

"Wh-what? I—" The guard sent a baffled look from Dom to me before finally looking at the open cell. His eyes widened, and the color seeped out of his face. "Wait, hold on…"

Night took a step forward, his eyes blazing green. The guards didn't know that Night was still recovering from the silver bullet and couldn't shift, but it didn't matter.

All they knew was that he was angry and could make them pay for it.

I moved between Dom and Night, roiling emotions taking hold of me. "Why weren't you four at your post?" I demanded. "Why didn't you tell us Troy disappeared?"

The guard began to babble. He couldn't seem to form a coherent sentence with four enraged wolves staring at him, so one of the other guards stepped forward, his hands clasped tightly in front of his chest.

"Please, Alpha," he said. "We didn't know! When the attack started, we left our posts to help the pack." Behind him, the other guards nodded emphatically. "No one has ever broken out of the cells before. The walls are so thick, escape is supposed to be impossible! We were trying to make sure everyone was safe and didn't even think to check on the prisoners."

Dom dropped the guard to his feet. He stumbled back against the wall. Fear seeped from the man's pores, but that didn't mean the guards weren't involved in Troy's escape. I wanted to believe their intentions had been good, if a bit misguided and shortsighted. But they would need to be questioned.

"How many prisoners are here?" Night demanded.

"We usually only have a handful," the guard responded. "The cells are only supposed to be used when an outsider trespasses onto our territory. But with Troy, that number increased." He gestured around us to the rock walls and torches. "This area is reserved for the most dangerous wolves. The cells are supposed to be impossible to break out of, and he wouldn't be able to shift while inside."

I turned away from them. This conversation was getting us nowhere. "We need to start looking for Troy." I looked at Tavi. "We need to send out a search party and drag him back here."

"Right," she said.

"I'll put a party together," Night said in a tight voice. He was so angry, his fists shook at his sides. I couldn't tell if his anger was directed at our situation or if he had also realized it was my fault Troy had escaped.

We left the holding facility with the guards in tow. Clear azure skies greeted us. It seemed wrong for the sun to shine so brightly on the day we discovered Troy missing.

The elders, the council, and a few of the Kings' top fighters and trackers had left the meeting room. It seemed they were on their way to meet with us, which was good timing. Night must have called his wolves because he and Dom separated from Tavi and me to speak to them. They were probably getting the search party together. While they took care of that, Tavi and I informed the elders and the others of the situation.

"We were right," I said. "Troy is gone."

A ripple of shock passed through them. Even Dana, the only female council member, was surprised enough to hold back her snide comments.

"Those four guards were supposed to be watching the holding facility but weren't at their posts. I want them questioned."

Theodore, one of the Kings' top fighting wolves, nodded. Night had kept his son safe during the ferals' attack, and that was enough to make him loyal to us. "I can make sure that happens, Alpha Hunter."

I stopped myself from shifting awkwardly on my feet. It still felt so strange to hear the word "Alpha" before my last name. I doubted I would ever get used to it, especially when I would only be alpha for a few more weeks.

"Thank you, Theodore. I don't want them harmed until we know for sure whether they were involved in Troy's escape."

He nodded again. "I understand."

As he and his men took the guards to be questioned, I addressed those who remained. "Finding Troy must be our priority, and we need to find more information on the ferals and why they're working for him. Some of you mentioned that there are banished wolves who might not be as insane as a typical feral. Do we have any records of those wolves? Any records of the wolves that have been banished from our pack?"

"Of course we keep records of that," Elder Queene said, his wavy dark hair lifting in the breeze. "But we have no idea if they became feral. After all, they might have been accepted into another pack after banishment." His voice was a low monotone, his expression grave.

"Well, I'm willing to bet that at least *some* of them were within the feral pack," I said, crossing my arms. "Why else would they have helped Troy escape?" Harlon and Samson were both deeply loyal to Troy. They had arranged for the ferals to do what they wanted, and I was positive they were working under Troy's orders.

Elder Queene inclined his head, accepting my point.

"If we track down those who've been banished, we might be able to find leverage to get them on our side. If we do that, they might tell us more about what Troy's planning. The sooner we do that, the sooner we'll be able to find Troy."

"We will look for them, Alpha Hunter."

Despite those words, the elders' lingering looks told me they still doubted doing so would do any good. I could hardly blame them. So far, my ruling had only resulted in an attack on the pack and Troy's escape. According to the guards, Troy was the first escapee in the pack's history. I was sure that looked great on my record.

"It wasn't your fault, Bryn," Tavi said as we left to join Night and Dom. "You couldn't have known Troy would escape."

I sighed. Logic told me she was right, but that didn't make this situation easier to swallow. Troy wasn't even here, and he was still making my life as difficult as possible. I tried to ignore the sting of that as we caught up with Night.

"...want Troy found as soon as fucking possible," he was saying. To my surprise, there were a few Kings' men gathered along with Night's men. It seemed his actions during the battle had really earned their respect.

"Now get moving, all of you," Night finished, and the search party immediately dispersed, Dom included.

Night turned to me. There was still a lot of stiffness in his posture, and I knew it wasn't only from the pain he had to be feeling. "Bryn, mind if we talk?" he asked.

"I don't mind."

"I'll take a walk around the compound and note the buildings with the worst damage," Tavi said. "Let me know if you need me." She patted my arm before leaving. The old Tavi would have hugged me, but she hadn't been the same since we had been rescued from Troy.

"See you later," I said. As Tavi left, I looked at Night. "Lead the way."

The alpha cabin wasn't a far walk from where we stood. I wanted to grab a notepad before we assessed the damage the feral attack had done to the pack. To be honest, I would have loved to head up to our bedroom to talk, but that wasn't an option. I felt exhausted, but there was still so much to do.

Night took a deep breath, and I knew I was in for a lecture.

"I understand that you didn't want to kill Troy before," he began, "but now it's time for you to reevaluate the situation."

I held back a wince. I should have known Night wanted to talk about this. "I know Troy has been the bane of our existence from the beginning, but—"

"That right there," he cut in. "There shouldn't be a 'but' after that. Not only has Troy been fucking with us all this time, he's also become a threat to the Kings and the Wargs—and probably the Idaho panhandle, with the ferals on his side." He shook his head. "Leaving him to rot in his cell was a risk to morale, but I let it go because I understood and respected what you were trying to accomplish. But now he's on the loose and has an army of unhinged wolves on his side. He's not just a threat to morale but to the lives of every wolf we know. It's not a search party we need; it's a fucking hunting party. And I'm going to tell them to kill on sight."

I was prepared to take Night's lecture because I thought I deserved it, but he had gone too far. He was not only telling me he no longer respected my goals for my pack, but he was also about to exert his will over mine. I thought we were past this. I thought he respected me as an alpha and his equal, but his words had proven me wrong.

What he didn't seem to get was that the Kings were *my* pack, not his. The Kings were under my rule until the alpha ceremony. Though I wouldn't be in charge for long, I didn't want to be the kind of alpha who killed other wolves. I would never be as prepared for bloodshed as Night was. I had already killed Evan, and I didn't want to add Troy's blood to my conscience. I just couldn't do it. It wasn't the kind of environment I wanted to foster as alpha.

But with all that said, there wasn't an alpha around who would let someone else undermine his orders. My wolf bristled at the thought. What Night was saying would piss off anyone in my position. *He* wouldn't stand for another wolf telling him that they were going to ignore his orders and do what they wanted. So, why did he think that was okay to do with me?

"We don't need to kill Troy," I said slowly, trying to get control of my emotions so I didn't bite my mate's head off. "We just—"

"What are you going to do when we find him? We can't leave him in a cell. He just proved he can get out."

My temper flared. Night had no idea how difficult it was for me to keep myself in check. "No. Troy proved he can escape *if* he takes the entire pack by surprise. When we find him, he won't have that same chance. And even if he tries to pull that shit again, I'll be ready for him. My pack will be ready for him."

Night continued to frown. "Bryn, I know you want to avoid as much bloodshed as possible, and I know you don't want to rule with violence. Your compassion is one of the many things I admire about you. But sometimes, if a wolf is too dangerous and a threat to the whole pack, you have to kill them because leaving them alive puts everyone at risk."

I shook my head. "You say you understand, but if you send a hunting party after Troy, you will *show* me you don't. Gregor was a violent alpha who ruled over the Kings with an iron fist; then they had it even worse with Troy. I need to prove to the pack that there is an alternative. I want to be the start of something good here." *I want to create the kind of pack I wished I had growing up.*

"Bryn." Night's hard expression and stiff tone softened as he said my name. He reached for my face and used his finger to wipe away a tear that slipped down my cheek. "Mate…"

I turned away from him and angrily swiped at the next tears that escaped. I hadn't even noticed them building up. Why were the tears coming so quickly when I wanted to show him I was a strong alpha with convictions?

"This conversation isn't over," I said. "I don't need you to pity me just because I got a little emotional."

"I'm not pitying you, Bryn, I just…" He let out a tight sigh and pushed his hands through his thick black hair. "You're right that you are the alpha now, but there's no telling who will be the next alpha a month from now. I hope it's me—and I will do everything I can to make sure it is me—but if I fail, we don't know who the next alpha will be. What if it's someone who's on Troy's side? That person will ruin everything we've fought for." He put his hands gently on my shoulders, and despite my frustrations, I couldn't help but notice how warm they were. "We have the chance to eliminate a future threat, and we need to take it."

I hated that Night was making some good points. We didn't know who the next alpha would be, and we couldn't bank on it being Night. He couldn't even shift at the moment. But that didn't change my mind. I was making good points, too, whether he wanted to acknowledge them or not.

"Don't forget, Night," I said, raising my chin to meet his gaze, "I will be on the council as den mother even when I'm not the alpha. I will have some influence." I moved away from his touch and crossed my arms. "All of this arguing won't matter if we don't find Troy. When we have him, we'll reevaluate what to do with him, okay?"

"Okay." But it was obvious that Night was reluctant to leave things like this.

"We should get back out there to evaluate the damage Troy's attack has done," I said in a monotone.

"Yeah. Let's do that."

As we moved to leave, I saw Night wince.

"Wait a second." I jogged into the kitchen to find the closest first aid kit, grabbing a bottle of painkillers and shaking a few into my hand. After filling a glass with water, I went back to my mate.

Crossing my arms, I looked away as Night swallowed the pills.

"Thanks," he murmured.

"Mmhm." I grabbed the notepad and a pen, and we headed back into the sunlight.

It hurt to know we weren't on the same page about something so important, but I couldn't see a way to compromise. It wasn't that I didn't hate Troy; I *loathed* him. If we found out his army of ferals had killed him, or he'd fallen into a ravine and died, I would laugh before shedding a single tear. I wished for nothing but the worst to happen to him for all he had done to me and the people I cared about. That went for Samson, Harlon, and anyone else who had helped him commit all that evil—which was why it was so important that I didn't kill him.

Before I realized I was a shifter, the Kings had tormented me because of the Redwolfs' anti-human stance. The Kings had thought of me as prey back then, and many of them probably thought of me as a pushover even now. It would be *so simple* to kill Troy and show them my authority. Doing that might earn me their respect, but would it get me their loyalty? Would they view me as someone who fostered the kind of pack they could feel safe in? No. Killing Troy would show the pack I was no different from the Redwolfs. Getting rid of him was the easy way forward, and it would go against everything I'd worked for.

Why couldn't Night see that?

Chapter 2 - Night

By the time Bryn and I finished assessing the areas that had suffered the most damage after the feral attack, the painkillers finally started to kick in. Every inch of my body had pulsed with aches; now the pain was just a numb memory. But my mind still raced with worry, frustration, and impatience.

Our disagreement about what to do if—*when*—we found Troy hadn't helped with things. Bryn's decision to keep him alive would never make sense to me. I would have thought that killing him would be a no-brainer after everything he had done to her. I'd heard what she had to say and tried to understand what she wanted for the future of the Kings, but I just didn't get it. It irked me that we couldn't see eye to eye about this, considering how important it was, but Bryn was stubborn and determined. I couldn't just ask her to go along with what I wanted to do.

I spotted Dom talking with a smaller group of Kings. After sending out the search party, I had him patrol the territory on his own. Given the unusually messy state of his blond hair, he must have just gotten back.

"I'm going to catch up with Dom," I said to Bryn.

"That's fine." She didn't look at me, keeping her eyes on her list of facilities that had suffered the worst damage. "I'm going to find Tavi and discuss the damage. Maybe we'll reconnect later."

I watched her for a bit longer, but she didn't return my gaze. My chest tightened when I remembered the tears swimming in her eyes during our argument and the moment she'd handed me the painkillers. Bryn didn't use her emotions as a weapon when she was distressed. And even though she was angry with me, she still worried about me. Still cared.

That caring side of her persevered even when she felt low—it was part of what made her so amazing. As frustrated as I was with her, I still loved her deeply, which made this situation suck even more.

My wolf whined as I turned away from her. He didn't like that we were on opposite sides of the Troy issue any more than I did. I wasn't planning on changing my mind about Redwolf, though. I planned on living long enough to see that line die out, but if Bryn had her way, that wouldn't happen as quickly as I wanted.

Dom nodded at me as I approached, but his attention was trained on the men in front of him. They were Kings, and from their quick, decisive gestures, it was obvious to me that they were either pissed, stressed out, or some combination of the two. Those conditions didn't bode well for wolf shifters, but at least they were still in their human forms, which made them easier to reason with.

"I'm telling you that we're handling this," Dom said to the group. "We've got Wargs and Kings working for this."

"What can *we* do?" one of the Kings demanded, stepping toward Dom.

"Hold on," I said, moving between the two. "What's going on?"

"We heard that Troy escaped," the same man responded. He had a decade on Dom and me, and he, like the men behind him, had the bulky physique of a fighter. "We heard he's the reason we were attacked. That true?"

I shared a look with Dom. "*Might as well tell them,*" his voice entered my mind. "*If there are already rumors, it won't be long before the entire pack finds out who was behind the attack.*"

Good point. "From what we've discovered, yes. Troy sent the ferals to attack so he could escape."

The King turned his head and spat on the ground. "Fuck that. Fuck *him.* I've gathered up some men, and we're going to hunt him down."

I arched a brow. "On whose authority?"

He raised his chin and met my gaze. "Our own."

I narrowed my eyes, and after a few moments, the pressure of staring down an alpha got to him. He looked away. These men were serious about going out there and finding Troy. I really, really couldn't blame them, but we couldn't afford to have rogue groups of wolves running through the forest, covering up tracks and scents with their footsteps.

"We've already got people on that," I said, looking from him to the other wolves behind him. "I know you're all concerned, but your alpha is handling it." *Maybe not the way I would want her to, but...*

"No." He shook his head. "I can't just sit around waiting for that. I need to do something. My mate, my pups..." His eyes flashed as he thought of his family. "They need to know I'm out here helping and making sure this doesn't happen to us again."

"What's your name?" I asked.

"Donald."

"Donald. Are you and everyone else fighters? Hunters?"

He puffed up his chest. "We're fighters."

"Yeah, I figured as much. You all look like you could take Troy down easily." A bit of flattery went a long way to calm wolves, and I hoped it would work here. "But Donald, I can't let you do what you want. There's something else you could be doing, something more effective than going blind into the forest."

He stared at me, waiting.

"I want you and your men to gather every able-bodied wolf you can find to stand at the border. If any of you see a feral wolf, catch it before it reaches the compound."

"You want us to just stand around and wait for something to happen?"

"No, I want you to *protect* your pack. That's what you all really want to do, right? You want to make it so that your families can sleep easily?"

The Kings glanced at each other. They had to concede my point.

"What better way to ease the worst of their fears than to watch over the territory?" I asked. "Your pack needs you and your men out there doing that."

They were coming around, but Donald still looked uncertain. "What about Troy?"

"It's like Dom said. We're on it. We'll find him."

He looked behind him to his men, and they all nodded reluctantly. "Alright. We'll watch the borders."

I nodded. "Do it in shifts. Everyone at the border needs to be as alert and aware as possible."

He nodded before he and the wolves with him went to do as I said.

I released a long sigh and turned to Dom.

"I didn't think you'd be able to calm him down," he said. "A couple of times while speaking to him, I thought he might shift and make a mad dash into the forest."

"Luckily, we avoided that." I ran my hands through my hair. "But I can't say I don't get where he's coming from."

"Yeah, I know exactly how he feels." Telepathically, he added, *"Are you sure a search party is what we want? I think everyone would feel better if they were ordered to kill Troy on sight."*

I appreciated my beta's discretion. *"Believe me, there's nothing I'd like more than to send hunters out there, but Bryn doesn't want to order his death."*

Dom frowned. *"She just wants to put him back in a cell?"*

"That's right."

"She won't be alpha forever. When her term ends, Troy will either be killed by the next alpha or let out."

I sighed, the irritation from my argument with Bryn returning. *"That's what I tried to tell her, but she won't budge. She reminded me that she'll still be on the council as den mother, but we don't know how influential that position will be."*

Dom scratched the stubble on his chin. He hadn't had the chance to shave with all the chaos going on. Come to think of it, neither had I. There was nothing I would have loved more than taking a dip in the hot springs to release some of the tension between my shoulders.

"I guess we'll just have to find him and see what happens."

"If we're lucky, he'll try to fight one of our men and end up being killed. I think even Bryn would be okay with that." Out loud, I said, "For now, let's help get everything organized for repairs. While you're doing that, I'll head back to Warg territory to make sure everything is protected in case of a feral attack."

Dom eyed me, one eyebrow raised. "Night, did you forget that you can't shift? How are you going to get to our compound?"

"Shit." Those painkillers had made me forget I was still recovering. I needed to shift, but according to Dr. Stan, I wouldn't be able to do that for another few days at most. I was itching to see my pack, but that wouldn't be possible for a little longer. "I guess there's no other option. I'll have to send you."

Dom gave my shoulder a sympathetic pat. "I'll be back as soon as possible."

"I know you will." Despite my bad mood, I felt some comfort knowing my beta was on top of things. "I want a detailed report of everything."

"Of course." He grinned. "When have I ever let you down?"

Five days after Troy's escape, which marked twelve days into Bryn's rule as alpha, I was washing the dishes from the rabbit stew I'd made for dinner. I heard Bryn walking around deeper in the house. Since our argument, we hadn't really connected with each other.

While I was recovering, Bryn, Tavi, and I corralled the Kings and put together a solid organizational plan for rebuilding. It would be best to start from the perimeter and work our way in, prioritizing the homes and places necessary for the pack to function, like the wood storage and emergency rations buildings.

While the Kings set to work restoring their pack to tip-top shape, Bryn and I shied away from the Redwolf issue. And as the days passed, and the search party had few updates for us on Troy's location, it seemed like things would never get better between us. This was the first huge fight we'd had since the claiming ceremony, and we'd both walked away with wounds.

I was still licking mine, and given the sad shift of Bryn's mouth whenever we made eye contact, she wasn't doing any better. It was tough feeling so distant from my soulmate, but what made it even tougher was being unable to shift. Running had always been the best way for me to let off some steam, but when I tried to push myself even a little, the pain in my side flared up so badly, it left me gasping and sweating on the floor.

That was earlier on in my recovery. Now the pain in my side had faded from searing to a dull throbbing. Another day or so, and I'd be back to form. I just hoped Dr. Stan agreed.

A knock came from the front door, and I set down the pot I was scrubbing. I wiped my hands on a kitchen towel and answered the door.

Dom was standing there. "Hey, Night," he said with a smile.

I smiled back, relieved to see him. "Dom. Come on in."

We returned to the kitchen, and I grabbed us a couple of beers. I sat on the counter and twisted off the tops. If Bryn saw me, she would've made me get off, but she was doing something else—I didn't even know what. That bothered me more than I wanted to let on.

"How are you doing, Night?" Dom asked. "You're looking a little constipated."

"If you value your life, you'll shut the hell up, Dom."

I knew he was tempted to make some joking retort, but fortunately for *both* of us, he kept it to himself.

"Status report?" I asked.

"Our pack is healthy and happy. Everyone's working as hard as they normally do, though morale's a bit low because it's been a while since they've seen you."

Guilt gnawed at me, even though I'd expected that update. I was still recovering, but I felt like I was neglecting my pack. "What about ferals? Or Troy?"

"As far as we could tell, there has been no increase in feral activity around our territory. And no signs of Troy lurking anywhere near our borders. Things have been normal."

"That's a relief," I said. At least I didn't have to worry about the ferals and Troy on top of everything else on my plate. "Anything else to report?"

"Yes, actually. It's about the council."

My brows shot up. "Do they want to meet with me?"

"Yes, they do, and it sounds pretty serious," he replied. After a moment of hesitation, he reluctantly added, "They didn't seem very happy."

I was glad to know Troy was leaving my pack alone, but hearing about the council set me on edge again. I wanted to visit my pack ASAP to assure myself that things were okay, but I would much rather avoid seeing the council. We were on good terms, but they were more traditional than I cared to be.

"By the way, how's Bryn?" Dom asked.

I hesitated. "She's…good. She's…you know, the same."

"Uh-huh." He crossed his arms. "I guess you two haven't made up yet."

I sighed and took a long swig of my beer. "No."

"Well, you should try to make up with her before you head back to our territory. We both know you'll miss her like crazy if you don't."

"Yeah, yeah, I know. It's tough to talk to her when we're like this. When we do talk, I feel like I'm bothering her or somehow making things harder on her."

He gave a sympathetic nod. "Well, you are terrible with your words. When's the last time you two had sex?"

I sent him a steely glare. "And how is that your business?"

He snorted. "I'm asking because maybe you're better in bed than you are at having a difficult conversation with your mate."

My eyebrows twitched with annoyance. "Perhaps I'll take your suggestion into consideration. Is that all?"

He smirked at me. "Yeah. For now."

"Good, then get to your cabin. I'm sure you'd like to get some rest after making the trip."

He snickered as I walked him out. I shut the door, annoyance still thrumming through my veins.

For some reason, Dom's comment had gotten under my skin. It was still on my mind the next day when I went to the cabin where Dr. Stan was staying with the other Wargs.

The cabin was pretty empty because I'd sent some Wargs out as part of the search party. When Doc saw me, he got me a beer and had me stand still while he unwrapped my bandages.

"Hmm…looks like the wound has healed nicely," he said. "It'll scar, of course, but I doubt you care much about that, alpha."

He was right; scars meant nothing to me, but when I examined the wound in the mirror he gave me, I couldn't help staring at it. I'd never been shot with a silver bullet before, and the roundish scar looked different from the old slashing wounds from teeth and claws that covered most of my body.

The scar would serve as a reminder of Evan's betrayal. It still hurt that he had been on Troy's side the entire time, but soon, the scar he had left me would fade like the other scars. The pain of losing someone who had once been so close to me would also fade, and it would become yet another fucked-up memory.

"Alright," Doc said, moving away from me to grab the tea he'd left steaming near the sink. "You should be well enough to shift now, Alpha Night, but—"

"Great." I could already feel the blood pumping in my veins. The urge to get out there and run was pushing me to leave almost as quickly as I'd arrived. My wolf hovered just beneath the surface, and it was getting more difficult to hold him back now that we knew we could shift.

"—but don't push yourself too hard, okay?" Doc finished. "We don't want that wound opening up again."

"Don't worry, I'll take it easy, Doc," I said, almost at the door. "You ought to think about heading back to the Warg compound soon."

He nodded. "Believe me, I know. I'm planning to head back in a few days. Would you mind letting the infirmary know?"

"I'll do that."

It was a short run back to the alpha cabin, which wasn't near enough time for me to get everything out, but it was a start. I headed inside and heard Bryn rummaging around on the west side of the cabin. I followed the sound to the study, where she was rifling through drawers.

"What are you doing?" I asked.

She jumped with a little squeak and turned around. "Night, don't scare me like that."

"Sorry." Technically, we were still fighting, but I couldn't stop the smile forming on my face as I walked farther into the study. The bookshelves, desks, and tables were all made of matching cherry-stained pine.

"I wanted to make sure there weren't any documents hidden in here," she said. "I don't think Troy or his father would keep them in their study, but you never know."

"Oh."

"Yeah."

Silence passed between us, and that silence leaned more toward awkward than I would've liked. Dom's words came back to me yet again. I didn't want to be the kind of man who wasn't willing to put in the emotional work a relationship needed. Just because Bryn and I were soulmates didn't mean the hard work of being together ended. I needed to try to bridge that gap.

"I'm heading back to Warg territory tonight," I finally said. "Dom is going to stay behind, and he'll be around to help you with whatever you need. I wanted to tell you before I left."

"Oh." She lowered her hand and glanced away. "Dr. Stan said you were healed enough to go?"

I nodded.

"Oh," she said again. "Well, have a safe trip."

"Thank you." The awkwardness returned, but I wouldn't let it linger this time. "Bryn, can we just…talk about this? I don't want to leave you with *this* hanging between us."

She crossed her arms, still not looking at me. "I don't think we'll ever see eye to eye on this particular topic, Night. You want to kill Troy; I want him back in prison. I don't see how we can compromise."

I sighed.

"But…" she said, glancing at me through her long lashes. "I think we can at least call a truce for now. I don't want you to be thinking about our argument while you're checking on the Wargs."

My heart beat hard with love for her. I appreciated her kindness and understanding nature. She always thought about others before herself, even when she was irritated with me.

"If this is a truce," I said, walking closer to her and offering my hand, "maybe we could shake on it?"

Her eyes fixed on my hand before traveling slowly up my arm to my face. An easy smile spread across her face. "You're going to be gone a few days, aren't you?" She ran her hand over mine up to my chest, her fingers splaying across my bare skin. "Maybe your hand isn't the part of your body I want right now."

A slow smile found its way to my face as she pulled me closer. I covered her mouth with mine, and she moaned, grinding against me. My arms started to wrap around her, but she turned her pert ass to me instead and pushed back against my growing erection.

She looked at me over her shoulder as she leaned forward a bit, pressing harder against me. "The hardest part about fighting with you is that we don't get to make love," she told me, swaying her hips from side to side. "It would be such a shame if I didn't see you off."

"Oh, Bryn." I smoothed my hands over her hips. "I had no idea my mate was so eager."

"Maybe next time you'll remember." Smiling, she reached between her legs and pulled her panties down. "I'm waiting, Night."

Fuck, I didn't need another invitation. My pants joined Bryn's panties on the floor, and I pushed her skirt up to her lower back. That perfect alabaster ass was at the perfect height for my cock. I rubbed my length against her warm slit, and she inched her legs slightly further apart.

Steadying myself with one hand on her hip and the other holding her dress at her back, I entered her as deep as I could go. I felt the shivers of her pleasure against my thighs as I leaned over her.

"Yes," she breathed as she braced herself on the table. "Night, my love…"

I hissed and fucked her hard, her heavy breaths and our skin slapping together the only sounds in the room. Her occasional moans set my blood on fire and sent goosebumps across my skin. Bryn was warm and soft inside, and I trembled every time she clenched around me. I smoothed my hand higher up her back, exposing more of her skin.

Releasing my grip on her hip, I slid my hand to her side and over her breasts. Her nipples were hard against my palm, and she whimpered when I squeezed them. She started moving against me, matching my every thrust. I bit my lip and caressed her stomach down to her pussy. Slick wetness coated my fingers as I found that coveted, sensitive bud.

Bryn gasped, throwing her head back, her hair falling over her back and across my arms, feather-light and smelling of flowers and earth. *Mine. Mine. Mine.* The scent and feel of her overwhelmed me. She was everywhere, and I was drunk with it.

"Night, I'm gonna—" she cut herself off with another gasp, goosebumps rising along her ass, down the back of her legs, and up her back.

"Yes," I groaned back, upping my pace slightly.

We came at the same time. Our juices mixed, dripping to the floor. Bryn hummed with satisfaction, swaying her hips in a slow, sensual figure-eight against me.

"I love you," I told her as I kissed her back, tasting the salt of her skin.

"I love you, too," she said. "Travel safely, okay?"

"Always." And I kissed her back again.

Chapter 3 - Bryn

I smiled as I walked out of our bedroom. I'd woken alone, but my body was still deliciously sore from the previous night. On his way out, Night had kissed me goodbye, and I could almost taste him on my mouth.

I headed to the alpha's office with the key to the office study. I wasn't looking forward to going through all the files and records the Redwolfs had left behind, but at least the memory of Night's touch would see me through it.

When I reached the door to the office, I slid the key into the lock. It clicked open, and the door creaked as I pushed it. The office was a mess. Papers were piled haphazardly into piles of varying sizes; documents were spread out across the floor as if someone had been rummaging through them before being interrupted. At a glance, it looked like these papers held the Kings' census information and notices of those who had died or gone missing over the past decade.

As I picked up the papers and collected them into a neat stack, I wondered why Troy would be interested in this information. What was he planning on doing with population records? Maybe once I had a chance to really look at them, I'd find an answer to that question. But first, I needed to do some organizing. There were reams of paper collected in seemingly random piles. My stomach churned just looking at the mess. Having another person around to help me with this chore would make this so much easier. I could always rope Tavi into helping me.

"*Um…hello?*"

I jumped, almost dropping the small stack of papers. A sense of something *else* lingered at the edge of my mind, another presence, a sense of magic. With that feeling came a voice, but it wasn't mine, and it wasn't my wolf's. It sounded a bit like…

"*Tavi?*" I asked. "*Is that you?*"

"*Bryn!*" Tavi responded. "*Yes, it's me. I felt…another person in my mind, and I thought I was going crazy. I had no idea that was you.*"

"*But how are we…how is this happening?*"

"*It's part of our bond!*" She had so much excitement in her voice that she almost sounded like the old bubbly Tavi from before Troy had kidnapped her. "*Alphas and betas can communicate like this, but I didn't think* we *would be able to do this because this was supposed to be temporary.*"

"*This is amazing!*" I had tingles. Despite the setback of Troy's escape, the fact that I had an alpha connection to

Tavi made me feel like it hadn't been a series of misunderstandings that had led to me being alpha. *"I was just thinking I could use your help."*

"You needing me must have formed our connection. What can I do to help you?"

"I finally got into the alpha's office, but it's a mess. I could really use some help organizing everything."

"I can be there in a few minutes. See you soon."

I was already downstairs when Tavi arrived. She wore a large gray hoodie and jeans, and her long black hair was tied back in a messy ponytail. When I hugged her, she stiffened but warmed up to the hug after a second and patted my back.

"I guess Night already headed back home?"

"That's right." I led her upstairs to the office. "He left this morning. He's probably about halfway there by now."

"It's not like him to leave us unsupervised," she joked.

I laughed. "Well, Dom's still around."

"He didn't go with Night?"

At her surprised, somewhat squeaky tone, I glanced over my shoulder at her. "Yeah. He's probably overseeing the rebuilding."

Her cheeks reddened. "Oh. Okay."

"Tavi, is something going on between you and Dom?"

"What? N-no." She shook her head vehemently. "There's nothing at all.".

"You seem a little…flustered?"

"No. I'm just surprised he didn't go with Night, is all." She forced a laugh. "Anyway, aren't we supposed to be organizing things instead of gossiping?"

I enjoyed teasing Tavi a bit, but I couldn't push it too far. The excitement she'd shown at our alpha/beta bond and the fact that she wasn't looking for a place to hide at the mention of Dom's name showed me she had made real progress from when she was more reclusive.

When we stepped into the office, Tavi let out a gasp. "Wow. You weren't kidding."

"Yeah. I wanted to go through the accounts, but at this rate, I'll be lucky if we can finish organizing before the end of the day."

"Well, I don't know about that. Let's just see what we can do now."

"Sure."

The most intimidating mountain of paperwork was on the birchwood desk. Corners of paper stuck out at random points of the messy stack. If we weren't careful, we'd pluck out one of the pages holding the pile in place.

Tavi and I took each side of the mass and carefully dismantled it. Though I hadn't set out to look through the papers until they were more orderly, I couldn't help but glance at them as we collected them.

There were a lot of overdue bills, requests for repairs, complaints about various goings-on around the pack. Unsurprisingly, it looked like Troy hadn't taken his responsibilities as alpha very seriously. Very little, if anything, had been handled as far back as a few months ago when Gregor showed signs of being sick. It was as if Troy had never intended to do a good job as alpha. His methods of dealing with his pack were deplorable, but some of these requests were for things the pack needed, like a construction request for a new shop at the market.

My stomach lurched. I pressed a hand to my mouth and closed my eyes. A wave of nausea hit me like a brick.

Tavi glanced at me when I dropped a sheaf of papers. "Hey, are you okay, Bryn?"

"I don't know…I think so? My stomach hasn't been agreeing with me the past few mornings."

"You look a little pale." She came over to me and pressed the back of her hand against my forehead. "You don't feel feverish. Something you ate, maybe?"

"That's what I thought at first, but it's been pretty consistent since Troy escaped. I've also been getting these headaches." I touched my temples—the pain had lessened, but I felt the lingering ache as I talked about it.

"It could be stress," she said.

"Stress?"

"Yeah. You say you've started feeling this way since Troy escaped, right? *Everyone's* been on edge—and I'm including myself in that. If you're so stressed that you're experiencing physical symptoms, I think you should take a break."

I frowned. "I don't know…I can't afford to take one with all this overdue paperwork."

She quirked a brow. "You're talking to your beta right now. It's my job to keep you as healthy as possible."

I smiled even as my stomach continued to churn. "That's true, but how can I leave all of this behind?"

"Why don't you leave the organizing to me and head to your mom's? It's been a while since you've seen her, hasn't it?"

I tried not to wince at the reminder. I'd been so busy that I hadn't visited Mom in days. Going to see her would be nice. It had been a while since we had talked, and she might have tea or some other remedy to take care of my nausea. If nothing else, a bit of fresh air would probably help.

"Okay," I said. "I'll leave the organizing to you."

"Great." She smiled, then added telepathically, *"And I'll reach out if I need anything, okay?"*

I laughed. Being able to talk to each other at any time would take some getting used to, but I was glad for it. Having Tavi in my mind wasn't unpleasant at all. In fact, it was as comforting as having my wolf.

"Sounds good. We'll catch up later."

The walk to my mother's cabin took about fifteen minutes. The morning air was clear and fresh, and the sky a bright azure. As I walked through the compound, nobody jeered at me or sent me strange looks as they had after I beat Troy in the alpha ceremony. It seemed to finally sink in that I was their alpha. *You'd think nearly killing Troy right in front of them would have been enough. At least they're giving me some space now.*

One familiar face stood out to me from a group of male wolves near one of the rebuilding sites. He looked around my age, with short, wavy auburn hair. He was very muscular, maybe even bigger than Night or Dom, and had sky-blue eyes tinged with silver when the light hit them. He didn't look like the type who would sell wares at the market; with that kind of physique, he was probably a fighter.

His name came to me when he met my gaze. Lance. I'd seen him around the compound when I was a teenager. I'd always kept my distance from him because he was close to Troy. He smiled at me, and I looked away. He had never participated in the bullying Troy and his goons had put me through, but that didn't mean he wasn't just as mean as them.

I jogged up the steps to Mom's front door and knocked. "It's me," I called.

"You know you don't have to knock, baby," she called back. "Come in!"

I laughed and pushed open the door. The moment I did, I smelled mint, chamomile, and rosemary. Mom was already making tea.

"That smells great," I said. "Could I have some?"

"Of course, baby." Her eyes twinkled as she gestured for me to sit. "Sit, sit. I'll make you a cup."

I sat at the table, and she filled two mugs with hot water and tea leaves before handing one to me. "I had a feeling you would come and see me today," she said as she sat across from me.

"I'm sorry I haven't come by to see you. Things have been—"

"Hectic, I know." She nodded. "Bryn, anyone with eyes can see how hard you're working. You don't have to apologize to me for taking care of business."

"I know, but still…I've missed you."

She patted my hand, her fingers warm from handling the hot cups. "I've missed you, too, love. So, let's catch up a little before you get back to work."

I sipped the tea and found it warm, comforting, and refreshing. I loved Violet's teas, but there was something special about my mom's. Probably just bias on my part, but I felt thoroughly relaxed as I leaned back in the chair.

The more I drank, the better my stomach started to feel. I wasn't sure if the tea, the walk, or just my mother's presence helped. Maybe Tavi was right, and my nausea was stress-induced. If so, a few minutes of relaxing with my mother was exactly what I needed to refresh.

"I wanted to ask if you might have some tinctures or herbs that would help with stress," I said. "This tea is already working wonders."

"I'm glad it's helping, but I'm sorry you've been uncomfortable, honey. What's been going on?"

"I feel okay usually, but in the mornings, I get headaches and nausea that last until lunchtime. I thought it might be something I ate, but it's been days now, and it's making it harder to get work done."

"Describe the headaches for me?"

"Okay," I lifted a hand and touched my forehead. "The pain kind of wraps around here, if that makes sense? Like a rope that's tightening around my forehead."

She nodded. "Hmm. And the nausea? Is it more of a dizziness?"

"Well, I do feel dizzy, but I also get sick. After I get out of bed, I have to rush to the bathroom."

Mom pursed her lips in thought for a few seconds, running her thumb back and forth over the handle of her mug, then she pushed her chair back and got to her feet.

"I'll be right back," she said, heading toward the bathroom. When she came back, she had a small box in her hand. "I like to keep one of these in my medical kit just in case someone comes to me with symptoms like yours."

"Oh?" I took the box, and immediately, my eyes went to the words PREGNANCY TEST typed in purple lettering across the box. The sight of it confused me, and if I was being honest, it also scared me a little.

"Mom, why did you bring this to me?" I demanded, my face flaming. "I'm not pregnant, just stressed out. Probably. And…and anyway, Night and I have only been having sex for a few weeks or so." It was hard to believe that Night and I had met only a few months ago. It felt like an era had passed between the day he'd kidnapped me and now.

"I've never been pregnant myself," she said, easing into her chair again. "But I know the signs. Go on and take it. What's the harm in being sure?"

She made a good point, but the walk to the bathroom seemed to go on forever. My hands trembled as I held the box up to read the instructions. I felt like I was having an out-of-body experience as I went through the motions of taking the test—I had no idea how to feel about this. Never once had I thought about having a baby. I'd spent my life believing I was human. I never thought I'd find a mate or a lover, let alone have children.

With Night, everything changed, and now it seemed there was a chance I could be pregnant.

I sat on the toilet and waited for the test. The box told me I would only have to wait a few minutes, but each second felt like an hour. If I was pregnant, what would that mean? The timing wasn't exactly ideal. Troy was out there planning something with who knew how many ferals at his command, and my position as alpha would only last for another couple of weeks, at which point the alpha ceremony would determine the new leader.

There were so many unknowns, and the certainty of having a baby wouldn't clear any of them up…though I had to acknowledge that the thought of having a baby with Night electrified me. What if our child had his gorgeous emerald eyes? His smile or my hair? I became giddy just at the thought of it.

But what about Night? He had so much going on— a baby would just be one more thing for him to stress about. I also had no idea how he felt about children. He was good with them, but did he want them? Did he want them *with me*?

I looked at the sink where I'd left the plastic stick and took a few deep breaths before getting to my feet. It was time to see the truth with my own eyes. The too-small rectangular screen revealed two vertical red bars. My stomach flipped.

I double-checked the box to make sure I wasn't misinterpreting the results, but no. The truth was right in front of me. Those two bars meant that the test was positive.

"I'm pregnant," I breathed in the quiet of the bathroom. *There's a life growing inside me right now...*

An overwhelming dizziness settled over me. I pressed my back to the wall. Bubbles filled my stomach, bubbles that could have carried me away to a level of happiness I'd never known before. The dark questions plaguing my mind vanished in the wake of the two red bars. My body felt warm, light. *I've got to tell my mom and Tavi and Night...*

But as soon as I thought about all the people who would need to know, the weight of those worries began to creep back in.

I ran a hand through my hair. Night and I hadn't been together very long, and with everything going on, we hadn't really gotten to know each other. I mean, I should know if Night—my mate—even wanted children, shouldn't I?

I dragged in a deep breath and tried to get my thoughts together. Mom would be worried if I spent too much longer in the bathroom, so I knew I might as well head out now.

In the kitchen, she took one look at me, then let out a cheer and got up from the table. She pulled me in for a tight hug, and I laughed and embraced her.

"Congratulations, love!"

"Thanks, Mom. It doesn't feel real."

"That's not surprising. But you should know that everything will be fine." She kissed the top of my head, then pulled back and took my face in her hands. "As exciting as this news is…how do you feel?"

"Happy! Well, mostly happy."

"Only mostly?"

"I mean, it's just a lot right now." I pulled away and sat at the table. She scooted her chair to sit next to me. "Night and I…our claiming ceremony was only a few days ago. I thought we'd have more time together before we had a baby."

My mother rubbed soothing circles on my back. "I understand where you're coming from, honey, and I'm sorry the universe doesn't work that way. The Fates want you to have a baby right now, and you'll have to embrace it to see what destiny has in store for you."

I nodded. It was exactly the kind of thing Mom would say. On one hand, it was comforting to hear things were proceeding exactly as they were meant to, but on the other, it felt like my life was no longer in my control—if it ever had been. Things were progressing quickly, and there were still so many things I didn't understand about myself. Could I really bring a baby into the world when I was still so uncertain about myself?

"What's wrong, honey? Aren't you happy?"

"I am, but…I guess I wish I had more insight into what fate has planned for me—or my baby. I mean, there's so much to worry about, and knowing that there's more in store, I can't help but worry about it."

She nodded. "After the things you've endured, Bryn, I don't blame you for worrying. But you need to remember that you've come out on the other side of your hardship a stronger, savvier woman. No matter what destiny has in store for you, you've proven again and again that you're strong enough to survive it."

"But I'd like to have some comfort in *knowing* that."

"I think we'd all like that, honey. It would be wonderful if we could have some sign that everything will work out, but that isn't how fate works." She had stopped rubbing my back as she talked about fate, but now she resumed. "Is there anything that might ease your worries a bit? Something else you could focus on for now?"

"I mean, there's still tons and tons of paperwork I haven't had the chance to—"

She poked the back of my neck. "No, silly— something other than work. Something that makes you happy or gives some respite to your soul."

"Oh." I mulled that over. Something that would give "respite to my soul?" I enjoyed reading and cooking and taking care of children, but I didn't think those things would take my mind off my work or worries about the future.

I had other questions about myself, things I'd never been able to answer. I had no idea what fate had planned for me. With so many unknowns, I wished I had more control over my life—and I wished I understood myself a bit more.

"I think…" I began slowly. "I'd like to know more about my birth parents."

Her soothing strokes slowed on my back. Fearing I'd hurt her feelings, I turned to her.

"Oh, Mom, you've been wonderful and amazing. Believe me. It's just that…now that I've got my own baby on the way, I wish I knew more about who I am. I want to be able to tell my baby about its biological grandparents and the kind of people they were."

Mom nodded and gave me a small smile. "Don't worry, Bryn, I'm not taking any offense. I understand where you're coming from. I don't have answers for you; the heavens only know how badly I wish I did have them. But, honey, I'm committed to helping you in whatever way I can."

I smiled, relieved that I hadn't hurt her feelings and she would help me. "Thanks, Mom. I love you so much."

"I love you, too, sweetheart. But I want to add one thing."

"Yes?"

"You don't need to know your biological parents to be a good mother. You have plenty of experience watching pups, and you're a very patient and nurturing young woman. You're going to be a great mother. I know it."

"I hope that's true, but I can't seem to stop doubting myself." I forced a laugh, but it sounded fake even to me. To break the awkwardness, I asked, "Do you think Night will be happy to hear the news?"

"Oh, Bryn, he's going to be *thrilled!* Most alphas want a child, though not all of them are the greatest with children."

"He's really good with them. You should see the way he walks around his compound and interacts with the families."

She grinned. "Well, it sounds like you have your answer."

"I guess that's true." I blushed as a grin spread across my face, my heart pounding. "I think I want to make the announcement really special for him. It's our first child, and I want to do something romantic."

"That's a wonderful idea, but now that you two are together, he'll be able to sense the change in you soon enough. If you want to go all out, you must do it quickly."

That was good to know. I filed that information away in my brain. "Okay, I'll make sure it's soon." *I have so much paperwork to get through, but I should try to spend my free time planning something for him*, I thought. *I hope I can get something planned before he gets back from the Wargs. But what would Night like? Should I get some candles? Buy something for him at the market?*

"Are you listening, Bryn?"

Mom's voice pulled me from my thoughts. "Huh?"

She chuckled. "I was telling you that you shouldn't lift anything too heavy, and you need to rest as much as you can."

"Oh. Right. I hear you."

"I'll give you a few ounces of this tea." She lifted her mug. "It ought to help with your aches and pains. But you must listen to your body and give it what it needs."

I couldn't help but smile. It would be difficult to pay attention to my body when so much needed to be done around the compound. I would try, for my baby's sake, but I doubted I'd have the opportunity to take it easy in the near future.

Still, I said, "I will, Mom."

"That's my girl. Here, let me refill your tea."

After the visit with Mom, I headed back to my cabin. I'd promised her I would get some rest, but I needed to return to the office to stay on top of things. I had a lot to do before the baby arrived. I needed to prove myself to the Kings and the council, get a handle on pack finances, and make sure that the Kings and the Wargs were in good places before the baby arrived.

I sighed. If nothing else, at least the nausea had disappeared, though in its place, I felt a slight headache building at the back of my skull. With more tea and a pill or two of ibuprofen, I was sure that the ache would vanish. Unfortunately, there was little I could do about the uncertainty swirling inside me.

Chapter 4 - Night

After days of being unable to shift, I rejoiced in getting in touch with my wolf again. Paws digging into the ground, crunching leaves and twigs, the wind through my fur, each breath a silver fog in the cool pre-dawn morning…my wolf, naturally, had missed it even more than I did. It'd been too long since he had been let out. Getting to let loose after that recovery period was such a relief.

I reached my territory within a few hours. I shifted and changed into jeans and a T-shirt. As I tugged my shirt down over my stomach, I sensed some tension, a shift in the air. *I've been gone too long.* The thought echoed in my mind like a warning. My pack missed their leader. I had been focusing far too much on the Kings, and my people were suffering because of it. They needed to know I was there for them and would always protect them.

I was planning on meeting with the council first thing, but Wayne Hudson, the oldest member of the council, told me they wanted to meet in the evening. That worked out perfectly—I'd have time to reconnect with my pack and meet with the council after.

I sent some wolves to gather all available bodies to the training grounds. It was the same place I'd spoken to them before, with Dom at my side, but that was when Troy abducted Bryn and Tavi. It was time to have another meeting.

It took about twenty minutes to get everyone together. Once they were all gathered, I climbed on top of the roof of the elders' cabin. As I looked over the crowd, the chatter gradually died down.

"Thank you for coming," I said, my voice resonating over the crowd. "It's been too long since I've been home. I was injured and helping my mate settle into her role as alpha, but I should never have left you all for so long. I apologize for that, but I know apologies aren't enough, so I'm here to reconnect with all of you and listen to what you need from me."

My announcement was met with silent stares until a voice spoke up.

"Is Bryn all right?" Mabel asked. "And Tavi and Violet?" Mabel was an older woman who loved working in the mess hall. She and Bryn had really built a connection when Bryn first arrived in my territory.

Dozens of Wargs nodded. They, too, wanted to make sure Bryn was all right. I smiled. It was a relief to know that my pack cared about my mate's well-being.

"Yes, they're all doing great," I said. "Bryn is settling into her alpha role well. As soon as we're able, she'll come round to see everyone."

"Well, it's nice to hear *someone's* doing their duty for their pack."

I heard the words even though the speaker had muttered them under their breath. It had to be someone standing near the elders' cabin.

"Who said that?" I asked. Silence greeted me. "You're not in trouble. I'm holding this forum because I want to hear how you've been feeling. I need you all to be comfortable enough to speak your minds so I know what's up."

There were a few seconds of silence, and then someone spoke up.

"I wasn't the one who said it, but I might as well have been," Iren said. She liked helping my mother in the gardens when she wasn't teaching the children. "I heard you have been rebuilding Kings' land. Is that true?"

"Yes. Troy attacked them. He—"

Before I could finish, Iren spoke again, anger seeping from every word. "We have projects that have been abandoned! Roofs with holes and supplies that need replenishing from Colville. We need more hunters bringing meat for the winters, but you've got them searching for Redwolf."

I frowned. "I wasn't informed that our stocks were low."

"Well, we're fine on food now," she admitted with some reluctance. "But if our hunters and trackers don't return soon, we won't be in time for winter."

The food stocks not being an immediate concern was a relief, and I was glad Iren had brought it up. If she was worried about such things, others were, too.

"Iren, as your alpha, I'd never let the pack suffer—not even when I'm helping the Kings with their Redwolf problem. Regardless of whether or not we find Troy, I will make sure the pack is fed and our medical supplies stocked."

"No!" This voice came from somewhere deeper in the crowd. "That's not enough. You have been getting cozy with the Kings and ignoring us. You've only come now because the council wants to speak to you."

I scanned the crowd for the speaker, but now other wolves were talking, too. It was difficult to pick out individual voices, but I caught enough.

"Kings steal our alpha. What'll they take from us next?"

"Why should anyone care about those fuckers?"

"Might as well just move to King territory. I'll see my alpha more."

I gauged the crowd's mood. They didn't speak with one voice, but from their general unhappiness, they might as well have been. The last time I'd held a public forum, I'd been sick because I hadn't claimed Bryn. It had been tough to accept the brunt of the emotions they had leveled my way. This time, I was stronger.

I didn't want to use my alpha voice to silence them—that would only be controlling them. Words could only go so far, and obviously, my pack wanted action from me.

Instead of raising my voice or asking for silence, I dropped down from the roof. That was enough to catch the attention of those closest to me. I nodded to the crowd to follow me and started walking toward the tool shed for some nails and roofing material. Part of the mess hall's roof near the conference room where I met with my closest men had a leaky room. The summer had been dry, and fall was looking to be the same, so we hadn't fixed it even when other holes had formed.

My pack trudged behind me, some still talking, and watched me climb onto the roof. I inched over to one of the larger holes and started working on it. The sound of my hammer sent a hush over the crowd.

"I'm here now, and I will always be here for you. I would never abandon the Wargs like Gregor Redwolf." With the hole covered, I stood and looked over my people. "Let's fix what we can while I'm here. We'll figure out what supplies we need before I head back to King territory."

Many of my pack seemed doubtful, but as I returned to the repair work, a few joined me. As they started working, I moved to the edge of the roof and spotted Iren standing near a group of wolves who seemed hesitant to join in. On the walk over, we'd passed her cabin, and I realized that her mate, Anthony, was one of the men I'd sent after Troy. Of course, she wanted him home. Other families would also be feeling the absence of their mates.

"Iren," I said.

She winced but held her chin high. "Yeah?"

"If you've got the time, could you see what supplies need to be replaced? Once you have a list, head into Colville with a group of your choosing to replenish them."

She blinked. "Me? Why?"

"Because I know things have been hard for you and your pups, and I want to make sure that families like yours are taken care of." I smiled at her. "Don't worry about how much you can spend. I trust your judgment."

She hesitated for another second or so, then nodded. Even the arms crossed over her chest relaxed. "Sure. I can do that."

I directed another group to grab some spare wood and supplies so we could get all hands on deck. Beer and food were served, and time passed in friendly productivity. Before I knew it, it was time to speak to the council.

I reached out to them telepathically.

"*We've been expecting you, Alpha,*" Wayne replied. "*Meet us at my cabin, please. The five of us have already gathered.*"

It seemed I wasn't the only one who wanted to get the meeting over with.

Wayne's cabin was farther inside the compound, a few yards from the library, where I was repairing one of the reading benches. In Wayne's sixty years of life, he'd had six pups. Because of that, he lived in one of the larger cabins that were impossible to miss.

I walked up to the door and knocked before stepping inside. They were expecting me, so there was no need to wait for an invitation.

I found the council members sitting at the varnished wood table in Wayne's living room. They stood as I entered. Jasmine Howler, the second-oldest in her early fifties, had her lips pressed into a slight, thin smile. Her chocolate-brown hair was threaded with gray, and she kept it shorn to her chin. Her chin had a scar from her old battles with the Kings. She was among the first women to sign up to be more than just a mother and caretaker of the pack.

Wayne grinned at me with his arms crossed. He had a full salt-and-pepper beard, silver hair, and a round stomach. But his grandfatherly looks didn't match the sharp look in his eyes. Not unlike Dom, who could smile in the face of his enemy, Wayne could switch his friendly grin to a glare when someone said something he didn't like or spoke out of turn.

The rest of those on the council were in their mid-to-late forties. Ida Kells kept her blond hair in two braids down her back, and her arms were covered in tattoos. Most of the rest of her body was also inked. Besides serving on the council, she passed down the art of stick-and-poke tattooing in the pack.

Graham Hanks was bald, and his limbs were corded with muscle. He had been Gregor's beta before Gregor abandoned the Wargs for the Kings. Graham had almost become alpha in Gregor's absence, but because he was so ashamed of not preventing Gregor's betrayal, he'd refused to take up the mantle. Instead, he had served as a fighter until a couple of years ago when his bad knees forced him to retire. Even with shot knees, he was one of the strongest members of the pack.

Finally, there was Ellen Grousby. She served in the infirmary in addition to being on the council. She and Dr. Stan were second cousins, and they had learned about medicine around the same time.

The five of them had such rich, honorable backgrounds serving the Wargs. Though I was their alpha, it was hard not to feel a little starstruck around them. Normally, I'd ask to hear a story or seek advice from them. Given the circumstances of this meeting, however, sharing a beer and a steak with them was out of the question. The tension in that room was even more intense than the tension outside. I felt a twinge of regret for not having Dom along with me. At least then, I wouldn't have to stand before these titans while delivering my progress report.

"Thank you for meeting with me," I said.

"It's good to see you alive and well, Alpha Night," Ellen said. "We heard about your awful injury, as well as young Evan's betrayal."

I nodded in acknowledgment of her well wishes. "It'll take more than that to keep me down, Ellen. As for the betrayal…it was an unfortunate blow, but nothing we couldn't overcome."

"Very true." She nodded. "We're glad you've recovered and seemed to have worked the pack into a fervor to repair the compound."

"I'm only doing what I should've done a while ago." I had to be humble, but to be honest? I was living off the high of getting so many pack members happily buzzing with activity.

"Alright, now that the formalities are out of the way…" Wayne and the others took their seats while I continued to stand. "Let's talk."

I took a short, quiet breath, then launched into the story about the ferals' attack, Evan's betrayal, and Troy's escape. Dom had likely already mentioned some of this to them, so I stuck to the facts and answered whatever questions they had.

When I finished, Graham leaned back in his seat. "We've heard whispers about the feral attack. We've already started to gather wolves to shore up our borders."

"I heard as much from Dom," I said.

"Then he's also told you that he briefed us about Troy." Wayne's dark eyes narrowed. "I guess I shouldn't be surprised that the Kings would be so shoddy about their prisons, but this is very, very far from good news."

As a pup, I would have shuddered under Wayne's harsh glare, but as an adult, I could meet his gaze without flinching. I understood his anger—after all, I was still pissed Troy's escape had happened under my watch. I wished just as much as Wayne did that I could find Troy and put an end to him with my own hands.

"We need to send out our own wolves to hunt him down. It's the only way to ensure we stop him before he does anything worse," Jasmine said.

I nodded. "That has already been handled. Bryn sent wolves to search for him."

At the mention of Bryn's name, the council members shared a look that made my hackles bristle. It wasn't outwardly disrespectful, but it was far too close to that for comfort.

"We expected as much," Jasmine said. "She couldn't exactly do nothing after Troy's escape. But from what we've heard of your Bryn, she seems a soft-hearted sort."

"Did she send out a party to arrest him or kill him?" Wayne asked.

"Arrest him," I answered.

At Wayne's sigh, annoyance flared in my chest, and my wolf began to growl. Wayne's children and I had grown up together. Frankie was his youngest, and she was two years younger than me. Wayne's position on the council and my closeness in age to his kids made him think he could speak to me like he spoke to them.

I leveled my gaze at him. As alpha, I was irked by Wayne's attitude toward Bryn. But because he was on the council, he had more leeway than others in the pack. His authority wasn't something I could easily usurp, but I didn't want to do that, anyway. After all, he was an asset on the council as he had the most experience and was among the oldest pack members. Given all the struggles that we Wargs had endured through the years, it took a tough-as-nails person to have survived as long as he had.

"My *mate*," I said, reminding Wayne and the others whom they were talking about, "is not the kind of alpha who believes in unnecessary violence. The Kings are her pack to rule, and it is my opinion that we should respect her decision." Even if I didn't agree with Bryn's decision, I intended to support her no matter what.

Unfortunately, the council didn't seem moved by my words.

"That may be true in an ideal world," Jasmine said. "But you are the alpha of the Wargs. Your duty is, first and foremost, to your people. You need to make sure Troy is dead and buried."

I met Jasmine's gaze, annoyance flaring up again. I stepped forward and pressed my palms to the table as I met each of their gazes. "With all due respect, Jasmine, I'm aware of what my duties are. I hate Troy just as much as any of you. I'd love to have him dead at my feet, but—"

"Excellent," she interjected, a small smile touching her lips. It wasn't a friendly expression but one with bloodthirsty intent. "As alpha, you understand the threat Redwolf poses to us. You'll see no problem with sending our own hunting party and nourishing our lands with his blood."

I raised a brow. "And all five of you have come to this same conclusion?"

There were nods around the table. I frowned. I wanted to send a hunting party out badly enough to argue with my mate about it, but the fact that the council wanted me to send one made me feel…torn. I didn't want to go against my mate and undermine her status. If the Wargs' hunting party found Troy first, it would show the Kings that Bryn wasn't a strong leader because her search party had failed.

But if I didn't show a strong hand here, or if I opposed the council's rule outright, there were other risks to consider. Someone could go over my head and send out their own hunting party, thus weakening my alpha status. I would have to challenge the guilty party and kill them in front of my pack to regain the pack's respect.

The absolute *last* thing I wanted to do was kill one of my own wolves, especially when Troy was on the loose and doing fate only knew what. My hands were tied, and the easiest path forward was to go along with their desires and send out a hunting party. *Bryn's team has a head start,* I reminded myself. *My men are on that team as well, and there's a good chance they'll find him first.*

Guilt coiled tight in my stomach. Bryn would eventually find out about the hunting party, so I'd need to make things right with her when I returned.

"Alright," I said, stepping back from the table. "I'll send one out after our meeting."

"Great." Wayne smiled. "What else do you have to report, Alpha?"

"My men have been helping rebuild the Kings' buildings after the feral attack, and we're establishing more of a presence there," I said. "Our goal to eventually merge the packs gets closer and closer with each cabin we repair. I genuinely feel that we're on the right track."

I'd hoped the good news would break some of the lingering tension in the room. But if anything, it only thickened.

"Right. The merger." Wayne's smile disappeared. "I never much liked the idea."

His response blindsided me, and I couldn't catch myself before raising my eyebrows toward my hairline. I knew the older generation of Wargs hated the idea of getting close to the Kings, but the council had never said they disapproved. They'd even encouraged me when we talked about it in the past.

"I know there are decades of bad blood between our packs, but the alpha challenge will put an end to that," I said. "That challenge is happening in a couple of weeks. When I win, they'll have no choice but to merge with us."

"Alpha Night." Ida was a woman of few words, so I was surprised when she started speaking. "Take a minute to consider something. Don't you think it'd be better if we had control over both territories without compromising at all?"

My wolf started to growl low again, but this time, it was a warning to me. I didn't like the sound of this, either. "*When* I win the challenge," I began, not wanting to preface this statement with "if" the way I had with Bryn and Dom, "I will become alpha of both packs. The packs will merge either way. I don't see the point of your question."

She shook her head. "No, Alpha, once you win the ceremony, you will be alpha of fresh territory. That territory—that land—will become the Wargs', and the Kings will be no more. We will scrub their existence from the face of the earth."

My hackles rose. "And what exactly does that mean for the Kings, Ida?"

The five of them exchanged another glance, then Wayne met my gaze. He looked at me with some sympathy, like he was about to deliver disappointing news to a pup.

"Well, they won't be welcome unless they assimilate completely," he said. "They'll have to abandon their pride as Kings and take on new identities as Wargs. If they don't want to do that, they can leave or be killed. Likely, it will be the latter."

"But your experience with the Kings is now decades-old," I protested. "I have seen this pack with fresh eyes, and after spending time with them, they've shown me that they are capable of accepting change. Of course, there will be Kings who hate the merger and abandon the larger pack, but there's real potential for them to—"

Jasmine let out a harsh laugh. "Potential, Night? Potential for what? For the Kings to accept living with a pack they have *always* viewed as lesser? Not a chance."

My wolf growled at her disrespect. I bit back the retort my wolf and I desperately wanted to make, forcing my voice to remain calm. "I'm saying that a violent takeover won't be necessary. If we want to end decades and decades of hate between our pack and the Kings, there's a peaceful way to do it."

Graham steepled his fingers in front of his face. "Do not misunderstand, Night—we Wargs are not trying to make peace with our former oppressors."

The shock was a lance that speared me where I stood. "The council," I managed to get out, "has never expressed this position. None of you have ever mentioned that you didn't want a merger. You all seemed open to it just a few weeks ago. What changed?"

"For us, nothing has changed." He shrugged. "Up until now, your goals and ours aligned. With the work you have been doing with the Kings, they will expect us to play nicely. They won't attack when we start to move in after you've won the ceremony—not until it's too late. The only difference is that now we are letting you in on our thoughts, Night."

I shook my head, my thoughts barraging me with negativity and worry. "No. That was never my plan. What about the women and children? You know they're treated like second-class citizens, don't you? You want to punish them for things they had no say in? How is that any better than what the Kings did to us?"

None of them rushed to answer me, but their silence said enough. It took everything I had not to lash out at them. To take things so far…it was *wrong*. The traditional hostile method of taking over a pack was killing the male wolves loyal to the previous alpha. That had been my original plan before I met Bryn, and everything changed. But what the council was suggesting was unnecessary and dangerous. Sneakily and underhandedly forcing so many wolves into the wilds could result in even more feral wolves, which meant a greater threat to *everyone*—not just the Wargs.

And if Troy managed to escape the search party and the hunting party, more ferals would give him an even bigger army. I opened my mouth to tell the council that, but as I looked from face to face, I could see their minds were made up.

Damn them. I could never be that alpha. I refused. I would send out a hunting party as they'd asked—I'd already promised them I would—but there was no fucking way I'd oversee the slaughter of an entire pack.

I could be ruthless when necessary, but doing it this way would put me on the same level as Gregor and Troy. Needless cruelty went against everything I believed, and it went against everything I'd thought the council believed. I remembered what Bryn had said about wanting to give the Kings an alternative to violence. Was this the sort of thing she was worried about? A forever-escalating scale of violence to the point of outright cruelty? If so, I could see her position much more clearly than before. What a shame that my own council had brought her argument into such focus.

"Do not forget," I said in a low growl, "that when I win the challenge, *I* will be the alpha, not the five of you. And once I've claimed the land that should always have been mine, *I* will decide what happens to it. Do not overstep your bounds as council members."

Wayne smiled, but none of his usual joviality shone in his eyes. "We'll have to agree to disagree for now, Alpha Night. But I hope we'll see eye to eye when the time comes."

"So do I, Wayne." I took the time to meet each of their gazes, my fists clenched at my sides. "If there's nothing else, I'll end this meeting here."

Wayne inclined his head. It looked like a dismissal, which only increased my temperature. Gritting my teeth, I turned and stormed out of the cabin.

I could hardly think with the angry rhythm of my heart beating against my ribs. The last thing I'd expected was the council to drop that kind of bomb on me. Still, I shouldn't have shown so much emotion in front of them— it wasn't becoming of an alpha to lose his cool in front of his council. I ran my hands through my hair and took a few deep breaths. If I had time, I'd have loved to head to the hot springs and clear my head, but I didn't have that luxury.

Instead, I gathered my best fighters and trackers and told them I wanted them to seek out and kill Troy. Among the members of this team was Jasper, hanging onto my every word.

"I want this as discreet as possible," I said. "There's also a search party looking for Troy. Don't get in each other's way. Even better, don't cross paths with them unless you can't avoid it. Do you understand?"

The group of seven nodded. Their eagerness to get out there and tear into Troy blazed from their eyes. I couldn't blame them for their excitement. Part of me felt the same, despite my meeting with the council. I couldn't summon even an ounce of pity for the shitstorm that was headed Troy's way.

"Report to me the moment you've found something," I said. "Don't make a move until I give the word."

"Yes, Alpha."

"Good. Get going."

With their orders given, they shifted and sprinted into the forest. As their quick footsteps faded, I pinched the bridge of my nose. I had nothing pressing to do now. My mind was free to return to uncomfortable territory: the council and their thirst for blood. I had to figure out what to do about them.

As old and as esteemed as they were, the council had a lot of sway within the pack. As the alpha, I had a ton of sway myself, but if we were publicly in opposition, it would cause a huge rift among the Wargs—those who were most loyal to me and those who were most loyal to the council would be in direct conflict with each other. From what I remembered of wolf history, conflicts like those ended poorly for everyone, and those who survived the turmoil either tried to rebuild or were forced to join other packs.

It was a shitstorm waiting to happen, and I couldn't let it reach that point. Fortunately, I had over two weeks before the alpha challenge. I was sure I could come up with a plan by then.

Chapter 5 - Bryn

I rushed into the bathroom and dropped to my knees in front of the toilet. The contents of my stomach burned my throat as I heaved into the porcelain bowl. My thoughts became a swirling mess, tears stinging my eyes as I trembled. I gripped the bowl, willing the sickness to pass quickly. I had so much to do today and so little time to get it done, but here I was, reduced to a shaking, sweating mess in my bathroom.

When the sickness finally subsided, I dabbed at my forehead and wiped my mouth with some toilet paper. Feeling a little more in control of myself, I flushed the toilet and sat on my ass with my back pressed to the bathroom wall. I closed my eyes and rubbed my stomach back and forth. I hadn't slept well last night, which had probably made my symptoms worse. My body pulsed with a bone-deep ache while my stomach swam with nausea. My brain was starting to function properly again, but all it did was tell me that I needed to get up and go to work.

Was this what I had to look forward to for the next nine months? I hoped the Fates would spare me months of this torture.

This was the first time I couldn't rely on my body. Even when I was unable to shift, and my body lacked the strength and speed of the wolves around me, it had always gotten me where I needed to go. It operated exactly as I wanted it to, and even when I got sick, I got better within days. Now that I was pregnant, things were different. The only thing I could count on was ending up on my knees in the bathroom each morning.

I ran my hands through my hair and took deep breaths. I needed to get up, make some tea, and get to the office. If I was quick, I might be able to make up for the work I'd missed by being stuck in the bathroom.

I opened my eyes. I'd spent two nights alone in bed, but I hadn't come any closer to figuring out how I wanted to tell Night about my pregnancy. There were only a couple of weeks left until the alpha challenge, and I still had so much confusing paperwork to wade through. I had to meet with the council today about the duration of my service as their alpha, and I wouldn't have Night at my side.

The alpha challenge itself was still a mystery to me. I knew Night would have to fight, but I wasn't sure about the specifics. Would it be a battle royale with wolves fighting wolves, or more of a tournament setting where one wolf fought another, progressing until the final two contenders faced off? What if it was a different setup altogether? Night was strong and used to fighting, but I didn't want him to get hurt again. He'd looked so weak the day after Evan shot him, and I didn't want him to go through that pain again.

The council, of course, hadn't been very forthcoming about the rules. That meant I needed to be firmer when I met with them, but I wasn't looking forward to the potential pushback.

I had so much on my mind, but I couldn't catch a break. I wished I could push my worries onto someone else while getting work done. Unfortunately, I had to bear the full burden.

My butt was starting to hurt from sitting on the cold, hard floor, so I pushed myself to my feet. Fortunately, by the time I straightened, I felt well enough not to throw up again. There was still a bit of dizziness, but that went away when I stepped into the hot shower. I cleaned up, and when I was done, I pulled my hair into a bun. With a towel wrapped around me, I went to my vanity and tried to cover the bags under my eyes with makeup. Knowing this pack, any sign of exhaustion would be taken as weakness, and the last thing I needed right now was some asshole trying to challenge my authority.

I blended in the makeup, set it with some spray, and looked at myself in the mirror. My shoulders slumped; I still looked exhausted even after all that effort. Why did I even bother?

"It's the best you can do," I whispered to myself. "Just take it one thing at a time."

I repeated those words like a mantra, and after another deep breath, I dressed and headed out.

Tavi was waiting for me outside the council meeting room. She was wearing her usual oversized shirt and leggings. I'd sent a telepathic message to her to meet me there and was glad to see her. She gave me a half smile, which I returned. I wouldn't have Night by my side, but at least I wouldn't face the council alone.

We headed inside together. Colby, Ross, Dana, Edward, and Grant were already seated. They rose as Tavi and I entered, but Dana took the longest to get to her feet. I knew it was because she didn't like or respect me, but whatever; her pettiness wasn't worth picking a fight.

"Thank you for meeting with us today, Alpha Hunter," Ross said. His salt-and-pepper hair normally fell down his back, but he'd tied it back in a low bun. Long strands of hair were in their usual place over the scar on the left side of his face. "We wanted to talk to you about the alpha challenge."

I nodded as Tavi and I took seats across from them. "I wanted to talk about that, too. I'm unclear about what the specifics of the challenge will be."

"We are still deciding on a system," he replied. "We want to ensure this is a fair struggle between the contenders, and to do that, we need to vote on the rules."

Tavi shot me a quick look. I didn't need my telepathic connection with her to understand her meaning. *They're* still *deciding on rules with only a few weeks left before the challenge?*

I agreed with her disbelief. "Do you have an estimated time for when you'll have that decided?"

"We're hoping to settle on the ground rules at least five days before the challenge. We will let you and your beta know what we've decided."

"Very well." That wasn't much, but at least I'd followed up with them about it. "Then what are your concerns?"

"As you know, the council will nominate a candidate for the ceremony," he began.

Again, I nodded. I and each member of the council could nominate someone for the challenge ceremony. I would, of course, nominate Night, and I expected the choices from each council member would be fearsome. I hoped to find out their picks in this meeting so I could let Night know as soon as possible.

"But if your Night Shepherd wins, it is the opinion of this council that we do not push back against the win. In other words, we see no point in standing in his way."

That surprised me, and I didn't try to hide my reaction from them. I looked at their faces, and only Dana refused to meet my gaze. If they were planning on accepting the tournament results no matter what, it would make for an easier transition between Night becoming alpha and merging the packs.

"This wasn't expected," I said.

Tavi added, "Does that mean most of you support a merger between the packs?"

"'Support' is far from accurate," Dana said. Her cinnamon-brown hair was slicked back into an elegant updo. "We don't support a Warg getting his filthy claws—"

"Dana," Grant, the oldest council member, growled. "That's enough. We are not here to sling insults back and forth, and we will not retread the same territory of previous conversations."

She looked away, and Grant sighed.

"But Dana is right, 'support' isn't the word we would use. We are interested in beginning the next phase of our pack's future as seamlessly as possible."

"For the health of the Kings pack," Colby added, "we would prefer to make the transition to new leadership as easily as possible for everyone. And if that includes a discussion of a merger, should Shepherd win," he continued with some reluctance, "we want to be sure of what to expect."

"Oh, I see," I said. The council's reasoning made sense—they were trying to be pragmatic to get ahead of any potential conflicts. If they were considering the real possibility that Night would win, that was a good sign. I was sure there was a time not too long ago when they would have been diametrically opposed to having a Warg in the alpha seat.

Having the Wargs initiate repair and reconstruction efforts throughout the compound had been an excellent idea. The goodwill we had fostered made it more difficult for the council to hold an openly hostile position.

"*At least they have some sense,*" Tavi thought to me. "*It's good that they're not trying to drag this out but are hoping to meet us halfway.*"

Agreed. "So, what are your concerns?" I asked the council.

"Well, there's the matter of allocating resources and housing, and there's the matter of outside threats." Colby's gray mustache moved up and down as he spoke. It completely covered his upper lip. "Merging two packs usually leads to the two packs sharing enemies, and we're concerned about the Wargs' enemies and how they will react to the two packs merging. Would they stage an attack?"

"These are reasonable questions," I said. "And I appreciate you all showing initiative for trying to get answers now. To be honest with you, the biggest threat to the Wargs has always been the Kings, so in the event that Night wins the ceremony, that threat will be eradicated. I am unaware of any significant threats outside of that."

I glanced at Tavi, but she shook her head. "*None that I am aware of. I'll ask around to double-check, though.*"

"That said, I can't speak for how other packs will react to two powerful packs combining," I continued. "I imagine we'll want to be prepared for anything."

"Well, that's a relief to hear," Ross said. "The Kings have enjoyed dominance of this area for decades, and we have an uneasy peace with neighboring packs for at least as long. The only physical conflicts we've had have been with the Wargs. If there is a negative response to a merger, we won't have to deal with any unknown threats."

"That's good to know," I said. We'd have to monitor the response that the Camas Pack and other packs in the area had to the merger, though I imagined the Camas would remain peaceful. *We just need to make sure we find Troy in time*, I thought. *He's still the big question mark in this situation.*

"As for resources and housing," Tavi said, "we would need to consider moving families into Warg territory and having Warg families move into King territory. Once the pack has recovered from Troy's attack, I imagine we'll be able to take a better look at what space is available for new families to move in."

The meeting ended shortly after that. It took everything in me not to smile too hard as Tavi and I said our goodbyes. It was such a relief to know that although the majority of the council wasn't completely on board with our plans, they wouldn't stand in our way. In the wake of such good news, the sickness that had left me bathroom-bound for so long that morning was a distant memory

"This is fantastic," Tavi said as we walked to the cabin she shared with Violet. "If the council won't be standing in our way, it's more likely that the Kings will fall in line. That's a great sign that things are finally coming together."

"I agree. Everything is still up in the air until Night wins the challenge, but we both know his chances of winning are very good." I grinned at her. "I can't wait until he gets back to tell him the good news." *That, and the baby...*

"Yeah, he'll be excited." She returned my smile.

"So, we didn't get the chance to talk before we went in," I said. "How are you today, Tavi? Are you holding up okay?"

"I have good days and bad days," she said. "Today started out as a terrible day."

"Really?" I glanced at her as we walked. It wasn't easy to tell which days were bad and which were good. Before we were kidnapped, a day when she didn't wear eyeliner or had bags under her eyes told me she was having a bad time. Now she looked tired and vaguely sad most of the time. Maybe there were other subtleties that I could watch out for.

She nodded. "Last night was a bad one for nightmares. I think I had maybe two hours of sleep."

"Oh, I see." I touched her forearm and gave it a gentle squeeze. "I'm sorry it was so rough on you."

"Well, considering everything we've been through, a few sleepless nights is inevitable, right?"

"That's true, but it's still a bitch to deal with."

She snorted. "You're telling me."

We walked in silence for a bit before Tavi spoke again. "So, do you ever get those? Nightmares about Troy?"

"Yeah, way more often than I'd like," I replied. Lately, I'd been dreaming about my baby, but I knew the nightmares about Troy would come back in full force. "I've had bad dreams about Troy most of my life, but after he kidnapped us, they've gotten worse and more graphic." I pushed my hair behind my ears as I quietly added, "They're worse when Night's not here."

"I can imagine. I almost wish I had someone like…" Tavi trailed off, her cheeks turning pink. "Never mind. I think I'll ask Violet if she has any advice on what to do about nightmares."

"That's a good idea."

It sounded like Tavi was about to say that she wished she had someone around who could make her nightmares easier to deal with. I would have liked to tease her about Dom, who obviously still very much wanted to be with her. But it was too soon to joke with her like that. She had only recently started warming up to him again.

But maybe it would be okay to bring him up? No harm in trying.

"Have you thought about talking to Dom?"

"D-Dom?" Her head popped up, the pink in her cheeks turning bright red. "Why would I talk to him?"

"I don't know. Just to talk. He might have some advice about nightmares, too."

Her blush deepened. "No, I haven't really considered talking to him about this. I don't know if I'd want to get into personal stuff, but I think I wouldn't...I wouldn't exactly hate the idea of spending a little time with him."

I smiled and bumped her shoulder with mine. "You've missed him."

She sighed. "Yeah, I have." She looked down and purposefully stepped on the leaves in our path. "It took me a long time to be near him without wanting to hide, but I miss his silly, goofy smile and stupid jokes."

"I think you should tell him that. I think he'd love to hear you say that."

"Well, we've both been busy with pack stuff lately, and I've been satisfied with seeing him around the compound."

"I see." Maybe it wasn't too soon for the two of them to have a real conversation. They just needed some excuse to talk.

When we reached the cabin, Violet was having tea with Dr. Damon Stan. The two were giggling together, and Violet had her hand on his knee. They looked up as we neared the table.

"It's good to see you both together," she said. "Were you out handling pack business?"

"That's right," Tavi said. She smiled at Violet and Dr. Stan before she headed toward the staircase. "I'm going to lie down for a few hours. Bryn, I'll look through paperwork with you later."

"Sure. Thanks, Tavi."

She went upstairs, and I looked from Violet to Dr. Stan and back again. It was so obvious that we'd walked in on them flirting with each other. I hadn't known they were interested in each other, never mind that they were an item. I'd need to ask Violet more about how their relationship had gotten to this point, but I didn't want to interrupt them with embarrassing questions now. Though, if the roles were reversed, Violet would be relentless with her uncomfortable questions.

"You look like you're doing well, Violet," I said. "You've come really far with your healing."

She nodded, and her emerald eyes returned to Dr. Stan. "Thanks to Damon's help, this awful alpha wound rarely bothers me anymore. He has the best salves for me." She patted his leg.

I pursed my lips to keep from smirking. "I'm glad he's been helping you so much. Having a doctor on call must be a huge relief."

Dr. Damon's face reddened. "A-anyway, did you need to talk to Violet? I don't mean to keep her from you."

"No, no, I just wanted to check in and say hello," I said, still smirking. "I'll catch up with you both some other time." I winked at Violet, then headed back to the alpha cabin.

On the walk back, I noticed a small group of women talking and laughing near the tree line. Tanya and Tara were among them. They were two-thirds of the Terrible T's, the women who had tormented me almost as horribly as Troy. Trisha was usually the ringleader, but I hadn't seen her around the pack lately. I suspected I knew why. Given her obsession with Troy and her deep hatred of me, she'd probably either abandoned the pack or was in hiding.

The group looked up as I neared, and their conversation slowly faded. I kept my head high. This was my territory, after all, and I had nothing to fear. I knew they would never attempt to attack me while I walked by, especially not if I kept my guard up.

I walked past them with a nod of acknowledgment, the way I'd seen Night do when he interacted with others. I didn't intend to speak to them but just go about my business and get home as quickly as I could—

"Hey, Bryn—I mean, Alpha Hunter."

I stopped. I knew it was Tara's voice. There was a moment of the old fear, of wanting to run away and hide from whatever fresh hell they had to dish out, but I didn't act on that old urge. Tara had corrected herself and called me Alpha Hunter. The least I could do was see what she wanted.

I turned and met her gaze. "Yes?"

Tara and Tanya shared a brief glance before peeling away from the group to close the space between us. Tara's thick, curly, dark auburn hair was cut to her chin; it was the shortest I'd ever seen it. Alternatively, Tanya's dirty-blond hair was the longest I'd seen; the straight locks hung down to her shoulders when before she'd usually kept it in a severe bob. They weren't wearing the latest in human fashion, and if they wore makeup, it was a very modest amount.

When they were within a yard of me, I raised my hand. To my surprise, they stopped in their tracks.

"That's close enough," I said, lowering my arm. "What do you two want?"

"It—um, well…" Tara hesitated and glanced at Tanya.

"We have something we want to say to you," Tanya finished.

I waited. The last time they'd spoken to me over two weeks ago, they had tried to turn the Kings against me after I'd become alpha. They accused me of being a witch and a fake wolf. But they didn't look like they wanted to call me out or ruin my reputation. They looked almost…sheepish.

Tanya took a deep breath. "We wanted to apologize to you."

I just stared at her, but when her words finally clicked, anger surged from deep inside me.

"Really," I said dryly. "You want to apologize to me after all these years?" I crossed my arms, looking from Tanya to Tara. "What caused the change of heart? Is it because I'm coming into my own as an alpha?"

The Tanya and Tara I knew would have tried to hurt me for talking back, but neither of them even raised a hand against me.

"I…I guess it would be a lie to say that wasn't part of it," Tanya admitted. "But that isn't the main reason we wanted to do this."

"Then what?" I demanded.

They winced at the sharpness in my tone. A few moments of silence passed, and one of the women separated from the group to stand beside them. It was Claire, the young mother I'd spoken to the day before the elders swore me in as alpha. Mom and I had watched her children, along with many other children. It was a surprise to see her hanging out with Tara and Tanya when they'd never been close before.

She stood next to them and put her hand on Tara's shoulder. "Just hear them out, Alpha. Please. They've wanted to approach you about this for a while now."

I raised a brow. I liked Claire because she was always cordial with me, so I had greater faith in her intentions than in Tara's and Tanya's. Still, angry words formed at the tip of my tongue, burning to be unleashed on my former bullies. It was so, so tempting to say them and continue home, but I held back.

I didn't want to encourage the kind of environment I'd grown up in, the one that played favorites and mistreated those with no power. If I wanted to improve things for my pack as a whole, I needed to face my former tormentors without biting their heads off—no matter how badly I wanted to.

The angry curl of my lips relaxed into a flat line. I didn't even pretend to look happy about hearing them out. "Fine. Say what you want to say."

Tara and Tanya looked up at me, hopefully now. "We're not hanging out with Trish anymore," Tara blurted. "The truth is after the ferals attacked the compound, Tanya and I realized we regretted how we were living our lives. We were terrible to you, Bryn, and we were awful to so many women who had pups because they couldn't compete with us for Troy's attention. And then we said those awful things about you after you were alpha..." she trailed off, shame coloring her cheeks.

Tanya added, "During that attack when people were wounded and crying and panicking, we felt like our world was crashing down. But you took control, and because of your leadership and the Wargs you brought with you, you saved a lot of people. We saw how much you cared about this pack, even though it's full of people who had mistreated you all your life. There was so much blood and chaos, but it didn't stop you, Bryn. And seeing you in that light…it changed everything."

I stared at them again, but this time because I was stunned by their words.

Taking my silence as encouragement, Tanya said, "Trish tried to go back to being a bitch after things started to calm down, but we didn't feel right about that. We stopped going along with her games, and she stopped hanging out with us."

"We don't miss her," Tara said, anger flashing in her dark brown eyes. "We don't want to be the people we were before."

Tanya nodded in agreement.

Some of the rigidity left my posture as their words bounced around in my head. Were they being genuine? Or were they trying to ease their guilt?

"Are you asking for forgiveness?" I asked, my voice little more than a whisper.

"We can't ask you for forgiveness after how we treated you," Tana said. "We just wanted to tell you that we aren't the same people anymore, and we support you as our alpha."

That was another surprise. "You do?"

"More and more people support you every day, Bryn," Claire said. "A lot of us see how hard you're working, and we really admire the fact that you haven't given up on us."

I gathered myself and focused on the three of them. "I need some time to think about all of this."

Tara nodded. "Right. Of course you do."

"Still, I…I appreciate your apology," I looked from Tanya to Tara. "I'll let you know how I feel when I'm in a better headspace."

"There's no rush, of course."

"Right." I felt awkward leaving them like that, but I couldn't think of a more diplomatic way to peel away from the conversation. So I nodded at them again, turned on my heel, and hurried away.

Chapter 6 - Night

I returned to the King compound after being away for three days. I arrived long after the sun had set, fully expecting to find Bryn fast asleep. I entered the cabin quietly, hoping not to wake her. I had spent most of my time in Warg territory dispatching the hunting party and handling my pack's complaints and concerns. I was exhausted, and I couldn't wait to crawl into bed with my mate.

I crept up the steps and pushed open the door, but I didn't find Bryn asleep under the covers. Instead, I found her sitting on the bed with reams of paper around her. She looked up as I closed the door behind me. Her smile was so warm and soft, my chest ached. I had been so busy handling alpha business at my pack's compound that I didn't realize how desperately I'd missed her.

"I heard you come in," she said. "What took you so long to get up here?"

I chuckled. "I was trying to be quiet."

"Oh, really?" She laughed.

"Yes, really. If I'd known you were awake, I'd have raced up here instead."

"Mmm. How sweet of you." She lowered the paperwork and started to gather the papers into piles. "Sorry about all of this."

"It's okay. You didn't know I'd be back tonight. What are you working on?"

"Ugh." She rolled her eyes as she placed the papers on the floor beside the bed. "The Redwolfs did *not* keep things organized. Tavi and I have spent the last three days trying to get things into some semblance of order, and it's only now that I could start really looking into the accounts."

"Sounds like you haven't had an easy time." Now that the bed was clear, I crawled in. Bryn's sweet floral scent surrounded me, making my wolf and I feel at ease, even as another part of me started to get excited.

"No, I haven't." She kissed me, and she tasted like peppermint tea, the remnants of which were cooling on her nightstand.

"Are you okay? You seem tired and a little pale." Her weary appearance was more apparent now that I could study her up close. Dark circles ringed her eyes. It looked like she hadn't slept since I left.

"I'm fine. It's just been a long day."

"Well, I'm here now, and I'll help you with anything you need."

She grinned at me. "I know. I'm happy you're back." She rested her head on my shoulder. "We have a lot to talk about, Night."

"Yeah, we do." I touched her chin and kissed her again, but this time, I took my time tasting her, relishing the softness of her lips on mine. I kissed her a third time, even more slowly, and let my tongue slip out to meet hers. When I pulled back, her face was bright red, and those blue-gray eyes were hazy with lust. Mm. Good.

"Let's save the talking for later," I murmured, pulling off my clothes.

Her grin showed her agreement, and she removed the pastel-blue nightgown. Her warm skin smoothed over mine as she wrapped her arms around my shoulders. She was still under the covers, but I felt every curve of her as I covered her body with mine. Kissing her deeply, I took my time to explore every corner of her mouth.

I dragged my tongue lower, to her neck, then to her breasts. Bryn groaned low in her throat as I took one nipple into my mouth. Her hands found my hair, tugging gently on it as I fondled and sucked her skin.

"Night," she murmured, squirming below me. The sheet began to slip down, allowing me more access to her. "I missed you."

Her nipple fell from my mouth with a slight *pop*. She shivered, grinning up at me. "I missed you, too," I said, pressing against her. Her heat seeped through the thin cover as I rubbed myself against her. She cooed, tugging harder at the strands.

"You're teasing me," she whined.

"Me? Tease you?" I nuzzled her and licked the spot where I'd claimed her. She jerked like electricity had just sparked across her skin. "Mm," I growled, looking up at her flushed face, her mouth slightly open as she panted. "Maybe I am teasing a little bit."

"No more." She stroked her hands lower over my neck, moving beneath me and kicking off the cover so we could be skin-to-skin at last. "I want you."

I chuckled and caught her lips again. Her legs opened, and I sank deeply between them. I reached down to take her leg, lifting her knee higher as I filled her.

"Ah." She broke the kiss to sink her head into the pillows. "Ah—Night!"

"That's right, baby," I whispered in her ear. "Say my name."

"Night," she murmured, turning her head and running her tongue along my jaw.

Bryn's muscles tightened around me, eliciting a groan from me. She gave a breathless giggle and did it again, holding it longer. I exhaled sharply.

"Dammit, Bryn, I'm trying to go slow."

She continued to give me that devious grin and tightened around me again. "Maybe I don't want you to go slow…"

I thrust once inside her until I was buried to the hilt, swallowing her cry with my mouth. My hands dipped low to grip her ass and lift her for even better access.

She tugged at my hair, and I growled into her mouth, pressing her into the mattress. Bryn broke our kiss with a moan, her thighs tightening against my body. The wood of the bedframe cracked beneath us.

"Yes, yes, yes," she panted with each thrust. "Night!"

I dragged my mouth down to where her neck met her shoulder, sinking my teeth into her soft flesh. The salt and sweetness of her blood dripped into my mouth and pooled on my tongue like magma. She clawed at my back, raking her nails down my skin. Her next moan was more of a howl as her wolf moved closer to the surface. We both drew blood, and the slight pain only heightened the pleasure.

Bryn threw her head back and screamed as her orgasm quaked through her. She came in ecstasy, juices flowing from her and across the bed. I clenched my teeth as my own climax hit me.

After, we lay tangled in each other, her head nestled against my chest and my arms wrapped around her.

"I'm glad we didn't break the bed," she said.

I gave a tired chuckle and kissed her forehead. "This time," I said. "But who knows what will happen next time?"

She giggled and ran her fingers up and down my chest. "So, how were things when you went home? Is the pack doing well?"

"Yeah, the Wargs are doing great. And there hasn't been any increased feral activity at the borders."

"That's good to hear. What about the council? Dom mentioned that you met with them."

I wasn't sure how to respond. I hated the idea of ruining the moment by describing how bloodthirsty the council was, but I couldn't keep everything about that meeting a secret from her.

"I'm not looking forward to sharing my news," I admitted. "Why don't you go first? I got the impression that you had good news."

I read some worry in her eyes, but she shrugged and propped herself on her elbow. "Sure, okay. I think having the Wargs do work around the compound has done a lot of good. The council seems to be warming up to us."

My eyebrows raised. "What do you mean?"

"Tavi and I met with them yesterday. They said that in the interest of the pack, they wouldn't oppose the next alpha."

"No kidding? That *is* good news. Did they say why?"

"I think their exact words were: 'We are interested in beginning the next phase of our pack's future as seamlessly as possible.' They brought us in to discuss how a merger between the Wargs and Kings would look."

"That's fantastic news." In my wildest dreams, I had never thought the Kings would take the initiative with the merger. I guessed we truly had made an impression on them…which made my council's desire for conflict all the more confusing. Doing things peacefully was working. Why fuck all that up by shedding unnecessary blood?

"I think so, too." She stopped petting me, her hand stilling on my chest above my heartbeat. "Now it's your turn. And don't try to hold anything back to keep me from worrying. You know I'll worry either way."

"Alright, alright." I sighed and placed my hand over hers on my chest. "I didn't have the greatest meeting with my council."

She nodded. "I figured. What's going on?"

"They don't want a peaceful merger; they want things to be as brutal as possible."

There it was—the tightness around her mouth, the furrowed eyebrows…I hated telling her things that made her worry. "Wait, what do you mean?" she asked.

I sighed, then explained the way the meeting had gone. It still made my blood boil that they were so determined to make the takeover of the Kings as bloody as possible. Bryn's expression went from concern to shock. She was seething by the time I finished.

"I never thought they would want to do that to the innocent wolves in my pack," she said. "It's disgusting."

"I hate it, too, love." I kissed her brow, hoping to smooth it out. "I promise you I won't let that happen. I just need to come up with a way to bring the council over to our side as effectively as we've done here." Before they did something we'd all regret.

"Well, you don't have to feel alone in that. I'll help you in any way I can."

"I know. You're always so willing to fight on my side." I couldn't help but smile as I pushed her hair behind her ear. "You've already done good work here. It'll make the merger so much easier now that the council won't oppose it. I'm sure that once the dust settles, our packs will be in a good place. Once the repairs are done, things will be even easier."

She nodded and let me coax her back down to the mattress. She rested her head on my shoulder. "During our meeting with the council, they mentioned that they were worried about Warg enemies becoming theirs, but I hadn't considered that issue."

I scoffed. "It's funny they asked about that when Kings have always been our biggest enemies. I'm sure the Kings have more issues with nearby packs than we do, considering how arrogant Troy and Gregor were."

She nodded. "That's basically what Tavi and I told them."

My hand was on her hip, and I caressed her skin in lazy circles. "It's not your fault you didn't think about those finer details. Mergers between packs as large as ours are rare. Most mergers happen with smaller, newer packs, but the Wargs and Kings have hundreds of years of history on this land. There's no need for one large pack to absorb another when things are peaceful, but our situation is different. Things have never been peaceful between our packs."

I felt her sigh, and my hand stilled.

"When we do finally merge them, I guess we'll have to be ready for conflicts," she said. "I'm not looking forward to that. It's impossible to let our guard down as it is."

"I know, baby." I wished I could deal with everything on my own and keep her far away from any danger or anything that would make her cry. But I couldn't have things my way. Bryn was the alpha of the Kings, and she couldn't just turn a blind eye to what happened in her pack.

"A merger between our packs won't happen all at once," I assured her. "It'll be slow, so both packs can have some time to get used to each other. There will still be conflict and pushback, but it'll be like…an arranged marriage. It's not love at first sight, but over time, you get used to the person next to you and eventually grow to care for them."

She laughed. "Are you using arranged marriages as an example because you know I've read about them?"

"I might have skimmed the backs of the books you've read," I admitted with a grin. "I'd love to hear you tell me about your favorites."

"You could just read them yourself."

"Nah. They're not really my thing."

She grinned and snuggled next to me. "Thanks for talking to me about this. I know things will get harder before they get better, but I'm glad you'll be by my side to see them through."

"Same here." I looked down at her when she yawned. She wasn't usually this tired when we had these longer conversations. "I know I've asked you already, but are you sure you're okay? You seem even more exhausted than I am." And I was the one who'd made the trek from the Wargs to the Kings.

"Oh, yeah. I, um, had to pull a couple of late nights to try to keep up with the workload. That, and I might have talked with some of my bullies earlier today. It took a lot out of me."

"You did?" I touched her cheek, my eyebrows knitting together in concern.

"Basically, they apologized for the way they treated me in the past."

"They're asking for forgiveness?" I scoffed. "If you wanted to banish them, I'd stand behind you."

I meant it—mostly—as a joke, but her little frown told me I hadn't stuck the landing. "Night, I feel really conflicted about this."

"I'm sorry, love." I brushed a gentle kiss over her lips. "You know you have zero obligation to accept their apology, right? They were terrible to you."

"I know, but I don't think I would embody the alpha I want to be if I turned them away."

"Well, you don't have to decide anything right now. You have more than enough on your mind as it is." I kissed her cheek. "Give it some time, and when you feel ready, you can do whatever you think is best."

"Isn't it bad to make them wait? Wouldn't I show them I'm a stronger leader if I give them a quick response?"

I shook my head. "Not every decision you make as an alpha needs to be the day of. Some things need more time to simmer. With experience, it gets easier to tell when you need a quick, decisive response and when you need to pull back."

"Oh." She let my words sink in, and her frown lifted into one of her sweet smiles. "Thank you, Night. I think that was exactly what I needed to hear."

"I'm glad I could help." I kissed her again and nuzzled her neck. "Let's get some sleep."

I decided to leave our conversation there, even though something told me there was more to her tiredness than work and an encounter with her old bullies. I couldn't put my finger on why, especially when her explanation made perfect sense. But she was tired, I was tired, and it was best for both of us to get some rest rather than try to get to the bottom of everything now.

I settled in more comfortably at her side and closed my eyes. In minutes, I was asleep.

Chapter 7 - Bryn

As soon as I sat up the next morning, a wave of nausea sent me hurtling into the bathroom. I made it to the toilet before everything I'd eaten the night before rushed up my throat. It forced me to my knees, and my hands turned to claws as I gripped the bowl.

A combination of embarrassment and dread hit me as I coughed and sputtered into the toilet. *Dammit! What if Night figures out I'm pregnant before I can tell him? Will he be upset that I didn't tell him last night? Will he be mad about the timing of the pregnancy in general?*

I squeezed my eyes shut and tried to force the nausea away. I needed to calm down. Freaking out now would only make everything worse. There was no way I could pretend everything was fine when I went back out there. I'd have to find out how Night felt about having children today. Once I knew where he stood, I would tell him about the baby.

When my stomach settled, I got to my feet and washed up. As I stepped out of the bathroom, I found Night sitting on the edge of the bed. He looked at me, the smooth, handsome lines of his face drawn in concern.

"Are you okay?" he asked, reaching for me as I walked over to the bed. "Are you coming down with something?"

Despite my anxiety about how to break the news to him, his worry for me warmed my heart. I settled on his lap and twined my arms around his neck. He held me against his chest and nuzzled into my neck. I let my hands drift through his thick black hair. It was getting a little long these days—not that I minded.

I could tell him the truth right now. The thought sent a small burst of electricity down my back. I could get it all over with, but it didn't feel right. Though time was running out, I wanted to make the announcement more special than revealing it right after throwing up my guts.

"I think I caught something while I was working," I said, loving the press of his warmth against my body.

"You should take it easy today," he murmured against my throat. "Maybe Tavi and I could take over looking through the paperwork for you."

"I am tired, but I don't think I can sleep. My mind is working a mile a minute now that I'm awake, you know?"

"Mm." He didn't sound pleased with that, and that made me giggle. I remembered a time not so long ago when it seemed like he disapproved of everything I did, whether it was good or bad. Back then, neither of us knew we were soulmates. And now, we'd come so far, although there were still things we didn't see eye to eye on.

Maybe I should tell him here and now. "Night…" I pulled back so I could look into his warm, jewel-green eyes. "Take a walk with me."

"Sure. I'd like that." He kissed me once, twice, and then we got out of bed.

After we got dressed, we headed out onto the compound. It was a cool morning, not quite summertime, and the compound seemed peaceful for once. These days, Night and I hardly drew any attention when we walked around together. In the past, there was always the danger that I'd run into Troy or one of his lackeys, but since I became alpha, I could finally enjoy a stroll through the land I'd grown up on.

I slipped my hand into Night's much larger, rougher one, and he squeezed it gently. I looked up at my mate and subtly ran my free hand over my stomach. I would soon have a family with this man, which was so scary and so exciting at the same time. I just needed to tell him.

"Where are we going?"

"There's this place nestled in the woods. It used to be my escape." It was where I'd taken Tavi when I asked her to be my beta. "I used to have little picnics there—either by myself or with my mom. Sometimes, I'd take a book with me, or I'd draw pictures." I'd packed extra paper from school and used the broken crayons and pencils the other kids didn't want anymore.

He looked at me and smiled one of his rare, warm smiles. "Then I can't wait to get there."

Night and I walked into the forest until we reached a small clearing. It looked the same as when I'd taken Tavi here, with tall, thin spruces circling us. But there were other wildflowers out now, and it was the middle of the morning instead of the afternoon.

Golden yellow wildflowers mixed in with the white and purple. There were camas, fairy bells, dogtooth violets, and trilliums. I took the presence of the trilliums as a good omen—my mother used to tell me they were used to aid expectant mothers in childbirth. I imagined I'd need to start picking them as my pregnancy progressed.

We sat on the soft grass, close enough for our shoulders to touch. The grass was still a little dewy, but it didn't bother us. When the trees shifted and let more sunlight reach the forest floor, the light reflected off the beads of dew, casting an ethereal aura over the area. The dancing butterflies only added to the fairytale-like scene.

"This place is beautiful," Night said, plucking a bright purple camas and placing it behind my ear. "No wonder you love it so much."

"I'm glad you see why this place is so appealing," I said with a grin. "I never had friends I could show this place to, but some part of me always hoped I'd be able to bring someone here." *Tell him! Tell him now!* "But lately, I've been thinking about my future child sitting here with me."

"Yeah?" He was smiling. That was a good sign, right?

"Mmhm. The two of us could play together, and I could teach them about wildflowers. I could read to them or make up stories and go from there."

"That sounds like heaven." He leaned back in the grass and looked up at me. "Am I included in that vision of yours? I'd love to experience that with you two."

"Of course." I lay next to him and cuddled close to his chest. His arm automatically wrapped around me. "As long as work permits it."

His lips brushed over my forehead. "I don't care how busy I am; I'll always make time for you and our family."

Butterflies danced in my stomach, mimicking the little white butterflies flitting from flower to flower around us. Night always knew what to say to fluster me.

"It means a lot to me that I can bring my soulmate here," I said. "I'd given up on my dream of having a mate and a family because I didn't believe anyone would want to have that with me."

"It pains me that you suffered so much while you were here," he said. "But I'm happy to prove you wrong."

He lifted my hand. His hands, scarred from the years of battle and hard work he'd done as a Warg and an alpha, contrasted sharply with my smooth and unblemished skin. Considering I had blood on my hands now, it jarred me to see them so unmarred. But I pushed that thought away. I didn't want to think of Troy or Evan, or anyone else. This moment belonged to Night and me.

"I feel so lucky we found each other," he said softly.

"Me too." I rubbed his arm before slipping my fingers between his. I knew I should just spit out my secret, but for some reason, I wanted to stall. "You know, I grew up wishing I had a father like the other kids. A big, strong wolf who would protect me from the things my mother couldn't."

Night nodded. "I get that. Before I knew what a monster Gregor was, I would tell myself that my dad was off fighting in a battle somewhere, and he'd come home to us when he won. My mom never talked about him when I was a pup, but when she felt I was old enough to know the truth, she didn't sugarcoat anything. It shattered a lot of my ideals for who I believed my father was." He paused, then added, "To be honest, even after I knew what Gregor was, I used to wish he was different, that he'd change his ways and come rescue us. Just a silly dream, I guess."

"I'm sorry," I murmured. "It must have been so hard for you to accept the truth about your father. I don't know how I would have dealt with it if I were in your shoes."

"It's okay. Mom was more than enough for me, and I did have some positive father figures in my life. Dom's dad, for example, was very good with me."

"Oh, yeah? Tell me more about him." I didn't know anything about this aspect of Night's past. A bubble of excitement stirred in my chest at learning new things about my mate.

He nodded and lowered our arms to his chest, squeezing my fingers. "Lucian Slate. He made sure Dom and I grew up as brothers. Lucian went out of his way to include me when he and Dom went hunting or fishing or to the market. He taught us how to fight and what it meant to be a strong wolf. I still hold a lot of what he taught us as principles."

I relaxed against him as he talked. He never spoke about his past like this, and I felt honored that he was revealing these things to me now.

"Dom and I wanted to live our lives making him proud," he said. "I know for a fact that the strength and support Lucian gave me at a young age made me a better alpha. It made Dom a better beta, too. And I see a lot of his dad in him."

I almost hated to ask, but I needed to know Lucian's fate. "What happened to him?"

He let out a sigh. "He was killed twenty years ago. His body was never found, but according to Mom, there was enough of his blood around the area that he couldn't have survived."

"Goodness," I breathed. "It sounded like it must have been a huge battle."

He nodded. "Must have been. We did find the bodies of the wolves he fought and killed. Lucian would never have gone out without putting up a fight."

"I'm sorry you lost him, that both you and Dom lost him."

"It was hard," he admitted. "But we managed to get through it somehow." He squeezed my hand again and sighed. "Wow. I haven't thought about these things in years."

"I'm happy you revisited some of those memories. They sound like good ones."

"They are." He turned his head to me and gave me one of those rare, soft smiles. "I appreciate you giving me the opportunity to go down memory lane with you. I owe it to Lucian to think about him more often."

"I'm sure you honor him by being an incredible alpha every day." I propped myself on my elbow to kiss his cheek and settled back down again. "Do you think you would want to be a father one day?"

He chuckled. "I can't believe you have to ask. Yes, I've always wanted to have a huge family. Growing up with Dom and, later, Tavi in my life was the best part of my childhood. I've always wanted my future pup to have at least one sibling to form that same kind of bond with. That kind of relationship is unbreakable...well, it's supposed to be."

Night rolled onto his side and pulled me against his chest. I rested my head on his arm and slid my hand under his shirt. His warm, muscular chest felt divine under my fingers. If I concentrated, I could remember the pattern of tattoos covering his shoulders. He shivered as I traced them.

"Maybe once all this shit with Troy and our packs blows over, we can try and have a pup. What do you think?"

A sliver of worry shot down my spine. Maybe this was a bad idea. Maybe the news would upset Night, and he wouldn't want our baby right now...

My wolf barked, startling me. She ran back and forth, growling gently. I smiled to myself because I understood her well enough. She was trying to tell me not to be stupid, that Night loved me, that he would love our baby—no matter what.

"That sounds wonderful," I replied, my face boiling. "Do you think nine months is long enough for everything to blow over?"

He paused, then looked down at me, his eyebrows furrowed in confusion. His eyes had darkened from bright emerald to pine green. "Bryn, what are you talking about?"

I smiled hesitantly. "Well, I...I'm pregnant, Night."

Another moment of silence passed, and then it finally hit him. His eyes widened, and a range of emotions passed through them: shock, followed swiftly by worry, fear, and then, finally—thankfully—joy!

He rolled me over on the grass and peppered my face with kisses. I shrieked with giggles at the sudden onslaught of affection, my arms wrapping around his neck. When his kisses finally slowed, I took his face between my hands and kissed him, tasting his happiness on his tongue. As we kissed, his heart pounded quickly against my chest, matching the exact rhythm of mine.

He pressed his forehead to mine. "How long have you known, baby?"

"I found out while you were away," I said. "I'm sorry I didn't do something more spectacular to tell you. I wanted to do something special, but when you saw me being sick this morning, I knew you would figure it out soon enough."

He laughed and kissed the tip of my nose. "Coming out here was more than special enough, sweet girl. I'm glad you shared this news—and this place—with me."

I could have melted into a puddle of relief. Night was happy; he wasn't angry or disappointed—just happy.

"Is there something you haven't told me?" I said. "You seemed a little scared after I told you the news."

"There's a lot to be worried about with Troy still on the loose, but I swear to you, I am happy about this. I've always wanted children, and ever since the day we realized we were mates, I've imagined that future with you."

I kissed him again. My heart was about ready to burst from my chest. Inside, my wolf purred, content that we had finally told him the news.

Later, when we finally pulled ourselves away from the wildflowers and the soft, sweet grass, Night and I walked back to the compound. He was still grinning from ear to ear, and an answering joy bubbled inside me. I had Night and my baby, and there was nothing else I needed. Except…the conversation we'd had about Night's father reminded me how little I knew about my parentage.

"Why so quiet? Something else on your mind?" Night asked.

I nodded. "I wish I knew more about my birth parents. I tried talking to my mom about it, but she didn't know anything more than what I already knew. I'd really, really like to be able to tell our baby about who they were."

"You want to know about them just for our baby's sake?"

"Well, not just for them," I admitted. "I also want to know more about who I am and where I come from. I mean, for all I know, I could have another family out there somewhere. What if they think I died with my mother?"

I was relieved when Night nodded. "I get where you're coming from. I don't know if it's possible to find any answers, but if they're out there, I will help you find them." He paused, thinking a bit more. "My mother might be of use here. I'll talk to her. Perhaps she knows something more. I mean, we know you're the daughter of a pack mother, so that's already a starting point."

"Thank you, Night. Really, it means so much to me that you understand."

He leaned down to kiss the top of my head. "I'm here for you, love. Don't forget that."

I smiled to myself. "I won't."

We walked a bit farther before slowing to a stop. "I wish I could spend all day with you, Bryn, but I should probably find Dom and let him know how things went with the council," he said.

I shivered, remembering how heartless Night had told me they were. "I also have stuff to do today." *For one, I want to head back to the office to finally put a dent in that stupid mountain of paperwork.* "We'll reconnect later, okay?"

He kissed my forehead. "Don't work too hard, okay? If you feel tired, please get some real rest, okay?"

"I will. And I'll have Tavi with me—" I cut myself off with a gasp. "Tavi doesn't know about the baby yet. Only you and my mom know, and that's because Mom was with me when I found out."

"I'm surprised you were able to keep it a secret for so long." He laughed. "I'm glad you told me first."

"Well, it's only right that you're one of the first to know," I grinned. "Maybe we could have Tavi and Dom over for dinner? Then we could celebrate with both of them at the same time. And they'll have the chance to talk to each other."

"Are they still avoiding each other?"

I nodded. "More on Tavi's side, I think. But she told me she wouldn't mind having some excuse to reconnect with him."

"Good, good. I'll talk to Dom and see if he has time to come over. Do we want to do this tonight?"

"Yes, absolutely." I stood on tiptoe and hugged Night tightly. "I'll see you later, okay? I'll be in the office."

"I'll find you." He kissed me deeply and passionately, and then we parted ways.

Chapter 8 - Night

Dom was helping a few Kings with a construction project. This project was taking place near the market along the southern edge of the compound. We were showing Kings different ways to build their buildings and cabins, instructing them on the various methods that could be used and the benefits and negatives of each one. Most of these cabins were built with the post-and-beam method, with logs placed vertically to hold up and support the horizontally placed ones, but there was the occasional timber frame, which had a similar construction, except the logs were squared off.

The Kings had adapted quickly to our teachings. While they worked independently, it always helped to have someone around to oversee the project. Dom and another group of male wolves raised one of the four walls of what would be a cabin. When one side dipped, I stepped in to keep the frame level.

No verbal instructions needed to be exchanged. I held up my end of the frame, Dom held the other side, and a couple of wolves inserted drills and nails into the structure to keep it from falling again. It was an hour of hard, mindless work, which turned out to be exactly what I needed to sort out my feelings about Bryn's pregnancy.

I was overjoyed. In fact, I could have howled about how fucking ecstatic I was that we were about to have a pup. I'd always wanted to be a father, and I didn't even care about its gender; I just loved knowing there would be a pup in the near future who would carry on my line. The timing was a little inconvenient, but Bryn and I hadn't used protection after the first few times we'd had sex. It was only a matter of time before this happened.

Dom turned to me, wiping sweat from his chin with the back of his hand. "Long time no see, Night. I hope things went well back home."

"Eh." I raised my hand, seesawing it from side to side. "More importantly, I have news, but I don't want to mention it here where there are eager ears."

He inclined his head toward the nearby tree line.

I nodded. Before we headed to the forest to get some privacy, Dom let the King wolves know that he'd be back in a bit and to shout for him if they had any issues. With that, the two of us moved between the trees.

I paused, listening closely to make sure we were alone. The only sounds I heard were the slight whistle of the wind moving between the trunks and the rustling of a pair of rabbits. Good, we were alone.

"What's up?" he asked. "The council give you trouble?"

"Oh, I've got things to say about the council," I began, "but that's not what I wanted to tell you."

He tilted his head, staring at me like he could figure it out from sight. "Okay?" He raised the hem of his shirt and dabbed at some sweat that dripped down the side of his face.

I let him sit in suspense for another moment or two, then I grinned because there was no way he'd be able to predict the news. "Bryn is pregnant."

A beat passed, then another, and finally, Dom let go of his shirt and charged me. He looped an arm around my neck, holding me in a headlock.

"You're fucking with me," he said. "You're not telling me I'm about to be an uncle!"

"No, it's *true*," I laughed, hooking one of my legs behind his. I leaned back, and we fell together in the grass, Dom laughing hard with me. My chest warmed and filled with pride, love, and wonder. It was such an incredible feeling.

"Night, congratulations!" he said when he finally got control of himself. "Congratu-fucking-lations!"

"Thank you." I sat up, offering my hand to help Dom get to his feet. I hadn't expected to end up in the grass for the second time that day, but the Fates always had their own agenda in mind.

He took my hand, and I pulled him to his feet. "How far along is she?"

"I don't know. Bryn said she found out while I was gone. We'll have to set up an appointment with a doctor to find out." I paused. "Preferably a Warg doctor."

"Oh, absolutely. I think Doc is still around."

I nodded. If Doc hadn't left for our territory yet, he'd be the best person to ask about Bryn, especially since he'd examined her after we rescued her from Troy. They already had a relationship.

"Tell me more, man," Dom said. "How did Bryn take the news?"

I thought about her smile when she asked me to take a walk with her, the way she laughed when I kissed her, and the softness of her Aegean-blue eyes. My heart stuttered. I put a hand over my chest.

"She's happy about it," I murmured. "Excited."

Dom grinned so hard, you'd have thought *he* was the one expecting a pup. "I'm so happy for you, Night. Truly."

"Thanks." I contemplated the future with a little pup running around, just as rambunctious as Dom or I had been—or maybe they'd be a quieter kid like Tavi. It warmed me, but almost immediately, Troy's ugly mug burst into my mind, shattering the vision. "To be honest, I would've preferred to already be alpha of the Kings or at *least* have Troy dead at my feet before I considered starting a family."

He nodded. "Naturally."

"But I'm not going to let my anxieties get in the way of my and Bryn's happiness. This is huge, but we have months until the baby comes. That should be plenty of time to get things where we want them."

"Absolutely. We have plenty of time to get our shit in order before the little one comes. Of course, you already know I'm willing to do whatever it takes to make things as comfortable for you and Bryn as possible."

"I do know that." I patted his shoulder. We had to do so many things for our packs, but with good people like Dom on our side, I felt confident we could accomplish them. And if anyone tried to stand in our way, we'd have the power to take them out.

"Have you told Violet or Tavi yet?" Dom asked.

"I think Bryn is on her way to tell Tavi, if she hasn't told her already. The only other person who knows right now is Glenda. But no, Mom doesn't know yet. Bryn wants to know more about her birth parents, and I told her I'd ask Mom if she could help her find more information."

"I see. So Bryn wants to know more about where she comes from before the baby gets here."

"Exactly. She wants to know herself better, and wants to be able to tell our child about the kind of people their grandparents were. I can't say I blame her."

"Neither can I. A lot of wolves in our own pack were adopted by other families because of death or illness. People like you and me…we're lucky we know anything about our parents." He paused. "Not that you had it easy with your father."

"No, no, I get what you're saying."

He seemed relieved that I wasn't offended. "Bryn is bound to have questions and feel like some part of her is missing. There's no telling what kind of family she could have out there or what her parents got up to in the months leading up to her birth."

"It's true…but I'm worried there won't be any answers to find. I just don't want her to be upset if we can't get the information she feels she needs."

"I get that. I don't want more pain to come Bryn's way, either. But if I were in her shoes, knowing that there's nothing more to learn about my parents is better than living in wonder for the rest of my life."

I nodded. "I think that's how Bryn feels. She'd rather have some answers than nothing at all." And I knew I would be there for her, even if there were no good news. "By the way, do you have time to come over tonight for dinner? We want to celebrate, and Bryn is going to try to get Tavi to join us."

Dom's cedar-brown eyes had lit up at the mention of a celebration, and when he heard Tavi might be there, his face softened. I wondered if he knew how obvious his feelings for her were. "I'll be there," he said.

"Good." I would have loved to stay on the topic of Bryn and my future pups, but I needed to tell him how things went with the council. "You asked me how things went when I went home…" I began.

Dom, sensing my shift in mood, dropped all excitement from his expression and focused. "Tell me."

"The council wants a complete takeover of the Kings, not a merger. And from the way they were talking, it was clear they wouldn't mind if things turned bloody."

As I recapped what they'd said, I watched Dom's eyebrows draw together and his upper lip curl. I'd begun to think I was going crazy—that I'd somehow missed the council's real intentions the entire time, so it was a relief to read the disgust on his face that matched mine.

Hearing the council's true opinion had blindsided me so much, I was second-guessing whether the people in my circle wanted the same things I did. I never really doubted Dom—he was my beta and my right hand. My goals would always align with his, even if we differed on which paths to accomplish those goals. Still, I was glad to see we were still on the same page about how we wanted to achieve peace.

"I don't know why they made us think they wanted things to go peacefully," he said when I finished. "If they had just been upfront about it, we wouldn't feel like they were yanking the rug from under us after all the progress we've made."

"That's exactly my feeling. That meeting made it clear they were manipulating us from behind the scenes, encouraging us to get the Kings to let their guard down before we turn around with our teeth at their throats." It had me seething all over again. Maybe Pete, the pathetic man who had been alpha after Gregor and before me, would have rolled over for them, but I never would. "The Kings have shown they're willing to put in the work to make their pack better. Why would we want to fuck up that progress with a hostile takeover?"

"There's no point to it but revenge for old wounds." He shook his head. "How do you plan on handling it?"

"Very carefully," I said. "I want to wait until the alpha challenge ends before I take a stance against them. Better that than risk forming a rift in the pack between those who side with me and those who side with them. If worse comes to worst, I want the power to protect my people."

Dom nodded. "It might be difficult to get the council to sit tight for a month, but I've got your back. Not that I like the idea of my niece or nephew being used as a tool in any way, but don't you think telling them about the new heir might get them off your back for a bit?"

I sighed. "Possibly. But I think it would be better to make that announcement after I'm alpha here. That'll give us time to meet with a doctor and find more information about the baby's due date."

"Good point. You're right—maybe waiting is the best thing to do for now." He hesitated, then asked, "So, about the hunting party you sent for Troy…"

I winced. "Let's just take this one thing at a time, huh?"

"Oh, so you didn't tell her about that?"

"Not yet. Once we're sure the baby is healthy, I'll feel more comfortable letting Bryn know. I don't want to put any more stress on her."

Dom gave a resigned sigh that dripped with disapproval. "I understand why you're not telling her right away. But all you're doing is delaying the inevitable." He crossed his arms. "But I'm sure you already know that."

"I'm just trying to avoid a fight."

He raised a brow. "For Bryn's sake or yours?"

"For *both* our sakes."

Dom didn't look convinced. "I just hope you know what you're doing."

A moment of silence passed between us, one that felt like a stalemate. When Dom spoke again, I knew it was because he didn't want the conversation to end on that note.

"Speaking about the alpha challenge, you need to start training. Like yesterday."

"I know. After we finish up here, I'll get started on that." I had a training regimen in mind that I wanted to try. "Mind sparring with me at some point tomorrow?"

Dom grinned, and an answering smile played on my lips. He was the closest to me in terms of raw power and endurance. If I wanted to see real improvement in my fighting—and quickly—Dom was the best person to train with. He'd helped me train when I became alpha of the Wargs. My wolf growled and hopped about in anticipation of battle.

"Today, I'll focus on agility and cardio," I said. "But after…"

"Any time, any place, Night," he said. "Just know I take no pleasure in whooping my alpha's ass."

I snorted. "You haven't beaten me since we were kids."

He smirked. "How do you know I haven't just been taking it easy on you?"

"I'm glad to see my beta's so fired up about fighting me." I chuckled. "After dinner, we'll talk more about where and when we'll spar."

"Sounds great to me."

Dom returned to the building site while I headed deeper into the forest to get started on my training regimen. I began with a jog to get my blood flowing and loosen up.

As I jogged, I allowed my mind to wander. When I took over the Wargs from Pete, I'd trained for weeks beforehand. I ran for miles and miles, bulked up, and worked myself until I was too exhausted to do anything but sleep in my off time. I remembered everything I did back then to get the hard physique I had now.

Compared to the first time I fought to be alpha, this challenge would be different. It wouldn't just be older wolves who didn't expect me to hold my own in battle; it would be men like me, who were trained to be protectors for their pack. All the competitors would know how to fight, and they would all be strong. I would have the advantage of already being an alpha, but I couldn't rely solely on strength. My training would need to focus on full-body workouts and honing my existing abilities. I needed to make each strike deadlier, sharper, and quicker.

I didn't get to show my best at the alpha ceremony with Troy. I knew some Kings believed I wasn't strong enough to rule them. This time, I wanted to eliminate all doubt. I'd prove to everyone that I deserved to be the alpha of the Wargs and the Kings, no questions asked. It would probably be tough to keep up my regimen and help Bryn around the King compound, but there were still a couple of weeks before the challenge. I had time.

I'd create the kind of environment where I could keep Bryn, my pup, and my people safe. That was my mission.

Chapter 9 - Bryn

Tavi was already in the office when I got there. I hadn't even needed to reach out to her through our telepathic bond. She was sitting on the floor, a large binder open in front of her, but she looked up as I walked in and gave me a tired smile. The office itself was still pretty disorganized, but at least the messy piles that once decorated every surface had been cleared.

"Anything interesting?" I asked.

She snorted. "Not really. I was curious about the meeting minutes that Gregor kept, but it's putting me to sleep."

"That sounds riveting." I laughed. "Well, I've got some news that should wake you right up."

"Yeah?" She snapped the binder shut. "What's that?"

"I'm pregnant!"

Tavi gasped, and seconds later, she was on her feet, across the room, and wrapping her arms tight around me. She didn't often initiate physical contact these days, so it was a tremendous gift for her to do it now. When she pulled back, tears shone in her cinnamon-brown eyes.

"How far along are you?" she asked. "Oh my gosh, I can't believe there's going to be a little version of you running around your heels soon!"

I beamed. Now that Night knew I was pregnant and his reaction wasn't anything like I'd feared, the excitement was really starting to seep in. I was going to be a mother!

"A few weeks along, at least, because I've been getting morning sickness, but we'll need to talk to a doctor to know more."

"You poor thing. That can't be fun." Her empathy for my morning sickness shifted when another question entered her mind. "Wait! Who else knows? I'm sure Night is aware, but what about Violet and Dom? Your mom?"

"My mother gave me the pregnancy test," I explained. "Violet doesn't know yet, but I'm sure Night is on his way to tell Dom now. I'm not sure when we'll break the news to Violet."

"You've got to tell her as soon as you can. She's going to be so excited to have a grandchild!"

It was so lovely to see this excitement from Tavi. I couldn't help but pull her in for another tight hug, and my heart soared when she returned the embrace. Maybe it was my hormones or just the emotions of it all, but I started to tear up.

"How are *you*?" she asked when I let her go. "You seem excited, but you must be all over the place, right?"

"That's putting it mildly," I said, plucking a couple of tissues from the box the desk. The first few were dusty, but eventually I found a couple that weren't so old. "I'm ecstatic about the baby, especially now that Night knows it's coming, but it's all happening so fast. It's too late to slow things down now, but I feel like I haven't been able to catch my breath, you know?"

"I can imagine. But I'm sure things will have slowed down by the time the baby gets here. And there's no doubt in my mind that you and Night are going to be kick-ass parents. You're the kindest person I know, and Night will do everything he can to protect you both."

I grinned as I thought of Night. His reaction to my pregnancy had been so precious, it would forever be a core memory for me.

"Do you want it to be a boy or a girl?"

The question pulled me back to the present. "Oh. I don't know. To be honest, I never thought I'd get to have children, so I haven't given much thought to whether I want a son or a daughter. I think I just want a healthy baby, no matter what gender it turns out to be. I'd think Night would want a boy as an heir, right?"

"Oh, Night will be happy either way. If it's a girl, maybe she'll become the first female alpha."

That surprised a laugh out of me. "I thought *I* was the first female alpha."

"Technically, yes. But interim alpha isn't really the same thing for the Kings." Her voice entered my mind. *"Like I said before, I didn't even think we would have the ability to talk like this, even though it doesn't seem to apply to the pack at large."* She switched back to verbally say, "I'm sure there are still people who oppose you and the Wargs in general. Can you imagine how much it'd shake things up to have a female alpha with full control over two powerful packs?"

"When you put it like that, I see what you're saying." It was rare enough to have a male alpha with that much control; a female alpha was unheard of.

I pushed the tissue box out of the way and scooted onto the desk. "Why hasn't there been a female alpha yet? Was it because they weren't allowed to commit to a challenge? Or hasn't one succeeded yet?"

Tavi considered the questions. "I think ability has to be part of it. The Kings aren't the only sexist community of wolves. Female wolves are definitely discouraged from competing so they can bear children. And the fact that, on average, male wolves are stronger than female wolves doesn't help. But you're already aware of that."

"I am. I guess what I really wanted to know is whether there have been *any* female wolves who challenged a male for the position before I did it."

"I don't think so. Pretty sure you're the first."

"Huh. Okay."

I wasn't sure which gender I wanted. A girl might have to spend her entire life fighting just to be viewed as someone who could do more than work in the gardens and care for children. A boy would have it easier, but he would still have to prove to everyone that he was as strong—if not stronger—than his father. There were pros and cons, expectations and shortcomings, to either. I guess questioning ultimately had no effect on which gender I would have; nothing I said or did would change the baby's gender.

"Oh, before we dig into more of this paperwork…Night and I were thinking we could have a little celebration tonight. You're invited, and so is Dom."

At Dom's name, Tavi flushed and looked away from me, busying herself with the meeting book. "Yeah, I'll be there," she said. "Should I bring anything?"

I bit my lip to stop my smile, then hopped off the desk so I could sit in the office chair. "Just your beautiful self."

She scoffed and moved into one of the chairs with the binder so she could continue reading. A few minutes passed. I should have started looking through the documents in front of me, but I was still watching Tavi. She pushed her long jet-black hair over her shoulder, braiding it so it would stay out of the way while she read.

She didn't wear makeup or flowy skirts the way she used to, but she didn't need to wear those things to be every bit as gorgeous and intelligent and important as she was before she was hurt. I didn't know how to communicate all that to her without sounding like I was forcing it.

"Bryn," she said.

I jerked in my chair. "Yes?"

"I think this ledger is missing a page. Do you have it in your stack?"

"Oh. I don't know. Let me check." It only took a few seconds to find the page she was looking for. "Thanks for your hard work," I said as I handed her the paper. "I don't know what I'd do without you at my side."

Her eyebrows rose. I worried that my words had come out awkwardly, but then she smiled, and my fears dissipated.

"Same here, Bryn," she said. "I'm glad I met you."

I shared her smile. As she stapled the papers together, I turned to the pile of overdue complaints. Getting my work done would be easier with my best friend at my side.

A few hours later, after the sun started to go down and the sky was the color of lavender and peach, Night and I finished our day. I had gone through more of the paperwork, and though I felt closer to understanding the state of the pack, there were still reams and reams to get through. When I got home, I changed into a sky-blue dress and arranged my hair into two long braids.

Night had spent the day training for the alpha challenge. When he walked through the front door, he was shirtless, with his chest and shoulders glistening with sweat and his shorts clinging to the powerful muscles of his legs.

The heady, masculine scent of him filled the living room, and it set me on fire. I was tempted to say we should forget the dinner so he could have his way with me on the couch. He smirked at me as he walked by. I was sure that my desires were written all over my face, but instead of indulging me, he gave me a long, sensuous kiss that blazed all the way down to my toes.

"Later, love," he said, sealing his words with another quick kiss, and then headed upstairs to wash off.

When he got back downstairs, we talked about what I'd planned for dinner. I wanted to keep things simple, so we had pasta with a meat sauce, a fresh green salad, and garlic bread. Night handled the meat sauce while I took care of the salad and bread.

We used beef, beef bones, and a combination of fresh and dried herbs for the sauce. The scent of savory tomato sauce filled the cabin. Night's knowledge of cooking surprised me. Beyond the occasional question about whether he was holding parsley or rosemary or if the heat was on too high, he handled himself well in the kitchen. Using the same meat cleaver, he easily cut through bones at one moment, then finely chopped herbs the next.

"Not bad," I said after tasting the sauce that had simmered for forty-five minutes. "You really know what you're doing, huh?"

"I ought to," he replied with a grin. "You know my mother. You think she'd let me leave her house without knowing how to boil liquids?"

I giggled. "Fair point, but you should cut me *some* slack. I don't think there are many alphas who know how to cook for themselves. Most of them would have their mates or lovers do it." I slipped my arms around him from behind and pressed my cheek to his spine. His body was warm under his T-shirt. "You're constantly surprising me."

"I'm glad." As he stirred the sauce with one hand, the fingers of his free hand caressed the back of my arm. "I'd hate to think you were getting bored with me."

"Me? Bored with you?" I squeezed him tighter. "Never."

It had taken me no time to throw the lettuce, tomatoes, and cucumbers together for the salad, and the bread was toasting in the oven with butter, garlic, and cheese. That meant I could turn on the battery-powered radio and put on some music. I kept the radio on a station that played the latest hits, turning up the volume to let the music fill the kitchen and dining room.

Human music wasn't as deep and bass-heavy as the traditional sounds played by pack musicians, but it was still fun to dance to. I was used to reading and working in relative silence, so the music was a real treat. I spun around to a particularly boppy song, and the pleated skirt of my dress swished around my knees. As I completed the turn, I found Night nodding along to the beat.

"Tell me, Night," I said, sashaying my way into the kitchen, "can my big, strong alpha dance?"

He laughed, looking at me over his shoulder. "Not as well as I can cook."

I offered my hands to him. "Care to show me?"

He lowered the heat and covered the sauce with a lid to let it simmer. "Alright, but you have to keep what you're about to see between us."

"Oh? Is it that bad?"

He took my hands and let me pull him to the open space of the living room. "I guess you'll have to decide for yourself," he said.

As it turned out, Night wasn't nearly as bad as he let on. He didn't know the most impressive dance moves, but he could hold the beat, which was more than I could say for some of the other male wolves I'd seen dancing at the few wolf celebrations I'd attended. And despite how large and imposing he was, my mate was very light on his feet.

He took my hand and spun me before pulling me against him again. We swayed to the music, and his hand slipped down to my lower back. He gazed down at me, his eyes a brilliant jade-green, and my heart skipped a beat.

A slow smile spread across his lips as he heard the tempo of my heartbeat speed up. He leaned down and brushed his lips across the top of my ear.

"What do you think?" he asked. "Do I pass your test?"

"With flying colors," I murmured. "I never get to see this side of you, Night." I inched my hands up his chest to his shoulders. "Promise me when things get really busy, we'll make time to do things like this once in a while."

"I promise," he said. "I love spending time with you like this."

I stood on my tiptoes to nuzzle him. "I love you, Night."

"I love you, Bryn." He pressed his lips to mine, and my eyes fluttered closed. He kissed me for a long time—so long, I couldn't think of anything but the softness of his mouth or the warmth of his hands on my back, my hips, my ass...

But we had company coming, and before things could go further, there was a knock on the front door. Night and I pulled away from each other, and I hurried to answer the door, smoothing my clothing as I did.

Tavi was the first to arrive. She'd dressed up for the occasion in a dark teal sheath dress and black flats. Her black hair, which she normally wore pulled back in a messy bun, hung down her back in soft waves. There was even a touch of makeup on her face—mascara and tinted lip gloss.

"You look gorgeous, Tavi," I said, hugging her. Tears stung my eyes because she reminded me of her old self before Troy and his goons got to her. It meant so much that she was willing to celebrate with us tonight. "Come in, come in. We'll put the noodles on."

"Already on it," Night called from the kitchen. "They'll be done in ten minutes."

"It smells great," Tavi said as I closed the door behind her. "But I'm surprised you convinced Night to cook. It was always like pulling teeth to get him to do anything more elaborate than put together a box cake."

"No, Tav, I was like that with *you* specifically," Night retorted. "For you, I don't do anything for free."

She snorted and rolled her eyes at me.

I giggled.

There was a second knock on the door, and unsurprisingly, that turned out to be Dom. He had dressed up as well, wearing black slacks and a navy-blue button-down shirt that accentuated his muscular torso. His curly golden-blond hair was combed out of his eyes.

"Nice to see you, Dom," I said, hugging him.

"Same here. And congratulations, Bryn." He lifted his hand, which held a bottle. "I brought some apple cider for you."

"Thank you so much." I beamed at him and accepted the bottle. After I closed the door behind him, I watched his eyes find Tavi's. There was an immediate connection there, the air between them electrifying as I stood there, and then Tavi looked away.

"It's good to see you," she told him.

"Yeah, good to see you, too," he said gently. "You look beautiful."

She smiled and pushed her hair behind her ear. "Thanks. You...you clean up pretty nice."

Dom grinned, slipping his hands into his pockets. I sensed this was my cue to give them some alone time, so I excused myself.

"I'll set the table," I said. "You two can change the radio station if you want. Just make yourselves comfy."

I went into the kitchen and took my time getting plates and utensils. Fortunately, Tavi and Dom were standing in the sitting room, and I wouldn't have to walk in on their conversation to get the dining room ready.

"Dom's here," I said to Night.

"I heard. Is he in there with Tavi?"

"That's right."

He paused, and I could sense where his thoughts were going. He wasn't oblivious; he noticed the depths of their feelings for each other. I imagined that as the big brother to Tavi and best friend to Dom, Night was torn about the two of them getting closer.

I set the plates on the counter and touched his back. "It'll be okay," I told him quietly. "Whatever happens between them, you know Dom will do right by her."

He sighed. "I do. It's just hard to let her go. Especially after all she's been through."

"But that's why it's okay. Dom has been nothing but respectful to her, and he's given her space while she deals with her trauma. He's a good guy, Night."

His answering sigh acknowledged the truth of my words. I fell even deeper in love with my big, strong, protective alpha.

"Do you need help setting the table?"

I shook my head. "No, but I'd like some."

He took the plates, forks, and apple cider from me, and I grabbed three beers from the fridge. When the table was set, and the pasta was ready, the four of us sat at the table to chat about the baby and how the repairs were going around the pack.

"By the way, Bryn," Tavi began, "whatever happened to the bitches who went out of their way to make your life difficult when you were growing up?"

She was talking about the Terrible Ts. "They've left me alone after the attack on the compound," I said. "I think the way the Wargs and I showed up for the pack showed them that I'm not the same girl they used to know."

"Damn right," Dom and Night said at the same time. Laughter went around the table.

Once the laughter died down, I said, "Tanya and Tara let me know that they felt real remorse for the way they treated me and that I had their support. I wasn't sure what to make of it at the time, but I think I'll let them know that I accept their apology."

Tavi seemed taken aback by that. "Wow, Bryn. I couldn't even imagine forgiving them. Do you think you might be friends with them?"

I scoffed. "No, I wouldn't go that far. With our history, I don't think we'll ever be that close. But they won't feel like I have it out for them, and I don't have to hold on to those bad memories so tightly."

Of course, those awful memories would never go away, but this was my way of proving to everyone—myself included—that people can change. The way Troy had treated me and the competitive environment he and his father had fostered in the Kings wasn't permanent. We could change as long as everyone had the space to do so.

"What about your training, Night?" Tavi asked.

"Hm? It's going well. I'm sore every day, but what kind of training would I be doing if I didn't have constant soreness?"

"Maybe you could train publicly with the rest of the wolves," Tavi said. "Show the Kings what's in store for them when you're alpha."

There was a pause, and we all turned to look at Tavi.

"What do you mean, Tav?" Night asked.

I thought she might blush under the attention, but she tossed her hair over her shoulder just like the old Tavi would have—a gesture that showed her confidence. It was so unexpected and welcome, I nearly laughed.

"Well, you've been training in secret, but maybe it would be more effective to show them what you're capable of."

Night thought for a moment. "I could do that. Before, I thought I needed to train privately because it would keep the other men on their toes. But you're right,

Tav. Maybe a little demonstration would be better." His grin was sharp. "Thanks."

Tavi grinned as if knowing how Night would take her suggestion. "It's what I'm here for."

The second little hair flip sent me over the edge. I started giggling, and soon that giggle became a laugh. It was such a relief to be here with three of the most important people in my life, and it was so, so wonderful to joke and laugh with them.

Chapter 10 - Night

After finishing the bottle of apple cider that Dom had brought for her, Bryn found a spot to curl up and fell asleep while the rest of us talked. I found her on the couch with her knees tucked toward her chest, surrounded by throw pillows. She looked like a doe curled up for sleep in the woods. The sight was so sweet, it almost hurt to look at her.

My mate, I thought with an intensity that surprised me. *Mother of my pups.* The deep, growling purr from my wolf showed me his agreement.

Tavi turned off the music, and I sent her a grateful look. "I'm going to put Bryn to bed," I said, speaking quietly so I didn't disturb my mate. "Good night, you two. Thanks for coming."

"We'll catch you later, Night," Dom said. "Tavi, wanna take a walk with me?"

She nodded, ducking her head slightly. Before they left, she turned to me. "I keep forgetting to tell you this, Night. Violet asked me to tell you that she wants you to come by and see her soon."

"I'll swing by her place tomorrow morning."

She nodded but hesitated instead of following Dom to the door. She looked up at me for a few moments, then moved forward to hug me.

"Congratulations, Night," she whispered. "I'm so happy for you and Bryn."

I hugged her back. I hadn't realized how much I'd missed her affection. It felt like years had passed since the last time we were so close with each other. "Thanks, Tav. Have fun tonight, okay?"

She nodded, and when she stepped back, she was smiling shyly. "We'll see ourselves out."

I carefully scooped Bryn into my arms. She moaned slightly, leaning her head against my arm. She felt so small and light in my arms, it was difficult to envision that she'd one day have a fuller, rounder stomach. The thought almost made me laugh because it was so different from how she looked now.

I helped her out of her dress and gently put her in bed. As I pulled away, my shirt caught on something. I turned, and it was Bryn holding the hem of my shirt between her fingers, her blue-gray eyes peering up at me through long dark lashes.

"Stay," she whispered.

I smiled. The expression on her face, sleepy but insistent, made my heartbeat quicken. "I was just getting to my side of the bed."

"Good." She slowly let go of my shirt, and I pulled it off before crawling on top of her. Her hands clasped my shoulders.

I kissed her. "Are you awake enough to have some fun?"

A smile spread slowly across her lips, and she nodded.

"That's my girl." I pressed my lips to hers again, slowly this time.

I kissed her jaw and the spot just underneath her chin. Her fingers pressed into my shoulders, and she let out a sweet, soft moan. The sound, the smooth warmth of her skin…every caress was like heaven to me.

I trailed lazy kisses down her chest and sucked one of her hardened nipples into my mouth. Bryn moaned loudly, and I moved to the other nipple. I was careful with her because I knew how sore her body had been lately. I didn't want to remind her of her aches and pains; I wanted her to feel beautiful—like the queen she deserved to be.

"Night," she whimpered, pushing gently on my shoulders.

She wanted me to head further south, and I was all too eager to oblige. I trailed kisses down her stomach, enjoying the texture of the goosebumps that my lips sent rippling across her skin.

Sliding my fingers under the waistband of her panties, I pulled the fabric down and tossed it aside to join my shirt and her dress. The intoxicating, heady scent of her pussy had my wolf purring. I flattened my tongue against her mound and dragged it slowly between her fuzzy lips, and it was all I could do not to howl when the salted honey taste of her spread across my tongue.

She gave a small cry as I devoured her, slipping my tongue inside her warmth before clamping my mouth down on her clit and sucking gently. Without my shoulders to hold onto, her hands pushed through my hair. Her legs bent, and her thighs tightened against my head.

It wasn't long before each pass of my tongue made her body quake. She gripped my hair, holding me still as my tongue delved into her. Her orgasm rocked through her. She arched her back as she came hot on my face. I lapped at her. She was delicious.

After, when her thighs relaxed enough that I could slip free, I looked up at her. She was a mess, her hair spread across her pillow, her skin glowing with sweat, her chest rising and falling with each quick breath. Her smile was full of satisfaction, which was all I needed to see.

I left the bed to wipe my face, and when I came back, Bryn was still awake. I climbed into bed next to her, and her body curved into mine. I wrapped my arms around her.

"You're going to tell your mom about our baby tomorrow?" she asked.

"That's the plan." I sighed. "I'm a little nervous."

"Why?"

"I don't know. I know she'll be happy, but I guess it's just the anticipation of talking to her about it." I shook my head. "I don't know."

Bryn patted my arm. "It'll be okay."

"Yeah, I know. Maybe I'm just tired."

She yawned and snuggled closer. "Let me know how it goes, okay?"

"Of course." I kissed the top of her head. "Sweet dreams."

She laughed a little, but within seconds, she was asleep. I closed my eyes and tried to empty my mind to let my exhaustion take over.

The next morning, I gave Bryn a kiss on her forehead before I left. Heading out into King territory at night wasn't something I often did. I was always on alert when out and about in what had always been enemy territory. Maybe that was why I felt a little nervous about announcing to Mom that Bryn was pregnant.

I was proud of Bryn, proud and unbelievably happy that I was going to be a father in a matter of months. Still, the weight of the news was heavier than the logs I'd carried earlier that day as part of my training. My mother would also want to hear about my trip back home, which I wasn't looking forward to rehashing.

When I got to Mom's cabin, I took a deep breath, exhaled, and walked inside. She was in the living room, snacking on some bacon she'd crisped up on the stove. A quick sniff told me her cup contained lemon ginger tea.

"There's my son," she said. "Look at you, coming to see me the day *after* I requested it."

I chuckled and eased into the seat across from her. "You know I like to be punctual."

"Mmhm." She sipped her drink. "So, I wanted to talk to you about the council. Dom said you were meeting them."

I let out a deep sigh and pushed a hand through my hair, wishing I was drinking something that would burn on the way down. For the third time, I went through the council's demands, and for the third time, I felt a seething frustration rise in my chest.

"Dammit," she said when I finished speaking. "I wish I could say I was surprised. The five of them have done so much good for the Wargs, and I would never take that from them, but those fools are too stuck in the old brutalist way of doing things. Not to mention," she added with a scowl, "they assume they can control you the way they were able to control Peter."

"Fuck that."

"So, what are you going to do about them?"

"My plan right now is to take things slow. Bryn had a pretty encouraging meeting with the Kings' council, and with the reconstruction projects, we're getting in the pack's good graces. I think I'll have some real support after the challenge—whatever that challenge turns out to be."

"Mm," she hummed, considering my words. "I know we all hate biding our time, but I think you're right—that's the best way to handle things right now. I can't believe the council is dragging their feet on this. I guess that's bureaucracy for you. What's the plan for the challenge? Have you started training?"

"I have. And I've got Dom keeping an eye on my competition. We know of two threats, but they won't be impossible to beat."

"That's good to hear. Is there anything else to report?"

Now was as good a time as any to tell her about the baby, but after talking to her about the alpha challenge, I wasn't sure why I'd been so nervous before. Mom would be over the moon with joy.

"Yes, actually," I said. "Bryn's pregnant."

She gasped, hopped to her feet, and rushed to embrace me. I hugged her and spun her around before setting her back down.

"Ah, my boy, my boy!" she exclaimed, pulling back to take my face in her hands. "Going to be a father already!"

I couldn't keep my grin from spreading ear to ear.

"You met Bryn only a couple of months ago, and already you're giving me grandbabies," she teased. "You certainly didn't waste any time."

I chuckled. "Mom, come on."

She pinched my cheek, then gently patted the same spot. "Honey, this is incredible. Why is Bryn not here with you to announce this?"

"She's exhausted. We had a little celebration with Tavi and Dom last night. She was still asleep when I left this morning."

My mother nodded and returned to her seat. I did the same as I snagged a few pieces of bacon.

"It sounds like you all had a great time last night."

"We did, yeah." We'd laughed a lot, and danced and talked about the future with my family, and…if I had space on my face to smile wider, I would've. "With all the shit that's been going on lately, I don't think I realized how much I missed relaxing with them."

"Oh, Night, I'm so glad you all had a good time." She reached across the table to touch my hand. "How far along is she?"

"We're thinking only a few weeks, but I want Dr. Stan to take a look at her. Dom told me he hasn't left for home yet."

"Oh, yeah, he's still here," she said. "I'm planning on seeing him tomorrow. I'll ask him to pay you two a visit."

I frowned and lifted the cup to take a drink. "Is it because of your alpha wound?"

"Oh, no, honey. He and I have been arranging a date."

I choked on my tea. She watched me recover from my coughing fit with obvious amusement.

"D-date?" I managed to get out.

My mother had the audacity to chuckle. "That's right."

I sighed and drank the tea, wishing again that I had something much stronger. "Between you and Tavi, I don't know how I'm going to survive the year."

"How was Tavi last night?"

"She was good, sociable even. Dom walked her home."

"Ah. Good for her. Good for them." She leaned back in her seat. "She has been hurt so deeply, and it puts me at ease to know she's starting to come out of herself a bit more."

"You and me both, Mom."

Tavi's shyness and introversion…it was hard to see. She had been quiet and withdrawn after the Kings killed her family, but as she grew up, she was such a vibrant, outgoing personality. I missed the person my sister used to be, the Tavi who could smile and talk for hours about nothing. But dammit, that didn't mean that I loved her any less.

To see her like this now…if it took *me* back to those hard days, I couldn't fucking imagine what it must be like for her. Rage burned in my chest thinking of Troy and the sons of bitches who had hurt her.

I felt bad about not telling Bryn I'd sent a hunting party after Troy, and I hated that the council had forced me to send one. But when I thought about the possibility of my wolves finding him, catching him unawares, and ending that fucker's life right then and there, I couldn't help but feel deep satisfaction that he could no longer hurt my family.

"Night?"

Mom's voice yanked me out of that dark place. "Sorry, what?"

"I asked when you were planning on revealing the news."

"I told Dom earlier that I don't plan to tell our council about Bryn's pregnancy yet. We're happy about the baby, but the timing isn't exactly ideal. There are still so many unknowns, still so much to get done."

"I imagine we're the only ones who know about it?"

"That's right. Bryn's mother and Doc will know, but other than the seven of us, we're keeping it quiet."

"At least until the alpha challenge is over," she agreed. "The Kings' council won't be too happy to know their temporary *female* alpha is pregnant. They'll throw that in her face."

"One hundred percent." I crossed my arms. "I'm not worried that they'll retaliate against her personally, but they might try to replace her with someone else. If that happens, it could undo all the progress we've made with the Kings."

She sighed. "We'll just have to wait and see. I'm sure the Fates have a plan for this, but I hate waiting to find out what it is."

"Same here." I blew out a breath. "By the way, Mom, I have a favor to ask. Bryn wants to learn more about her biological parents, but she's hit a brick wall there. Is there anything you can do to help her out?"

Her eyebrows shot up. "I wasn't expecting you to ask me that." She scratched her chin.

"I know it probably won't be easy with how little we have to go on."

"Honey, you know I'm at my happiest when I'm needed." She patted my hand. "Don't worry, I'll find out what I can, but as you said, I doubt there's much to find."

She smiled. "I'll reach out to our elders, the Kings' elders, and anyone else to get more information about Bryn's mother."

"Thanks so much, Mom." If she could find out where Bryn's mother lived, it would lead us closer to finding out who her father was. "Bryn wants to be able to tell our pup about their grandparents. I think she feels lost because she doesn't know anything about them."

Mom nodded. "Wolves have always been pack animals. We must have family and community around us all the time. And equally important, we need to know they accept us. Bryn was denied both community and acceptance her entire life. If there's even a chance that she has siblings or cousins, it's only natural that she'd want to find them."

"Exactly." Bryn had recently learned that not only was she never human, but also that she was the daughter of a pack mother. All that new information would make anyone want answers about their heritage.

"Thank you for doing this for her, Mom. Really."

She waved a hand in dismissal. "If I can help ease Bryn's worries, that'll be all the thanks I need." The corner of her mouth twitched. "You know, Night, you had such a kind, gentle nature when you were a little boy. You cried every time you and Dom had one of those silly fights, or one of the other kids didn't want to play with you. Whenever I told you stories, your little heart broke when the hero didn't make it."

"Aw, Mom." I couldn't remember being so tender-hearted.

"I was beginning to think the harshness of Warg life had weeded out the soft little boy I raised. I worried I was one of the lucky few to see your sweetest smiles….but I was wrong. Bryn brings out the warmest parts of you, Night. You're much quicker to show your gentler side. Not just with Bryn, but with how you talk about the merger and being alpha, of trying to foster a better, healthier community. It's lovely to see." Tears misted her jade-green eyes. "It's lovely to see," she repeated.

I got out of my chair to kiss her forehead and hug her. "I love you, Mom."

"I love you, too, honey." She sniffled and patted my back. "Now, listen. The first three months of pregnancy are the hardest. The best thing for Bryn to do is to get as much rest as possible and drink peppermint tea when her stomach aches. But to be honest, I imagine Glenda's already got her covered on that front."

"Got it. I'll make sure she doesn't push herself too hard. But you know it'll be a struggle to get her to listen to me."

She laughed. "Our Bryn is stubborn, but she'll do right by her baby. That's just the kind of person your mate is."

Chapter 11 - Bryn

The warm water in the bath was filled with so many herbs, I felt like I was steeping in tea. The aromas of rosemary and chamomile drifted through the air, thanks to the things Violet had sent with Night. A cup of the tea my mother had mixed for me sat on the stool next to the tub. The soothing scents and tea helped ease the aches in my body, but I still felt like a pincushion.

Some of the bubbles had disappeared in the twenty minutes since I'd gotten into the tub. I reached to add more, but a wave of nausea rocked me before I could grab the bottle. I closed my eyes, willing away the urge to vomit. Now, in the tub, would be the worst time to lose my breakfast.

Thankfully, the wave dissolved without incident. I sighed and leaned my head against the hand towel draped over the edge of the tub. "Dammit, I should be working." I groaned.

I was here because I'd vomited my entire stomach into the toilet that morning. Night told me I needed to rest—what else was new? Everyone had been telling me to do that—and that he'd take over the paperwork for me. When he offered his help, I assumed the two of us would be working together. Not that I would be soaking in a tub while *he* did all the work.

Even Tavi was busy checking up on the reconstruction today, so Night was working by himself. I loved him, I appreciated him, but it irked me to no end that I had to rely on him so completely. I'd never felt more useless and out of the loop. And he wouldn't even bring me some documents to pass the time while I "relaxed."

What a joke. How was I supposed to take it easy when my pack needed me?

Growing up, Mom was the only person I could rely on, and even then, I was always a pretty self-sufficient child. Having a mate meant I should rely on him when I needed to, but I hadn't thought I'd have to rely on him like this so soon.

While I understood that the first few months would be the toughest on me, I'd never expected it to be like this. As much as I had already fallen in love with my baby, I wish I'd known ahead of time that it would feel like my life was being drained out of me. At least then, I could have planned for the days when I was too weak to get out of bed—or out of the tub.

Night didn't mind catching up on work for me, but that didn't lessen my guilt about taking a bubble bath while he and Tavi combed through that mass of paperwork.

I sighed and closed my eyes, sinking under the water until the suds covered my mouth. Maybe I could convince Night to bring some of the paperwork home. I could handle some light reading.

As if thinking about him had summoned him, I heard his heavy footsteps headed up the stairs. Night was normally light on his feet, but because I hated when he snuck around, he didn't mask his footsteps.

Moments later, he came into the bathroom. I opened my eyes and spotted the envelopes he held.

I sat up, wiping away the suds that clung to my chin. "Did you read my mind?" I asked, resting my arms on the rim of the tub. "I was just thinking of asking you to bring me something to look at."

He chuckled as he bent and kissed my forehead. "Are you so bored that you *want* to look through these old receipts and invoices?"

"It's not about boredom; it's about getting things done." I gestured for him to sit. "Sure, reading a book is nice, but we need to get this done. These old ledgers will help us understand the pack better."

Many of the complaints I'd read involved issues with access to resources. I'd always been under the impression that Kings lived luxurious lives, but in reality, it was just a front. Most of that money had ended up in the pockets of either high-ranking families or the Redwolfs. Many of the issues could have been addressed with a simple reallocation of funds.

Night moved my mug so he could sit on the stool. "You're supposed to be relaxing."

I scoffed. "As if I could focus on a bodice-ripping romance in the middle of all this chaos."

He smiled and brushed the back of his hand across my cheek. "Fair enough. It's impossible to get you to slow down. Paperwork shouldn't put too much of a strain on you."

"Right."

"So, how are you feeling?" he asked.

"Like crap," I said with a sigh. "It's like I've got a bad flu with all the aches and pains and vomiting but none of the sneezing and coughing." My body already felt like it was carrying the weight of two, but the baby wasn't much larger than a pebble right now.

Night frowned in sympathy and peered into my mug. It was almost empty. "I'll make you some more tea. Will that help?"

"Thanks, love. I'm still a bit queasy, so that'll help a lot." I glanced at the envelopes. "What did you bring me?"

"Oh, right." He looked like he'd just remembered why he'd come up here. "A wolf dropped these off. They need your signature. He wanted to bring them to you directly, but"—he grinned and showed his sharp canines—"I told him that wasn't necessary. I'd bring them right up to you myself."

I snorted. "Uh-huh. And I'm sure you terrified the guy in the process." I noticed the papers stuck out of the envelopes. "Did you trip and open the envelopes on accident?"

A mischievous glint flashed in his eyes. "Well, I admit I was a little curious about them. I *might* have taken a peek before coming up here."

I raised a brow. "And how long have you been sitting on these important documents?"

He tried to look innocent, but with those sharp features, the attempt fell flat. "No more than an hour."

I knew he was joking, but a new worry formed in my chest. Night was not the alpha of the Kings, so his seeing the documents was probably against pack law. Allowing a once-enemy-pack's alpha to look through these documents was likely very ill-advised. Hopefully, the council wouldn't find out how much Night was helping. There hadn't been any pushback thus far, and I hoped things stayed that way.

I dried my hands on the towel. "Alright, hand them over."

The documents were approval requests for repairs within the pack and checks to pay the shopkeepers and workers. I signed the papers with the pen Night handed me. At least I was doing *something* productive.

"By the way," he said, "I found some irregularities when I went through the ledgers."

"The ledgers? You're already looking through those?" I'd set those aside to look over tomorrow or the day after. He'd moved through the documents quicker than Tavi and me.

My emotions must have shown on my face because he gave me a gentle smile. "I'm used to looking through these sorts of things, and I know what to look for. Don't be too hard on yourself, Bryn. You're still getting the hang of all this."

"Right, yeah, of course." I tried not to feel like a little girl who was more out of her depth than she'd thought going into all of this. I should've been the one who had discovered the irregularities, not Night. "What irregularities did you find?"

"For the most part, everything was as I'd expect, but the Kings have been making slightly less of a profit than expected for a pack this size."

"Less of a profit," I repeated. "Is that due to the markets bringing in less money, or is it because Gregor and Troy spent more of the pack's funds than they should have?"

"It's hard to say for sure, but I think it's probably a bit of both. Starting in January, it looks like the market sales went down at a steady rate. They were probably neglected when Gregor became sick. Sales took a major dip a couple of months ago, and I'm sure that's because Troy didn't bother to keep things up and running."

"Okay. Could we check in with the shop owners and see what they have to say?"

"Absolutely. I think we ought to ask them how well their sales have been lately."

I nodded. The commons was where packs made their money. If the shop owners weren't bringing in the profits we needed to see, the pack as a whole would suffer. "Does the pack have enough money in savings to handle payroll?"

"From what I see, that shouldn't be a problem. It's not that the markets aren't making any money; their sales are just lower than expected."

"You said it might be more than just the markets, so where else have we been losing money? I could totally see Gregor or Troy stealing money from the infirmary or the gardens, for example."

He snorted. "So could I, but it's not quite that. It's not just one account that's missing money—it's all of them."

I tilted my head. "What do you mean?"

"It's not unusual for a pack to have multiple accounts; the Wargs have one for payroll, one for renovations and general pack upkeep, and one for emergencies. Everything else is a surplus. It's easier to keep it all separated because then you can see what you have in each account to take care of specific things. It can get confusing looking at the whole sum without some organization."

"That makes sense."

"The Kings work the same way, though they work with larger sums of money and have more accounts. Someone has been taking medium-sized sums from each account and citing 'taxes' for these withdrawals. The money that's moved into this supposed tax account is never the same amount, and the funds are never withdrawn at the same time."

I was starting to feel cold even though the water was still pleasantly warm. "And how much money is in the tax account?"

"It should be close to two-hundred-and-fifty-thousand dollars."

"Why 'should be?'"

"I can't find the tax account in any of the documents, so I don't know the exact amount."

"Wait, what do you mean you can't find it?"

His expression darkened. "It's not connected to any of the main accounts. These withdrawals go back at least five years, but the tax account is hidden. I can see the discrepancies and the reasons given for the withdrawals, but I can't find even one official statement that shows the tax account exists."

My heart started to race. "I don't even want to imagine what someone could do with a quarter of a million dollars. But Night, you have to give it to me straight."

He ran a hand through his hair and sighed. "Bryn, I don't want to stress you out any more than you already are, but that money is more than enough to start a new pack."

"Oh, shit," I whispered. My blood chilled thoroughly. *Troy.* "Do you think Troy has the account?"

"That's exactly what I'm afraid of, but without knowing more about the account, I can't say for sure."

"Who else would have access to these accounts?" I asked.

"I wish I could tell you, but I don't know how the Kings operate. My pack had an issue with theft under Pete, so when I took over, I made it so only the council, the elders, myself, and Dom could access our accounts. I'm hoping the Kings work similarly."

"I guess we'll have to ask the council if they know anything about it."

"That's what I want to do today, but I can't do that without you present," Night said. "I hate that I have to ask you to do this when you should be taking it easy, but we should get to the bottom of this as quickly as possible."

"I agree," I said, setting aside the documents. "Let's do this now."

His eyebrows knitted together. "If you're sure you're feeling up to it, we'll do it. I wanted to give the doc a visit and see if everything's okay with you and the baby, but perhaps we should do that another day."

I shook my head. "No. We'll see Dr. Stan after we've seen the council. Making sure the baby is healthy is a priority, but I want to confront the council about this."

No matter how horrible I felt, I couldn't keep sitting on my ass when there were so many unknowns. If Troy had access to that tax account, there was no telling what kind of evil he'd do with that kind of money. If he had been squirreling funds away all this time, I had no doubt he'd use them to benefit his feral army.

The thought pushed me to my feet. Startled by the sudden movement, Night reached out to steady me, but I was already standing on the bath mat and reaching for my robe.

"Bryn, it could be taxing—"

"Night, I don't care. This might explain why the ferals were so willing to risk their lives to help him escape. If they're on Troy's payroll, we're probably in for more attacks."

His lips pulled back into a snarl. "Shit. You're right. We needed to get to the bottom of this *yesterday*."

I nodded. "Let's get going."

Chapter 12 - Night

Bryn sent Tavi to gather the Kings' council members while she got dressed. Worry churned in my stomach as I watched her get ready. She seemed so pale and fragile, and I hated that I had to drag her out of the house. True, the stakes were incredibly high if Troy had access to that money, and there was no way I could approach the Kings' council with this info on my own. But at the same time, Bryn was pregnant. She needed to take things easy, but every time I saw her, I brought news that increased her stress. It was only a matter of time before that stress took its toll on her.

"If it were up to me, you wouldn't have to leave this cabin," I said as she brushed her hair.

She put down the brush and turned to me. "Don't say that. This is bigger than either of us. You uncovered some crucial information, and we can't just let this go. We need to handle it now while there's still time. If Troy is behind this, there's no telling when he could strike."

"I know, but…" What kind of man was I to force my pregnant mate out of bed instead of handling it myself? A shitty excuse for one, that's what. Bryn was right—this was out of our hands, and it was clear that she felt a little inadequate that she hadn't handled the ledgers herself. I understood her wanting to feel useful through this process, but that only settled the guilt more firmly on my shoulders. Was I being the mate she most needed? How did I know I was supporting her the way she needed most?

After she dressed, we left to meet the council at the usual spot. Bryn must have reached out to Tavi telepathically because she was waiting for us by the double doors.

I had hoped that the next time I saw my sister would be under more casual circumstances, but given her grave face, she had been brought up to speed as to why we'd called this meeting. But to my delight, her expression lifted a bit when she saw me.

"Hi, Night," she said.

"It's good to see you, kid."

She chuckled. "Likewise." She held her fist out to bump, and I obliged. "Let's hold these folks to task, huh?"

"Absolutely," Bryn said with a bright smile. She was getting better and better at hiding the effects of her pregnancy. Her ability to adapt was impressive and intimidating at the same time.

I pulled open the door to find the council assembled and waiting for us.

"Good morning, everyone," Bryn said, taking charge before any of them could speak.

"It would be a better morning if we were privy to the nature of the meeting," Dana said.

"Then I won't waste your time. I'll get straight to it." Bryn tossed the documents on the table in front of the council members, drawing their attention to the circled and highlighted sections. "There are discrepancies in the pack's financial accounts. Going back at least five years, thousands and thousands of dollars have been moved into an account labeled 'for taxes,' but there is no evidence of a tax account. Do any of you know where that account is?"

Edward looked through the paperwork before handing it to Colby, who was sitting next to him. His frown told me he was about to say something stupid, and the man didn't disappoint.

"I'm sorry, Alpha Hunter," he said in an unapologetic tone. "Maybe there's something more at play here? It's likely you don't understand some of the accounts because you're still so young, and your mind...your mind just isn't wired to understand how our accounting systems work."

Bryn leveled a scathing glare at him, but Tavi stepped in before Bryn or I could retort.

"That's going too far, Edward," Tavi said. "Are you saying because she's female, she doesn't know how to read?"

Pride swelled in my chest. Though Edward's comments pissed me off, I was glad my sister had said something before I could. It was a beta's job to have their alpha's back, and it seemed Tavi had taken to that part of her role.

"That isn't what I said—" Edward began.

"It's what you implied," Tavi interjected, putting her hands on her hips. "I recommend you rethink how you speak to your alpha."

Edward shut his mouth. Instead of arguing the point further, he settled on glaring at Tavi for calling him out.

"Councilman," I said, stepping forward. "My mate is more than intelligent enough to read bank statements and track money." I trained my gaze on Edward. "And Tavi is right—don't try to bullshit us. One way or another, we'll track down the truth, and you will want to be on our side about this."

"That sounds like a threat," Dana said. "Is the alpha of the Wargs trying to usurp our authority?"

She had no idea how badly I wanted to say "yes."

Bryn crossed her arms. "Dana, you're not changing the subject so easily. What Night said wasn't a threat; it's the truth. We'll find out the purpose of that tax account somehow, and when we do, I doubt the Kings will be happy to hear that members of their council got in our way. Let's not forget we're talking about *pack funds*—money that's meant to benefit the Kings. This isn't just a little skimming off the top of some surplus account."

An uneasy silence filled the room. Dana tried to stare Bryn down, but Bryn wasn't having it. She crossed her arms and met her gaze without flinching. If I didn't know any better, I would never have guessed she wasn't feeling her best.

Had I been in her position, I would have threatened the council with death to find out what they knew. It would be well within Bryn's right as alpha to have them killed for concealing the truth, but that wasn't my mate's style. Not for the first time, I felt real pride for my mate. Being alpha suited her much better than even I would have thought. I was so attracted to Bryn at that moment, I would've pulled her against me in full view of the council had I not known it would undermine her authority.

The silence broke when Grant collected the papers and tapped them into a neat pile. He was the oldest member of the pack, and from his solemn expression, he understood the stakes more than Edward and Dana.

"You don't look surprised," Tavi pointed out to Grant. "Were you all aware of this already?"

"Yes," he said. "The tax account you are talking about is over five years old. We've known that money was missing as early as *seven* years ago."

"Why wasn't I informed of this?" Bryn demanded. A reasonable question.

"It's the way things have been for decades."

"That's not good enough. Every alpha—even interim ones—should be informed of the pack's affairs. It's ridiculous to keep something a secret just because you've gotten complacent."

Grant inclined his head to take her point.

Bryn's shoulders lost some of their stiffness. We were finally getting somewhere, and she didn't need to keep herself as rigid.

"So the account is at least seven years old," she said. "Did you confront Gregor about this?"

"We did. Alpha Gregor claimed he would handle it, but the money continued to disappear."

Encouraged by Grant's willingness to talk, Councilman Ross said, "We waited a little while for Gregor to put a stop to the payments, but he never did. The only thing he seemed to do was lessen the amounts withdrawn from each account."

"Do you think he was the one hoarding it or someone else?" Bryn asked.

"We suspected Troy was squirreling the money away," Councilman Colby said. "We figured that was why Alpha Gregor didn't stop the withdrawals. We tried to stop it ourselves, but he wouldn't stand for it. He demanded we stop looking into it and prioritized his son over his pack."

He let that silence sit for a few moments. Bryn, Tavi, and I weren't the least surprised by Gregor's selfishness, but we gave the council some time to mourn the man who had been their alpha.

"The day before he died, I spoke to Alpha Gregor," Grant finally said. "I asked him to tell me the truth behind the missing money. Even after he made me promise I wouldn't reveal anything to anyone outside of the council, he wouldn't give me any details about the account or what it was for; all he told me was that Troy was doing what he had to do to ensure the pack's future. I don't have any proof of this, but I got the impression that Gregor was the one who advised Troy to take the money and hide it."

I frowned. That speculation only raised more questions. Gregor had been the alpha and a tyrant who no doubt used money however he wanted. Why would he cover up that money was being moved around? And why would he let Troy, of all fucking people, take that money? Gregor had known his son was a loose cannon, so why give him access to such a huge amount of money?

Bryn was on the same page. "Troy wasn't exactly the most stable or rational man. Why would Gregor let him do that?"

Grant shook his head. "We have no idea. I can only imagine his love for his son was greater than his rational mind."

I said nothing to that. From what Bryn had told me, I doubted very much that "love" was why Gregor had let Troy do what he wanted. It would make more sense if Gregor had thought Troy was the only person capable of carrying out their sinister plans.

"As Colby said," Grant continued, "we brought up the issue multiple times, but we were shot down every time. And when Troy became alpha, it was too dangerous to try to get information out of him. As a council, we couldn't go against our alpha."

"Do you have any idea how much money was in the account?" Tavi asked.

Edward sighed. Now that most of his fellow council members had revealed this information, he was apparently no longer interested in bullshitting us. "We suspected it was in the hundreds of thousands. But we don't know where the account is, nor do we have any way of finding out an exact amount. We've never seen a statement from that tax account, which leads us to believe it might not be a wolf account."

"Wait…you think he's got a bank account in the human world?" Bryn asked.

She sounded as shocked as I felt. The Kings had always believed that humans were beneath wolves. According to Bryn, only Kings' men were allowed to go into human towns, and they only ever went to get gifts for a female wolf they liked or to have sex with human women. The idea that the Redwolfs, who hated humans the most, had a financial account with a human bank was preposterous. Would Gregor have been desperate enough to hide this money in a human account? If so, we had even more reason to be alarmed.

"We've been trying to find the account for years," Edward said. "We pulled every string we could, but it was nowhere to be found. The only way an account could be hidden so well is if it belonged to a human bank."

"But I thought we couldn't transfer money from a wolf account to a human account?" Bryn said.

"No, it's possible," I replied. "But you have to withdraw the cash from the pack's bank, then go to a human town and deposit the cash into an account there."

"Well, Troy would have had plenty of time to do that—he went into Colville all the time." Bryn frowned, chewing on the inside of her cheek. "If they were stealing money, why did they record the missing money in the ledger?"

"Alphas have to keep track of every penny that moves in and out of pack accounts," Ross explained. "It's an ancient law to which alphas are bound. Hundreds of years ago, alphas and the lucky few in their inner circle were treated like royalty. Back then, they claimed there wasn't enough money for the entire pack to survive while spending lavishly on themselves. Packs revolted against their alphas. Riots and infighting made life unbearably difficult, so to bring peace, a new law was created. All money had to be marked in the ledgers to keep the alpha accountable. If an alpha doesn't keep detailed ledgers, they risk being executed."

"But there is a loophole," Grant added. "The law doesn't expressly state that alphas have to disclose which account the money is going into; just that it has to be noted that it's gone somewhere. That's why our hands were tied."

"That *is* the loophole," I said, fury making my voice little more than a growl. "But no alpha worth his salt would take advantage of it."

The council didn't have a response to that.

"We need to speak with the Kings' banker and see what they can tell us," Bryn said. "And we need to go through everything Troy and Gregor owned. There must be information on this account somewhere."

I sighed and pinched the bridge of my nose. This was turning into a much bigger nightmare than I'd thought. If Troy had used a human bank account, it would be very complicated to gain access to it.

"Don't any of you have ideas about what the Redwolfs were planning?" Tavi asked. "It's been seven years—you must have some kind of theory?"

The councilmen exchanged looks. "Well," Colby began hesitantly, "it's possible they were trying to expand King territory, but not from neighboring packs."

"Wait, wait." I held my hand up. "Are you saying they were after human land?" That was a disaster waiting to happen and much more trouble than it was worth. Humans were physically weaker than us, true, but they had guns and tanks and heavy machinery—all of which made them a significant threat. Gregor hated humans, anyway, so why would he be interested in living among them?

Colby shook his head. "No, not human land. I'm talking about land from other realms. From other shifter species."

We stared at him in puzzlement. "You lost me. Wolves are the only shifter species," I said.

Colby sighed and rubbed his forehead. "From what I remember, this was a little above my head."

"I'll try to explain it as I understood it," Grant said. "Around the same time we learned about this tax account, Gregor started collecting old maps of the Idaho panhandle and ancient texts on wolf legends. We have no idea where he got these documents or where he stored them. They're not in the pack library or his personal library because we've had those places checked thoroughly. We asked Gregor about the books, but all he would say was that they held information that would bring the Kings to new levels of greatness."

"What the hell does that mean?" I asked. "How would old texts and maps help him?"

"Well, there is a very old fable about an ancient version of our world." He glanced at Dana, who had been sitting in quiet disapproval since the others told us what they knew. "Dana, please, you know the story best."

She heaved a long, exhausted sigh, but she spoke. "Everyone knows pack mothers started the wolf shifter species, but this legend states that hundreds of years ago, the world was populated with more than just wolf shifters. Dragons, bears, birds, foxes, and big cats lived alongside us, and each species had their own pack mothers who brought them into existence.

"Each shifter species had their own territory to rule over, but over time, some of them became greedy. Dragons descended from their mountain caves to seek out treasure and hoard wealth, leaving nothing for the others. Smaller species like the birds and rodents were hunted while in their animal forms, powerless to stop it. Bigger species like the cats and wolves became increasingly territorial as their populations grew.

"Wars and deep blood feuds broke out, and before long, all shifter species were getting closer and closer to extinction. To stop their children from killing each other, the pack mothers came together and used their magic to open portals to new realms. They created one for each species and separated them forever. We wolves were the only ones who remained in the original realm."

Tavi, Bryn, and I exchanged glances. It appeared none of us had heard this story before, but it sounded far too crazy to be real. No wonder Dana had called it a fable.

"What does that have to do with the Redwolfs?" Tavi asked.

"I don't understand why everyone is struggling so much with this," Dana huffed. "It's clear—Alpha Gregor believed that if he opened those portals, he could travel through different realms. When he arrived, he could use the might of our army to expand our territory."

Silence followed her words, then Bryn spoke up. "You supported this?"

Dana's lips twisted with annoyance. "I supported the spirit of it. Everyone seems to be forgetting that we are *Kings*. We are meant to have kingdoms. If Alpha Gregor believed he could make it happen, why should I care if his methods are unorthodox?"

"He was screwing over this pack in the pursuit of something impossible," Bryn argued. "And what did it amount to? Hundreds of thousands of dollars stolen? A divided council? You should care a lot, Dana."

She scoffed. "He was working in service of the greater good."

This conversation was getting so frustrating. I hated sharing blood with a man who'd been crazy enough to believe such a story. *Dragons? Really?* It was far more believable that Troy had used the money to build himself an army of ferals.

"I can believe that Gregor and Troy would want to get more land," I said. "I simply can't wrap my head around the possibility that they would believe in some ridiculous bedtime story. There's no proof that those events ever happened."

"It's one of those things that can only be proven when achieved," Ross replied with a shrug. "We didn't say it was reasonable for them to believe it was possible."

"But we have to admit it's possible that they believed the story was true," Bryn said. "If Troy and Gregor believed in other realms, that would explain the ancient maps and books Gregor collected. He needed some intel on the locations of those portals."

This was all so ridiculous. I was on the verge of storming out, taking my mate and sister with me. But Bryn was right. We had to consider every avenue to track down this money.

"Do any of you know how a portal could be reopened?" she asked. "Or even where the closest portal is supposed to be?"

"Of course not," Dana snapped. "We didn't give it any thought because we don't believe it's possible. There are so many myths about the ancient world that most wolves don't know. None of them have been proven true, and there's no reason for anyone to take them so seriously."

"If your precious Alpha Gregor was determined to find out if it was true," Tavi began, glaring at Dana, "at least one wolf took it pretty damn seriously."

"Maybe the idea of more power and control was too appealing for them to resist," I replied. "*If* this is what they were doing with the money, it's because the chance to conquer foreign land was too good to pass up, no matter how far-fetched it sounded."

"If Troy is the only one left who believes in this story, couldn't we just find some way to cut Troy's access to the account?" Bryn asked. "No money, no way for him to fund his army or open a portal, right?"

"I doubt it'll be that simple, Bryn," I said. "We need to find the account first, and if it's in the human world, there will be a lot of hoops for us to jump through before we can close it. It could take a lot of time." I paused because something Bryn had said filled me with unease. "Troy might not be the only one who believes this story. There could be wolves in your pack who are loyal to him and want to open the portals. Wolves who might be helping him from the inside."

Bryn clenched her eyes shut briefly and addressed the council again. "I know it's a long shot, but are there any records that would tell us who would be most loyal to the Redwolfs?"

"We don't keep records like that," Edward said. "You'd have to ask around. As far as we know, the ones who were most loyal to Troy left either when you were appointed alpha or shortly after the feral attack."

She sighed and nodded. "I should have expected as much." Looking from Tavi to me, she said, "We've asked them what we needed to ask, so let's head to the bank to see what they know."

"That sounds like a plan." I stared hard at each member of the council. "If we have more questions, we'll be back."

Chapter 13 - Bryn

After that strange meeting, Night and I headed to the commons. We were determined to get more of our questions answered. Tavi had opted to look through the Redwolfs' belongings to find some link to the missing account. *I knew being alpha would be hard, but I would* never *have thought I'd have to deal with a financial mystery. And* of course *it all goes back to Troy.*

It was so like Troy to be the bane of my existence even when he was nowhere to be found. I was beginning to wonder if I'd ever be free of his chokehold on my life.

The commons had shops on either side of a wide walking path. People were selling all sorts of jewelry, clothes, salves, sauces, groceries, drinks, street foods, and toys. It was a bustling place, and a few wolves played music for money. I'd rarely gone to the commons because I felt exposed, but my mom went all the time. She said her favorite thing about the market was haggling down the prices.

I grinned as I recalled how she'd gush about talking down the price of a dress or a new pan. But the memory also angered me. Ross had made it sound like the monarchical system was a thing of the past, but Mom and I never had much money. People had treated us much like the "peasants" Ross had talked about.

I shook my head and focused on the task at hand. Let the past be the past for now. We needed answers.

The Kings' bank was in a red brick building at the end of the long strip of shops. People crowded the inside, either withdrawing or depositing money into their accounts. But when the doors shut behind Night and me, the chatter stopped immediately.

I didn't have time to be offended or embarrassed by the attention—what we had to do was too important. I took advantage of the quiet to announce, "I want to speak to the owner."

There was a pause, and then one of the tellers spoke up. "I-I'll go get him, Alpha Hunter," she squeaked, scurrying off to do so. We waited for just a few seconds, and then the teller returned. "He said he'll see you now in his office, Alpha."

"Great." Night and I followed the teller to the back.

The owner's office had a window that overlooked the tree line. A scent of vanilla wafted from the candles burning on his desk, giving the room a relaxing vibe. The shelves to the right of his desk held binders of the pack's financial information, and on the left of his desk were some dried snacks and candies. I wondered if they were for him or the people who came into his office.

The owner, a scrawny man in his early seventies, sat behind his rectangular oak desk. The nameplate revealed him to be Jefferson Boyle. The top of his head was bald, while white hair puffed out at the sides. He wore a black blazer over his eggshell-blue button-down shirt and black slacks.

"Greetings, Alpha Hunter and Night Shepherd," he said, bowing to me before sitting again. "To what do I owe the honor of seeing the two of you?"

"Hundreds of thousands of dollars have gone missing over the last seven years," I said as Night handed over the ledgers. "We know they've gone into a tax account, but no one—not even the council—knows anything about it. We're hoping you could give us more information about it."

Jefferson took a few moments to skim through the ledgers. He set the papers down and reached into one of his desk drawers for a large black binder. "Let me double-check something." The binder was labeled "Pack Accounting." He opened it, flipped through the binder, then nodded to himself.

"It's just as I thought," he said, flicking the binder closed again. "We don't have an account with that name."

"What? How do you explain all of these transfers, then?" Night asked.

"Well, I see in these ledgers that these transfers were indeed labeled for some kind of tax account. But Alpha Gregor told me to officially mark them down as 'community expenses.'"

"What is that?" I asked.

"As you've seen, we keep multiple accounts, and one of those accounts is called 'Community.' It's used for events and parties within the pack. Alpha Gregor had me mark down the withdrawals as being for the community."

"But there weren't any events around the time of these transactions," I said.

He nodded. "I'm aware, but it is not the place of a banker to question what his customer is doing with his money. Especially not the alpha himself."

I understood what he wasn't saying: if Jefferson had tried to question the alpha about what he did with his money, he definitely would have faced consequences. Maybe even deadly consequences.

"Were you concerned about the missing money?" I asked.

"Not particularly." Jefferson's dispassionate face and monotonous voice showed exactly how little he cared about it. "As long as the pack thrived and there was plenty of money in the accounts we needed, I had no reason to be concerned."

"I understand." That didn't mean I was happy about it, but I sympathized with his logic.

"Can you tell us who took out the money?" Night asked. "Was it Troy or someone else?"

"Well, I'm not here every day. Sometimes my job calls me to the market to help with disputes, so I can't say whether it was him one hundred percent of the time…but yes, it was usually Troy. He would come in with a leather satchel, the money would be placed inside it, and then he would leave to do whatever he did with it."

Dammit. A human bank account was looking more and more possible. "Well, do you have any idea if there's a way to find this missing account?"

"Every pack bank has a different eight-digit identification number with two or three letters at the beginning or end. All our accounts are labeled KP, for 'Kings Pack.' Please correct me if I'm wrong, Mr. Shepherd, but I imagine the Wargs' accounts are labeled WP, correct?"

He nodded. "That's right."

"If you can find the code related to the account's identification, I can tell you into which pack bank he deposited the money."

"What if he used a human bank?" I asked.

"Oh, I can't imagine Troy or Alpha Gregor using a human bank," Jefferson dismissed. "But if there are only numbers and no letters in the account code, that would tell you he dealt with a human bank. If that's the case, only a human banker could tell you where it was deposited."

Night and I shared a look. We were getting answers to some questions, but the main one was still a mystery.

I tried not to let my frustration and defeat show when we thanked Jefferson and headed out. My head felt heavy with everything we'd learned, yet we still hadn't gotten to the bottom of it. We knew Troy had been making the withdrawals in cash, and we knew Gregor had actively covered it up for Troy. What we didn't know was why or where the money was located.

This headache would follow us to our next destination—meeting with Dr. Stan to see how the baby was doing.

"I feel like we're in a dream," I said as we walked away from the commons. "Like we're chasing something that's getting farther and farther away from us. What do you think about all of this?"

"I feel the same," Night said with a sigh. "It's frustrating that Troy and Gregor would do all of this just for more power, but I can't be surprised. We both know how power-hungry my father was, and he raised Troy to be the same way. Unfortunately, they were smart enough to cover their tracks so we can't quickly find the information we need."

"What about this portal stuff? Do you think any part of the story could be true?"

He shook his head decisively. "There's no way. I'm forced to admit that the Redwolfs believed it possible, but it can't be real. I can't even wrap my head around bird and dragon shifters. How would a man my size shift into a bird?"

The mental image that his question elicited had me chuckling, but my good humor only lasted a few seconds before the seriousness of our situation crept back in. "Do you think Violet might have more information about this? Gregor might have discussed the legend with her at some point."

"That's not a bad idea, but I've tried to avoid talking about Gregor after Troy gave her the alpha wound. I didn't want to stress her out while she was healing."

I shuddered, the shock of seeing her blood splattered across the floor after Troy bit her still fresh in my mind. Night pulled me close to his side, which helped a little.

"I won't make you bring this up to her," I said. "We can find another way to get more information."

He nodded. "How are you feeling? Are you up to seeing Doc?"

"Yes. I mean, I'm a little on edge from talking and thinking about Troy, and I'm a little nervous about being examined. But I'm eager to learn more about our baby."

He kissed the top of my head. "Don't worry. I'll be with you the entire time."

I smiled. "I know. It would be much harder if I had to do this on my own."

He smiled back, and for a few seconds, I felt a little less like I was in the middle of a wild goose chase and more like a woman going to the doctor for a mundane checkup. Something normal and not drastically important for the pack's safety and well-being.

We met Dr. Stan inside the infirmary, and he led us to an exam room. He directed me to sit on an examination table before leaving to grab some equipment. I shifted from side to side as I sat.

The infirmary walls were white-painted wood. It smelled sterile and antiseptic, making my nose itch and putting me on edge. I had never sat inside a doctor's office like this. I was used to going home with scrapes and bruises from my bullies, but I'd never been injured to the point that a pack doctor needed to see me.

Night's hand was warm and reassuring on my shoulder, and a wave of calm stole over me. "Don't worry, I'm here," he reminded me.

I put my hand over his and leaned against him. "Thank you. I needed that."

So many problems felt insurmountable, but as long as I had my mate at my side, I knew we could conquer anything—including a brief doctor's visit.

Dr. Stan returned a moment later, wheeling a bulky device with a flat black screen. The screen looked like a solar panel, but I knew it was meant to show images. I'd seen similar screens around the pack.

"I have to say, Alpha Night," he said, closing the door with his foot, "the Kings have remarkable technology.

We don't have any ultrasounds as advanced as this one back home. We must get some of these ultrasound machines as soon as we can."

Night smirked and nodded. "We're working on it, believe me." I knew he was referring to the alpha challenge. With his win, the Wargs would have access to the Kings' resources.

That seemed to please Dr. Stan, and he brought the ultrasound closer to the examination table. "Congratulations on your pregnancy, Bryn. How have you been feeling?"

"Thank you, Doctor," I replied. "Honestly, I haven't been feeling all that well. I've been sick and exhausted."

His gentle, handsome face was sympathetic as he nodded. "That doesn't surprise me. Having a baby is no easy feat. Why don't you lie down, and we'll get started?"

"Sure. I'm a little nervous about all this."

He smiled. "Don't worry. There's nothing invasive about this process; we'll just see how your little one is growing. Could you lift your shirt, please?"

When I did, he squirted clear gel on my stomach.

Night took my hand again, and I squeezed it. "It's a little cold."

"Sorry about that. It'll warm up once I've started the examination." He pressed a device with a smooth head to my stomach and spread the gel around. It *did* warm up pretty quickly. "Now, you're just at the beginning of your pregnancy, so we probably won't see much."

As Dr. Stan slowly moved the device back and forth over my stomach, I squeezed Night's hand again, and he ran his thumb back and forth over the back of my hand.

"There it is." Dr. Stan grinned. "It's just the size of a pea." He turned the monitor toward me, showing me a black-and-white image. Near the middle of the image was a black circular shape and a little circle attached to the inside of that shape.

"That's the baby?" I breathed. I didn't know much about fetuses, but I hadn't expected mine to be that small…and cute.

"Yes, indeed. Tiny, right? I'd say you're around six weeks along."

"Why is it pulsing like that?" Night asked, pointing to the throbbing bean.

"That's the baby's heartbeat."

"In real-time?" he asked, awe filling his voice.

"Yes, Alpha. In real-time." The doctor's smile was so gentle, I got the impression that he loved having consultations with parents-to-be.

I returned my attention to the screen, my vision suddenly blurry with tears. It was one thing to know I was pregnant, but it was another thing to see the baby—to see it living. I was seeing the little life that was forming inside me, and I'd never seen anything more amazing.

Dr. Stan looked around a bit more. "Bryn, you should know that you're very lucky."

I tore my gaze away from the screen to look at him. "Hm? Why?"

His happy expression had smoothed into a more neutral one. "It looks like you've got only one ovary and a very low egg count. Because of that, the odds of you getting pregnant are quite low."

I gaped at him. I'd had no idea there was anything wrong with me. True, my periods had never been regular, but my mother and I had chalked it up to female wolf hormones in the air throwing off my cycle.

"Will I be able to get pregnant again?" I asked.

"Most women with this condition only have one child, if they are able to conceive at all. It's very unlikely that you will be able to have a second child. A condition like this is genetic, something you would have been born with."

Shock pierced me like a lightning bolt. I couldn't bring myself to look at my mate. Night had said that he wanted a big family, but I probably wouldn't be able to give my baby even one sibling. Night had done so much for me, but I couldn't even do that much for him.

"Um, so, what happens now?" I whispered.

"Well, I'll need to see you every two weeks for a checkup. I'll want to monitor both your and your baby's health. In the meantime, you need to do what you can to ensure you and the baby are as healthy as possible. Listen to your body, especially when it's telling you to rest."

I was certain his words weren't meant to sound accusatory, but they hit me like a blow. All the times I'd pushed back when Night asked me to take it easy, the times I'd insisted on getting out to look around at the pack—even this morning when I insisted I had to be there while he went to the council and the bank. I hadn't even realized I was risking our baby's life. I could've just sent Tavi and saved myself some strain.

The doctor pressed some buttons. The machine started to make a new sound, and it took me a minute to realize it was printing off the image like a Polaroid camera.

"Miscarriages can happen at any time without warning. But the best thing you can do to prevent one is to stay away from smoking and alcohol. Don't do any heavy lifting, avoid stress, and spend as little time on your feet as you can. You will experience cravings. It's perfectly fine to indulge, but keep your diet healthy overall."

"Okay," I murmured.

"I've got to put this thing back where I found it." He turned off the machine and handed me the picture. "Don't hesitate to see me if you have questions or concerns, even if it's before the next appointment."

Night and I thanked him, promising we would come by if necessary. Then Dr. Stan got up to wheel the ultrasound away. When we were alone, Night grabbed some tissues to help me wipe off the gel.

"How are you doing?" he asked.

"I'm okay." After a second, I added, "Night, let's go home."

"Of course."

When we arrived home, I immediately went to our bathroom to take a long hot shower. I wanted a few minutes to myself. I leaned against the shower wall as the water streamed over me.

The diagnosis Dr. Stan had given me had blindsided me. If I had known more about my mother, I might have known about my low egg count and only having one ovary. I could have warned Night he was getting involved with a woman who could only bear him one child.

If he'd known ahead of time, he probably would have been with someone better. Someone stronger.

My wolf whined, and I shivered. I was a lot better at reading her at this point—she was telling me not to think that way, reminding me that Night and I were soulmates, destined to be together. But that didn't stop me from feeling bitter. I wished I'd come with a warning label.

When I got out of the shower, Night was waiting for me. He stood in the doorway, leaning against the doorframe. His deep emerald eyes searched my face as I wrapped a towel around me.

"You wanna talk?" he asked, his deep voice gentle.

I hesitated, standing on the bathmat like a drenched puppy. "I promise to do everything I can to deliver a healthy baby," I blurted.

He stepped towards me and took me in his arms. "I know you will, baby. I'm not worried about that at all." He gave me a gentle smile, but for some reason, I couldn't tell if it was genuine or not. Maybe it was only because my mind was still reeling from the information Dr. Stan had given us, but I suddenly felt very insecure.

"Night, how do *you* feel about what the doctor said? About me only having one baby?"

He took my face in his hands. "Bryn, I don't care if you're able to have one child, zero, or a hundred. You're my soulmate. I love you no matter what happens in the future."

Tears pricked my eyes. "But you said you wanted a lot of kids, and I just can't—"

He cut me off with a sweet, gentle kiss. "If all we have is one child, that only makes our pup all the more special," he murmured. "I promise you I will protect you both to my last breath. Nothing and no one will hurt either of you."

I let out a breath and kissed him again, wrapping my arms around his neck and pulling him close. It was a relief to hear that he was okay with us only having one child, but I wondered if my guilt would ever go away.

"I'm getting you all damp." I sniffled.

He chuckled. "Let's fix that. I'll help you dry off."

He pulled away to grab more towels, then he tugged me into the bedroom and nudged me onto the bed. With one of the towels, he started to dry my hair. He was as gentle as he could be, but the vigorous motion of him running the towel back and forth over my hair—just the way I'd seen him do after he had taken a shower—wasn't exactly sensual. When he pulled the towel away, he suppressed a laugh, but a small snort escaped.

I looked at myself in the mirror, saw the incredible bedhead he'd given me, and burst out laughing.

"Sorry," he said. "I'll do better down here."

He crouched in front of me and lifted my right leg. The Redwolfs had kept very luxurious, plushy towels. I'd felt them on my skin dozens of times before, but the way Night used it to caress my foot and ankle set my skin on fire.

He rested my foot on his stomach while gently drying my calf, his touch soft but firm as he moved on to my thigh. His jet-black hair fell across his shoulders as he moved on to the other leg. I wanted to brush the lock away, but his touch had put me in a trance.

Taking my hand, he kissed the wetness from each of my fingers, peering up at me through those long dark lashes. I shivered even as tears stung my eyes once again. Did I deserve such tenderness? Did someone like me really deserve a mate as wonderful as Night? My wolf whined at me again for having these thoughts, but the questions lingered.

As if sensing my doubts, Night slid off the towel covering my body and tucked me into bed. He crawled in with me and turned my face to his to kiss me slowly and gently. His touch stroked my neck, my breasts, and down my stomach to the apex between my thighs.

His tongue politely asked for entrance to my mouth, and I obliged him. It immediately stroked across mine. It moved in time with his finger against my clit. I moaned against his mouth as he caressed me. The circling of his finger in my warmth sent delicate, sparkling pleasure across my skin. Each movement told me again and again, "I love you, mate."

As bliss fluttered through my body and the tears slipped free, I told myself I wouldn't let my feelings of inadequacy hurt my chances of bringing a healthy baby into the world. I needed to be strong and hold my head as high as I could. Night was chasing my worries away for now, and I had no doubt they would return, but it was alright. I would try to be brave for him and our baby because my mate was right. The baby was a blessing, one he and I would cherish forever.

Chapter 14 - Night

By the morning of the third day after the ultrasound, Bryn and I were falling into a routine: she'd wake up, I'd rub her back while she was sick in the bathroom, and afterward, I'd bring her tea and plain toast for breakfast. It never felt like enough food to me, but Bryn assured me it was all she could stomach in the morning. Glenda also came by often to check on her.

"How are you, love?" I asked my mate, setting the plate and the tea on her bedside table.

A pale, exhausted face looked back at me. Her silence was more than enough of an answer.

"That great, huh?" I pressed a kiss to her forehead and sat next to her on the bed. "I wanted to talk to you about something, and then I'll leave you alone to get some more rest."

She reached for the tea and took a little sip, wincing when she burned her lip. "What is it?"

"Do you want to keep living here when the baby comes, or do you want to have a new cabin for the three of us? In addition to the one we have on Warg territory?"

Her eyebrows rose, and she completely forgot about the tea. "What brought this on?"

"Well, it's just that I know this place has a lot of bad memories for you—for good fucking reason. And I know you still have nightmares about what happened with Troy. I don't care if we live here or get a new cabin. What I want is for you to be comfortable in your own home without dealing with trauma every day."

"But…would you really leave the alpha cabin? I thought you'd want to live here after you won the alpha challenge."

I shrugged. "Actually, I've always kinda wanted to burn this place to the ground."

She gasped and laughed. "Night! We can't do that."

"I know, I know. Destroying the cabin would be a waste of resources and a destruction of history, and all those other reasons Mom gave me to keep the building intact." Bryn giggled and lightly smacked my chest. The sound of her laughter made my body feel lighter. "Anyway, it's only a building, Bryn. I just want you to feel comfortable and safe in a place that's your own. If you decide you want to move, we can use the building for something else. It could be the official meeting room for the council or elders or for pack meetings. Whatever we want."

Her fingers, hot from the mug of tea, caressed my cheek. I leaned into her touch, my wolf purring in delight.

"I'll think about it, Night. Thanks for sharing your feelings with me."

I turned my head to kiss the palm of her hand and enjoyed the goosebumps that trailed up her forearm. "Remember, I'll be happy with whatever you decide." I kissed her lips, then got to my feet. If I didn't leave now, I'd be tempted to crawl back into bed with her, and I had things I needed to do. "I have to go out for a while to see how things are going with Dom and Tavi, but I'll check in with you after lunch, okay?"

"Okay."

"I love you, Bryn."

"Love you, Night." She blew me a kiss on my way out.

I resumed the search that Tavi had started into the Redwolfs' stuff. She hadn't found anything useful during her search, and we had combed through everything we could find. It was worse than looking for a needle in a haystack because at least a needle would stab you when you found it.

I flipped through more documents and found a recorded log of all the wolves that had disappeared or were killed, banished, or imprisoned over the past twenty years. I doubted the account number would be here, but Bryn had asked whether the council knew who was still loyal to the Redwolfs. Finding that account number was important, of course, but these records could point me to someone who might know more about what the Redwolfs were doing with it.

Tavi arrived a short while later. She came into the office, nodded at me, and immediately took up a spot on the floor. I told her I was looking into the records instead of searching for the account number and why.

When I finished explaining, Tavi nodded. "Cool. Hopefully, that'll give us a better lead than what we have now. I'll keep looking for the account number."

"Thanks, Tav."

I'd been alpha of the Wargs for over a decade now, but I hadn't had to banish or kill more than fifty people in that time. I could remember the names and faces of all of them. I doubted Troy or Gregor could say the same. Troy, for one, hadn't been alpha for a year, but he'd gotten rid of over fifty people; Gregor's number was in the hundreds. The Redwolfs were far more likely to kill their enemies.

Troy rarely bothered to give reasons for his punishments, but Gregor's reasons ranged from a very reasonable "stole large sums of money" to "committed assault" to "refused to work when commanded" to "looked at another man's woman with lust." The punishments were usually a lot worse than the crime itself.

The kidnappings were the most interesting to me because they seemed to follow a pattern. A decade prior and for four years straight, most of the victims were males, and all were between the ages of five and seven. They had apparently gotten lost in the woods and were expected to have died from "exposure, starvation, accident, or animal attack." The Kings had sent search parties, but the children's remains were never found, and the trails went nowhere.

It wasn't strange to lose pups in the woods; when they were young, they weren't able to track their way back home, and unfortunately, that often led to them getting turned around. But to lose dozens of children over a few years without ever finding their bodies was unheard of. It was strange, too, that this had happened ten years ago. At that time, I had just become alpha.

"I'm going to talk to the council," I said.

"Yeah?" Tavi looked up, and I noticed that she'd gotten through a lot of documents as well. "Find something?"

"I might have, but I need to ask them more. Do you know where they are now?"

"They're probably in the meeting room. They handle pack business there for a few hours every day."

"Good to know. I'll be back."

I left her to her search and went for the door. On the way, Bryn's scent drew my attention to the staircase. She was wrapped tightly in her robe, and the color had returned to her face. The few hours she'd had to herself had done wonders for her, setting my wolf and me at ease.

"Where are you going, love?" I asked.

"I was just about to ask you the same thing." She finished coming down the stairs.

I smirked. I was on a mission to speak to the council, but some banter with my mate wouldn't matter in the grand scheme of things. "I asked first."

She quirked a brow, a light smile on her lips. "Alright. I was coming down to get more tea and make some toast."

"I could've brought it to you. Or Tavi could have."

She shook her head. "I'm feeling better, thankfully. Now it's your turn."

"I'm heading to the council. I have questions about some of the ledgers...what is it?"

Bryn's lower lip, pink now that she was feeling better, poked out as she frowned. "On your own? I don't think so, Night. They might see that as overstepping."

I started to say that they would listen to me, anyway, but it occurred to me that Bryn was right. I couldn't just burst in there demanding the Kings' council to give me answers about something that had happened a long time ago.

"I think you should take Tavi with you," she said.

I nodded. I was glad Bryn hadn't suggested going herself, but she must not have felt up to walking around. "I'll go get Tav—"

"I'm here," Tavi spoke from behind me. I hadn't even heard her coming. "Bryn already filled me in."

I smiled. I wasn't used to being outside the alpha-beta telepathic connection, but I didn't mind. Knowing my mate and sister had that connection pleased me to an unreasonable degree. "What if they ask where you are, Bryn?"

She shrugged. "Just tell them I'm reviewing documents. I'll be doing that, anyway."

"You're sure you're feeling up to that?"

She patted my chest. "I'm fine. Now you two go on. You can fill me in on how it goes later."

"Okay, love." I kissed her forehead and then her lips. "See you soon."

Tavi and I headed out, and I filled her in on what I'd found on the way. She was right.

The five council members were discussing something in the meeting room. Their voices died down as we entered.

"Here without your mate?" Dana asked with a slight smirk. "That's unusual."

Tavi crossed her arms. "Your *alpha* is busy," she replied, rising to Dana's taunt. "She sent us in her stead, but you can be sure that if we need a follow-up, we'll have her with us."

"A follow-up?" Grant asked. He pushed aside some of the paperwork piled in front of him. "For what?"

"We've found some reports of pups who went missing ten years ago," I said. "Do any of you remember what was happening back then? Why were so many kids going missing during that four-year period?"

There was a brief pause. Tavi and I waited as the council members exchanged looks. I was even happier that Bryn had caught me before I left. They'd have no reason to answer my questions if Bryn or Tavi weren't with me.

Eventually, Grant nodded. "We remember. It's devastating to lose a pup, and it was even more so back then. Our trackers never found their bodies."

"I can imagine. Why did things slow down after four years?"

"Our only explanation is that there was a killer within our territory and possibly within the pack. When things stopped, we believed the killer had died or been killed, but we never found out who it was."

"If Troy hadn't been so young, I would have assumed it was him," Colby admitted.

Tavi frowned. "Yeah, I don't blame you."

Troy would have been thirteen or fourteen back then—old enough to be coming into his strength but not capable of kidnapping on such a large scale.

"You mentioned your trackers couldn't find the children's remains."

Grant sighed. "Yes. To this day, we still don't know what happened to them. Back then, we were all so paranoid that some families even left the pack with their young pups to protect them."

"Were there any witnesses?"

"Well, there was one…" He hesitated, and his fellow council members exchanged uncomfortable looks.

Even Edward and Dana, the two least friendly council members, looked uneasy. I guessed even they had to show reverence when it came to the missing children.

"What's wrong?" Tavi asked.

"It's just that he's not a very reliable witness," Grant replied.

"Tell us about him," I said.

"His name is Samuel Granby," Ross said. "He was with one of the children who went missing. When we started searching for them, we found Samuel wandering the woods. When we found him, he couldn't answer any of our questions. Whatever he saw affected him so deeply that he hasn't been the same."

"Where is he?" Tavi asked.

"At home with his parents. They live on the southern end of the compound. The cabin's door is painted sky-blue with white clouds." Ross hesitated for a few moments, looking pained. "If you're planning to talk to him, I assure you that you won't get anything useful. It will likely be a waste of your time."

Tavi shook her head. "We'll decide whether or not it's a waste of our time, Ross, but thanks for your concern."

"This information is appreciated," I echoed. "Thank you all. We'll let you continue your work."

Tavi and I left them to their business, releasing deep breaths as soon as we stepped outside. Overhead, the sun had slipped lower in the sky. It would be evening soon.

"The atmosphere really shifted when you brought up those kids," she said. "God, those poor things. My heart aches for them and their families."

I suppressed a shiver. "Same here. I can't even imagine the pain that they've dealt with."

She ran her hand through her hair before pulling her hood over her head. "I'm going to head back to the alpha cabin. Are you coming?"

"No, I think I'll train for a bit before heading back. And go visit Mom." Hearing about the pups made me want to spend some time with her.

"Sure. I'll keep an eye on Bryn and catch her up on the meeting."

I grinned. "I knew I could rely on you, Tav."

Tavi walked me to the tree line, then veered off to the alpha cabin. I pushed deeper into the forest until dense trees surrounded me. I chose a new spot each time I trained, just to keep things interesting. This spot was my favorite thus far. Because of the packed trees, I couldn't hear the Kings—only the sounds of nature.

I wanted to work through my lingering discomfort after that meeting with the council. I started with cardio, climbing up the trees and leaping from one to the other. Birds were startled into flight in my wake. Afterward, I did hundreds of chin-ups and squats in quick succession.

When my heart was pumping and a sheen of sweat covered my body, I started training in earnest. I used my claws to mark a circle on a thick tree, then punched and kicked it in the same spot each time.

Hours later, the sun was much lower in the sky, and I was drenched in sweat. I ran a hand through my damp hair and caught my breath before walking back to town. When I reached Mom's cabin, I was relieved to see she wasn't with Doc—and that she recently made bread because her cabin smelled like butter and baked deliciousness.

"Come in, come in," she said, coming down the cabin steps. She paused, her nose scrunching. "Get in here and wash up, Night. You smell like you've been rolling around in the dirt."

I chuckled. "I was training."

"Yes, that's what I said." She moved out of my way and ushered me upstairs. "Go on, go on. I refuse to hug you before you're clean."

I grinned. This was the sort of interaction I wanted, this normalcy. I washed in her shower, the hot water relaxing my taut muscles. When the water sluicing down my body ran clear, I stepped out of the shower and toweled off. Mom had left me some clothes while I was washing, so I dressed in them and headed downstairs.

"Ah, now that you're clean," she said from the kitchen, "come and have some dessert with me."

"I shouldn't since I'm training…" I pretended to hesitate. But the blank look she gave me made me laugh. "Yeah, I'll have some. Do you have blueberry jam?"

She swatted me gently as I passed her. "Of course I do."

We went into the kitchen, and she made us milk tea and brought out the blueberry jam. "I had a feeling you'd visit me today," she said. "What's going on? Is Bryn okay?"

I sighed. "She's still waking up with morning sickness. It sucks, Mom, it really does. I had no idea it would be so hard on her."

"Neither did I, poor thing." She gave an empathetic frown. "What did Damon say?"

"He told us the baby was six weeks and seemed to be doing well. And he said that Bryn has only one ovary and a low egg count. She probably won't be able to have any more children."

"Ah. That's unexpected."

"It was for Bryn as well. Damon said she would have been born that way. She didn't say anything, but I think it bothers her. She wouldn't have been so shocked if she knew more about her birth mother."

"I can imagine. I wish I had an update about Bryn's mother, but I haven't heard back from our elders yet. I'm sure they'll get back to me, but, like everything, it's a matter of waiting." She chewed a slice of bread laden with butter and honey. "And how are you holding up with everything, Night?"

"I'm more than okay with having one pup, but knowing this is our only chance has hit me differently now that I've had time to sit with it. I mean, Troy is still out there, and neither of the parties we sent out has any leads. We're swamped with the amount of work the Redwolfs left behind, and the alpha challenge is coming up. I'm trying to make sure everything is handled, but we're not planning to tell anyone about the pregnancy until the challenge is over."

"Well, I don't think you should worry about the challenge, Night. You will win," she assured me. "You were born to be a leader and a fighter."

I smiled a little. "I appreciate your confidence, Mom. I'll probably feel better about it once I've trained more."

She nodded and patted my hand. "Well, you let me know if you need any help with paperwork or the challenge. I'm happy to help anywhere I can, even with ledgers or with watching over Bryn while you train."

I didn't know if we would ask her for that help, but it was nice to know she was open to it. Mom was always willing to support me, and it made me feel like shit that I was here to ask her about her past with Gregor.

Sensing my hesitation, she patted my arm again. "How are the Wargs? I'm sure they're missing you."

Thinking about my pack pulled me away from my darker thoughts. "Things went well there. It started out rocky, but by the end of it, we ended up repairing dozens of buildings and getting some supplies from Colville that we needed. I think you'll be surprised when you go back."

"I'm glad I asked," she said. "Your eyes look brighter when you talk about our people."

I nodded. "I just wish everything else could be solved with a hammer and some paint."

"Wouldn't that make things easier?" She chuckled. "Now, tell me more about whatever mess you have, Night. I can tell it's weighing you down."

I caught her up on the missing money and the search we were doing through the Redwolfs' belongings—a search that was going nowhere—and the fable about portals to realms holding other shifters.

She nodded as I spoke. She digested the information easier than Bryn, Tavi, or I had. I wondered if it was because few things surprised her or because of her connection to the spirits and belief in fate and destiny.

"I hate having to ask you about my father," I said after I finished. "But I have to know if he mentioned anything about this strange story to you?"

"It's not easy for me to talk about my history with that man," she said slowly, "but it's much easier now than it was even a few months ago." She took a few breaths, then continued. "I've told you more than once, but I'll say again that Gregor wasn't always a monster. He and I grew up together with Damon, and back then, he was sweet, gentle, and even kind. He grew up to be a strong, capable fighter and leader, and he was ready to take over as alpha for the Wargs. It was kind of a given that we would end up together—we were always hanging out with each other, and even though my connection to the spirits wasn't as strong as it is now, I had a feeling that my future was inextricably tied to his.

"When I told him I was pregnant, he was happy and excited at first. He'd always wanted a boy, and when we found out your gender, he was even more thrilled. But after a couple of months, he became more withdrawn and exhausted. He wasn't sleeping very well. He took over as alpha for the Wargs when I was about four months pregnant with you, and then his behavior changed even more. I don't know what happened, but it was like his heart had been replaced with someone else's.

"He got irritable and angry with me, he'd disappear at night, and he would stay at his beta's home instead of mine if I annoyed him even the slightest bit. It all came to a head one night when he told me he didn't love me…or you." She closed her eyes briefly. "It hurt, Night. It hurt me deeply. At first, I suspected he'd found his real mate, but that wouldn't have made him treat me so badly or say such awful things about you. He'd always wanted a son, and I couldn't figure out why he would say he wanted nothing to do with you. I asked him to tell me what was making him behave like this, but he wouldn't answer me. Not long after that, he abandoned us and took over the Kings' pack."

Hatred burned in my chest for the man who had hurt my mother. "Did you see him again after that?"

"No, but a couple of years after you were born, I heard he'd had a son with a woman from the Kings' pack. It tore my heart to pieces." She shook her head. "I'm sure you know this, but the Wargs and Kings have always had conflicts. After Gregor took over the Kings, relations between the packs got worse, not better. The Kings were much more hostile toward us, even coming into our territory to hurt us or mess with our things. Peter, of course, rolled over and did nothing, and the pack suffered.

"The pack mother we were hiding was probably the only one left in the world we knew. Everyone believed the Kings had killed her, and that deepened the rift between the two packs. But Gregor had kidnapped her first."

"What?" I jumped to my feet, and my chair clattered to the floor. I couldn't believe what I'd just heard. "He took her?"

"Yes, he did. Lucian tried to get her back because he was the strongest and best fighter in the pack. Peter didn't want him to risk his life for the pack mother, but Lucian ignored him. He tried to get them out, but they were both killed. You and Dom were just little boys when we lost him."

I picked up the chair and set it down. I had no idea that was why Dom's father had died. "That pack mother was Bryn's mother, right?"

"I believe so, but it will be hard to prove that. No one knew she was a pack mother. After she was killed, I suspected she might have been. The pack immediately loved her, and there was her kind yet firm way of dealing with pack conflict. But it was her skill with the soil that confirmed it the most for me. That's a skill Bryn also has. It's only with hindsight that I'm able to put these things together."

"Who was she?"

"I'm sure you will remember her in time."

"Okay. Who was Bryn's father?"

"We were never sure. She was as secretive about that as she was about everything else, and we weren't going to press someone we were sure was a pack mother for information. I'm waiting to hear from the elders about whether there's a ritual that would allow Bryn to see what happened through her mother's eyes. That's the best way for her to find the answers she seeks."

"Would that be safe for her to do while pregnant?"

"It should be, but it's ultimately Bryn's decision whether she wants to do it. We can talk more about that after the Warg elders have gotten back to me."

The idea of letting Bryn do some random ritual didn't sit right with me, but that was something I could raise with her some other time. "So, what about the realm portals?"

"Oh, Gregor was always obsessed with that story. His father told him about it when he was a pup, and he loved going on research adventures to gather books that were said to have mentioned it. I'd tell him it was a waste of time, that there was no way those books would prove it was true, but he was determined to find out more."

"You never believed in the legend, then?"

"Hell, no." She grimaced. "If it had happened, we would have other proof than just a legend. And the spirits would give some indication that it was true. The idea that there are other shifters somewhere in the universe doesn't sound far-fetched, but that legend mentions bird shifters." She shook her head. "Could you imagine a man as large as you shifting into a kestrel? Or a hawk? I just don't see how that would work."

I grinned as she continued her rant. I deferred to her on all matters of ancient wolf history and stories, so I was glad to hear my mother also regarded this fable as bullshit. But this made me wonder…could we use Troy's belief in the portals to our advantage? Maybe there was a book or an artifact supposedly connected to the legend that we could use to set a trap for him? The best way to find out was to find the books he'd hidden. I was sure they'd have something we could use.

Chapter 15 - Bryn

I'd been cooped up in the alpha cabin for three days straight, and I had to get out of there. Night said he was against it, but I promised all I would do was check on the progress of our rebuilding projects. The fresh air would be good for me, and it would show the Kings that I was still around and taking care of them. Plus, I hadn't been sick that morning, and I even felt well enough to eat a small omelet with my usual toast and tea. I wanted to take full advantage of my strength while I had it.

Tavi asked if I wanted her to come along, but I told her to stay behind so she could continue searching for that account information. She agreed, and I stepped out on my own.

The sun was shining that morning, which I hoped was a sign that I'd made the right decision. I went to the commons to buy something for Night and Tavi. Alphas were given a generous monthly stipend, and when I received mine, I hadn't known what to do with it. Mom suggested I save it or spend it on something that would make me feel good. I didn't know what to get for myself, but I wanted Tavi and Night to know how much I appreciated their hard work while confined to my bed.

I looked around for a moment, taking my time to find the best gifts. Eventually, I decided on a stall that sold braided leather bracelets. No one was manning the store when I arrived, so I browsed the goods on display.

There were a lot of beautiful bracelets for sale, some with metal clasps or trinkets attached to them, others with simple three-strand braids, and some with much more complex weaves. I was tempted by more than one style, but when I considered Tavi and Night's personalities, I knew they would prefer simpler styles.

"See something you like, Alpha?" The deep voice made me look up.

It was as if Lance had just appeared next to me. I stepped to the side and eyed him. He wore the kind of smile a person reserved for someone they hadn't seen in a long time. I wasn't sure what that smile meant, but I didn't return it.

The first time I ever saw Lance, he was hanging out with Troy, his pale eyes staring dispassionately forward. I'd never known him to smile or laugh or have a kind word for anyone. Why was he here if he was so close to Troy? Was he keeping tabs on us? After what happened with Evan, we couldn't be too careful.

"Yes, actually." I pointed to a chestnut-brown bracelet and a cranberry-red one. Both bracelets had brass clasps to keep them securely closed around the wrist.

Lance started to respond, but the shopkeeper returned at that very moment.

"You have a good eye, Alpha. I'll give you a good price for the pair of them."

"How much?"

"Forty-five dollars."

I reached for my purse. My mother would be disappointed that I wasn't haggling over the price, but I wasn't in the mood for it. Besides, Lance was standing right next to me, and I didn't want to try talking down the price with him watching me so closely.

I went to give the money to the merchant when Lance's hand covered mine.

"Hold on there, Alpha," he said. "I happen to understand the work that goes into bracelets like these. He's taking advantage of you by asking for anything more than thirty."

Both the merchant and I looked at Lance in surprise. The transaction was almost complete. Why was he stepping in for me?

"I can assure you," the merchant began slowly, "that my daughter put everything into making these bracelets. How can you put such a low price on her hard work?"

Lance smirked, amusement twinkling in his eye. "Oh, really? Then why was Charline selling them to her friends for fifteen dollars each? Wouldn't she know the value of her own work?"

"Charline—what?" The mention of his daughter's name seemed to throw the merchant off. But he recovered quickly. "Well, regardless, what passes between friends is different from what happens in real commerce. I'm sure Alpha Hunter and I can settle for paying forty dollars for the bracelets."

"Mmm." Lance pretended to consider the offer. "No. I still think thirty is more than enough for two."

"Thirty-five."

"Nope. Thirty, or we walk."

I didn't remember agreeing to walk away from the sale. I really wanted those bracelets, but honestly, this negotiation was a little entertaining. What would the merchant do next?

He gritted his teeth, his face reddening the longer this went on. I hadn't noticed until that moment, but a small crowd had formed behind us. I should have expected as much—Lance was handsome and a rare sight around the compound. That mystery kept people curious about him.

"Fine," the merchant said. "Thirty it is."

"Excellent! I knew we could come to a reasonable agreement."

I handed over the haggled-down amount, and the merchant gave me the bracelets in a paper bag, which I slipped into my purse.

"That was...kind of you." I didn't even try to mask my confusion. One of Troy's people helping someone out? That didn't sound right—unless he had some kind of vendetta against that merchant.

Or maybe he had a greater plan in mind.

"Hardly," he scoffed. "I'm just having some fun. Maybe next time, you'll do the bargaining yourself."

"Um, yeah, maybe."

He raised his hand by way of goodbye. "I'll be seeing you, Alpha."

"Sure. Bye."

He went in the opposite direction to the alpha cabin. That had been a bizarre interaction, to say the least. He didn't make me feel unsafe, but he seemed to be testing me or trying to figure me out. I also had the strangest feeling that he and I were supposed to meet when we did. I wondered if the spirits were trying to give me a warning about him.

"Hey, Bryn!"

I whipped around, but it was only Jasper. "Oh, Jasper." I pressed a hand to my chest. "I wasn't expecting to see you around the compound."

"My bad. Didn't mean to scare you," he said with a sweet, apologetic smile. "I thought you heard me calling."

"I probably should have, but I guess I was zoned out." I relaxed. "It's been about a week since I've seen you. What've you been up to?"

"I wish I could say I've been having a good time, but that hasn't been the case." He gave me a sad smile. "I've been hunting down Troy, and I needed to give Alpha Night an update." He obviously had some bad news. "I'm glad I bumped into you, Bryn. You'll probably want to hear my update. Want to walk with me?"

"Oh, sure." We fell into a comfortable rhythm as we walked. All that was missing was Tavi. A pang of guilt hit me in the chest. Maybe I should've asked her to come with me after all. She might not mind seeing Jasper after all this time.

I frowned. Something he'd said stood out to me.

"Hey, Jasper?"

"What's up?"

"When you say 'hunting down Troy,' you mean you're part of the search party, right? You're hunting him down…to arrest him, right?"

He laughed like I'd made a joke. "Oh, we're searching for him, alright. But no, not to bring him in. Our orders are to kill on sight. The only thing we need to bring in is proof of our kill."

His answer rattled around in my head until it finally clicked into place. My confusion turned to fury hot enough to boil a kettle.

"A hunting party, you say," I repeated, my voice low. "How interesting."

Night had broken his promise to me. I stopped walking, and Jasper continued for a few steps before stopping and turning to me. When he saw the expression on my face, his smile fell.

"Jasper, when did Night give the order for this hunting party?"

"The day he got back to the compound. I think that was about eight days ago or so?"

That was the day he met with the Wargs' council. I'd thought he'd told me everything, but he must have "forgotten" to mention this part of it. How convenient.

"How interesting that he didn't tell me about this."

His eyes became as wide as dinner plates. "Bryn, I'm sorry. I thought you knew—"

"Well, I didn't." I shouldn't have snapped at him. It wasn't his fault that Night had kept me in the dark, but I was pissed off, dammit, and I needed to speak to my mate now. "Follow me, Jasper," I said, storming towards the construction site. Night had mentioned he would be assisting Dom with repairs.

We found Night and Dom standing together and laughing about something, but when they saw us approaching, they stopped.

"Bryn, what's—"

"When the hell were you going to tell me you sent a hunting party after Troy?"

Night blinked, looking like a startled buck. "What?"

"Night, I want to know *right now* why you'd send a *hunting* party after Troy when I told you I didn't want him killed." I looked at him expectantly, my rage wafting off me in waves.

Night didn't answer right away. He looked from me to Jasper, who held his hands up in surrender and took a step back.

"I saw Bryn when I arrived," he explained quickly. "I didn't know you were keeping it a secret, Alpha. If I had, I wouldn't have told her."

I stepped in front of Jasper. If I were calm, I would have found it funny and maybe a little nostalgic that I was getting between the two men again, just like I had when Night and I denied our feelings for each other. But I wasn't calm; I was ready to rip someone's head off his shoulders.

"Don't you dare blame him, Night Shepherd," I snapped. "*You* are the one keeping secrets from me. Why didn't you tell me that you did this? No, forget that—why did you send a hunting party at all?"

He sent one more glare at Jasper, then put his hand on my shoulder. I allowed him to steer me away from Dom and Jasper to a more private spot, but I jerked free the minute we had gone far enough.

"Stop stalling and tell me," I demanded.

He closed his eyes briefly, and when he opened them, he looked a little apologetic, but not in a way that said he knew he'd fucked up. He just looked like he was sorry he'd been caught.

"Bryn, look, I'm sorry I didn't tell you, but my hands were tied, alright? The council wanted a hunting party sent after Troy, and I couldn't say no. They were right to request it."

"They were right to request it, but I wasn't right to forbid it?"

"It's different, Bryn. I'm the Wargs' alpha, and I need to do what's right for my pack. This is what my pack wanted."

"Then why didn't you just tell me the truth? You had plenty of time to tell me, and you never did. I thought we agreed that we wouldn't keep secrets from each other anymore!"

He squeezed his eyes shut for a few seconds before reopening them. "I didn't mean to go behind your back, Bryn," he said, speaking at a calmer, slower pace. You're right—I should have told you—but there was no way I could do that without stressing you out or coming off like I was undermining your authority."

"You *decided* that this would stress me out, so you also decided not to tell me. You kept this a secret so I wouldn't get mad at you. You see how well that turned out, Night, because I'm fucking pissed off."

He stared hard at me but seemed unable to come up with a good response.

"I can't believe you would do this," I said, running my hands through my hair. "I bet you're happy the council asked you to send them, aren't you?"

He paused, and I saw the debate raging in his forest-green eyes before he said, "To be honest, Bryn, yeah, I am. After I found out about the baby, I can say that I'm fucking glad the council forced me to send them. At least with him dead, we don't have to worry about him trying to kill you or our baby."

"I knew it," I shot back. "But now that we know about the secret account, we need him alive more than ever, don't we? We have no leads without him!"

"Bryn, you know as well as I do that he's not going to tell us anything," he retorted. "Even if we captured him, you know that all he'll do is lie to us."

"Troy's crafty, but he's not that smart. Night, I was stuck with him for a week in that damn cave, and he was more than willing to give away family secrets without much of a push from me. I could get him to talk."

"You don't seriously think I'd let you interrogate him alone?"

"I didn't seriously think you would go behind my back, Night! Maybe you're willing to do all kinds of things that I wouldn't have imagined you capable of doing."

He let out a tight breath. "Listen, Bryn, even with the account in play, Troy is still too dangerous to be allowed to live. He's a fucking psychopath, and he's crafty. If we captured him, he'd just escape again."

I gritted my teeth. We were retreading the same argument. Night claimed he wanted to avoid stressing me out, but now my stress levels were through the roof because he hadn't been honest with me…again. Why did he insist on making it so hard to believe when he was telling the truth? I loved him, but I needed to trust that he wouldn't keep important things like this from me. It was true that I was in a more fragile state because of the baby, but I was pretty damned sure that Night still wouldn't have told me if I wasn't pregnant.

I stared at him, feeling pressure build behind my eyes. "I am your mate, Night, and because of that, you should have trusted me with the hard news," I said finally. "If you didn't tell me because you thought I was too weak to take it, you're no better than Edward or Dana, who think I'm too stupid to understand a ledger."

The anger on his face faded, and he looked like I'd thrown ice water on him. "Hold on, Bryn—"

I held up my hand, and he stopped talking. "Is there anything else you've been keeping from me?"

It took him a few seconds to answer. "I wasn't keeping this from you, Bryn," he said gently. "I just hadn't had the chance to tell you. Tavi told you about the missing pups, right?"

"Yes, she told me," I said. The reminder of the missing boys cooled some of my anger, replacing it with sadness. "I was only a few years older than the boys who went missing. Mom wouldn't let me out of her sight."

During that time, I was hardly ever bullied because Mom was with me all the time. The pack's mood had changed. Their paranoia, worry, and grief had put me even more on edge.

"Do you think the disappearances have something to do with the ferals?" I asked.

"I don't know, Bryn. It could be nothing."

But I recognized the determination in his eyes. "Your gut is telling you that it's not nothing."

"Yeah, something feels off about it all, but I can't prove that they're linked. I'm planning on talking to a witness, but I don't know how well that will go.

Apparently, the poor kid was traumatized by what he saw, and he might not be the most reliable source of information."

"I want to be there when you talk to him."

He was about to say something—maybe to argue against me going or maybe to agree that he wanted me there—but before he could, I noticed Jasper approaching cautiously from behind Night. Night sighed instead of speaking and turned to meet Jasper.

"I'm sorry, Alpha—I really am—but I need to catch you up on what's happened. The others are waiting for me to get back to them."

Night cursed under his breath and put his hand on my shoulder. "I'll be back, Bryn. Don't go anywhere, okay?"

"Fine. Whatever."

Almost as soon as they walked away, my stomach flipped. Nausea rushed to my head, and I ran to a nearby tree. I threw up in the grass behind the tree. Having an omelet for breakfast had been a mistake. I felt a soothing hand on my back, and I assumed Night had come over to help me through it. When I finally stopped heaving and looked over my shoulder, I saw that it was Dom, not my mate, helping me through it.

"Are you okay?" he asked. "Do you need to lie down?"

"No." I straightened and stepped away from him, leaning my back against a different tree. "I had a right to know about the hunting party," I said. "Night should have told me."

"You're right. He should have."

I let out a long sigh. "There's a 'but' there, Dom. I can hear it in your voice."

He gave me an apologetic smile. "*But* things are complicated. The council is up his ass about Troy, and they want him to take the Kings over by force."

"No, I get that they're putting pressure on him, but I'm an alpha, too. I'm not saying I wouldn't have been upset, but I am saying I would've understood what he was going through if he had just *told* me. He chose not to, and now I'm pissed off." And hurt. But I was too heated to admit that to Dom.

"Night is trying to balance a lot—and so are you," he quickly added. "But that also means he has to make calls that neither of you will be happy about to keep his pack healthy. He can't risk the council trying to usurp him, especially now."

"I don't want to go back and forth with you about this, Dom. Night Shepherd should be explaining all of this to me, not you." I glanced at my mate, who was still in deep conversation with Jasper. "We could have avoided this conflict if he'd just come clean, but he chose not to."

He sighed. "You're completely in the right about that, Bryn. He should have been smarter about it but I think Night's trying, you know? He'll get better at communication with time, but he'll mess up along the way."

I felt stilting pressure behind my eyes, but I gave a small chuckle instead of crying. "You know, it feels a little like I'm being scolded by my big brother."

He smiled. "I'm sorry, that's not what I meant to do. You have every right to be upset with him, Bryn. I really am on your side about that." He put his hand on my head, which might have annoyed me under normal circumstances, but I found it strangely comforting now. "I'm sure you two will work things out eventually."

I wanted to get to the bottom of this sooner rather than later, but the hurt in my heart went pretty deep. I wanted us to be equal partners in this relationship, and Night sparing my feelings made me feel like he didn't trust me. And I still felt bad about not having the ability to give him more kids. Were I a stronger wolf, a wolf with the capacity to give him as many pups as he wanted, would he rely on me more?

Night's conversation with Jasper wrapped up, and they jogged over to where Dom and I stood. Their expressions were grim, and I felt a pit form in my stomach.

"What's wrong?" Dom asked.

"There's been another feral attack on a smaller pack about a three-day run from here. The pack was just starting to form and hadn't even decided on an official name for themselves. From what Jasper tells me, none of them survived. Not the women or children. No one."

"No." I covered my mouth with both hands. Horror poured through me, ice forming in its wake.

Dom scowled. "How do we know it was ferals?"

"We caught a trace scent of Troy in one of the buildings," Jasper said. "The rest of the hunting party is tracking down the scent, but they had me come back to give the report. I intend to meet up with them again once I'm done here."

"Were they looking for something?" Dom asked.

"We couldn't tell. The compound was ransacked, and cabins had been burned to the ground. It was an awful mess."

Night said, "I'm planning on sending word to other packs near the site of the attack to inform them of the situation. I don't want anyone else caught unawares like that. Bryn..." He looked at me, and I tried to decipher the expression on his face. But I couldn't—it was too muddled. "We'll talk later," he finished.

I nodded, not trusting my voice to keep from shaking.

"I'll go with you, Night," Dom said. "Jasper, make sure Bryn gets home safe."

"Of course." Jasper turned to me. "Bryn, follow me."

I went with him, but my legs were numb as I walked, and my body felt drained. *Dammit.* I clenched my hands. *How could things have gotten to this point?* Troy was out there killing wolves, and we had no idea why or how to stop him. I felt useless and small, and I hated feeling that way. I wished I could be out there with them looking for Troy, but I knew I couldn't risk the baby. All I could do was wait and hope this wouldn't end in disaster.

Chapter 16 - Bryn

"I want to go to my mom's," I said as Jasper and I walked through the compound. The last place I wanted to be right now was the alpha cabin.

"Sure, of course," he said. His hands were in his pockets, and he hadn't looked at me since we started walking. It sharply contrasted with how things had started—just before he revealed that Night had sent a killing squad after Troy.

"Bryn, I feel awful about what happened back there."

"It's fine," I replied. But my tone was so flat, I wouldn't have believed myself.

He winced. "Still, it sucks that I broke the news to you like that. If I had known—"

"It's fine, I get it. It's not your fault. I don't blame you, Jasper." I really wanted to leave it at that. I'd talked with Dom about Night's secret, but my heart was still tender. The queasiness in my stomach didn't help in the slightest. "You were just following Night's orders, after all."

He chewed the inside of his cheek and looked down. He looked so guilty that *I* felt guilty by proxy. That was frustrating because I knew I wasn't wrong to be upset about the situation, though I was trying not to take it out on him. I really, *really* wished I could let it go, but the more I thought about it, the tighter the angry fist in my chest got. That was the reason I wanted to get to my mom's. She was great at putting things into perspective for me.

I sighed as we got closer to her cabin. "Listen, Jasper," I said. "Night is my soulmate, so it's not like I'll be mad about this forever. We'll work through it somehow. Eventually. I'm sorry I haven't been better company on this walk—"

"You don't have to apologize for that," he protested.

"—but I need some time to think and process all of this on my own time, you know?" We stopped at my mom's front door, and I patted Jasper's shoulder. "I hope I see you again before you head back home."

He still looked guilt-stricken, but he pulled up a smile for me. "I hope so, too. And I hope it's under better circumstances, huh?"

I tried to smile back, though my heart wasn't in it. Jasper was a good guy, if a little sensitive. We said our goodbyes, and I went into the cabin just as my mother came down the stairs.

"Oh," she said. "I thought I heard you talking outside. Were you with Night?"

I shook my head and headed into the living room. I collapsed onto the old couch with fabric sewn patchwork style over the exposed tufts of filling. We'd had to make a lot of repairs over the years, but it was still the most comfortable couch I'd ever sat on.

"Ah." Mom followed me into the living room but leaned against the doorframe. "I take it things aren't going well between you and your mate?"

I heaved out a sigh. "Not really. We're kinda in the middle of a fight."

"It's not about the baby, is it?"

I shook my head again. "No. It's something else."

"Okay, well, before we get into this fight, how are you feeling? Still nauseous?"

I nodded. "I threw up before I came over here."

"I'll get you some tea." She turned and headed into the kitchen. She was gone for just a few minutes, and the familiar sounds of boiling water and pottery clanking against the counter was soothingly nostalgic. Mom was back quickly, handing me the tea. She'd also gotten herself some salsa and corn chips.

"Thanks, Mom," I said, accepting the mug.

She offered the paper bag of chips, and after a moment of hesitation, I accepted a handful of them, munching on them while we spoke.

"Now," she said, easing into the old armchair, "tell me what's been going on."

I took a deep breath and told her about the hunting party. I wasn't sure whether I should mention that Troy had attacked a small pack. Night and I hadn't discussed whether it was safe for other people to know, so I wanted to give that development the gravity it deserved. The whole compound already knew that Troy was on the loose, so there was nothing wrong with talking about it.

When I finished, I took a long sip of my tea, which had cooled down.

Mom's lips were pursed in thought. "So, it sounds to me," she began, "like the issue is communication."

"That's the long and short of it."

"You feel Night doesn't respect you enough to tell you the important things."

I nodded. "I know the Wargs' council put him in a difficult position, but when he got back, he omitted the part about the hunting party because he knew it would upset me. He told me everything else the council told him, and that's arguably just as upsetting. He left out the bit about the hunting party because I'd told him not to do it."

"I understand why that hurts you, baby. It's awful when you don't feel like you're on equal footing in a relationship."

I nodded, relieved that she could empathize with my position.

"That said, from what I've seen of your mate, I think it's likely that he was trying to protect you from anything that would elevate your stress too much. All mate pairings can have communication issues, especially if they bond as early in the relationship as you and Night have. The two of you didn't go through the dating process that non-soulmate pairs go through before they decide to mate. The connection between you was so strong that the two of you just acted."

I felt that familiar stinging sensation behind my eyes, but I didn't have the same impulse to keep the tears from falling around my mom. "Did we do all of this wrong?" I asked. "Did we mess things up?"

"Oh, honey." She lay her hand on my knee in reassurance. "No, that's not what I'm saying at all. All I'm saying is that you two aren't talking things through. You need time to learn each other's strengths and weaknesses and work through them together."

I nibbled sadly on a chip. "I feel like I put more effort into communicating."

"You didn't tell Night about the baby right away."

"I wanted to make it special," I argued. "And I *did* tell him. I didn't wait for someone else to break the news to him."

She chuckled. "That's true, but that wasn't the real reason you didn't tell him immediately. It was because you were worried about how he'd react to the news. If Night didn't have the ability to sense you were pregnant, how long would you have waited to tell him?"

I opened my mouth to argue more, but dammit, she had a point. I had worried Night would reject me when I told him about the baby. Looking back, though, it was stupid of me to think my mate would react that way. And I would have probably waited a while to figure out how best to tell him, especially now when things were so busy.

Mom patted my knee again. "Give Night some time, Bryn. He should have told you about the hunting party, but he is an alpha and used to keeping things from the people he cares most about to protect them and the rest of his pack.

It will take him a while to realize and accept that he doesn't need to hold things back from you."

I sniffled and wiped away a tear with the back of my hand. Mom's words reminded me of my conversation with Dom. I appreciated that they were considering both my and Night's perspectives. Those two were more correct than my ego was willing to admit, but I needed to let that go if I wanted to move forward with Night. He had been pulling double duty all around, and other than this secret, he was nothing short of amazing.

"You've given me a lot to think about, Mom. Thank you...I think," I added jokingly.

She chuckled. "That's what I'm here for. Was there anything else you wanted to talk about?"

I was about to say no, but then I remembered the doctor's appointment. "Oh, I got an ultrasound at the infirmary." As happy as I'd been to see the life growing inside me, the other stuff Dr. Stan told me brought me low again. "Mom, getting to see the baby was...amazing. It's so tiny, this life inside me." I touched my stomach. "But Dr. Stan told me I wouldn't be able to have more children."

Her eyes widened, eyebrows scrunching together in alarm. "What? Why not?"

"Apparently, I only have one ovary and a low egg count." Admitting it out loud was like a slap to the face. "I never knew about that, but Dr. Stan said I was born with this condition."

"So you've had this all your life?" She slowly absorbed the news, slumping back against her chair. "Oh, Bryn, I should have taken you to get a physical when you were younger. We could have done something to try and save the eggs you had."

I shook my head. "You can't blame yourself, Mom. It's not your fault. You were working yourself down to the bone to keep me clothed and fed while the rest of the pack shunned us." I finished my chips and picked up my tea. "It's just how things worked out."

Mom sighed but didn't push against my words. "I guess that means we have to treat this baby with extra special care," she said, trying to smile. "Have you and Night given much thought about a nursery?"

I was glad for the change in subject. "Not yet. We've been a little preoccupied. But he's willing to move out of the alpha cabin if I want to."

"Oh? How do you feel about that?"

"It surprised me. The pack is his birthright, and I know having the alpha cabin means a lot. But…I'm not sure how I feel yet."

Mom nodded for me to continue.

"The cabin has symbolic importance to the Kings, and the alpha has lived there for generations. But Night and I are trying to change so much about this pack…perhaps it's for the better that we switch up that tradition, too. Just think about the location. It's in a good position for the Kings to have easy access to us, but if we merge the packs, shouldn't we think about positioning ourselves somewhere more accessible to the Wargs as well?"

"A lot of pros and cons to leaving the cabin," Mom remarked.

"Yeah. I'm still weighing them. I need to decide soon so we can get everything ready for the baby."

"You do, but you've got time, honey. You have a lot on your mind right now, so don't stress too much about it. Whenever there's some time for you two to address things, do it."

I nodded and smiled. "Thanks again, Mom. I'm sorry I haven't been by more often."

"It's okay, baby. I cherish every moment we get to spend together, even if some of that time is devoted to you venting about your mate." She grinned. "I thank the Fates every day that you come to me when you need to."

Her words were enough to make me want to burst into tears. I tried to get some control of my emotions by taking a long drink of tea.

Chapter 17 - Night

Dom and I went to the training grounds after Jasper and Bryn left. After I'd instructed a few wolves to let neighboring packs know what had happened to the small pack, Dom suggested we head to the training grounds to check out the competition I'd be facing during the alpha challenge. I thought it was a good idea to get my mind off things, but it was hard to focus on anything but the feral attack and the hurt on Bryn's face.

I should have told her, I cursed myself. *I should have been a man about it and come clean.* I'd fucked up with her again. I'd known it would eventually come up but hoped it would be on my terms and Bryn would be in a better place with the pregnancy. My not telling her had sent her into a borderline panic attack. The guilt burned like a brand searing into my chest.

It sucked even more that Jasper had been the one to tell her. Bryn and I had claimed and mated each other, but jealousy lingered inside me. Jasper would never be stupid enough to try to get between an alpha and his soulmate, but it irked me, anyway. I was a mess of pent-up emotion and aggression and had no easy way to deal with it. I tried to

shake myself out of it. Bryn and I would talk more later—
no use in getting all worked up about it now.

I tried to keep an eye on the Kings' fighters. My
men were also sparring, but none of them would try for the
alpha spot. Only the Kings would be getting in the ring
with me. I would take Tavi's suggestion to heart and train
in full view, but I wanted to scope out the competition first.

"Have you heard anything about which men will be
participating?" I asked Dom.

"Not as much as I would've thought," he said. "The
Kings have been pretty tight-lipped about it, but I did hear
from the elders that the Redwolfs came into power in the
last alpha challenge."

"Interesting."

Dom nodded toward a brown-haired kid who
seemed to have the most skill. I put him in his early
twenties. Every punch and kick he threw had deadly
precision. It surprised me that he was so agile when he had
about the same muscle mass as Dom.

"That's Lance," he said. "He's supposed to be the
Kings' best fighter."

"What's his story?"

"Don't know. I asked around about him, but no one
had much to say. He's twenty-three, and he wasn't born

into the pack. Apparently, Troy found him seven years ago and recruited him into the pack, but he's been a mystery ever since."

I frowned. Troy had personally brought in this kid? That meant Lance had a connection to Troy and was possibly loyal to the Redwolfs.

"He's good," I said, watching Lance grapple with a guy almost a foot taller than him. In seconds, he had taken the guy to the ground.

"He is," Dom agreed. "To be honest, Night, his fighting style reminds me of you when you were younger."

"Sure," I scoffed.

"I thought you'd say that." He chuckled. "Anyway, it bothers me that no one seems to know anything about him. Not a single wolf could tell me his last name."

"Dig deeper," I said. "This guy is an unknown, and we can't ignore that he might still have a connection to Troy."

"I'll do that."

"Any other fighters who plan on competing?" I asked.

"Xavier is the next pack favorite."

I followed Dom's gaze to a man who was about my height and build. He was older, probably in his forties, and the hair above the nape of his neck was shaved, leaving enough up top for him to put into a small bun.

"He was one of Gregor's personal guards and had been since he was twenty-five. It was like pulling teeth to get anyone to talk about him, but those who were willing said Xavier is ruthless and excessively violent."

I could see as much from the kick he planted in the chest of his sparring partner. The man fell to the ground with a thud, gasping for breath. He struggled to get up, but Xavier put his foot on his shoulder and pushed him down again.

Other wolves were waiting to spar with Xavier, but their faces told me they didn't want to. I bet he'd left many of them with serious injuries.

"He believes the Kings need to be a small, powerful pack instead of a larger one," Dom told me. "And he's been open about how he plans to cull half his own pack to achieve that goal."

My upper lip curled back in disgust. "He sounds like an idiot. A dangerous idiot." I leaned close to Dom. "Have our men keep an eye on him and the wolves he hangs around. They might also be in league with Troy."

"Of course. Need me to do anything else? Any work you want me to take off your plate?"

"Not right now." I had a lot going on, but I was dealing with it. My biggest problem right now was how my conversation with Bryn would go. I was certain I'd really hurt her this time. My wolf whined inside me. He hated when we fought.

"Xavier and Lance are high-priority right now," I told Dom. "But I'll let you know if I need you to do more."

"Sounds good."

We watched the fighters a bit longer, and then because I wanted to distract myself from my thoughts, I asked, "So, how have things been with you and Tavi? Have you seen her since the dinner?"

"Not really." He put his hands into his pockets. "After dinner, we walked around the compound and got some dessert at the commons, but I haven't had a chance to spend time with her since then. She's determined to look through the Redwolfs' documents and says she doesn't have much free time."

I heard the slight hurt in Dom's tone. It still felt a little weird to think of him and my sister as a couple, but as Dom's friend, I wished I could do something for him. The reality was that only they could work it out, and if Tavi said she was too busy or wasn't ready to spend more time with him, there wasn't much he or I could do about it.

"I guess the best thing is to give her the space she needs for now," I said. "She's made a lot of progress, but she still needs time."

"I know, it's just tough. I...I miss her." He shook his head as if trying to physically shake off his pain. "Anyway, I should probably head back to check on the rebuilding project."

"I'm going to spar with Vince. I've got some stuff I want to work out."

Dom and I hugged goodbye, and I went into the ring. Vince's partner was taking a break, so when I offered to take his place, Vince agreed.

"Don't go too easy on me, Alpha Night," he said as we squared off.

I grinned. "I won't go too hard on you, either, kid." I just wanted to let off some steam and get in a good workout; I wasn't going to leave more than a bruise on one of my best men.

As Vince and I traded blows, I kept an eye on Xavier and Lance to note their style. I didn't want to make it obvious that I was watching them, and Vince provided good cover.

"Keep your elbow pulled more toward your chest when you go to punch," I said to Vince, blocking one of his fists. "You'll be able to put more power behind it."

"Thanks, Alpha." He tried it again, and when I blocked, I felt the hit vibrate up my arm.

"Good," I said. "Just like that."

We sparred for another minute, and then Vince spoke again. "Alpha Night, there's something I wanted to tell you."

I ducked under his kick. "What is it?"

"I got back from our compound yesterday, and while I was there, I heard rumors that the council might be looking for a new alpha if your takeover doesn't work."

"Were you able to verify the rumor?" I asked, keeping my expression as neutral as possible.

"No, nothing concrete. Just rumors." He hesitated, then added, "I wanted to tell you about it as soon as I could. Most of us are rooting for you, Alpha. Not whoever the council has in mind."

"I appreciate that, Vince." I caught his arm, twisted it, and tossed him to the ground over my shoulder. It wasn't a powerful takedown, but he blinked up at me in surprise. I helped him to his feet. "Do you have any idea who they might be looking at to challenge me?"

He shook his head. "I'm sorry I don't have more for you."

"That's alright. Keep an ear on the ground for me, would you? And let me know if you learn anything else."

"Of course, Alpha. I've got your back."

I wasn't shocked to hear the council was coming up with a backup plan in case I didn't follow through with their wishes. They knew I wouldn't give up my position without a fight, so whomever they had in mind to take my place would have to be a real threat.

Sparring with Vince allowed me to let off some steam, but I still wasn't ready to face Bryn. Still, she and I had talked about going to Samuel's house together. I would follow through, even if we were in the middle of a fight.

I went up to the alpha cabin, but before I opened the door, I heard Bryn's voice behind me.

"Night."

I turned to see her coming my way. The sun chose that moment to move out from behind the clouds, just long enough to bring the shine out of her hair and accentuate the gold hue of her skin. She was so beautiful, my heart twisted. I wanted to take her in my arms, but I didn't.

"Hey," I said. "Did you go somewhere else?"

"Yeah, I went to see my mom. We just…talked."

"Oh." A chilly breeze intensified the silence that settled over us. There were only a few feet between us, but the distance seemed so wide. I ran my fingers through my hair.

"So, are you ready to go?" I asked.

"To talk to Samuel and his family? Yeah. I'm ready."

We set off with that chilly breeze drifting between us.

"We need to be delicate," Bryn said as we walked. "From what Tavi told me, he's pretty fragile."

I nodded. "Do you want to take the lead on the questions?"

She hesitated, then said, "That might be for the best."

"Sure. I agree." I paused. "Did you know Samuel?"

"Not really. I'm a couple of years older than him. His parents, Adam and Cathy, seemed like nice enough folks. Normal, you know?"

"Yeah."

"After Samuel experienced whatever he experienced, they were much more withdrawn. I don't think I've seen more than a glimpse of them in years."

"I see." I couldn't blame Samuel's parents for being reclusive. It was good that Bryn was taking the lead on this. On my own, I'd probably come off as intimidating. Her gentle nature was more suited for these kinds of conversations. Still, I wanted to be there with her, both to find answers and make sure nothing dangerous happened.

The council had told me the Granby cabin was on the southern side of the compound, with a door painted to look like the sky. Whoever had painted it had talent—the clouds were shaded very realistically.

I knocked a few times. In moments, Adam and Cathy Granby, both petite and gray-haired, answered the door. Their eyes widened when they saw me, and the male wolf shifted slightly in front of his wife. His reaction didn't offend me; it showed he was the kind of man who put his family first. I'd be a fool not to respect that.

"Uh, yes?" he asked. "Can I help you? Oh—" He saw Bryn step out from around me, and his eyebrows raised. "Alpha Hunter?"

"We're sorry to come here unannounced," she said with a kind smile. "We were hoping to speak with your son."

The Granbys shifted from side to side. Cathy placed her hand on Adam's shoulder and squeezed.

"My son...isn't well," he said. "What could you possibly want to speak to him about?"

"We want to ask him about what he saw that day," she replied gently. We had no reason to lie to them. "Night and I are looking into the disappearances."

"Oh, but Samuel is...he's such a delicate boy," Cathy blurted, her fingers digging deeper into her husband's shirt. "He could get hurt." She paused, her eyes narrowing at me. "*You* could hurt him."

Her words didn't offend me—I'd expected this pushback. I glanced at Bryn, and she nodded for me to speak.

"I promise I won't touch your son or make him talk if he doesn't want to. All we want is to try to get to the bottom of what happened all those years ago. As far as we know, he's the only witness."

"Forgive me for asking, but why do you care about missing King pups?" Adam asked. "They're not part of your pack."

"I care because the disappearances are strange." I saw no reason to lie, but I wouldn't give them every detail, either. They didn't need to know the disappearances might be related to Troy. "So many pups went missing in those four years, and it devastated your pack. Maybe in some ways, this pack is still dealing with the fallout of those disappearances."

Bryn nodded. "We just want to find some answers. Even if we can't get much, we'll be happy if you let us into your home."

The parents turned to look at each other, speaking with only their eyes. After a minute, they stepped aside. Wringing her hands, Cathy went into another room as Adam led us upstairs.

"Did Samuel paint the front door?" I asked.

"Yes, he did." Adam kept the answer short.

Shit. I must have overstepped.

"It's beautiful," Bryn said, saving the moment. "He's very talented."

"Yes," he replied, his voice softening. When we reached the landing on the second floor, he turned to us. "Listen, the minute Samuel has had enough of your questions, you must leave," he said. "Is that clear?"

"Absolutely," Bryn said. "We won't make him talk if he doesn't want to."

"Alright." Still, he was hesitant. "He can be pretty excitable, so whatever you do, don't spook him."

He led us to a door painted to look like the sky at sunset, with pastel-pink and purple melding together. The clouds looked similar to those painted on the front door, only less puffy.

Adam knocked on the door, then opened it. I stepped inside, and my eyes widened. It wasn't really what I was expecting from an artist.

The room was so dark, it took my eyes a few seconds to adjust. The curtains were nailed down over the window. Samuel was taller than either of his parents but wiry and thin. He was seventeen, but he had the haunted face of a kid who had seen too much too early in life. He paced back and forth in the middle of his room, mumbling to himself. Sketches covered his walls.

Bryn took a few steps inside while I stood near Adam by the door, trying to make myself look less large in the small room.

"Hey there, Samuel," Bryn said. "Do you mind if I ask you a few questions?"

He didn't respond and continued to pace.

"Samuel?" She took another cautious step forward. Though she was careful, her body language was relaxed. She looked like she knew what she was doing. "My name is Bryn. Do you remember ever seeing me around the compound? Back then, I was the only human in the village."

Samuel's mumbling quieted as he looked at Bryn. He still paced back and forth, but his eyes were riveted to her face. After a few seconds, he looked away again.

"Yeah, I thought you might recognize me." She smiled. "I like your art. You're obviously very talented."

He didn't visibly react to that, though I had no idea what he was thinking.

"Samuel, I'm going to ask you a few difficult questions, and I don't want to alarm you. We're trying to figure out what happened to you ten years ago. Could you tell me a bit about what you saw that night in the woods?"

Samuel stopped pacing and mumbling. He stood in the middle of the room, partially turned away from us.

"If you're afraid to speak, please don't worry. I brought my mate Night Shepherd with me."

"Hello, Samuel," I said. He turned his head toward me, and I felt rooted to the spot. There was so much behind that gaze, but nothing I could read.

"Night is strong enough to protect you, your parents, and the entire pack from what you saw that night," Bryn said. "If you feel comfortable, could you tell me what took you and your friend—"

Before she could finish, he rushed toward his wall, grabbed one of the sketches from it, and ripped it off. Then he stormed toward Bryn. My instincts pushed me to defend her, but she threw her hand back, stopping me before I could move. In my mind, I knew Samuel wasn't a threat to Bryn—and even if he was, his body language didn't show any bad intent—but my wolf and I were uncomfortable at his proximity to my pregnant mate.

He pushed the paper into her chest and quickly drew away, pointing at them.

"Th-the shadows," he said, his voice wobbling and eyes watering. "Took him. Hurt him."

Bryn glanced at the sketch, then handed it to me. The page was covered in charcoal marks, menacing shapes, and hulking figures. But other than how ominous they appeared, I couldn't tell what the drawing was supposed to be.

"The shadows?" she asked. "Was it a monster?"

He shook his head, and his long thin hair flew around his head. "Don't talk about it. Don't. It'll come back and get me, too." He went to his bed and crawled into the far corner of it. He trembled as he pulled the blankets up to cover him.

"Samuel?" Bryn asked.

"No!" He shouted so loud the entire cabin seemed to shake. "No, no, no!" He repeated this, winding the blankets tighter around himself. His shoulders trembled under the covers, and small sobs filled the room.

Footsteps stomped up the stairs seconds before Cathy shoved the door open.

She gasped when she saw Samuel's state. "Look what you've done to my boy!" She rushed inside and climbed onto the bed with him, pulling him into her arms and rocking back and forth. "Oh, get out, get out! Leave us be!"

"Let us help you, Cathy," Bryn said evenly. "I put him in this state. I want to help make it right."

Cathy seemed hesitant, but seeing the concern on Bryn's face made her ease her order.

"Fine. You can stay, Alpha. But *that* one"—she jabbed a finger toward me—"get out of his room. I don't want anyone like you near my boy."

Bryn turned her worried gaze my way. She wanted to know what I was going to say, wanted to know that I wouldn't be hurt if she stayed to look after the boy.

My heart pounded. Cathy's words stung. Her distrust of me came from the fact that I was the alpha of the Wargs, but Bryn's worry helped smooth things over for me.

"Of course." I inclined my head.

Adam gently touched my shoulder and guided me out of the room. "When he gets like this, there's hardly anything we can do to get him out of it."

"I'm sure Bryn will do everything she can." I folded the sketch in half carefully. Poor kid was even more traumatized than I'd thought.

Adam and I went outside while Bryn and Cathy calmed Samuel. He took out his pipe and lit the tobacco with a match. He took a few somber puffs and blew out the smoke.

"I'm impressed," Adam said to me. "Alpha Hunter was very good with him, and you were patient. The males of this pack treated him poorly, even when he was just seven. They asked him so many questions that he started to scream and cry. When they didn't stop forcing him to talk, he hit himself to get them to leave him alone."

It made me incredibly sad to hear that Samuel ending up in tears was the best-case scenario, and we wouldn't be able to get more information out of him because whatever he'd seen had affected him so terribly. I looked down at the pictures and tried to arrange them into a neat stack.

"I'm sorry they put him through that. It couldn't have been easy for him, or you and Cathy," I said.

"It was torture. I mean, we tried to do right by our son. We let him go out and play with his friends, disciplined him when he was naughty, and gave him all the attention he could want. But even when you do everything as best you can, things still happen that are totally out of your control." Adam clenched his hands at his sides. "You never think anything bad will happen to your child, but when it does, all you can do is hope they come back to you in one piece."

My heart broke for this small family and all they'd suffered, and it broke for the families who'd lost children and who would probably never know how or why they'd died.

"What do you think happened, Adam?" I asked.

He puffed from the pipe again before answering. "Well, when the investigation happened, and they couldn't get much out of my son, the official story was that the boys were scared by an animal or something and were separated. I think that's bull. Animals fascinated Samuel, and we taught him how to identify the ones he would likely see. To this day, he can look through a picture book and recognize each creature without being afraid.

"No...I think we had a child killer in our pack. I think someone waited until those poor boys were in the woods by themselves, then grabbed them and killed them. Fates know what he did with their bodies. Honestly, I don't even like to think about it."

"I don't blame you." That was what the council had said, too—that a killer had been hanging around the Kings' pack. "Why do you think the kidnappings stopped?"

"I'm hoping it's because someone killed the bastard," he said. "But in my heart, I know it's never that simple. In my head, the monster got what he needed from our pack, and either went to another pack to do the same thing or stuck around. He could still be in this pack somewhere, biding his time, waiting to do it again. Or at least, that's what my paranoia tells me. I don't know, but no one in this damn pack seems to care."

"I care," I said. "And so does Bryn. We want to figure out what happened and bring justice to the families who suffered."

"I can see that you're being honest. Like I said, you two were good with my son. When he walked up to Alpha Hunter with the sketch, I was worried you would push him or hurt him, but you didn't even touch him. I appreciate that." The expression he wore wasn't a smile or a frown, but it was open and friendly. "I know you're going to compete in the alpha challenge with the others. For what it's worth, I hope you win. This pack could use a leader who doesn't jump to a violent solution at every turn."

I winced inwardly, remembering the hurt and anger radiating from Bryn during our argument. I needed to talk to her as soon as possible. "I appreciate that, Adam."

He nodded. There were another few moments of silence, and then he said, "You know, Night, I heard a rumor in the pack that our current alpha is pregnant."

Shock coursed through me, causing me to straighten. "Who's saying that?"

"I don't know who started it, but not everyone believes it. It doesn't matter one way or another to me, but if it is true...congratulations. There's no greater gift than a child. It's hard with Samuel sometimes, but I thank the Fates every day that he is still with me because I know not every father is lucky enough to say that. It's important to always put your kids first and cherish every moment you have with them because they go so fast."

I wasn't sure what to say to that, whether I ought to acknowledge it as the truth or play it off. It bothered me that there were rumors about Bryn spreading around the pack, but I knew Adam didn't mean any harm by it. And I appreciated what he had to say. So, instead of answering, I just stayed in the moment with him and mulled over his words.

Chapter 18 - Bryn

While Cathy rocked Samuel back and forth, I told him one of the stories I had read to Pax about a knight who protected his princess. I was surprised I still remembered the story after so many weeks, but what surprised me more were the emotions that hit me as I recited it.

I associated the story with children, the adorable ones who still had wonder behind their eyes. Now, I was telling the story to a boy whose childhood had been stolen from him. Whatever he'd experienced or seen, it had done incredible harm. He still hadn't healed. And how could he heal? I thought of Pax, who was around the age Samuel had been ten years ago. If he were to die or go missing, we would feel insurmountable loss.

And with a little one of my own on the way, the weight of Samuel's fear and sadness hit hard. The more I spoke, the more he calmed down. Eventually, his sobs and whimpers died down, and he lay still.

Cathy gently pulled the blanket from her son's head. "Ah," she whispered. "He's asleep."

"I'm glad. I'm sorry we pushed him to this state."

She shook her head. "It's okay. To be honest, he gets this way after he has a nightmare or hears a loud sound. It's nothing new; I just let my worries get the best of me. It's hard not to be overprotective when it comes to your pup."

I resisted the urge to rub my stomach as I thought about the baby.

"I wish I knew more about what happened to him," she said. "If we had answers, we might be able to help him through this. As things are, he never really gets better. He hasn't said more than a hundred words to me since it happened."

My heart ached for her. For him. "He has his art, at least."

"That's true. But if he were mentally healthy, he could do so much more. We could show his art to the pack and not keep him cooped up in here. He should be out with his friends and impressing girls with the portraits he does, not hidden in here."

She touched her son's forehead and gently pushed his hair behind his ear. He nuzzled against her. The bond between mother and son was obvious. Just being in its presence brought tears to my eyes. I felt like I was intruding on something as beautiful and precious as it was quiet and sorrowful.

"I don't know if Night and I will find answers to what happened to Samuel and those boys, but we will try."

She gave me a small smile. "I think I speak for all the parents of those boys when I say I appreciate your efforts. There's nothing in this world that matters as much as the safety of your children. Nothing at all." She looked down at her son and stroked his hair again. "When you see your mate, will you tell him I'm sorry I snapped at him like that?"

"I will. He won't hold it against you, I'm sure."

She nodded. I could tell she wanted to spend time with her child, so I got up to leave, closing the door softly behind me.

I met up with Night, who looked about as shaken as me. We were technically still fighting, but I took his hand.

"Let's go home," I said.

"Yeah," he said, squeezing my fingers.

We were both lost in thought as we made the trek back home. I wasn't sure what Night was thinking about, but my mind was on our pup. I couldn't imagine going through what the Granbys had suffered. It was just too painful—and I hadn't even given birth yet.

When we got to our cabin, I started to go upstairs, but Night's grip on my hand was firm. When I looked at him, his eyes were the soft green of fresh grass, and there was a sad tilt to the frown on his lips.

"Can we talk?" he asked.

"Yes."

We adjusted our course, going to the living room instead of upstairs. Night sat on the couch, and I brought lavender and peppermint tea.

He took his mug when I handed it to him, and I sat on the couch next to him, curling my legs up on the cushion. After a moment, Night slid his hands over my legs and moved them into his lap. He let his hand rest on my thigh.

I touched his chest, and he looked at me. "I'm not ready to talk about Samuel yet," I said.

"That makes two of us," he agreed. "But that means we need to talk about our argument."

I nodded. It was a relief to hear that Night wanted to talk things out. The task had seemed so daunting when I left my mom's cabin, but after what we'd just experienced, talking things out seemed easy.

"Alright, I'll get things started." I took a long sip of my tea and let out a sigh. "So, it's come to my attention that the two of us have pretty shitty communication skills."

There was a pause, and he let out a short chuckle. "That might be an understatement, love."

I laughed with him but sighed again. "I know I've got to be better about coming to you when I have an issue. And I think you need to be more open and honest with me about what's going on with the Wargs. I don't want you holding anything back from me, and in return, I'll do the same." I touched his cheek; it was slightly scruffy. He'd probably shave it soon, but I didn't mind the stubble. "I understand now that your hands were tied with the Troy situation, but we should have discussed it one on one. I want us to be partners in all things, and I want us to trust each other with the good *and* bad news."

"I want that, too." He nuzzled against my palm and kissed it, sending delightful tingles down my arm. "To be honest," he said into my hand, "part of the reason I've been so overprotective of you is that I feel like I keep failing you."

I frowned. "What do you mean?"

"I couldn't protect you, my mother, or Tavi from Troy. The days you were gone were the hardest of my life, and I don't think I could survive it if I let something like that happen again. I was too weak to kill Troy during the challenge ceremony, and I couldn't keep him from escaping custody." He looked at me, and my breath caught at the jewel-like shine in his eyes. "I can't even keep myself from putting more stress on your shoulders, Bryn."

"Oh, Night." I pulled him close to kiss him, needing that closeness, needing him to feel how deeply I loved him. "I have no idea how I would've felt or what I would've done if things were reversed. But none of that was your fault." I pulled back, framing his face with my hands. "We can't keep letting fear of the unknown stop us from living in the present, or we'll keep hurting each other."

He let out a tight breath. "You're right. I'm sorry I've put you through so much."

"I'm sorry, too. I know I haven't been the most receptive to bad news lately. And before you say anything," I rushed when I saw him open his mouth to protest, "I know I should be avoiding stressful things and taking it easy, but I still need to be a good partner to you. I can be there for you *and* take things easy."

He chuckled and moved his hand up my thigh to my waist to pull me onto his lap. Resting his chin on top of my head, he said, "My brave little mate. You keep reminding me why I love you."

I laughed and relaxed against his chest. "So, I guess we should talk about Samuel, huh?"

"Yeah." He sighed. "That was so…heavy. I'm glad you insisted on going together. I doubt I would've been as successful by myself."

"If you can call that 'successful.'" I sighed. "Cathy asked me to tell you she was sorry for snapping at you."

His breath fluttered against my cheek. "Did she really?"

"Mmhm."

"After the way she looked at me, I was sure she hated me because I'm alpha of the Wargs. I'm surprised she'd apologize to me when she didn't do anything wrong." He sipped his tea and set the mug on the table. "I'm still reeling from all of that."

I nodded. "I think I told you that I remembered how tense things were back then. I'd heard about Samuel, but with him holed up inside his home, I had no idea he was like that. You were right when you said the Kings are still dealing with what happened ten years ago. I get the feeling that the entire pack just forced themselves to move forward, but you can't leave something like that behind. We all remember. And Samuel, his parents, and the parents of those missing kids are living proof of that tragedy."

Night let out a shaky sigh. "Bryn, seeing that poor kid so broken did something to me. All I could think about was our baby and how awful it would be if they went missing and were never found, or had come back so traumatized, they could hardly leave their room. Samuel's parents have real strength, but I don't know what I'd do if I experienced that."

I felt something wet on my head, and I looked up, surprised to see Night with tears in his eyes. With the tip of my finger, I gently brushed away the tear that had escaped.

"I know what you mean," I said. "All that time, I kept thinking how dangerous the world we're bringing our baby into can be." I kissed him gently. "But Night, my love, what happened to the Granbys couldn't happen to us. We can be smarter parents who never let their baby wander around unsupervised. And even if something did try to attack our baby, you are more than strong enough to protect them." I kissed him again, gentler this time. "And guess what? Together, you and I are even stronger than you on your own. After the baby is born, I want you to train me so I can be a warrior like you."

His eyes widened. "Bryn, are you sure? It'll be really hard work."

"I know, but when it comes to you, our baby, our family, and our packs, I know I can do anything. This way, I'll be strong enough to protect them."

"Bryn," he sighed, kissing me slow and sweet. "You're amazing."

I deepened the kiss, adjusting myself in his lap so I was straddling him. He moaned gently against my mouth, his grip tightening on my waist. I pushed his shirt over his head, and my hands took their time exploring every inch of his chest and back. His muscles were hard beneath my palms, his skin smooth but for the faint ridges of his scars.

"Bryn," he sighed again, sliding his hands under my shirt to caress my back.

I let him take off my shirt, then reached down to his pants, slipping my hand under the waistband. He let out a purring growl as I stroked his growing erection. I loved his girth in my hand, the warmth of it. I wanted it inside me, but I also wanted to taste him. I slid down to my knees in front of him as he watched me with eyes that had turned almost black with desire.

I ran my tongue up from the base of his cock to the tip, then back down. He held his lower lip between teeth that had grown slightly sharp since I started touching him. He twisted his fingers gently through my hair. Trailing my tongue back up, I carefully took him into my mouth, circling the head of his cock with the tip of my tongue over and over again.

His breathing was heavy as his head tipped back. His hand twitched in my hair every so often as I bobbed up and down his length. I tasted the tang of his precum and picked up the pace. Cupping his balls gently in my palm, I massaged them between my fingers. The muscles in his thighs tensed and relaxed, tensed and relaxed with my motions. His hand tightened briefly in my hair.

"Bryn, I don't know…" He stopped as pleasure shivered between his shoulders and down his back. "I don't know if I can hold back."

I looked up at him and smiled as best I could around his girth. My fondling hand and sucking mouth increased in speed, and he growled out a moan. His cock twitched against my tongue, and I kept up my speed.

Night gripped my hair, holding me still while he came. He gushed into my mouth—hot, salty, and slightly sweet. Cum flooded my mouth, so much that I couldn't quite swallow all of it. When I came up for breath, a bit trickled down my mouth.

"Fuck, Bryn," he said, looking down at me. "Fuck."

I grinned at him, my tongue snaking out to catch what escaped. "Are you sure you're up to that?"

He chuckled breathlessly. "Shall we find out?" He pulled me to my feet and into his lap again, but this time, my back was to his chest, and I was facing the decorative mirror on the opposite wall. Kissing my temple, he stroked his hand down my chest, fondling my breasts along the way. Transfixed, I watched his hand trailing down my stomach in the mirror.

He reached my panties, and his fingers elongated into claws to rip the fabric off me. He tossed the scraps casually to the side. I could see my wetness in my reflection, my pussy glistening even in the living room's low lighting. I pulled my lower lip between my teeth as the pads of his fingers—human again, no longer claws—circled my clit. He applied gentle pressure as he fingered me. Sighing, I shivered against him.

"Beautiful," he whispered, kissing my temple again and dragging his kisses down my neck. His fingers dipped inside me.

"Night," I gasped.

He nibbled at my throat while his other hand returned to my left breast, bouncing it a bit even as he caressed and massaged it. All the while, he continued to love me with those devious fingers.

I spread wider for him as he upped his pace, twitching and trembling against his chest. I watched him leave red and purple hickeys along my neck. I was already so turned on from giving him head that it didn't take long for him to bring me to orgasm. I climaxed hard, my juices dripping between his fingers.

"Good girl," he whispered, kissing my shoulder.

He was hard again. I could feel his erection pressing against my lower back. I met his gaze in the mirror and gyrated slowly against him. His eyebrow raised as he grinned.

"What a hungry girl," he said, lifting me just enough to position me above his hardness. "Is this what you want?"

"Yes," I moaned. He lowered me until just his tip was inside me. My pussy throbbed hard, desperate to be filled.

He pushed me down lower, and we both let out long, shuddering breaths. I reached behind me to wrap my arms around his neck, holding myself steady while he worked me up and down his length. He was slick with my wetness, and I watched myself take in every inch of him. I'd been terrified that he wouldn't fit the first time we made love, and now I couldn't help but get aroused by how easily he slid in and out.

His lips were on my shoulder again, nibbling my skin. My breasts bounced and jiggled as he increased his speed. If I could have opened wider for him, I would have. My ass smacked soundly against his thighs, his fingers dimpling my thighs as he held tight.

"Night, I'm gonna…I'm gonna…" A loud moan burst from my chest, and I clenched around him again. He grunted, twitching inside me, his teeth pressing into my skin.

After, Night was the only one with the strength to move, so he pulled me into his arms and carried me to our bedroom. Once we were under the covers, I nestled close to him and shut my eyes, still in the aftershock of all that pleasure. I felt safe in his arms and in our bed. What shadows lurked in the outside world seemed so far away.

Chapter 19 - Night

Bryn and I woke, still tangled in each other's arms. I made a sound halfway between a growl and a purr and pulled her even closer so I could bury my nose in her neck. I loved the sound of her giggle, but I loved feeling it bubble through her chest even more.

"I'm glad you're in bed with me and not making out with the toilet," I joked.

She scoffed and pinched my forearm. "Watch it, you."

I chuckled.

"I'm usually fine until I get up. That's when the nausea hits."

"Is there anything I can do to make it easier on you? I can make you tea all day, but if I could be doing more, I want to know."

A breath shuddered out of her. "I think I just have to wait it out. Hopefully, the morning sickness and constant energy drain will ease up soon, and I'll feel better again."

My chest tightened at the thought of her just smiling through the pain. She deserved to be as comfortable as possible. "If you'd like some advice from someone who's gone through this, you could talk to my mom. Apparently, she was sick through most of her pregnancy with me."

"Oh, I didn't know that. I think I will talk to her to see what she did to get through it." She turned in my arms so we were chest to chest, wrapping her arms around my neck. "By the way, I wanted to talk about our future living situation."

"Oh, yeah? Have you made a decision?"

"Yeah. I really don't mind living here with you, despite everything. I think you and I have made a lot of good memories to replace those old horrible ones. But I can't deny that it's tempting to have a fresh start for our family in a place that has no baggage and only the memories we'll make together."

"I get that," I replied. We were in the room where she had been kidnapped, tied up, and threatened with rape by a monster. I completely understood why she wanted a fresh start for our family. "If you want a new place, I'll find us the perfect spot to build a home or renovate one that already exists. You say the word, baby, and I'll find a spot today."

Her eyes softened, confirming that was what she truly wanted. Still, my sweet girl wanted to double-check with me.

"You're absolutely sure you're okay with not living in the alpha cabin?"

"I am positive. It's so much more important that you can come home and feel safe—physically, mentally, and emotionally." I kissed her neck and felt her pulse jump. "I have a question."

"What's that?"

"Should we live on King territory or Warg?"

"I don't know. Maybe we should have a house on both territories."

"I think that's a good idea. We'll figure out how to divide our time equally between the two."

"I don't mind staying in your cabin on Warg territory."

"My cabin could use a good sprucing up. I didn't bother to do that when it was just me, but for you and our pup, I'll put in the work." I kissed her neck again, more slowly this time. Bryn let out a small moan, and lust coiled in my stomach. "What's on your schedule today?" I asked lazily.

"I want to visit the gardens today. More Wargs will be entering our territory after you become alpha, and I want to make sure we're not short on our food stocks."

"Sounds good to me. Just make sure you don't work too hard."

"I won't, Night, I promise. The most I'll do is some gardening, but I'll have Mom there to keep an eye on me."

"Alright, I'll trust you," I said, moving so I could kiss her lips. She opened her mouth, deepening the kiss. Things grew hot and heavy until she pulled back with a gasp.

"Oh! I can't believe I almost forgot."

"Forget what?" I asked, a little startled.

She rolled out of my arms to open the drawer of her nightstand. When she turned around again, she held out a paper bag.

"I got you something."

"You did?"

"Yeah. I bought it at a stall in the market."

I watched her open the bag and remove a braided leather bracelet. It was the color of freshly roasted coffee before milk or cream was added, and there was a brushed red copper clasp to keep it closed.

"But I didn't get you anything." I looked from the bracelet to her, my eyebrows pinching together. "It's not even my birthday."

She laughed and sat up slowly, not wanting to trigger her nausea. "I wanted to show my appreciation for you and everything you've done for me. I bought something for Tavi, too, but I wanted to give yours to you last night. Hold out your wrist."

I watched her open the clasp and wrap the bracelet around my wrist. "There," she said, sliding the clasp shut with a slight *click.* "I was a little worried it wouldn't fit, but it seems I got the right size after all."

I never wore jewelry because it wasn't my thing, but I had to admit that the bracelet suited me. It wasn't bulky or flashy, and it sat comfortably on my wrist. It was exactly my style, and Bryn had picked it out for me.

My wolf yipped with pleasure at the gift, and a grin spread across my face. This was a precious gift because the woman I loved most had gotten it for me. I kissed her again, clutching her to my chest.

"I guess that means you like it?" she joked.

"Of course I do." I kissed her again. "I don't think I'll ever take it off. Thank you, Bryn."

A bit later, she and I got dressed and ready for the day. Bryn did get sick, but she assured me that she could follow through on her plan for the day.

I scoped out a few cabins and locations for cabins that had promise. Some were closer to the commons for convenience's sake, one or two that were settled in the forest and closer to Warg territory, and some that were closer to Glenda's cabin. I'd need to ask Bryn what she thought about them.

Looking at the locations and imagining what a future with Bryn and our pup would be like was a nice break from staring at financial accounts, stressing out about Troy's whereabouts, and dwelling on the state of Samuel and his family. I couldn't wait to get in bed with Bryn and talk about our future. When the two of us returned to Warg territory, we could have similar conversations about what needed to be done for the cabin.

I was standing near the commons again, only a few paces away from the Kings' bank. I still had things I wanted to do before the sun went down—namely, checking in with Dom and training for the alpha challenge—but for now, I wanted to go on a run. It was the perfect way to cap off the last couple of hours.

I walked between the trees and started to jog. Not so long ago, I had been laser-focused on taking over the Kings' pack through whatever means necessary. Now I was thinking about a future with my mate and planning the rest of our lives. When I thought about the conversation we'd had the night before, I felt relieved that we'd agreed on how we wanted to handle disagreements moving forward. It felt like we'd taken a step forward, and like I knew her better now.

After a couple of miles, I headed back to the compound. My heart was pumping, I felt exhilarated, and my mind was far away from the issues that usually plagued my mind. There were cabins in sight, and I was just a few yards away from the compound when I heard the sharp gasp of someone in deep pain.

It brought me up short. My wolf and I went on high alert, listening for another noise.

Moments later, I heard the sounds of a struggle. I focused on the noises and sprinted toward them. I cleared the trees in my way and found a pile of three men: the one lying on the ground was a Warg, a younger recruit who was here shadowing a fighter. The two standing over him were Kings. It was an obvious ambush, and it sent my blood to a roiling boil.

I shoved the two Kings off the kid and stood in front of him. "What the fuck is this?" I demanded, glaring at the men.

They pushed themselves up to their feet. Their surprise quickly shifted to annoyance when they saw it was me who'd stopped their fun.

"We don't want Wargs on our land anymore!" one of them spat. Given their builds, they were fighters.

"That's the way you speak to an alpha? Are you stupid enough to think you could take me?"

"You're not *our* alpha," the other growled. He was already close to shifting—the glow of his irises revealed it. "Go back to your shitty territory and stay the fuck away from ours!"

I stepped forward but caught myself. These kids were idiots, and I figured situations like this were bound to happen when I took over their pack and merged them with the Wargs. I needed to seize this opportunity to set them right.

"I don't control this pack, but I am an alpha, and you will yield to me," I said in a low voice. I was tempted to call on my power as an alpha to make them submit to me, but that would only last as long as I held it. It wouldn't ensure their obedience forever.

They hesitated for a moment. Then, to my surprise, they started inching toward me. Their eyes were glowing now, and suddenly I was in battle mode. I needed to protect the Warg lying at my feet, which presented some complications for a fight—

"Hey!" a new voice sounded from my right. I glanced in that direction and blinked. Lance was leaning against the tree with his arms crossed over his chest. "Mace, Charley," he said. "Get out of here."

The wolves—Mace and Charley, I guess—stood straight and faced Lance like he was their alpha. "L-Lance," Mace stuttered, "we were only trying to—"

"I think I told you to leave." Lance's voice was icy, but he looked bored, like he was watching paint dry. "So go. Now."

Mace and Charley didn't argue. They inclined their heads in respect to Lance and shuffled off into the trees, heading back to the King compound.

Annoyance jabbed me in the ribs. Though I didn't want to admit it, Lance's stepping in was a bit of a blow to my pride. He had ended the fight before it had started, not me.

Instead of thinking too deeply about that, I turned my attention to the young Warg and crouched beside him. "Your name's Ricky, right?"

"Yes, Alpha Night," he said, wiping blood from the corner of his mouth.

"What happened, Ricky?"

"I was out taking a walk, but those Kings jumped me." His voice trembled as he spoke—not with fear, I was happy to see, but with anger. "I should have seen them coming, but they got the better of me, Alpha. I'm sorry."

I offered my hand, and he accepted it, allowing me to pull him to his feet. "You're here to learn, Ricky. It's okay that you're not an expert at fighting yet. Besides, those two didn't exactly leave without a scratch. You held your own."

Some of the anger and shame burning Ricky's cheeks faded as he nodded. "Th-thank you, Alpha."

"No thanks necessary. Just head to the infirmary and get yourself looked at."

"Right." He nodded once more at me before limping toward the infirmary.

I watched him go. I sent a message to Dom to either keep an eye on him on his way or have another Warg go with him.

I turned to Lance, who was now within a few paces of me. I hadn't even heard the kid move. *Dammit, he* is *good.*

I kept my thoughts from showing on my face, but the slight smirk on Lance's lips irked me. Cocky bastard.

"We haven't met," I said. "I'm Night Shepherd."

"I know who you are," he replied. "Just like you know who I am." He slipped his hands into the pockets of his sweatpants. "I watched your fight with Troy. It wasn't what I'd expect from an alpha like you."

Another twinge of annoyance went through me, even though I knew he was trying to get a rise out of me. I ought to be unbothered, but everything about this kid set me on edge, and I wasn't sure why. He just screamed "threat" to me.

"You ought to know that wasn't a fair fight," I replied. "I won't let another wolf have any advantage over me."

I meant it as a warning. Lance was overly confident, even when he stood face-to-face with me. I knew he would be a hard fight during the alpha challenge, even with my history of life-or-death fights under my belt. But I had complete confidence in my abilities, especially after my days of training.

He ignored my warning, his face hardening. "Let's cut the bullshit, Night. I see what you and your pack are trying to do here, schmoozing up to the Kings by helping rebuild homes, but it's not going to work."

"And what are we trying to do?"

"Don't be coy. This pack will never let a merger between the Wargs and Kings happen. The few who would benefit are outweighed by those who are loyal to the Redwolfs. It won't be as easy as you seem to think it is."

Now I was the one smirking. "Well then, I have nothing to worry about. I've got Redwolf blood in me. But what about you? What blood flows through your veins?"

"Red." His eyes dropped briefly to my bracelet, and he frowned. "You and your mate should go as far away from here as possible before it's too late and you're killed during the alpha challenge."

My lips pulled away from my teeth as my wolf growled. I didn't like him mentioning Bryn. "You seem to forget that my mate is *your* alpha, Lance. You shouldn't make that mistake again. And I won't lose the challenge. Not that that's any of your business."

"It *is* my business."

"Why?" I stared hard at him, trying to spot any hint of deception. "Because you're loyal to the Redwolfs? I know Troy brought you in when you were younger."

He scoffed. "My loyalties lie with my family and no one else."

"Who's your family?"

A beat passed, and then another. Finally, that cocky expression was back on his face. "I've got things to do, Night. I'm sure you do as well. I'm sure we'll get another chance to talk later." He winked before walking back to the compound.

With him gone, the tension began to seep out of my muscles. I hated that I hadn't gotten more information about him, but the fact that we'd had a conversation was a start. What he had said only made me dislike and distrust him more. Part of me was really looking forward to seeing that confidence disappear during the alpha challenge.

I stood there a bit longer, letting the worst of my frustration drain out of me before I headed back onto the compound. I felt a mental nudge from Dom, indicating he was headed my way.

"Hey," he said as he reached me. "I made sure that Ricky got to the infirmary okay. He said he got jumped?"

I nodded. "I found two Kings beating him up. We need to keep a better eye on the newer recruits."

"Agreed. I'll make sure they step up their training."

"Appreciate that." I let out a sigh. "Lance was there."

Dom's eyebrows rose. "Was he one of the wolves beating on Ricky?"

I shook my head and explained. "I wasn't able to find out anything more about him or where his loyalties lie," I said. "It was overall a very frustrating conversation."

"That checks out," he replied. "Like I told you before, no one knows much about him. That said, a lot of wolves fear and respect him, but I haven't heard any reasons why that is."

"What do you mean?"

"He hasn't been involved in any fights or kills. The only thing he's known for is being one of Troy's men, but that alone shouldn't make people fear him so much."

I grunted in annoyance. "Let's make sure we've got eyes on him as often as possible. But tell the men to be discreet."

"Of course." Dom nodded. "So, how's Bryn? Did you two make up?"

"We did, and we're in a much better place. I spent the morning looking at a new home for us."

"You're okay with not living in the alpha cabin?"

"Absolutely. It's better if Bryn can start fresh in a new cabin. There are a few spots that seem promising, but I'll have to see what she thinks."

"That's good news. It would be cool if you and Bryn could find a place between here and Warg territory.

After you win the challenge and redraw territory lines, it'll be closer to the middle."

"That'd be nice for sure. We'll see, huh?"

"True. Let me know if I can help you at all, Night."

I snickered. "What, you don't have enough work?"

"I'm your beta, Night. You know I can handle anything." He gave me a cocky grin. Dom would follow any order I gave him, even at the cost of his life, but I'd never let that happen.

"Sure, sure," I said. "I think I'm going to find Bryn." The fact that Lance had brought her up made me want to see her again. My need to make sure she was safe overpowered anything else.

Chapter 20 - Bryn

Tavi accompanied me to the garden. I'd reached out to her telepathically, asking if she'd like a change of pace, and she agreed.

We entered the gardens, the scent on the air shifting from clear and pine-scented to the comforting aromas of moist soil and fresh vegetation. I'd heard that the crops had withered during the short span of Troy's reign, and as familiar as the garden looked, I saw that things were different.

In my memory, I saw lush fields filled with rich life, with bees and butterflies flitting from flower to flower. The growing plants looked healthy, but the fields weren't as plentiful. Harvesting of the vegetables would account for some but not all of that loss. It hurt my heart to see how Troy's evil had hurt the health of the land.

"Wow," Tavi said. "This is pretty amazing."

I blinked. I'd been so focused on the fields that I'd forgotten I wasn't alone. We walked along the perimeter of the garden. Mom and I had been among the only ones who worked the fields, but it seemed that Troy had sent a few more to help her while I was in Warg territory.

"What is?"

"Well, I knew the Kings had to have a huge garden to accommodate their size. But wow, you guys have, what, ten acres on us?"

I laughed. "That's probably true, but many crops suffered because of Troy. I wish you could have seen it in its prime."

"Don't worry," she said with a slight smile. "I'm sure things will get better in the wake of your and Night's leadership."

I looked at Tavi, my eyes wide. "Thank you so much, Tavi. It means a lot that you said that."

"Well, remember, you and Night are building a lot of goodwill, right? You're the descendant of the pack mother, and you and Night will have a baby who bridges the gap between Wargs and Kings. You're kind of a big deal, you know?"

I'd never thought about it that way, but Tavi's words sounded reasonable. "When you put it that way, you kind of make my baby sound like a prince or princess," I giggled. "Or at least the heir to a huge fortune."

She laughed with me. "I should've known you'd find a way to link what I said to the novels you read. But that's not too far off, right? I think I'm right."

"No, no, I think you're right. It just surprised me." I ran a hand over my stomach even though I wasn't showing yet. I was still a little sad I wouldn't be able to give my baby siblings, but I was happy to know I was continuing both Night's legacy and the pack mother's line. "Hey, Tavi?"

"Mmhm?"

"Did you know anything about the pack mother who stayed with the Wargs? I know you would've been a baby, but…"

She shook her head. "Not really. I'm sorry."

"Don't be. It just occurred to me that I never asked you."

"Yeah, the only thing I've been told was that it wasn't known that we had the pack mother until after she'd been killed. I think only a few Wargs knew she was living among us. And somehow, the Kings who killed her knew about her."

I was taken aback by that. "Really? I had no idea that it was a secret. Violet and Night never said that."

"I don't know why Violet never mentioned that, but I think Night never did because of how things deteriorated between us and the Kings. It's less important that her identity was kept a secret from most of us than the fact that the Kings killed the last pack mother, you know?"

"Oh. I guess that makes some sense." I mulled it over. "You're a huge comfort to have around."

"I'm glad you think so. I like being around you, too." We shared smiles.

We let a few moments of silence pass between us, and I was surprised when Tavi was the first to break it.

"Can I ask you a weird question?" she asked.

"Of course."

"Your term as alpha will be up in a few weeks. When you look back on being alpha, what will you think about it?"

I laughed because I wasn't expecting her to ask something like that. "Honestly? I don't even know how to answer that."

"My bad. That was a dumb quest—"

"No, no, that's not what I meant, Tavi. I'm just not sure how to put my emotions into words." I thought about it a bit more, and Tavi gave me that space as we walked.

Den mother was a position that neither the Kings nor the Wargs had. It was meant to be a more nurturing role, someone who oversaw gardening and kept track of births—things like that—but the Redwolfs had never appointed anyone for the position; the Wargs had been in survival mode for so long, they never took the time to fill the role. My future responsibilities were a mystery to me, but if I continued proving to the Kings that I was strong, I would have some influence and still be able to do some good.

"There were a lot of things that I wanted to do that I probably won't get to do," I said. "I would love to have a pack-wide meeting, but between my sickness and the mountains of paperwork we have to go through, there hasn't been a good time for one. I would love to spend more time with my pack individually—mostly to get to know them, but also to show them how wrong they were about me being weak. The most I've accomplished has been reading paperwork, signing documents, and getting the rebuilding underway. I wish I had more time to do more."

Tavi nodded.

"How do you think I did as alpha?" I asked.

"Well, when you consider what you had to work with—a pack where almost every wolf was against you and only a month to get anything done—I think you did well. I mean, I think what you got done was a net positive for the Kings, whether anyone wants to acknowledge it or not."

I smiled. "Thanks, Tavi. What about you? How will you look back on being a beta?"

She chuckled. "Well, it's been an interesting experience, to say the least. I never thought I could do this, even before all that stuff with Troy. My goal was just to stay by your side and be there when you needed me. I think I can say I more or less keep you out of trouble, huh?"

I laughed. "You know, you're right. As far as I'm concerned, you pass with flying colors, Tavi. And I'm glad you won't be obligated to read through all those boring documents once we're through. Unless you want to."

It occurred to me that without her job, Tavi might revert to the way she was just after we were rescued from Troy and his goons.

I studied her as she stared out over the fields. Would she retreat again? Pull so far into herself that none of us could get her to come back out? The thought terrified me, and for a few seconds, I wasn't sure how to ask her about it. I didn't want to pressure her, and I didn't want to diminish her good mood by asking about the past. Was it selfish of me not to want to lose my best friend again? Could I ask her to check in with us once in a while, or would that be going too far?

While my thoughts spiraled, Tavi laughed a little to herself. "Bryn, I have another question."

"Y-yeah?" I asked, trying to pack away those feelings and fears. "Ask me anything."

"Even after Night becomes alpha and you become den mother, could I still be by your side?"

I paused. That had been the last thing I'd thought Tavi would say. "What do you mean?"

"Well, I don't know what the future holds. But I know that being your beta allowed me to make some sense of life. I feel like I have a purpose now. That's not something I'm eager to leave behind, you know?" She took a few deep breaths and went on. "I don't know if there's an official term for it, but could I be your…wingwoman? Or assistant den mother? I'm probably not making any sense. I just want to keep protecting you and the baby to the best of my ability even when I'm no longer officially a beta." She looked at me, dark eyes shining. "Would that be okay?"

Tears once again pricked at the back of my eyes, and one slipped free before I could catch it. I sniffled, chuckling as I wiped my face on my shoulder. I'd always been emotional, but since becoming pregnant, it was even more difficult for me to keep it together. But I couldn't blame myself for getting misty-eyed now. My term wasn't over yet, but my best friend was asking to stay by my side long-term, and I didn't have to worry about her pulling away from us again. What a relief. What an honor.

"Tavi, I would be delighted if you stayed at my right hand. Whatever my duties as den mother will end up being, I don't think this pack will make our work easy for us. I'll need all the help I can get, and I can't imagine a better person to share that burden with."

Tavi grinned at me, and it was a genuine grin, not an echo of the old Tavi; she was fully herself in that smile. "Well, then I look forward to working with you." She held her hand out.

I nodded as I clasped it. "Likewise." We shook on it, and I pulled her in for a hug. I held her as tightly as she'd let me.

Tavi and I finished our inventory of fresh vegetables, also noting the stocks of food in the underground cellar. Despite Troy's ruthless leadership style, we would have more than enough food to last us through the rest of the year. Thankfully, Gregor had ensured the Kings were good about saving and preserving foods. That was one of the few compliments I could give to that man.

After, I went back to the alpha cabin, and Tavi walked me there. That worked out well for me because I still needed to give her the red bracelet I'd gotten at the market. I went up the stairs, grabbed the bracelet from my nightstand drawer, and hurried back down.

"What are you up to?" Tavi asked, eyeing me with faux suspicion.

I grinned. "Hold out your wrist and close your eyes."

She gave me another suspicious look, but she did as I asked. I carefully looped the bracelet around her arm so that it didn't touch her skin. I held it there until I said, "Okay, open them," and then let it fall against her skin.

She opened her eyes, gasping when her gaze landed on the bracelet. "Oh!" Then, a bit more quietly, "Oh, Bryn, you didn't."

"I did!" I beamed at her. "This is my way of thanking you for everything you've done for me, Tavi. You're a great beta, a wonderful person, and my best, best friend."

Tears welled in her eyes. "Bryn, I don't think I can…" She hesitated, then shook her head and sniffled. "Thank you so much. If I'd known you were getting me a gift, I would've gotten you something."

"I don't want anything in return," I assured her. "This was something small I wanted to do for you."

"This is *huge* to me." She wrapped her arms around me, surprising me; she rarely initiated hugs these days. "Thank you, thank you, thank you."

I embraced her as hard as I could. "You're welcome, Tavi. I hope this proves that I'm not going anywhere, and neither are you. You're my sister now and forever."

She chuckled. "Of course." And then she added telepathically, *"We're sisters for life."*

I could have held onto her for hours, but she pulled away, and we said our goodbyes. I went to the kitchen to make tea and toast, and then curled up on the couch because I didn't feel like walking upstairs again. After finishing my tea and snack, I napped for a couple of hours.

A knock on the door woke me. I yawned, stretching my arms over my head before getting up.

It was Violet. When I opened the door, she gave me a warm hug. "Hello, sweetheart," she said. "How are you?"

"Hi, Violet," I hugged her back. "I'm doing okay today, though I'm a little tired."

"Ah, I remember those days." She gave an empathetic smile. "Is my son around?"

"Not right now, but he'll probably be home soon. Did you need something from him?"

"Not really. I wanted to talk to you." I led her into the living room and sat on the couch, patting the spot beside me. "Night told me you wanted to know more about your biological parents," Violet said when she sat down.

I nodded.

"Do you think knowing about them will make you a better mother?"

"Honestly, I'm not sure. But it'll make me feel more secure in my own skin. On top of that, I'd like to be able to tell my kids that their grandparents were good people and not be lying. If we could find out whether my mother also had reproductive issues, that would be another huge help."

Violet nodded. "I understand where you're coming from. It's only natural that you'd want to know."

"Did you find something about my parents?" I asked, my heartbeat speeding up.

"Sort of. But let me explain a bit more." She cleared her throat. "The pack mother came to the Wargs decades ago when she had nowhere else to go. A few packs were after her because of the power she possessed, and the Kings were the largest and most powerful of the packs. We accepted her, and she lived peacefully with us."

"I spoke to Tavi, and she said that most Wargs had no idea she was a pack mother."

"That's true. I think only the elders knew her true identity."

"You've never mentioned this before. Is it because it wasn't the right time for you to tell me about it or something?"

She chuckled. "If the spirits were directing me, I wasn't aware of it, but I wouldn't have kept it from you intentionally. After the pack mother was killed, *every* wolf felt the ripple of it. I suppose the fact that we didn't know who she was at first didn't seem like a necessary part of the story."

"Oh, I see." I pulled my legs onto the couch. "What did she look like?"

"I wish I could recall her features with perfect clarity, but most of the details of her face have faded with time." She closed her eyes as she cast her mind back. "I remember she had hair as brown as yours, but her eyes were brown, too, not the pretty shade of blue that yours are. Of course, she was beautiful, with a bright, bright smile." She opened her eyes again and smiled. "Like yours."

It warmed me to hear that the pack mother and I shared a resemblance, but I wished there was more substance to the description, more certainty. "Is there a way for us to learn anything more about her?"

"There might be a way. But only you can do it."

I leaned forward, eager. "Yes?"

"The Warg elders have found a ritual you could do. It would allow you to see through your mother's eyes, and it could reveal a birthmark, her reflection, or reveal who your father was."

"A ritual…" I chewed my lip nervously. "Would it be safe for the baby?"

"Yes. It doesn't involve you doing anything or drinking anything that would put you or your baby in a compromising position, but I can't guarantee that you won't see anything unpleasant." She touched my leg. "It's your choice if you want to do this, of course."

I wanted to agree to do it right away, but I hesitated. As desperate as I was to discover more about my birth mother, I knew if I saw things through her eyes, I might see something traumatic. But if it was the only way for me to learn more about her, I didn't have much of a choice. Dr. Stan had warned me against doing anything stressful, but if

I could survive Troy, I could survive anything. The more I thought about it, the surer I felt about doing it.

After some deep thinking, I nodded. "When can we do it?"

"Tonight is a full moon, which will help the ritual."

"Okay. Where will the ritual happen?"

"The elders' garden."

My eyebrows shot up toward my hairline. "The Kings' elders are involved in this, too?"

She nodded. "This is a matter of spiritual significance, so they'll want to be present."

"Got it."

Violet grinned at me and stood. "Wonderful. I'll make some soup. It'll give you strength for the ritual and be easy on your stomach."

"That sounds lovely. I've only had tea and a few pieces of toast today." I followed Violet into the kitchen and sat at the table. "What's in it?"

"Well, the ingredients vary depending on what you've got in your kitchen—which is the best part about the recipe." She winked at me as she rummaged through the pantry. "It always has a tomato-based broth, beans, about a spoonful of peanut butter, and a bit of a spicy kick to it."

"Night told me you didn't have an easy time when you were pregnant with him," I said. "Was this soup something you ate a lot back then?"

"*Oh,* yes. That boy was an even bigger pain back then, and he wasn't even born yet." She chuckled to herself. "Those were some of the hardest months of my life, and this soup was pretty much the only thing I ate besides bananas, peanut butter, and pickles."

"I see." I made mental notes as she cooked the soup. When it was bubbling on the stove, she had me taste it. I found the broth rich and filling, with the peanut butter adding an interesting complexity to the flavor.

She fixed us each a bowl, and we ate at the table. The cabin felt warm and happy and full of potential. While Violet entertained me with stories of Night's childhood, I thought again about the ritual and my baby. I was so close to learning more about my birth parents, and I couldn't wait.

Chapter 21 - Night

I caught the savory scent of dinner even before stepping into the cabin. As delicious as it smelled, it worried me that Bryn cooked dinner when it was usually my responsibility. I called her name as I stepped inside the cabin.

"In the kitchen," she said. "Violet's here with me."

Oh. Well, that answered that question—Mom wouldn't have let Bryn cook on her watch. I walked into the kitchen and kissed Bryn on the forehead before kissing my mother on the cheek.

"How are you two doing?" I asked.

"Good," Mom said. "Just bonding over girl things."

I took that to mean that they were talking about pregnancy. I was glad Bryn had listened to my advice.

I went to the stove and ladled some soup into a bowl. Now that I was closer to the pot, I recognized the scent. I should've known Mom had been the one to make dinner.

"How are you?" Bryn asked as I grabbed a beer from the fridge. "And how's the pack?"

I joined them at the table, sitting next to Bryn. I told her about the cabins I'd seen that seemed like promising new homes for us. I hesitated to talk about the fight I'd broken up, and my conversation with Lance, but it was best not to keep anything from her.

"Huh," Bryn said after I recounted everything. "I'm glad you were there in time for Ricky, but…Lance is kind of weird, isn't he?"

I raised my eyebrow. "You know him?"

"Not really. He's been a mystery since he joined the pack. We never talked to each other. Well…actually, the first time we spoke was at the market when I bought your bracelet." She paused. "He bartered down the price."

I frowned at her, alarm shuddering through my veins. "What? Why didn't you tell me?"

She set her hand gently on my arm. "I'm sorry. I wasn't trying to keep it from you. It just…didn't seem important, I guess? He didn't threaten me or anything. It was just a weird conversation."

I knew the moment I met her bright aquamarine eyes that she was being genuine. I could believe she hadn't intended to keep it from me, but after our talk about being honest, I felt a little hurt. I forced myself to loosen my death grip on my spoon.

"Bryn, we promised to be open with each other about this stuff."

She winced and lowered her head. "You're right. I dropped the ball on this, Night. I really am sorry. I'll try not to keep you in the dark about anything like that again."

"I know. It's okay." I touched her wrist. "So, what did you and Lance talk about?"

"Not much. He and the vendor went back and forth about the price. For both bracelets, I was told it would cost forty-five dollars, but he dropped it to thirty because Lance said he'd seen the vendor's daughter sell them to her friends for fifteen each."

That told me Lance was very perceptive. It also told me he was familiar with everybody in the pack. Funny how he seemed to know so much about everyone, but no one knew anything about him.

"Did he say why he helped you?"

"He said he was just having fun."

I scratched my chin. There wasn't anything inherently wrong with the situation Bryn was describing, but she clearly wasn't sure what to think about it. I wanted to go out there, find the kid, and settle things right now, but that was obviously a bad idea.

"Did he rub you the wrong way?" I asked.

"I mean, I was cautious, and he didn't seem dangerous. But you know, now that I'm thinking about it, he came off as kind of…awkward?"

I scoffed at the thought that the arrogant guy I'd spoken to earlier would seem awkward, but I believed her. I wondered if he was hiding his true personality from her, but I couldn't come up with a reason why. How would he benefit from throwing Bryn off?

"Well, I see you two have a lot to talk about," Mom said, standing. "I'll go now. Bryn, I'll get things ready for tonight, alright? Meet me when the moon is at its zenith."

"Okay, Violet. See you later."

"Night, walk me out," my mother said.

"Oh. Sure." I walked her to the foyer. When we reached the door, she looked up at me.

"Listen, Night…" She looked at me. "Don't be too hard on Bryn. Believe me when I say that the little things can slip from a woman's mind when she's pregnant. It sounds to me like that thing with Lance was one of those things."

I wasn't sure what to say to that. My mother was sticking up for my mate, which I would normally appreciate…if it wasn't about something Bryn and I had talked about and promised to improve upon.

Instead of responding to that, I asked, "What did you mean when you said you were getting things ready for tonight?"

"I'm sure Bryn will tell you. It's not anything you didn't already know." She patted my cheek. "See you then, son."

I closed the door behind her and returned to Bryn. "What are you and Mom doing tonight?"

She smiled brightly at me. "There's a ritual that will help me learn more about my birth mother. We're doing it tonight!"

Her smile was so sweet that it took me a few seconds to comprehend what she'd just told me. "Wait, you're doing that tonight?"

She nodded. "Isn't that awesome?" But her smile slowly disappeared when she saw me frowning. "You don't seem happy."

"Mom told me about that ritual. She said she needed to make sure it would be safe."

"Well, I guess she made sure it was safe. She wouldn't have suggested it to me otherwise, would she?"

She was right, but frustration swarmed my chest. "How could you make that decision without talking to me about it first?"

When she scowled at me, I knew my question had come out the wrong way. "What are you talking about? I'm telling you right now. This was the earliest I could tell you. Anyway, Night, it's my body. I can do what I want with it."

"No, Bryn, it's *not* just your body while our pup is growing inside you. I think I should have a say if you're going to put our baby at risk." I glared at her. "I'm not saying you can't do the ritual at all; I just don't get why it has to be right now while you're pregnant. This is our only chance to have a baby. Why would you want to put that at risk?"

"I'm not putting anything at risk! I just told you that Violet made sure it was safe. She would never suggest something that would endanger me or our baby. You know that better than anyone else." She huffed, setting her spoon down with a clatter against the bowl. "I don't think I can put into words how deeply important this is to me, that it's something I *have to do.*"

I heaved out a long sigh. "I know it's something you need to do, but what if you see something that will affect you mentally? Or emotionally? There's no way to control what you'll see."

She closed her eyes, and when she opened them again, the hard look had softened. "Night, I know you're just looking out for me and the baby, but I've already considered the risks. I know I might see something upsetting, but you forget that I've already been through hell. Growing up was torture, and then I dealt with a week of horrors after Troy kidnapped me." She uncrossed her arms and took one of my hands between hers. "I know I can do this, Night. Please trust me."

I stared deeply into her eyes, finding her resolve and her desperation. She was so close to finding answers to questions she'd had all her life, and she couldn't wait anymore. If we were supposed to have an equal and honest relationship, I needed to trust that she knew what she was doing.

"Okay," I agreed, even though I wished I didn't have to. "But I'm going to be there with you, and if I see any sign that you might be in danger, I'm putting an end to it, okay?"

She nodded. "Absolutely. I *want* you there, Night. I wouldn't do something like this if you couldn't be there with me." Now that we'd both calmed down, she smiled without any anger or hesitation. "I wish I'd had more time to tell you, but I didn't make this decision without thinking it through. I *have* to know more about who I am."

"I know." I sighed. "Okay, I'm with you on this all the way."

"Thank you, baby." She brushed her lips over mine. "Thank you so much."

We had a few hours to kill before the full moon was in position, so I finished my dinner and went out to train. After I returned and freshened up, it was time to go.

The moon cast a silvery glow over everything as we headed to Mom's cabin. Though this night wasn't technically different from any other, something about tonight gave it some weight. It felt like something important would happen tonight.

Bryn must have felt the same way because she squeezed my hand as we neared the elders' cabin. I squeezed her back.

We walked up the steps to the cabin's front door, but Violet called for us to head around back. We rounded the cabin and found dozens of white candles lit around the small backyard. I wasn't surprised to see the three King elders standing with my mom, but I didn't expect to see Warg Elder Patrice Woods there as well. Bryn and I exchanged greetings with everyone, and I turned to Elder Woods.

"I'm surprised to see you here," I said.

She smiled kindly at me, her white hair glowing in the moonlight. "I'm sorry, Night. I didn't tell Violet I was coming, either. Considering the importance of this ritual, we decided one of us ought to be here, but I didn't get a chance to let you all know."

I would've liked more of a heads-up so I wouldn't be caught unawares, but her reasoning made sense. From what I understood, much of this had come together at the last minute. "It's just you?"

"Yes. The others and I decided I should be the one to make the trip. I arrived about fifteen minutes ago."

"I'm sorry to cut in," Elder Sage said, rubbing his thick silver beard, "but we only have so much moonlight. We should start before it gets any later." He inclined his head toward the center of the white candles, where a perfect circle had been drawn in white chalk. Other symbols drawn in chalk surrounded the circle. My wolf whined his unease at the sight of it.

"Elder Sage is right," Mom said. "Bryn, step into the circle when you're ready."

"Right." Bryn started walking toward it, but I pulled her back.

"Just a minute," I said. Elder Sage seemed displeased but didn't say anything as I pulled Bryn aside.

"Are you nervous?" she asked.

"Aren't you?" I pushed her hair behind her ear and bent so I could talk to her at eye level. "Are you absolutely sure you want to do this?"

She kissed the corner of my mouth, then looked up at me with love blazing in her eyes. "I haven't been this sure about something since the first time we made love," she whispered.

The kiss, followed by the memory of that first night, seared through me. Yet, it still seemed so unsafe. "Everything in me is screaming at me not to let you go in that circle," I told her.

"I know you want to protect us," she said, her hand on her belly. "But Night, you can't protect me from this. This will answer so many of my questions about who I am. I need to do this."

I let out a long breath. I wished with everything in me that I could do this ritual with Bryn, but I knew I couldn't. This was something only she could do, and I hated that she was going somewhere I couldn't follow.

I pulled her in for a tight hug and another kiss before slowly letting her go. "Alright, let's do this."

Bryn smiled at me one more time before turning from me and heading toward the circle, her fingers slipping free of mine. She stepped into the circle, and all the candles flickered at once. I stood behind Elder Forsythe, my hands buried deep in my pockets.

"So, how does this work?" Bryn asked.

"First, you must sit down," Elder Queene replied, pulling his long hair into a ponytail. "Then, we will perform a chant to activate the ritual."

"Once the ritual has begun, you'll be able to see through the eyes of your mother," Elder Woods said. "You'll be able to control which memories you see, but it can be difficult."

"Why?" Bryn asked.

"Because you'll have to remain calm through the process," Mom replied. She had moved a few candles closer to the circle. "You'll need to open your mind to memories that aren't your own so they'll flow naturally toward you."

"Gotcha." Bryn sat down in the circle, and the candlelight flickered again. "Now what?"

"Just close your eyes and take deep breaths in and out," Elder Woods said.

Bryn set her hands on her knees, closed her eyes, and breathed. When she looked relaxed, the elders and my mom formed a circle around her. They closed their eyes and raised them to the sky. At first, I could hardly hear them chanting anything, and then their voices grew louder until they were at a normal speaking volume.

They were speaking a language I'd never heard before. It was guttural and sounded as old as the earth itself. Their voices never went louder, but as they lowered their arms, the circle and symbols started to glow an ethereal white.

Bryn slumped forward. I cursed, heading toward her, but I stopped myself before entering the circle. I didn't know much about magic, but I knew it was a huge fuck-up to interrupt its flow. So, I clenched my hands at my sides, my eyes riveted on my mate, my wolf howling inside me.

When the circle was as bright as the moon, the elders' chanting lowered again to a barely audible whisper before they went completely silent. A second passed, and then another, and suddenly Bryn sat up straight. Her eyes shot open, but they weren't the silvery blue I knew. They had turned completely white.

Chapter 22 - Bryn

When my eyes opened, I knew I wasn't in my own body anymore. My soul had traveled to another plane of existence while my physical self had been left behind. I looked around and felt like I was peering through a membrane that cast the world in a faint gray hue.

Tall, densely packed coniferous trees surrounded me. I didn't know how I knew this, but I was certain this forest went on forever and ever. I didn't know what I expected when going into this ritual, but it wasn't an infinity of trees. My shoulders sagged with pressure at the vastness of it all. The trees weren't moving toward me, but it seemed they were somehow pressing closer, further illustrating how small I felt around them.

I had the sense that something was moving between the trees. When I turned toward whatever it was, I was thrown to the ground. Memories flashed across my vision, appearing and disappearing so quickly, I couldn't comprehend them. My head started to pound, and my vision swam. The dizziness took hold of me and made me spin. What little control I had started to slip from me until I remembered what Violet had told me: "... *you'll have to remain calm...open your mind...*"

I closed my eyes and gritted my teeth. I tried to focus. I had control over these memories; I just needed to quiet my mind so I could see one of them at a time. I breathed in through my nose and out through my mouth a few times, and when I opened my eyes again, I found myself standing on the Warg compound...but it wasn't the same as I remembered it.

This version of the compound was smaller, more like a little village. There were far fewer cabins, and they all looked rundown. I looked down and held my hands out. They weren't my hands; they were smaller and more delicate than mine, the skin a few shades darker. I turned them back and forth, but I saw no scars or tattoos or other markings that distinguished them. I lowered my hands, then spotted my protruding belly. My mom was pregnant. With me?

My hands rubbed my stomach in slow circles. I didn't have control over this body, so my mother was moving on her own. It was almost like she knew I was here somehow and was trying to show me as much as she could.

Suddenly, the sound of footsteps running toward me permeated my mind. A little boy, maybe six or seven years old, sprint my way. One hand stayed on my belly as the boy got close. I hadn't expected to hear my mother's voice, but

I felt her mouth open. I would have felt a shiver of anticipation had I been able to shiver.

"My, you're in a hurry, aren't you?" she said as a smile spread across my face. She had a slow, smooth voice, like a fresh honeycomb pulled from the hive. It was easy to listen to, which made me wonder if she had been a good singer.

The boy nodded. He couldn't immediately answer her because he was still panting from his sprint. His black hair was an adorable mess. She chuckled and tried to pat the unruly locks into a more presentable style, but it didn't work. If anything, she made the curls stick up more.

She gave a resigned sigh. "How are you doing today, Night?"

Shock arced through me. Night had known my mother? Why hadn't he ever said anything? *Maybe he didn't know. He looks so young. Maybe he doesn't remember her.* Amid the questions, I felt a pang of regret that Night had met my mother when I'd missed out on everything.

My mind swam as more questions filled my thoughts. As they inundated me, the image of the little Night began to grow fuzzy around the edges of my vision. I was losing focus, which meant I was losing my grip on the memory. I tried to push away my shock and open my mind again. Slowly, the memory cleared once more.

Night gave her a big toothy grin. My heart twisted at the unrestrained innocence on his cherubic face. I would never have imagined that my mate had ever smiled so openly. This version of Night had never known a day of real sadness in his young life, but that would change as he grew. Sadness overwhelmed me for a moment as I mourned for the little boy who had been forced to grow up too quickly.

"I rushed over here 'cause Dom and me are supposed to be practicing our tracking," Night said in one breath. "But I can't find him anywhere. Have you seen him?"

My mother laughed again. It was light and almost airy despite the lower, more mellow tone of her voice. "Silly boy. I don't think I should tell you even if I did know where he is."

"Why not?"

"Because if I tell where he is, you'll never get better at tracking."

Night paused and pouted. He looked up with large jade-green eyes, and my heart melted for him. There was no way I could have said no to that face, but my mother wasn't as easily swayed.

She patted his head. "Don't give me that face, young man. You know I'm right. And you know Dom will tease you for the rest of your life if you can't find him on your own."

He let out a dramatic sigh and put his hands in the pockets of his denim shorts. His little thumb poked through a hole in the denim.

"Okay," he said. "Anyways, how's your tummy?"

"My tummy? Oh, are you asking about the baby?"

He nodded.

"She's doing really well, thanks for asking." I felt a twinge at my back, and my mom straightened to ease the slight pressure. She rubbed her stomach in gentle, loving circles. "Did you know that this little girl is very special?"

"She is?" His eyebrows raised. "How come?"

"Well, for a lot of reasons. But one of them is because she'll be your mate one day."

He paused, and then he frowned, his nose scrunching. "Ew," he said. "Girls are boring and yucky."

She tilted her head back and let out a louder laugh. "You won't always think that way, sweet boy."

"Uh-uh. Girls never like wrestling with me or digging in the mud or doing any other important stuff. They just wanna play pretend or tell secrets."

She continued to smile, enjoying his little rant.

He took out one of his hands and pointed to his chest with his thumb. "*I'm* special," he declared. "That's what my momma tells me."

"She's absolutely right." She patted his head again. I tried to commit the feeling of his curls to memory—they were even softer back then. Her hand lingered in his hair as if she was thinking the same. "And because you're so special, Night, you'll need a mate to match, won't you?"

He considered that. "Will she like playing?"

"Of course."

"And wrestling?"

"Sure!"

"And we'll be friends?"

"She's special, remember? She'll like to do all the same things that you do, and you'll become closer than friends could ever get."

He still seemed skeptical, which made my mother laugh.

"My daughter is destined for greatness, Night, and so are you. It'll be on you to help protect and guide her so she can fulfill her destiny."

I expected Night to protest more, but he only tilted his head. "How do you know?"

"A mother always knows. Fate has intertwined your lives, and that tells me you'll accomplish some amazing things together."

"Oh." He pursed his lips, deep in thought. Then he nodded to himself and thrust his hand toward her. "Okay, fine. I'm already gonna protect you and my momma and the whole pack when I get older. Everyone except for Alpha Pete." He frowned, and he became the stern, stoic Night I knew. But almost as soon as the darkness appeared, it vanished. "But I'll protect the baby too if she'll help me. Deal?"

My mother accepted his hand and shook it. "A deal is a deal," she said with a smile. "She'll be by your side the entire time, and I can't wait to watch the two of you grow up."

The scene shifted suddenly. The membrane I was looking through began to shift and shimmer, obscuring my view of Night. When it cleared again, I was standing in a kitchen. My mother was holding a warm mug of ginger mint tea as she stared out of the window above the sink. It was impossible to tell the true color of the sky through the gray haze, but given the sun's position, it looked like it was approaching dusk.

Heavy footsteps entered the kitchen, and a pair of strong, muscular arms wrapped around my mother from behind. She leaned back against the man's chest, and he kissed the side of her neck, his hands on her belly.

My heartbeat quickened. Was this my father?

"How are my sweet girls doing?" he asked. His voice was even deeper than Night's, almost just a growl.

"We're happy and healthy," she said. "How is my mate?"

"Better now that he's with you." He kissed her neck again. "It's been a long day, but coming home to you makes it all worth it." They shared a quiet moment while she finished her tea.

She turned in his arms to look up at him, and I knew I was looking at my father. If I could cry in this state, I would have. But I couldn't make my mother cry in her memories.

My father was tall, muscular, and handsome in a casual, almost boyish way, with light brown hair and blue-gray eyes. There was something *so* familiar about him even though I'd never laid eyes on him before.

"Dominic and Night are out practicing their tracking again," she said.

"I know." He laughed. "I caught Dom hiding from Night in a juniper bush."

"Wow." She giggled. "I can just picture that. Those boys are so funny."

My father pulled her as close as he could. Her stomach put some distance between them, but neither seemed to mind. They swayed gently together as if pushed by a light breeze. I could feel the strength of the love my mother had for my father. It was like a tightly corded rope. But underneath it was a distant sense of sadness that marred her happiness and love.

"It won't be long now, Lucian," she whispered, trying to push that sadness away. "Soon, she'll be able to play with them, too."

"I can't wait," he whispered back. "Dom's already looking forward to being a big brother."

Another bolt of shock coursed through me. Lucian Slate? But that meant…

The memory began to lose focus, and I almost lost hold of it. I tried to do the same thing as before, bringing calmness inside me and holding tight. *Get a hold of yourself, Bryn,* I snapped. *Get. It. Together!* After a few seconds, I let go of the shock, and the memory steadied.

Relieved, I tried to look again at my father, but my mother's eyes were focused on the far corner of the kitchen.

I don't know how I didn't see it before. My father looks just like Dom! So, Dom and I were half-siblings.

I let that revelation wash over me as my parents continued to sway together in the kitchen. The more I sat with it, the more sense it made. I'd felt an instant connection to Dom from the moment we met.

I'd never imagined the two of us could be related. I'd have to tell him as soon as I returned to my own body. How would he take the news? Dom had definitely known my mother, but what if he didn't know his father had gotten her pregnant?

With that question lingering in my mind, the memory shifted again. I wasn't standing; I was flat on my back on a mattress. As far as I could see, the room had only one small bed, and the walls were covered in black, haphazardly painted symbols. I had no idea what the symbols were, but I felt my mother's alarm like it was my own.

Unlike the other memories, this one had a staticky haze to it, as if something was interfering with the signal. The light in the room was too bright, and the bed under my back was too hard. I just felt…off. What the hell was happening here?

I couldn't tell if my mother knew where we were. I tried to sit up, but my arms and legs were bound to the bedposts. I'd been in similar positions too many times, but I wouldn't have thought my mom had ever experienced something like this. Panic washed over me, but the vision didn't become distorted like the others. Maybe it was because she and I were experiencing the same emotion?

Suddenly, I heard footsteps running toward the door. Our eyes widened, staring at the door. Was her captor coming to finish the job? She clenched her hands into fists and flinched when the door was kicked open. She turned her face to the side, squeezing her eyes shut.

"I finally found you."

That voice. Warmth cut through the fear, and she turned her head. My father was there, covered in blood and bruises, his shirt a stained, tattered mess, but he was there to rescue her. Relief hit my mother and me hard as he rushed to her side and sliced through the bindings with his claws.

"We need to get out of here *now,*" he said, pulling her to her feet. "They're sending more Kings after us."

She took a step and winced as pain stabbed through her. "Luke, the baby—" She panted. "She's coming!"

My father cursed. Below, we heard the door burst open and the sound of several men running inside. Lucian sprinted to the window and kicked it out. My mother turned away from the spray of shattered glass. He cleared the most jagged bits of glass from the window frame before turning to my mother again.

"I'm sorry," he murmured, pulling her into his arms before leaping through the window into the cool night air. He hit the ground and started sprinting with her clutched in his arms.

As he ran, my vision finally cleared of that staticky haze, but he was moving so fast, I couldn't tell where exactly we were. The most I could tell was that the land smelled like King territory.

The minute I realized this, I understood that this was the night my mother died. I wasn't expecting to see it so soon, and I didn't know if I was ready to see what had happened. At the same time, I knew I couldn't look away. I needed to know what had happened to them. I owed them that much.

My father sprinted into the woods, with King wolves not far behind. My mother cried out as pain rammed into her, her muscles contracting. Her water had broken, and her body throbbed as the baby—*me*—started to push through. I wished I could tell myself to hold off. This was the *worst* time to go into labor, but the stress of the situation must have induced it.

My father had to stop when she screamed again. He set her down at the base of a large oak tree. She pushed his chest as if to tell him to go without her.

"I'm not leaving your side," he said, his eyes wet with tears. "I'll defend you to my last breath."

She was breathing hard as she stared at him, her hand still on his chest. After a few seconds, she stopped pushing him and nodded. "I know you will. We can't run from our destiny." She tried to smile, but the pain and the weight of her sorrow wouldn't let her. "I love you so much, Lucian."

"I love you, too, Blo—"

Guards burst from between the trees before he could finish speaking. Lucian released a roar, his hands turning to claws as he turned to face them head-on. He killed them quickly and without mercy. Dark blood splattered over the ground, through the air, across the trunks of the trees. He was a machine, cleaving through his adversaries before they even got close to my mother. A wolf bit into his shoulder, but my father didn't even grunt. He stabbed his claws through the wolf's underbelly, and its bowels sloshed to the ground.

My mother watched it all through vision that was slowly fading. She stared at her mate's back, calm stealing over her as she accepted that she was close to the end. She wasn't injured from anything external, but something inside had torn.

Once Lucian got rid of that first wave of wolves, he turned back to her. As their eyes met, my hold on my mom's mind began to slip away.

I scrambled to regain control, thinking I was losing focus again, but I realized at that devastating moment that she was dying. My father seemed to realize it at the same time.

"No." His voice cracked, tears spilling over his cheeks. He crouched in front of her. "What can I do?" he asked. "How do I save you?"

She gave a weak shake of her head and placed her hand over her stomach. *Save the baby*, she willed him to understand.

He sobbed once as he looked at her stomach, and then mustered up enough resolve to nod. He took her hand in his and tried to coax her through my birth. She was fading fast, but she held on long enough to make sure I was born. As she pushed, she simultaneously pushed me from her mind. I was no longer seeing through her eyes but hovering above the scene, looking down at them.

I tried to angle myself to see her face, but I couldn't get a clear view. The last thing I saw was myself as a newborn in my father's arms. Newborn-me opened her mouth, let out a cry, and then everything went black.

Chapter 23 - Night

I paced around the elders' backyard. My stress was at an all-time high. I couldn't even imagine what Bryn was seeing or what she was going through. For all I knew, she could be living through torture. It had only been an hour since her eyes started glowing white, but that time had passed so slowly. I willed myself to be patient, but how could I when my soulmate was enduring this by herself?

Mom watched me calmly. She and the other elders were grouped near the back door of the cabin. Elder Queene had brought water and snacks while we waited for Bryn to come back, but I had no appetite. Pacing was the only thing I could think of to pass the time.

"Night, she's going to be fine," Mom said. "We just need to wait a little longer."

My wolf whined, and I bit down on the inside of my lip. "I don't like this, Mom."

"I know, Night."

"I just can't calm down. I feel like it was a mistake to let her do this."

"It must be terrifying to know she's gone somewhere you can't follow, but sweetheart, this is what Bryn wanted. You know that this was Bryn's choice to make, not yours. She needed to do this to understand who she is."

"I know that," I snapped. "Bryn told me herself so many damn times." My tone was much sharper than I'd meant it to be. I stopped pacing and pinched the bridge of my nose. I was antsy and irritable, but letting my emotions get the better of me wouldn't help Bryn. "I'm sorry. I shouldn't snap at you like that. I'm just on edge."

"It's okay. I know you didn't mean anything by it." She smiled sympathetically. "Why don't you try thinking about something else? Maybe some paperwork you can go through? Or more training you can do?"

I shook my head. It was a good suggestion, but neither of those options worked for me because they involved me leaving Bryn. I wasn't about to let her out of my sight for a second. I ran my hands through my hair and tried to think of something else I could do to stop obsessing so much over Bryn's well-being.

And then a thought occurred to me. I hadn't talked to the Kings' elders about the children who'd disappeared. Now was the perfect opportunity to ask them what they remembered. It wasn't the happiest of topics to bring up, but the questions I had about the disappearances were relevant enough to hold my interest.

I took a few calming breaths, then walked over to them. They were talking to Elder Woods about something. Whatever it was had their full attention, but when they noticed me nearing them, they stopped talking. I might have found that suspicious under different circumstances, but I didn't care.

"I have a few questions for you three," I said.

"Yes?" Elder Queene asked.

"Do you remember the string of disappearances that happened a decade ago? The children who vanished without a trace?"

The three elders stared at me for so long, I wondered if they'd somehow forgotten about the children.

Elder Forsythe sighed. "My goodness," he said slowly. "I haven't thought about that dark time in ages." The other two elders nodded solemnly.

I gave them a few seconds to cast their minds back to that time before asking, "Were there any suspects you know of? Any leads?"

"We all suspected a wolf was taking them and killing them," Elder Forsythe replied.

"When I looked over the reports, I figured it had to be someone the kids knew and trusted," I said. "I can't see any other reason for so many pups to wander off the compound on their own."

"Your logic is sound," Elder Forsythe said. "At that time, everyone had their theories, but there was no evidence linked to a perpetrator. Whenever someone was suspected, there was a brief trial with circumstantial evidence. In the most benign cases, the accused was released without charges, and in the worst, they were put to death. But the kidnappings continued." His dark eyes became even darker. "All of us were so paranoid and desperate to find answers, but there weren't any. Lives were lost, relationships were ruined, families fell apart."

"If you don't mind the question," Elder Sage began, "why the sudden interest, Night Shepherd?"

"We found reports about the missing kids in the office of the alpha cabin," I said. "We were working through the paperwork for other reasons, but this mystery interests me."

"I believe there is one boy who survived the kidnapping. Samuel."

I nodded. "I tracked him down, but he was too traumatized to tell me anything I could use. It's just so bizarre to me that the kids were taken, and their remains were never found."

"If their remains were missing, how do you know they were killed?" Mom asked the elders. "They could be alive, couldn't they?"

"It's unlikely they would have survived," Elder Queene said gravely. "It's possible one or two might still be alive, but whoever took them would have had to keep them somewhere and discreetly provided for them for the past ten years. Maybe they could get away with a few pups, but a dozen would be hard to wrangle."

"How awful," Mom whispered, her hand on her chest. "My heart breaks for the parents who lost their children."

I patted her shoulder. "Is it possible that the pups were taken to another pack?"

"Possible, yes, but unlikely," Elder Queene replied. "Again, maybe they could get away with sneaking in one or two boys, but there would be too many new pups entering the pack. Not to mention, the children would smell like they were taken from our territory. People would notice. They would ask questions."

"Was it just the Kings pack who suffered such losses?" I asked. "Or did other packs lose pups?"

"Children have gone missing over the years in various packs, of course," Elder Queene said. "But those disappearances usually had clues and remains and viable suspects. Our disappearances had none of those things."

"You brought up Samuel before," Elder Forsythe said. "And it jogged a memory. One thing that always stood out to me was that the poor boy swore he saw a shadowy monster with long talons. Of course, that is probably just a child's mind scrambling to make sense of whatever horrors he witnessed that day, but there are ancient fairytales that use the same imagery. Those stories talk about shadow monsters with jagged teeth that were said to suck the mind out of a person, leaving them incapable of living. The fairytales were created to keep children from wandering too far into the woods by themselves."

"I know legends like that can be rooted in some truth," I said. "Did creatures like that ever exist?"

"Again, your logic is sound, but we don't believe creatures like that have ever existed outside of legend."

"We believed the children had grown curious about the story and wanted to see the creature for themselves," Elder Sage said. "They went out into the woods while no one was watching and were taken by whoever told them about the myths. We believed young Samuel was somehow able to survive, but his trauma manifested as the shadowy creature because that was why he ventured into the woods in the first place."

That made some sense. We'd need to track down the root of where the children had heard the story. But was that even possible at this point? Whether the children were lured into the forest by someone they trusted or tempted into it because of a story, both the elders' theory and mine pointed to an adult wolf who would have had time to gain their trust or get them interested in those old stories.

"The air was heavy with sadness ten years ago," Elder Woods murmured. "The other elders and I...we suspected something had happened with the King pack, but we weren't sure what." She looked at the Kings' elders with tears shimmering in her eyes. "Such a great loss as that...I cannot even fathom the toll it must have taken on these wolves."

"We appreciate that you can empathize with our tragedy, Elder Woods," Elder Queene said. "Likewise, I hope you can understand that we had little to do with Gregor and Troy's distaste for you and your people."

"Of course."

Elder Forsythe inclined his head in thanks. In response, Elder Woods patted his shoulder.

I hadn't planned for there to be any interaction between the Warg and King elders, but it warmed me to see them get along—not just from an emotional standpoint but from a political one as well. This connection could help bond the two packs.

"Night," Elder Sage's voice pulled me out of my thoughts. "It is honorable for you to look into this, but odds are, you will never get answers. After so many years, the young victims are likely dead, and the guilty parties have either died, escaped, or are so well-hidden it would be impossible to drag them out into the open without their confession." He shook his head sadly. "I'm not certain if solving this will help you win over the council or the pack."

"I'm not doing this to win any points with anyone," I said. "When it comes to those missing pups, I only want to give closure to their parents. They deserve it. As for the rest of the pack and the council…well, they'll have to deal with me once I win the alpha challenge, anyway."

The elders all smiled. "Ah, you're very confident," Elder Forsythe said. "Be careful, Night Shepherd. If you're too confident, you might miss the forest for the trees, so to speak."

Their warnings didn't faze me. "I won't miss anything," I vowed. I looked at my mate for the first time since I started asking them about the missing pups. "Because there's too much at stake."

Another thirty minutes passed, and Bryn was still in her trance. Talking about some of the elders' theories had kept me busy for a little while, but now the worry crept back in. I started pacing again.

"How long is this supposed to go on for?" I asked. Having Bryn this physically close to me but mentally far away was wrong. It only elevated the pricking anxiety in my chest.

"It depends on what Bryn wishes to see," Elder Woods said. "Remember, Alpha Night, Bryn will be experiencing the memories of a pack mother. Those memories span hundreds of years, if not thousands. She will likely be able to focus those memories on when her mother was with child, but it will take her some time to do that. Seeing through the eyes of someone else is a very complicated process."

I groaned. The elders weren't making this any easier on me.

"Night, what do you remember of Blossom?" Mom asked.

"Blossom? I remember…that she was pregnant," I said slowly. "And I remember she went missing."

I paused and frowned as I thought more deeply about her. "I'm starting to remember more now that she's on my mind. She was a huge fixture in my life, almost as huge as Dom's father." I hesitated. "I think she mentioned once that her daughter and I would grow up to be close."

Soon after Blossom went missing, she was presumed dead. Her death, and her baby's death, had depressed me and the rest of the pack for weeks and weeks. It was such a dark time for me that I couldn't believe I hadn't thought about her for such a long time.

"Are you sure that's all you remember?" Mom asked. "Think a bit more."

I closed my eyes and ransacked my memories of Blossom. More of that fog disappeared, and I realized with a slight jolt that I'd misremembered what she'd said about her baby. She hadn't told me we would be close; she'd said we would be fated mates. When I was a pup, I thought she was being silly. I was still at the age where I believed girls were a waste of valuable playtime, but I'd adored Blossom.

And as if a fog was lifting from my brain, I remembered the beautiful woman who was kind and graceful. She was always very sweet to me, sharing her treats with me and inviting me over to chat…though our chats usually entailed me talking without pause for hours on end. I'd forgotten how much of an attention hog I was.

And when I learned that she and the baby had died, I had this crushing sense that I'd lost something precious. Even when I started to become interested in women, none of the females in my pack ever felt like the right fit. I couldn't commit myself to them. Eventually, I thought I'd have to give up on the idea of claiming anyone. That deep sense of loss followed me until the moment I met Bryn.

"Mom, why are you asking me about Blossom?" I asked. But as soon as the question left my mouth, I started to put together the puzzle pieces. "Was Blossom the pack mother we were hiding?"

Mom just smiled instead of giving a verbal answer.

Shock rocked me, and I sat on the nearest seat—a tree stump. If Blossom was the pack mother, *Bryn* was the baby girl she was carrying. All this time, Blossom's baby had been my fated mate, and I'd had no idea. All this time, our paths had already crossed, and neither of us had known it.

At first, I couldn't process this huge piece of information. But the longer I thought about it, the more it made sense. I hadn't remembered who Blossom was until my mother asked me about her, and I knew that had to be for a reason—the Fates or destiny or whatever had kept me from knowing Bryn's identity until this very moment. As Bryn was learning more about her mother through her visions, I was making a few discoveries about my past, too.

A groan from Bryn yanked me out of my thoughts. The white light was fading from her eyes, and the circle was dimming, too. Soon, her eyes returned to normal, and she fell back, her body convulsing.

Chapter 24 - Bryn

When I came back to the present, I found myself on the cold ground, trembling in the wake of the ritual and everything I'd experienced. Night appeared at my side in an instant, crouching next to me and gathering me into his arms. I shivered against the heat of his body. All the warmth had left my body during that ritual, as if seeing through my mother's eyes had sucked some of my vitality out of me.

"Bryn, are you okay?" My mate's murmured words permeated the heavy cloud of disorientation.

I gave a shaky nod and a shakier thumbs up.

He let out a breath that wasn't quite a laugh and lifted me in his arms like a bride. I felt a pang of sadness as he carried me. Lucian—*my father*—had done this with my mother in the moments before her death. He'd been just as tender as Night was with me. I gripped Night's shirt in my trembling hand. I mourned for both my parents and the loss they must have suffered from being separated from each other so brutally.

"You can take her inside," I heard Elder Queene's voice from far away. I focused on it to stay in the present. "It'll be warmer there."

Night took me inside the elders' cabin, the others following. He sat on a bench with me in his lap, holding me gently as I tried to stop my body from shaking so much. Elder Forsythe built a fire in the hearth while Violet draped a blanket over me. I hadn't felt this cold since I was human. After all these weeks of living with a higher body temperature, I had no idea how I'd managed the cold.

"Don't worry, Bryn," Elder Woods said. "Your body is reacting to the strain of the ritual, but it will pass soon. We just need to get you warmed up."

"Strain" was the right word for what I felt. My mind was still swimming with all I'd learned, and my heart drummed against my ribcage. I felt exhausted and wired with energy at the same time.

I opened my mouth to say something but couldn't form the words. Night, Violet, and the elders were all waiting to hear what I had seen, but I wouldn't be able to tell them anything until I felt like myself again.

Closing my eyes steadied me. I hadn't been able to see my mother's features, but I'd heard her laugh and voice. My vision blurred at the memory, and tears poured down my cheeks before I could quell them. I hadn't been able to cry while looking through my mother's eyes, and it was such a relief to be in control of myself and my body again. To be able to feel and grieve and ache for the loss of who she was.

"Oh, Bryn." Night sighed, his lips brushing over my forehead. "What did you see?"

I was still shivering but not as much as before. After a few moments, I was able to find my voice. "I didn't see my mom," I said quietly. "But I heard what she sounded like, and I saw her hands and her pregnant belly. I felt what she felt as she experienced it. It was amazing."

His smile was full of relief as he loosened his tight hold on me now that I could speak. "I'm sorry you didn't get to see what she looked like, but I'm really happy you got some answers. Did you see where your mother was from?"

I shook my head. "I didn't go that far back."

"What was it like navigating the memories?" Violet asked after she brought me a glass of water.

I gingerly took the glass. I didn't trust myself not to drop it unless I held it with two hands. "It was bizarre," I replied. "It was so difficult to focus on a single memory at first, but once I got hold of one, the visions became clearer. In fact, I can confirm that she lived on Warg territory."

Violet nodded, a slight smile on her lips. "Anything else?"

"I was hoping to see some of the people she might have interacted with, and I got lucky." I looked up at Night, and I touched his cheek. "I saw you when you were little, my love."

His eyes widened. "Really?"

"Yeah. You were just a cute little boy. I think you were around six years old. Maybe seven?" I eased off his lap to sit next to him. "Why didn't you ever mention that you knew my mother?"

"I had completely forgotten that I knew her until tonight. And even then, I didn't start to remember her until Mom asked me about her." He nodded to Violet. "It was like your mother had been erased from my memories."

"Yes, that was how it felt for me," Violet said. "I hadn't thought about her until Night mentioned you wanted to know more about your birth parents, Bryn. Only then could I start to access those old memories."

"Why is that?" I asked. "Why was it important that so many of you forgot who she was?"

"Only the spirits understand why things happen the way they do," she replied. "I do, however, have a theory. I believe those memories were kept hidden from us because it wasn't important that we remember them until it was time for you to learn about your past."

"But why now?" I asked.

"I suspect it's because you're getting closer to achieving your destiny. Whatever the Fates have planned for you is approaching more quickly, so now is the time for things that were hidden from us to be revealed."

The enormity of her words made me shiver. I wasn't sure what to do with all of this. The surrealness made me feel like I was still in that dream world. I couldn't shake the impression that the Fates had wasted their time on me. After all, I was just some girl. Why was I so special?

Elder Woods cleared her throat, catching my attention. "What else did you see, Bryn?" she asked. "Did you see what happened to your mother?"

I finished the water and wiped my mouth on my sleeve. "I did. Sort of. I didn't see everything that happened the night she died, but she was tied to a bed in a strange room within the Kings' territory. My father rescued her, and they escaped into the forest. He helped her give birth to me, and she died right afterward." It pained me to remember how she'd faded away. It was such a quiet, tragic ending for someone so important. "I didn't get to see what happened to my father or how I ended up in the spot my mom found me in."

The ritual was a success, but disappointment lingered bitterly at the back of my tongue. I wished I'd seen more. There were still so many things I didn't understand about my mother.

"Did you see your father?" Violet asked.

I nodded. This was what I'd been slow to bring up because I was still processing the information. "It was Lucian Slate."

"Lucian?" Night blinked. "You and Dom have the same father?"

"Yes. I saw a memory where Lucian mentioned that Dom was looking forward to being my big brother." I shifted a little in my seat. "I saw Lucian. Dom looks just like him."

"That...that is huge," Night said. "We wondered if you had any siblings, but I didn't think your family would be this close."

"Neither did I."

"The more I thought about the pack mother, the more I wondered if you and Dom were related," Violet said. "She and Lucian were very close, but she was quite guarded about anything related to her relationships and personal life. It makes more sense to me now than it did back then."

"Violet, I never heard anyone say her name. What was it?" I asked.

"She asked us to call her Blossom. As far as I know, she never revealed her last name."

"Blossom," I repeated quietly, reverently.

"I never realized that Blossom was a pack mother," Night said. "But now that I'm thinking about it, it makes so much sense. She always seemed special to me. I got the impression that I could never misbehave around her." He ran his hands over his face. "She used to tell me her baby was going to be my mate, but I didn't know that was you. Like Mom was saying, it's like a fog is lifting from my brain, and the more I think about Blossom, the more I remember."

I could almost see the gears turning in his mind as he went through his memories. I envied that he had easier access to information I could only access through a ritual. But I would pick his brain about this later.

"Do you think Dom will take the news well?" I asked. "I'd hate it if things got awkward between us."

Night chuckled and clasped my hand. "Bryn, you don't understand how important this is for him. We all believed you'd died with your mother. We mourned both of you for weeks. We'd all forgotten about Blossom and you over time, but the minute Dom remembers, he'll be over the fucking moon to learn that you're alive."

I flushed at the thought. To think, my *brother* had been right by my side for weeks. In some ways, I should have known he was here with me because we shared the same blood. From the minute I'd met Dom, I'd felt close to him, but obviously, there would've been no way for me to know we were related without conducting a blood test—or performing a ritual that allowed me to see my mother's memories through her eyes.

"Violet, I have another question," I said. "Is it possible to be fated to someone?"

"Of course. That's what makes you and Night soulmates. Some wolves are destined for greatness, and the love of their mate helps them achieve it. Fated mates always find each other, but it doesn't always happen at your age. Your mother must have sensed that you and Night were fated even before you were born because you two were in close proximity."

"Wow," I breathed. It was a lot to take in—not just for me but for Night as well. We'd need to talk more about this when we were alone.

Elder Sage cleared his throat, and I almost jumped. The three Kings' elders had stayed quiet while we talked amongst ourselves in their cabin. I appreciated that they had given us that space, though they must have been curious about what I'd experienced.

"What do you remember about the room your mother was held in, Alpha Hunter?" Elder Sage asked.

"There was a small bed, and the walls and ceiling had strange symbols all over them. I'd never seen that room before."

"Can you draw those symbols?"

"I can try, but I'm not that great at drawing."

"That doesn't matter. Anything you can remember would be helpful. We never knew that the last pack mother was in our territory. We had heard that the Wargs blamed us for her death, but we weren't sure if there was any truth to it. Now that we have proof, I am ashamed that we couldn't prevent her death. Her loss was a great blow to everyone."

He lowered his head, as did everyone else. Killing a pack mother had left such an ugly stain. Blossom had deserved to live, and yet someone—likely a King wolf— had taken it upon themself to murder her. It was needlessly cruel.

"Can you think of any reason why there would be a room covered in symbols on your territory?" Elder Woods asked. "A place for rituals, maybe?"

Elder Forsythe shook his head. "No. As far as we know, there is no reason for a room like that to exist. Perhaps when we see the symbols, we'll be able to discern more. For now, we're just as unsure as all of you."

"I'll do my best to draw them," I said. "I'll do that tonight while it's fresh on my mind. I should have the drawings ready for you by tomorrow afternoon."

They bowed to me, and the gesture was so respectful that my cheeks heated. "Thank you, Alpha Hunter," Elder Forsythe said. "You are giving us the opportunity to atone for the tragedy that befell a pack mother. Your mother."

They asked a few more questions—what the quality of the visions were, and whether I could hear my mother's thoughts in addition to feeling what she felt—but their questioning lasted only a few minutes, and then Night and I were free to head home.

Before we left, I turned to Elder Woods to say my goodbyes. "Safe travels on your way back."

Her lips turned up at the corners. "Thank you, Bryn. I know Neil and Jacob will be eager to hear about what happened tonight."

"I'm sure they will. I'll be happy to answer any questions they have."

"Oh, believe me, they will have them. Once things calm down here, I'd love for them to come and speak to you in person."

"I'd like to go see them. It's been too long since I've seen Warg territory."

"I'm sure they will be happy to see you."

After Night said his goodbyes to Elder Woods, we headed out. I gazed at the sky as we walked. When the ritual started, the moon was high above us, but it had sunk from that position. Hours had passed since I'd entered my mother's memories, but I'd had no idea so much time had gone by.

"I'm sorry I doubted you," Night said, pulling my attention. "I should have listened to you and my mother and trusted that you knew what you were doing."

I hadn't expected an apology, but hearing it made me smile. It felt like we'd gotten through something difficult and come out stronger. "Thank you," I said.

He smiled back. "Well, where to now? I'm sure you're exhausted after all that."

"I am really tired," I said. "But I don't think Dom should have to wait to hear that he has a sister."

"I understand, but you look like you could fall asleep on your feet." He took my hand, intertwining our fingers. "Telling him can wait until tomorrow morning."

"Is that an order?" I joked.

He snorted. "No, it's a request from your mate who wants to see you safe at home and bundled under every blanket we have."

I smiled and squeezed his hand. I wanted to tell Dom the truth right away, but the thought of being home surrounded by warmth and cuddled close to Night was just too tempting. Besides, after everything I'd seen, I'd earned a good night's rest, hadn't I?

"Alright, alright," I said. "You've convinced me. But as soon as I wake up, we're telling Dom, okay?"

"Of course." He kissed the back of my hand. "First thing."

Chapter 25 - Night

I'd managed to convince Bryn to rest last night, but as I watched her dress now, unease pricked at the back of my mind.

I had no idea how Dom would take the news. I knew he would be happy eventually, but he might also be skeptical or at least hurt that he'd lost so many years with Bryn. After all this time, his sister had been held by the pack that had killed his father. If that upset him, he'd come around once the shock wore off, but I couldn't get comfortable with the fact that we were about to drop such a massive bomb on him.

Hell, *I* was still dealing with the shock of Bryn's revelations. Memories that were buried deep in my mind were coming to the surface. I should have prepared myself for this, but never in a million years would I have thought that what she'd seen would hit so close to home. I knew this would only bring Bryn and me closer, and that it would, as Bryn hoped, reveal more about who she was and what made her tick. But until we went through it, this information would weigh me down.

The lights were already on in Dom's cabin, which was a relief. At least we weren't rousing him from his sleep on top of everything else.

Bryn knocked on the door, and after a few seconds, Dom opened it. From his light blue short-sleeved shirt and shorts combo, he was obviously about to go on a run.

"Huh," he said. "Usually, I'm the one finding you two, not the other way around."

"Hi, Dom," Bryn said. She sounded adorably shy, but it was easier for her to find her voice than for me. "Sorry we're interrupting your workout, but could we come in?"

"Well, I wasn't expecting visitors," he said, his usual easy grin spreading across his face. "But yeah, of course."

He held the door open for us, and Bryn and I went inside.

"I'm glad you weren't still asleep," she said.

"Yeah, you two are lucky," he said as he closed the door behind us. "Usually, I'm still dead to the world, but I felt like going on a jog. So, what brings you two lovebirds around?"

"We needed to talk to you," I said.

He arched a brow at me. "Wow. Been a while since I've seen you so stiff and awkward, Night." He smirked. "Whatever you're here to tell me must have shaken you up. But it can't be bad news; otherwise, you'd be crossing your arms."

I glanced down at myself and then up at him. "Dom, I think you know me a little too well."

"That's my job, right?" He leaned against the wall. "So, what's up?"

I rubbed the back of my head and looked at Bryn. We shared the same expression. *Where do we even start?*

It took some time, but Bryn and I explained the ritual and what she had seen. The longer we talked, the more serious Dom became. By the end, Dom wasn't standing by the wall anymore; he'd sunk on the couch. He leaned forward, his elbows on his knees, his head hanging down. Hell, we probably should have asked him to sit before we started talking.

"Lucian saved my life," Bryn told him. "I saw him fight off dozens of wolves before he helped my mother give birth to me. If not for him, I don't know where she or I would be."

He ran his hands over his face as he processed the information. And then, he slowly got to his feet and headed to the cabin's back door.

Bryn started after him. "Wait, Dom—"

I caught her arm and tugged her to my side. "Don't worry," I told her. "He's just going for a run."

"Oh." She relaxed into my chest. "When do you think he'll be back?"

"Hard to say." I could have reached out to him telepathically, but that would have been overstepping. "I'm sure he'll be back soon. Do you mind waiting?"

She shook her head. "Let's give him all the time he needs."

Though it was early morning, I grabbed a beer from the fridge—I needed something to fortify myself—and got some water for Bryn. I moved some throw pillows to the armchair and sat on one side of the couch. Bryn finished her water and settled in beside me. She grabbed a book off the table and thumbed through the pages. The sight of it reminded me of when she and Dom first met. He had been able to do what I couldn't: get her comfortable enough to talk. They'd spoken about books all the way back to the Warg compound. At the time, I'd been jealous, but now it made me wonder if their connection as siblings had made it easier for them to bond.

Eventually, Bryn lay down with her head in my lap. I stroked her hair. It was lucky that the men Dom shared the cabin with were either back on Warg territory or searching and hunting for Troy. Otherwise, we wouldn't have this privacy.

Dom returned fifteen minutes later. He was still breathing hard, and his light brown hair was windblown. Bryn sat up, pushing her hair over her shoulder. She'd been on the verge of falling asleep.

"I'm sorry it took me so long to get my thoughts in order," he said. "It was like I had to dust off the cobwebs in my brain or something."

Bryn and I shook our heads. "There's nothing to apologize for," she said. "You needed time, and we were happy to give that to you."

"I appreciate it." He ran his hands through his hair. "So, then, you're my little sister, Bryn?"

"Yeah." Her eyes shone with tears, and she tried to smile. "It turns out you're my big brother after all."

Dom went quiet again. We waited while he ordered his thoughts. "My mom…" he said finally. "She told me the baby who was supposed to be my little sister had died with her mother. She said my dad had died, too."

"That's what everyone thought," I replied. "Glenda found Bryn in the woods near the outskirts of the Kings' territory. I think Lucian was trying to bring Bryn back, but that was as close as he could get her to Warg territory."

That last bit hurt to say. I was an adult man who had seen more than my fair share of tragedy. It shouldn't have been difficult for me to accept that someone as powerful as Lucian had died in battle, trying to protect his family as best he could. But there was a large lump at the back of my throat, like the pup who'd known Lucian was still in me somewhere, missing him. I hadn't let myself think about him for a long, long time, that even the man I'd viewed as a hero could fail.

Dom briefly closed his eyes and opened them again. "This is a lot to take in," he murmured. "But I believe what you've told me." He looked at Bryn. "I want to tell you about the people who raised me."

She nodded, sniffling. "I have so many questions, but I didn't want to overwhelm you."

He smiled. "I appreciate that, Bryn. You're just as kind as Blossom was to me."

She went to him and touched his shoulder. "So, then, you knew that the child Blossom was carrying was your father's?"

"Yeah, I knew. Things between my dad and my mom were complicated," he said. "She always loved him, and he, in the beginning, loved her, too. They had me, and they were happy, but when Blossom was accepted into the pack, he and my mom separated. Blossom was his soulmate, and my mother wouldn't stand in the way of that. It broke her heart, but there was nothing she could do. I remember there was a lingering sense of hurt when she and Blossom were in the room together, but she wasn't mean or cruel to your mother, Bryn. My mom wasn't like that."

"Of course she wasn't," she said, tears tracking down her cheeks. She wasn't trying to hold in her emotions like Dom and I were, and that made her stronger than either of us. "I'm sure your mom was a very kind person. I can't even imagine the heartache she endured."

"Thank you for saying that. She and Dad remained friends even after they stopped living together, and they shared the responsibility of raising me. By the time Blossom got pregnant, Mom was even excited about me having a younger sister. She wouldn't stop gushing about how beautiful you were going to be."

Bryn laughed and wiped under her eyes with her sleeves.

"I'd always wanted a sibling, but Mom was never able to give me one because she never fell in love with another man." He took a deep breath. "When we heard that the three of you had died, we were devastated. I think the shock of losing you all hurt her so much that she couldn't fight off the sickness that took her life. I wish she'd lived long enough to meet you, Bryn. She probably wouldn't have known you were Blossom's daughter, but I'm sure she would've loved you."

He paused, pushing his hands through his hair again. "I never thought you survived, Bryn. And to learn that you were alive this whole time, that I could have come and helped you at any time…I'm sorry the Kings were so awful to you and Glenda."

"Dom, no." She wrapped her arms around him in a tight embrace.

I watched them, waiting to feel some pushback from my wolf, but the jealousy I might have felt under normal circumstances wasn't there. I mean, what was there to be jealous of? A sister and brother hugging?

"You didn't know," she whispered. "You couldn't possibly have known. What my mom and I went through is not your fault, Dom."

He tentatively hugged her back, letting out a sound that wasn't a sob and wasn't a laugh. "I never thought I'd get to do this with my little sister."

She laughed and hugged him harder. It was so rare to see my beta so emotional. It felt like I was intruding on a private moment.

"I'm sorry for the way things ended," she said. "I'm sorry about what happened to your—no, *our* father. I wish I could tell you more about what happened to him, but the vision stopped when my mother passed away."

"You've told me more than I ever thought I'd get to hear." He pulled back but kept hold of her hands. "I made peace with my dad's death a long time ago. I've always been proud that he went down swinging. But I am sorry you didn't get to know him. He was an amazing man and an incredible father to me. And to Night."

I tried to clear the lump in my throat, but it touched me that Dom had mentioned Lucian being like my father. It meant a hell of a lot that Dom viewed me as his brother as much as I viewed him as mine.

Bryn smiled. "What little I saw of him told me as much. He cared so much about you and Night, and my mother did, too."

"Blossom was the sweetest woman I knew, next to my mother. There are so many stories about our childhood that I could tell you."

Her face brightened. "Tell me everything! I want to know as much as I can about how you and Night grew up." She glanced at me and stood on her tiptoes to whisper loudly, "Especially the embarrassing stuff."

I laughed and reached for Bryn's hand. She let me take it and pull her back to the couch. "I'm really not looking forward to you knowing that much about my past," I joked.

Dom smirked. "No, you shouldn't be. Bryn, I have *plenty* of stories that would make Night squirm. It's tempting to go into them while he's here." The smirk fell, and his face softened. "But I don't think I should do that right now. I need to process all of this and decompress, you know?"

"Of course." She nodded. "We have all the time in the world to go down memory lane, and I want you in tip-top shape so you can tell me everything."

He grinned.

"If you want, you can have the next few days off," I said.

"Why? So you can pawn my work onto some other poor wolf?" He chuckled. "No, I think I'll keep working."

I'd known he'd say that. Dom was the kind of man who processed things best while staying busy. He could be a real workhorse sometimes, but he always handled his tasks without getting overwhelmed or burnt out by them.

"The offer's still on the table if you change your mind," I told him. "You can take time off whenever you want."

He smiled, then looked back at Bryn. "So after everything you've been through, you're okay, Bryn?"

"Yeah, I'm fine. After the ritual ended, I was shaking so badly, I thought it'd never stop. But then it did, and it's over, and I'm fine. The ritual didn't answer all my questions about who my mother was, but I'm glad everyone knows about our father, so I can at least find out more about him."

"Well, of course everyone knows him." His eyes brightened. "My dad was more than just a fighter for the Wargs; he was a warrior. I mean, he was the stuff of legends."

Dom's excitement touched me, too. "His reputation went far outside our territory. I'm sure every wolf in the state heard of him," I said.

"We all expected him to take over as alpha one day, but that didn't end up happening," Dom said. "I guess he had other priorities than taking on Pete."

Hearing him say that made me question whether that was an example of the Fates intervening in our lives, crafting things so they happened just as they were supposed to…or if it was another coincidence. I didn't want to think too deeply about that because if I started worrying about it, I'd question whether any of us had an active role in our lives. That was a little too heavy for me.

To distract myself, I told Bryn a story about a fishing trip Lucian, Dom, and I went on and the massive catfish Lucian caught and cooked for us. We stayed for another hour or so, talking and laughing about our past. Dom had said he wasn't sure he could handle talking about our past, but once we got going, he couldn't seem to stop. Being Wargs, we'd had plenty of dark moments in our lives, but it was so nice to remember the happy, precious moments, too.

Chapter 26 - Bryn

Night and I left Dom to his thoughts. He needed to decompress, and now that I'd told him he was my brother, I realized I needed to process everything as well. I needed Night.

I tugged his arm, and he leaned down so I could whisper in his ear.

"Let's go home."

The moment he met my gaze, he instantly knew what I wanted from him, and he wasted no time in getting me home. Once there, he pulled me against him so our chests were flush. His hardness pressed into my lower stomach, and his deep, masculine scent assaulted my senses. It reminded me of rainfall and freshly chopped cedar, and I couldn't get enough of it.

As we walked upstairs, he trailed his fingers down the side of my body until he reached my ass. He smoothed his hand over my skin and lifted my leg to his hip.

Night kissed me as he entered me. I sighed, nuzzling his chest as he made slow, sleepy love to me. My eyes drifted closed as I traced the tattoos on his shoulder.

"You make me feel so good," I whispered. "I can't believe I get to wake up to this every morning."

His answering chuckle rumbled through his chest. "Imagine how lucky I feel," he said, turning and covering me partially with his body as he caught my mouth with his. His kisses were deep and tender, just like his even strokes.

I ran my hands down his back, his hard muscles shifting under my palms. I moved my leg a bit more, and he shifted, rolling fully on top of me. I reveled in the weight of him pushing me into the mattress. His thrusts grew less lazy and more intentional. Each one brought me closer and closer to release, dispersing electric bliss from my core and throughout my body.

I gripped his waist, gasping with each deep stroke of his cock. My orgasm swept through me, and I shuddered at the delicious tingling. I licked the spot where his shoulder met his neck and nipped at his flesh. He groaned as he came, filling me with his hot seed.

After, Night and I lay next to each other, enjoying being in each other's presence in the quiet of the bedroom. I turned my head to look at him and found him looking back at me. His eyes were a pair of bright chartreuse gems in the late-morning light, and he turned to me, brushing the back of his hand across my cheek.

My body was wonderfully spent, and if not for my racing thoughts, I would have fallen asleep again.

"I'm still trying to wrap my head around everything I learned last night," I said.

"Talk to me," he said. "Tell me what you're thinking." Night was totally focused on me, on hearing what I had to say. His devotion to me made me want to giggle and blush and hide, but the heaviness on my mind kept me from giving in to those impulses.

"When I saw you in Blossom's memories, she told you that you and I had a destiny to fulfill, but she didn't give any details."

"I...I remember her telling me that," Night said. It was fascinating to see how his eyes brightened when he recalled old memories. "I never really understood it. Mom told me that when something is fated or destined to happen, there's nothing anyone can do to stop it. All we can do is accept it and fight for our right to see it through. But that doesn't make it any less bizarre to know there's a future for you that you can't really control."

I nodded. He was just as uncomfortable with the unknown as I was. "I wonder what our destiny is and when it will happen. Violet said all of you are starting to remember more about my mother because we're getting closer to achieving our destiny."

He stroked my cheek again. "I don't know, love, but whatever it is, we'll face it together."

Those words sent shivers through me, and I touched his chest, letting my hands splay across his heart. "In the memory, Blossom said you were my protector."

"And she was right." He gave me a sharp-toothed grin. "I'm willing to fight anyone and anything to protect you. If I had to go toe to toe with fate itself, I would."

I snorted. "You talk a big game, Night, but you said that no one can go against fate."

"I'm sure I'd find a way. And it wouldn't stand a chance against me."

We laughed, and I knew for sure that the ritual had brought us closer. Night and I were on the right path with our relationship; we had both taken huge steps to treat each other as equals. As soulmates.

"You make me feel so alive," I said. "I want to know everything I can about you."

"Yeah?" He sounded hesitant.

"What's wrong, Night?"

"It's just…I'm not proud of much of my past. We already disagree about how violent an alpha is meant to be, and I'm worried about what you'll think of me when you find out what I've done to get to where I am."

I shook my head. "I want to know everything," I said again. "Good and bad. I can't guarantee I won't be upset about some of the things you tell me, but I won't stop loving you, and I won't abandon you. We can't change the past. We can only move forward."

"That's true." He relaxed again. "Okay. From now on, why don't we tell each other one thing about ourselves that the other doesn't know? We'll do that every morning, and we'll keep going until we run out of things to talk about."

I gasped. "Oh, I love that idea! Do you mind going first?"

"Nope. I thought Dom would tell you this story last night, but I'm glad he didn't." He smiled. "When I was a kid, I was terrified of spiders."

"Really? You?" I thought about the little boy from my mother's memories, the one who was full of energy and didn't yet know how to scowl. "Actually, you know what? I can see that."

He snickered. "Yeah, yeah. Anyway, when Dom and I were four, we were playing hide-and-seek in one of the caves near Warg territory. I wedged into a tight spot inside the cave, but I hadn't had my first shift and couldn't see that the crevice was literally crawling with the little bastards."

I suppressed a shudder at the idea of being surrounded by spiders. "Gross," I said. "My soul would simply have left my body."

"That's how it felt for me. For years after that, I was terrified of spiders. Just seeing one made me feel like death itself was breathing down my neck, tickling me like their little legs." He grimaced. "Dom, of course, liked being a dick about it. He used to catch them and leave them in my room, or put them on me when I wasn't paying attention. He used to say it was to help me get over my fear, but that was bullshit."

"That's terrible!" I shouldn't have laughed at young Night and his arachnophobia, but the way he told it, I couldn't help the giggles. It was no wonder that he and Dom were so close. They'd grown up attached at the hip. "I'm sure you're not still terrified of the creepy crawlies," I said. "How did you get over your fear?"

"That's the worst part. Dom's torture did help me…kind of. I knew the only way to get him to stop was if I stopped reacting to it. At first, I pretended I wasn't afraid of them anymore, but at some point, the fear actually disappeared. And then he found other ways to fuck with me."

"I guess it all worked out for the better, then." I rolled onto my back and looked up at the white ceiling. "When I was growing up, my mom was my number-one fan. She was always supportive of me and told me I could do and be anything I wanted…but the one thing she couldn't support was my dream of being a singer. Apparently, whenever I opened my mouth to sing, I yowled like a cat being electrocuted—or so she said."

Night burst into one of those full-belly laughs I loved so much. I grinned, staring at him.

"So, no lullabies for the baby, then?"

"Oh no, there will be. You'll need to be prepared for the sounds that come out of my mouth."

"Sure, I'll prepare for that…by getting earplugs for me. And tiny ones for the baby."

I smacked his chest. "You better not!"

He laughed again and pulled me against him so he could nuzzle into my neck and kiss me there. "I'm so in love with you, Bryn," he said. "Every day, I fall harder and harder for you."

"I feel the same way." I ran my fingers through his soft, thick hair. "But we can't stay in bed all day…as tempting as that is."

"Are you sure? Maybe we could take a sick day." His sexy grin stirred desire in my core, and I was this close to saying yes.

"You know we can't." I kissed his forehead. "I'm feeling much stronger today than I usually feel. I need to take advantage of that and get some work done."

Night gave a long mournful sigh. "I'll check up on Dom and see if he needs my help training our wolves or with any construction projects. I also want to see if there's been news about Troy."

I grimaced. "It's been too quiet lately. I hope they have an update."

"Me too, baby."

It took a little while, but Night and I finally pulled ourselves out of bed, freshened up, and got dressed. He kissed me goodbye and left. I decided to stay inside.

I grabbed some paper and a pencil and sat at the dinner table with a cup of tea. The first order of business was sketching the symbols I'd seen. I told the elders I'd do that last night, but the ritual had exhausted me. Fortunately,

I still remembered them clearly, which helped me hold the pencil with some confidence.

I used five sheets of paper, one for each wall that made up the room and the ceiling. I drew the symbols as I'd seen them from Blossom's position on the bed. Because I knew nothing about these symbols or how they worked, I wasn't sure if the positioning mattered. I wanted to be as accurate as possible so that the elders could give me some real information.

It took me about an hour and a half to complete the five pages, and when it was done, I dropped my pen and sat back in my chair, my hand cramping like it had when I was still in school. Now that it was done, I just needed to drop the drawings off at the elders' cabin, and then I could do some work here in the office while they analyzed them. I hoped I'd done a good enough job recreating what I'd seen.

I gathered the papers, keeping them in order as I put them in a canvas tote I'd found in one of the alpha cabin's many rooms. As I pulled the strap onto my shoulder, there was a knock at the door.

Weird. I wasn't expecting anyone to come by. I opened the door and found a middle-aged male wolf standing on my porch.

"Yes?" I asked. My suspicions had been raised, but I tried to keep that off my face. "Did you need something from me?"

"The council gave me the task of coming to get you, Alpha Hunter," he said. "They request your presence."

I raised a brow. "Did they say why?"

He shook his head. "They didn't give me that information, Alpha."

"Okay. Did they say why you're to escort me?"

He shook his head again. "That's just what they've asked me to do."

"Fine. I was heading out, anyway."

I was confused, but I tried to keep my expression impassive as I followed behind him. What on earth could the council want? And why did I need to be led there like a child who didn't know her way? It seemed pretty disrespectful to me, and that put me on edge.

He left me at the door leading into the building, and I went in alone. It occurred to me that I should have asked Tavi to come with me, but I was so taken aback by my "escort" that I hadn't even thought to reach out to her. Now that I was here, it was too late. *Maybe they wanted to get me alone. Just what the hell do they want from me?*

I stormed up to them, not bothering to hide my annoyance. "What is going on?" I demanded. "Why did you go to all the trouble of bringing me here like this?"

"Apologies, Alpha Hunter," Ross said. "This isn't exactly orthodox, but we voted on how we wanted to do this, and three of our council decided an escort was necessary."

I looked at each of them in turn. Ross obviously hadn't been one of the three to support the summons strategy, and the way Colby shifted uncomfortably in his seat told me that he hadn't voted for it either. That meant Grant, Dana, and Edward had been in favor of the theatrics.

The latter two I understood—they seemed to live to belittle me—but I would have thought Grant was above this sort of pettiness. Plus, he'd seemed supportive of me—or at least of Night—until now. But when I looked at him, his dark brown eyes stared back at me without a hint of regret. It reminded me of what Night had said about his council turning against the original plan to merge the packs. Was my council about to do something similar? And when had I lost Grant's support? Had I pissed him off in some way?

"The reason we've called you here today," Grant began, "is that this arrangement is no longer working for the pack."

"Meaning?"

"We have decided to move the alpha challenge up by five days."

I couldn't have hidden my surprise even if I'd tried. The challenge was supposed to be in *ten* days. "Why the sudden change?"

"We've noticed that you haven't been as attentive an alpha as you ought to be," Dana said. She was practically purring as she watched me seethe. "Your mate is the one handling the rebuilding, reading through confidential paperwork, and putting effort into working with the people. Not you."

"I've been a little under the weather lately, but I've *never* shirked my duties," I retorted. "I was at every meeting with Night, and there was nothing he brought up that we hadn't already discussed. I was present for every step we took and every decision we made."

"That all might be true," Ross started speaking before Dana could make some hateful comment. "And if we're being honest, you haven't done a poor job."

"Then why?"

"Because we know you're pregnant."

I froze. "You…what?"

"We know," he said again. "You were spotted heading into the infirmary, and someone caught you throwing up in the woods. Your mother was seen collecting herbs used for easing nausea, and someone overheard that you were getting an ultrasound at the infirmary. Did you really think you could keep this from us for so long?"

I couldn't refute the evidence. I cursed myself for not being more careful.

"Yes, I am pregnant," I admitted. "And yes, I did keep it from you, but I can still do this job just as well as before. And moving the challenge up by five days isn't a big change. What does it matter if I'm alpha now or even a couple of weeks from now?"

"Your duty as an alpha is to keep your pack safe," Grant said, his voice firm. "But you are operating under conditions that would make your job more difficult, and you kept it from us. Lying by omission is not something we want from our alpha. You should have known better."

My temper spiked, and my wolf started to growl. "Maybe you don't remember how distrusting you all have been of me," I snapped back. "How could I tell you something so personal when the five of you haven't been forthcoming about anything? You didn't tell us about the ledgers—*we* had to come to *you* about it. That should have been something we discussed together, but you left it for us to find on our own."

Grant sputtered at my accusation, but he couldn't argue. Edward, however, seemed more than willing to slide into the conversation while Grant recovered.

"Mothers must be protected so they can focus on bringing new life into the world, not dealing with paperwork or trying to facilitate a merger between two packs. The stress could injure you or the child you are carrying."

I stared at him while he spoke, blood simmering in my veins. "Don't pretend to care about me or my child, Edward. I know what you and Dana think of me. It's really not smart that you two were so open about that. Don't forget, once this is over, I'll be den mother, and I'll still have just as much influence over my pack as I have now."

"Is that a threat?" Dana demanded.

"I, as an alpha, would never threaten my council. But when I am den mother, I won't have the same constraints I have now. You can be assured that I will have my eye on the two of you." I glared at them, letting that sink in. For the first time, I had the satisfaction of seeing them waffle under my threats. The council would be up for reelection in less than a year. Given all the goodwill I'd fostered within the pack, I could make things difficult for them.

Colby cleared his throat, drawing my attention. "Please don't take this personally, Alpha Hunter," he said. "We felt it would be better to have a permanent alpha in place before you are forced to make major decisions for the pack. This is the perfect opportunity to pick our next leader rather than wait even a few days more."

"Think of it this way," Ross added. "If merging the Wargs and the Kings is what's best for the pack, that process can begin much sooner."

It was clear that Ross and Colby also favored shortening my term, but at least they came from a well-meaning place. That clarified my confusion about where they stood, but this situation still bothered the hell out of me. They had decided unanimously that I couldn't be alpha anymore because I hadn't told them I was pregnant. It wasn't fair.

It was almost equally annoying that I could see things from their point of view. For them, it was possible that Night might not win, so there was no point in letting me carry out my plans when the next alpha could undo all my hard work. I could see their logic, even if I didn't agree with it.

Their minds were made up, and I had no real power to go against them. It occurred to me, too, that this was how Night had been forced to kowtow to his council's demands. I thought I'd understood what he meant about making hard decisions, but now that I was sitting in the hot seat, I understood the tough position he was in a hell of a lot better. This really, *really* sucked.

But I still had my voice. "I want to make it clear that I think your reasons for voting me out early lack any validity considering the already short length of my term and the climate I was brought into. But you all have made a decision and voted unanimously on it. I have no choice but to accept what you have decided."

Colby cleared his throat again. "Your words have been...um, noted, Alpha Hunter."

"Good."

Grant, recovered from his earlier incredulity, resumed control of the meeting. "I'm sure you'll be happy to know that we have worked through the details of the challenge ceremony. On the day of the challenge, we will nominate a wolf we believe will be the best alpha for our pack. Any other wolf who wants to try for the position will nominate themselves. They will have to fight one on one in the order they step forward until only one remains. Our nominee will fight first."

I worked through that mentally. "So, if there are twenty challengers, then in theory, your challenger will have to fight twenty battles? If your nominee fails, the person who beat them might have to fight eighteen other wolves?"

"Exactly." Edward smirked, speaking for the first time since the meeting began. "Does that not seem fair to you, Alpha Hunter? The man who will be this pack's alpha must be strong enough to go multiple rounds without falling."

I frowned at him. I had complete faith in Night's ability to win, but fighting a dozen strong wolves one after the other wouldn't be easy for anyone. There was a good chance he'd end up seriously hurt. Worry wound tightly in my stomach.

"Who are you nominating?" I asked.

"Xavier has proven himself to be our strongest prospect," Ross said. "Given his history as a fighter, it will be interesting to see how he performs."

I filed that name away to tell Night. "Will I still serve as interim alpha until the challenge?"

"Yes. Once the challenge is over, you can move to your den mother position if you're up to it."

"I understand," I forced myself to say. "Was there anything else you wanted to discuss?"

Silence answered me, so I gave them a single nod of farewell and turned to leave. I still wanted to tell them off, but I needed to let that go.

The middle-aged wolf who had escorted me here was waiting for me when I left the building, but I snuck past him. Allowing a King to follow me around was a recipe for disaster. If I came across him again, I'd go off on him, and I wouldn't care who was around to see me do it.

When I successfully avoided him, I walked with purpose. Now that the time until the alpha challenge had been sliced in half, it was much more important to update Night as soon as I could.

Chapter 27 - Night

After kissing Bryn goodbye, I planned to meet up with Dom but decided to stop at the library. All the talk about fate and magic reminded me of the portal legend Gregor and Troy supposedly believed. I wanted to know if anything in the Kings' libraries had more information. Gregor had hoarded most of the books about it and stored them away somewhere, but he might have missed something.

I spotted Tavi in one of the rows, debating between two novels.

"Hey, Tav," I said, walking toward her.

She flinched but relaxed when she saw me. "Hey, Night. What are you doing here?"

"Oh, I just thought I'd do some light reading," I joked. "What about you? Looking through the romances?"

She snorted. "I haven't had the stomach for romance lately. I'm trying to decide if this novel about battles in space is more appealing than this one about battles in space." She put the books back on the shelf. "I want something that will help me relax, but I don't know if science fiction is doing it for me."

"Do you want to go outside for a bit?" I asked.

"Yeah, I'd like that."

We headed outside and moved into the trees until we found a massive oak tree. We climbed it the way we used to when we were kids. I sat on one of the thicker branches, and she took one a bit higher than me.

"Well, this takes me back," I said. "We haven't been tree-climbing in, what, ten years?"

"At least," she said. Smiling, she peered down at me through the leaves. "So what's going on? Is Bryn okay?"

"She's fine. Actually, I think she's doing a little better than fine after last night."

She wrinkled her nose in disgust. "Gross, Night. I hope you didn't interrupt me just to talk about what you and my best friend do in your alone time."

I plucked an acorn from my branch and tossed it at her. "Don't be an idiot, Tav."

The way she joked with me wasn't the same as the Tavi I'd grown up with, but the fact that she still joked eased some of my worries about her.

A warm breeze chased through the leaves, and Tavi let out a long sigh. Now was a good time to ask how she felt about Dom.

"So, you and Dom," I began slowly. "Are you interested in him?"

There was a pause, and then a handful of acorns bounced off the top of my head. I looked up at her bright red face. "Um, ouch?" I said.

She was still flushed, but her tone was teasing when she said, "That was probably the most awkward way you could ask me a question like that, Night Shepherd."

"Can you blame me? It's an awkward subject for me to bring up."

"Then why are you?"

"Because I care about you both, and from where I'm standing, it seems like you're interested in each other, but your relationship is staying in one spot instead of moving forward. I want to give you space, but I'm curious about where you stand."

She didn't say anything.

"You don't have to tell me if you don't want to," I said.

"No, it's okay." She sighed. "I guess I'm not sure. I do like Dom, and I care a lot about him, but after everything that happened when I was kidnapped…" She gave a slight shake of her head. "I don't think I'm the best person for him. I already feel like I fall short of being a good friend to Bryn or a good sister to you. How can I expect to be a good partner for Dom?"

My heart twisted painfully. "Octavia, that's not true. Dom doesn't think that about you, and neither do I or Bryn. You're an amazing person, and anyone with eyes can see that."

She shifted on her branch. "I don't see that in myself. Not anymore. I don't think I would be good for Dom as I am now. He needs a woman who can stand at his side, not someone who can barely convince herself to go to the commons."

"But what about what *you* need, Tav?" I asked. "Don't you deserve a man who will stand by you even when you're at your lowest? Do you genuinely believe Dom would reject you if you let him in?"

Tavi picked at the bark. "No…I don't know. I don't want to think that, but I'm not sure if I'm ready to find out what he thinks about me. I'm satisfied just being friends with him right now."

I nodded. "I'm not trying to push you into a relationship before you're ready. But you need to know that none of us—not Bryn, me, Dom, or Violet—would ever abandon you. We're all here for you as much as you want and need us to be. Because you're worth it."

She sniffled. "Thanks, Night. You're such a strong figure in my life, and I've always looked up to you. I think I needed to hear you say that."

"I'm sorry it took me so long to say it. I didn't want to make you uncomfortable or crowd your space or—"

"No, no, I get it." She wiped her eyes and smiled down at me. "You're a good big brother, Night. I hope you know that even when I'm feeling at my lowest, I'm glad I have you and the others in my life."

I grinned. "I couldn't imagine a better little sister."

She snorted, sniffled again, then moved to a branch closer to me. "So, what were you doing in the library?"

"I'm looking for books on old wolf legends and magic," I said.

"Oh, is this about the portal stuff?"

"Yeah. According to the Kings' elders, there are stories about shadow monsters. Those legends might be why the kids went into the woods."

"Sounds like you're after books about our mythologies. Need my help?"

I was taken aback by her offer. "I can't ask you to look into that. You were just talking about looking for a book that would help you relax."

She waved my words away. "Yeah, but I was going to look into the fantasy section next, anyway." She shrugged. "Might as well help you out. And besides, looking through books about myth and legends will be a hell of a lot more interesting than looking through old invoices for that elusive account number."

"I guess that's fair." I chuckled. "I'll leave it to you, then."

We didn't hug or kiss each other on the cheek, but I felt closer to Tavi than I had in weeks. It was a relief to reconnect with her like this, and I was glad we'd had the chance to talk again.

I arrived at the training grounds to find Dom already there. He was keeping an eye on our men as they did drills. Some Kings had decided to join them, which was nice to see. Off to the side, Xavier and Lance were each doing their own thing.

I hadn't seen them train for a while. Seeing them now reminded me how stiff the competition would be if I faced off against either of them. But I was preparing for that scenario, and I'd improved a lot as a fighter because of my regimen. I intended to win, and it didn't matter who got in my way.

I went to stand next to Dom, bumping him with my shoulder. "How are you doing?"

"Can't you tell?" He gave me a half-smile. There were bags under his eyes, and he looked paler than usual. "My brain hasn't been able to work through it all yet. I'm still shocked. Part of me feels like I imagined everything you and Bryn told me, even though I know it's real."

"It *is* real," I said, knowing he needed someone else to confirm it for him. "I'm sorry you had a rough morning."

"I just can't stop thinking about it. How's Bryn doing?"

"She's doing a lot better. I feel like an idiot, though. She told me over and over again that she wanted to find out more about her mother so she could learn more about herself, but I didn't want her to do the ritual."

"Why not?"

"I don't know, Dom. Everything in me told me it was dangerous to let her do it. It was like I was letting her walk off the edge of a cliff. But now that it's all over and she and I have talked, I have to acknowledge that my instincts were totally off. Bryn was fine at the end of the ritual, and it's helped us connect on a level we couldn't reach before."

"That's great to hear, Night. It was a *long time* coming."

I scoffed and nudged him. "Yeah, yeah…there is still one thing about it that worries me, though."

"Oh, yeah?"

"Blossom said Bryn and I had a destiny we needed to fulfill, but neither of us has any idea what it might be."

"I guess that's something you won't know until it's staring you in the face, you know? But in the end, it doesn't matter. Between you and me and everyone else who cares about us, Bryn is protected and supported. We're not going to let anything happen to her or the baby."

There was resolve in his voice as he spoke. He hadn't sounded that fired up in a while. Dom was already protective of Bryn, but now that he knew they were blood, his drive to keep her safe must have increased. I couldn't be happier about that. He was a powerful wolf, and I knew if something happened to me, he would keep Bryn and our pup safe and loved. I had no intention of dying anytime soon, but my beta made me feel more secure.

Dom and I watched the training a while longer, and my gaze wandered to Xavier and Lance again.

"Any new intel on those two?" I asked.

"I've got something on Xavier. He has a bad right knee. If you watch him long enough, you'll see he eventually favors his left leg and overcompensates for it."

I took a look at Xavier's leg. Dom was right; he always stepped with his left leg first and protected his right leg slightly more while he sparred.

"That's really good intel," I said. "What about Lance?"

"I haven't been able to dig up anything about him, and it's frustrating the hell out of me."

"Well, we've still got time. We should be able to figure something out about him."

"That's true, but it's bizarre that nobody knows anything about him. He could be a spy for Troy, but nobody is talking. It puts me on edge."

I agreed with him. I was sure there were spies within the Kings that we hadn't had time to weed out, and there was a real possibility that Lance was one of them.

"Night, Dom."

Bryn's voice pulled my and Dom's attention. She was striding toward us with a flat, unreadable expression on her face. Tavi was at her side, but she just shrugged when I shot her a questioning look. Bryn must not have filled her in, either.

"Night said you're not feeling so sick today," Dom said to Bryn when she and Tavi neared us. "Still true?"

"Yeah, I'm feeling great physically, but emotionally..." She trailed off and frowned in annoyance. "We've got a problem."

"What's wrong?"

She glanced over my shoulder at the training grounds. I glanced behind me and saw Lance looking at us—specifically at Bryn. There wasn't anything threatening about his look, but I didn't like it.

I returned my gaze to Bryn. She and Tavi looked just as wary of Lance as I was.

I took Bryn's hand and led her a few steps to the side, Tavi following. I blocked Bryn from Lance's view, and Dom, catching on to what we were doing, stood close to my shoulder, ensuring Lance would see no part of her.

"Tell me what's wrong," I said.

"The council found out I'm pregnant," she said. "They're using it as an excuse to move the alpha challenge up and replace me."

"They're what?"

She sighed, then went into more detail about what had happened. As she spoke, she became more agitated, her hands moving faster and faster with every word. I was right there with her. The council had no reason to vote her out just because she hadn't told them about the baby. They had never had a female alpha, so there was no precedent for their decision.

Tavi was so angry, she growled. "Those bastards. And to do that to you without me by your side? Fucking cowards."

"True," Dom agreed. "And they've moved the alpha challenge to five days from now, which means we have half as much time as we thought." He looked at me. "If one wolf ends up fighting each challenger after another, that could be bad for you, Night."

"I can handle it," I said immediately.

He rolled his eyes. "It's not about whether you can handle it; it's whether you'll make it through in one piece. Knowing how vicious Kings can be, I'm concerned they'll put you first."

But Bryn shook her head. "That's not how it works. They would have to nominate Night, and they won't do that. Xavier is their nominee."

"Oh." Well, that changed things. "I think that setup works in our favor. It sounds like I should nominate myself last and let the Kings kill each other." That would take care of either Lance or Xavier, and I would just have to fight the winner.

But Dom still looked doubtful. "I don't think that's the best play here. If you wait until the end, it'll be obvious what you're doing. Logically, your plan works fine, but you'll come off as a coward if you're waiting for your opponent to tire out."

I sighed. He had a point, but considering how often the Kings had cheated us, it was hard not to want to do it, anyway.

"You could try to go sometime in the middle," Bryn suggested.

"That's an idea." Tavi seemed calmer now. "Who knows? There might only be a handful of wolves who nominate themselves."

Bryn nodded. "And if that's the case, you might only fight five wolves. It shouldn't be hard for you to win, Night."

I grinned at my mate. Her confidence in me was a massive ego boost, and I was tempted to pull her away for some fun…but now wasn't the time.

"Don't look at me like that, Night Shepherd," she said, a pink tinge creeping into her cheeks. "I'm still worried about you. I'll have to watch every second of these fights, and I want you to be careful."

I couldn't resist pulling her against me and kissing her cheek. "I will be, love. I promise."

"Don't worry, Bryn," Dom added. "He's got too much riding on this challenge to do badly, and this time around, he won't have to worry about Troy hamstringing him with hostages."

It was true. I was five days away from everything I'd spent my life working toward. Soon, we could start building our ideal pack and bring peace. I could deal with the extraneous things, like the Wargs' council and Troy, once I had everything in my hands. I was too close to let things slip through my fingers again.

Chapter 28 - Bryn

After hugging Dom and kissing Night goodbye, I took the drawings to the elders' cabin. It was much shorter to walk in a straight line through the forest than follow the compound's curving path. In about half a mile, the trees would give way to the elders' cabin, and I decided it was worth being out of public sight for a few minutes if it reduced my travel time.

It was shaping up to be a bizarre day, but at least I felt more certain about everything. Night seemed confident that the challenge would work out. I needed to have faith that he knew what he was doing, but I'd never be able to let go of my worry for him.

Was this what it had been like for Night to watch me go through the ritual? If so, I could empathize a lot more with his position.

I let out a sigh. The tote bag hardly weighed anything but seemed to gain ten pounds with each step I took. When I thought about the drawings, I felt less sure they were legible. A lot was riding on my ability to draw them accurately. If things turned out well, I would know even more about what happened to my mother. I hoped with everything in me that I'd done a good enough job, but I felt so uncertain.

"Wait up, Interim Alpha."

I stopped walking, turning towards the voice. Lance was leaning against the tree closest to me.

I hopped away from him, immediately on guard. He'd just been at the training grounds, yet he'd somehow managed to catch up to me without me hearing. That should have been impossible.

Lance had never threatened me or said anything that seemed concerning on the surface, but he could be a spy, and Night viewed him as competition. All that told me he was powerful and dangerous.

"You sure it's okay for you to wander off by yourself?" he asked. "Wouldn't you be better off with an escort?"

I stared at him. The way he said "escort" made me suspicious. Did he know something about my meeting with the council?

"What are you talking about?" I demanded, thankful that my voice sounded every bit as powerful as I wanted it to. A wolf ought to present a strong stance in the face of potential opposition, and I didn't know what this guy wanted from me. "This is my pack. I can walk wherever I want, whether I'm alone or not."

"Ideally, that would be true, but someone in your condition should be guarded at all times, don't you think?"

"My 'condition?'"

"You know what I'm talking about." He glanced at my stomach and back up at me. "You could say I've got a sixth sense when it comes to things like this. Not that I needed that extra sense; anyone keeping an eye on you would have figured it out."

I instinctively stepped back from him, my arms covering my belly protectively. My lips pulled back from my teeth as my wolf growled. *Dammit.* With that one sentence, he'd put me on the defensive. How did he know about the baby? I had zero clue who he was, yet he seemed to know everything about me.

I continued to glare at him, and Lance took a small step back, which confused me even more. It was almost like he was giving me space, but if he wanted to give me space, why didn't he just leave me the hell alone?

"You should stick close to your mate," he said. "I'm sure I don't need to remind you that there are people in this pack who hate Night, the Wargs, and everything you represent."

"And what do I represent? Change?"

"Exactly."

"And how do I know you're not one of them?" I demanded. "You must be watching me at all times if you know so much about my personal business."

He didn't deny it.

"Why are you keeping tabs on me?"

He gave me a level stare, and I couldn't tell if he was trying to intimidate me or scold me. "Because I know that the alpha challenge is only five days away, and once it's over, no one will listen to you. Because I know that if there's one thing these small-minded wolves believe, it's that women are subservient to men. And because your being pregnant only makes that belief worse, but I'm sure you already had a taste of that when you spoke to the elders earlier."

I had to navigate this conversation with more poise. At the very least, I should try to be civil—for all I knew, I was talking to someone who was in direct contact with Troy. But the day had been too taxing, and I couldn't keep myself from getting pissed off.

"Do *not* patronize me," I said. My voice took on a growl, thanks to my wolf. She was also sick of whatever game he was playing. "I am not a child, and I'm not the stupid girl that you, the council, and most of the pack thinks I am. I've been through hell, and I've made the best of it. I've made mistakes, and I've tried to make up for them. I've reached my lowest point, and I've crawled my way back. You don't get to tell me what to do and pretend you give a damn about me or the people I care about."

Lance took another step back, and for a second, something bright flashed across his eyes, but it was gone before I could read it.

"Have you considered that you might have just gotten lucky?" he asked. "You're alive today, true, but that doesn't mean you'll keep succeeding. You're making a huge mistake if you think the wolves in this pack won't turn against you and your mate the minute they have the chance."

"Night is going to be the next alpha. They won't have a choice but to listen to him."

"It's never that simple, Bryn. And if your mate is telling you that, he's either lying to you, or he's an even bigger idiot than he looks."

My temper spiked again, and my wolf seethed within me. But I caught myself before I exploded again.

"If anyone is lying, it's you. After all, no one knows anything about you. Someone who's being truthful wouldn't need to keep so many secrets."

He let out a brief chuckle. "You'll know who I am when it's time, but until then, you really should listen to my advice. I say it with your safety and the safety of that little wolf in mind." He turned from me and started walking away.

"Sure you do," I muttered under my breath, staring after him until the trees swallowed him up.

It was only the second time Lance and I had interacted, but he left me more confused each time. I shook my head and resumed my trek to the elders' cabin at a much quicker pace. I didn't have time to parse my way through Lance's possible motives to seek me out and talk to me. I'd do that later with Night, hopefully in the safety of our cabin. Until we had the chance to talk, I'd file the conversation away. For now, I wanted to see my original mission through.

The sight of the elders' white cabin had never been more welcoming. I knocked on the door, and Elder Queene let me in.

"Hello, Alpha Hunter," he said.

"Hello, Elder Queene," I replied. "I thought Elder Woods would be with you?"

"I am still here." She came in from the side room and gave me a kind smile. "I will be heading back to Warg territory soon enough, but I wanted to be here when we discussed what you saw in your visions."

"I'm glad you're still around," I said, returning her smile.

"I trust you have the sketches?" Elder Queene asked me.

"I do, yes." I took off my tote and pulled out the drawings. I went to the nearest table and set them up the way I wanted. As Elders Forsythe and Sage entered the foyer, I explained which wall each paper represented. The three bent over the papers, poring over the drawings with obvious fascination.

"Oh, and I don't know if this helps, or if it means anything," I said as I finished my explanation, "but when I was in the room with my mother, I felt...different."

"Could you clarify what you mean?" Elder Forsythe asked at the same time Elder Woods asked, "Different how?"

"Well, in the other memories, I could see them clearly as long as I stayed calm," I said. "But when I was in that room, I felt weaker, and my vision had this weird, foggy quality. It was like I was looking through a curtain of mist. I wrote it off as a side effect of my mother going into labor, but it's occurred to me that it might have been because of these symbols. I think they might have affected my mother somehow."

"Fascinating," Elder Woods said.

"I suppose that could be possible," Elder Queene said. "There are oral histories that talk about the existence of symbols that can block magic, but those accounts are so old, it's difficult to verify their truth."

"It's also possible," Elder Sage added, "that the symbols were used to keep your mother from shifting. It's obvious that the symbols had some sort of magical effect. The real challenge will be trying to understand what effect it was."

"It made me feel awful," I said. "I don't think these symbols were meant to calm her down or keep her happy. I'm pretty sure they were meant to harm her."

"Given the situation you described in your vision, I understand your interpretation. However, we need to come at this reasonably. The symbols themselves might have a positive meaning—for example, to strengthen the bond between mates or friends or to calm someone. It's possible that this combination of symbols was meant to disorient her, not outright harm her. Until we've had some time to analyze them, it's far too early to discern their purpose."

I'd known before coming that I probably wouldn't get answers today, but it was disappointing all the same. The elders were almost as in the dark about the symbols' purpose as I was. Apparently, they weren't even sure if the individual symbols were meant to do something positive or negative.

I was pretty damn sure that they had hurt Blossom. The room itself had felt *wrong*. I couldn't see how it could strengthen a bond when it didn't make me feel anywhere near as nice as when I was with Night or someone I cared about. And if that was the effect those symbols had on me, I imagine Blossom had felt much worse. Who knew how long she had been cooped up in that awful room?

Furthering my theory that the symbols were meant to harm was how Blossom had been tied to the bed and held against her will in King territory. This, to me, was more than enough evidence to show that she had wanted to be as far away from that room as possible.

But I kept those thoughts to myself. I knew absolutely nothing about these writings, and my interpretation of the situation wouldn't be as accurate as what the elders would find in their research. I just had to wait and see what they were able to find.

"Thank you for helping me," I said. "It means a lot that you all are helping me find answers."

"Your thanks are unnecessary," Elder Queene told me, his eyes riveted to the pages. "We are very curious to find the answers to this mystery ourselves. If anything, we should be thanking you for giving us the opportunity to further our knowledge."

"Oh." I wasn't sure what to say to that. I appreciated the honesty, but I didn't know whether I should thank him again or tell him, "You're welcome."

"I guess I'll head out now," I told them. "I want to get back home."

"Make sure you're careful, Alpha," Elder Sage said as I picked up the empty tote. "Until we know where that room is located and what these symbols mean, it would be best for you to stick to populated areas of the compound or walk with someone you trust—just as a precaution. You are a descendant of pack mothers, and it's imperative that you stay alive and healthy."

I hesitated, unease curling in my stomach. The warning was eerily similar to what Lance had told me. It was like he was two steps ahead of me. What did he know that I didn't?

"I'll be careful," I promised.

I headed home. This time, I stuck to more populated paths rather than taking my usual shortcuts. I didn't want to risk coming into contact with Lance—or someone worse—again.

Within five days, things would start to change. I wasn't an idiot; I knew most Kings wouldn't be happy about Night becoming their alpha, but it was too cynical to assume nobody would be on our side. The Wargs had helped many King families, and that accumulated goodwill had to amount to something. I had to believe that because otherwise, how would I find the motivation to keep trying as hard as I was?

But I was tired and beyond done. I didn't intend to look at any work or think too much about the things that stressed me out for the rest of the day. I needed to make sure that I was keeping myself alert and healthy. Night would protect me, I knew, but I needed to do my part, too. I'd focus on growing the life inside me, and then when the baby was born, I could stand at Night's side to protect the baby and everyone else I held dear.

Chapter 29 - Night

With everything that was going on, I was sure Bryn was feeling the pressure. I felt the same pressure, but it was tinged with excitement at finally taking on the mantle of alpha of the Kings. I couldn't wait to put this struggle behind me and move forward with my goals. I just needed to get past this challenge first.

I'd been training as often as I could—alone and with Dom—and Bryn had been trying to distract herself from her anxieties by throwing herself into work with Tavi. We hadn't had a chance to enjoy each other's presence, and if it was getting to me and my wolf, I knew it had to be getting to Bryn and hers.

So, when the sun started to descend from its position in the sky but hadn't quite reached the horizon, I took Bryn out. I covered her eyes with a strip of cloth and took her hand so she wouldn't bump into or trip over anything while I led her through the forest.

"Remind me again why I have to be blindfolded?" she asked. "If you're trying to kidnap me, you've already done that once."

I snorted. "Kidnapping you was too much work. You're a terrible captive—far too annoying."

"I don't know," she sang. "I think it worked out okay."

I chuckled and brought her hand to my lips. "I couldn't agree more."

Soon, our destination came into view: an old, two-story log cabin. I removed the blindfold and watched Bryn intently. At first, she looked confused, but after a few moments, her eyes widened, and she gasped.

"Is this…?"

"It is. If you'd like for it to be." Threading my fingers between hers, I led her to the cabin.

There was no telling how old it was, but some logs had lightened with age. It was constructed with a timber frame, so the logs were squared off instead of round. Most of the planks were still in great condition, but others would need to be replaced. There were no solar panels on the roof, which meant it wouldn't have electricity, but that was an easy fix.

The corners of the interior were home to cobwebs, and a fine layer of dust coated the floor except where Dom and I had done our walkthrough. The furniture—a dining table big enough for two, an ice box, cabinetry, and chairs—stood strong, only in need of washing, sanding, and re-staining. It wasn't the prettiest sight, but it had a lot of potential, and the floorboards were largely intact as well.

"I know it doesn't look like much," I said, a flash of doubt hitting me as Bryn examined one of the cracked logs in the wall. "But it could be something amazing if given time. I'll make sure it's perfect by the time our son or daughter is born, and—"

"Hey, easy." Bryn came to and took my face in her hands. "You're my mate, Night. You think you need to go all out for me?"

My face warmed. "I want to impress you."

She laughed. "The location is ideal since it puts us closer to Warg territory, and I can see the potential of this place already." She stood on her tiptoes to kiss me. "It's beautiful. Now, give me the rest of the tour."

My wolf was grinning as wide as I was as I led her to the second floor. The cabin had three bedrooms, two bathrooms, and one half-bath on the first floor. I showed her the master bedroom first, where an old king-sized bed frame and one or two chairs sat.

Bryn went to the window and gazed out at the sky. The sun had sunk lower by now, and the clouds were lined in gold.

"What a beautiful view," she whispered. "And it's in such a quiet spot."

"Mmhm," I wrapped my arms around her from behind, my hands pressing flat to her stomach. Eventually, it wouldn't be so flat, and I couldn't keep from smiling about it. "I thought it would be good because it's not crazy far from the Warg territory."

She leaned back against me. "That's even better."

We stood, watching the sunset a bit longer before I led her away. The other two rooms were smaller. Both were big enough for guests to stay over if we wanted…but one would work well as a nursery.

Bryn's eyes went round the moment we went into the third bedroom. It was across from the master bedroom and had the same spectacular view of the skyline. She stepped into the room, the floor creaking under her. I reached for her, but she steadied herself right away. If she noticed the way the floor had dipped slightly, she didn't seem to care.

"This one," she said, looking from corner to corner. "This would be amazing for the baby. I could put a bookshelf there and fill it with all the baby's favorites, and put a rocking chair under the window. The crib could go opposite that, and maybe a changing table here."

I leaned against the door frame, watching her plan everything. I knew she'd had something of a mental block when it came to designing the space where the baby would stay, and it was such a treat to see her do it now.

"I take it this was a good choice, then?" I asked.

"Yes!" She whipped around and threw her arms around me. "It's perfect. Thank you so much for this, Night."

I lifted her and spun her once before setting her back down and pressing my forehead to hers. "That's not the only surprise I have for you."

"Oh, do you?" She kissed me. "Show me."

It was outside in the backyard. There, I'd set up a table with candles and a woven basket sitting next to it.

I opened the basket, showing her the brisket sandwiches, chips, and chicken soup I'd packed earlier that day. Also in the basket were a couple of glasses and a bottle of some non-alcoholic cider I'd bought at the commons.

"Oh, Night, this is perfect."

"It's been too long since we had a date, and I wanted to make it up to you."

"I had no idea you could be romantic."

I laughed. "That's my fault. Just consider this something new you learned about me today."

"Hmm. This is lovely, but I won't let you off that easily." Her silvery-blue eyes glittered with mischief. "I think I'd like to hear more embarrassing stories."

I snorted and started to unpack the basket. We sat next to each other, and I poured the cider.

"I had no idea this cabin was here," she said. "How did you find it?"

"Dom and I found it while we were training the other day. We already know how we're going to fix it up." I explained how we would deconstruct it before rebuilding. We would replace the rotten and cracked logs. Bryn said she'd like the cabin to be updated, so we'd add the solar panels.

As we spoke, Bryn covered my hand with hers and squeezed it. "I really appreciate you doing all this for me, Night," she said. "I didn't know how much I wanted this until…well, until now, I guess."

"Neither did I." I brushed away the breadcrumb on her cheek with my thumb. "Things are going to get complicated pretty soon," I told her. "So many things are going to change, and there's no telling when we'll get to spend time together like this. I wanted at least one night where we could be mates instead of alphas."

She scooted closer so she could rest her head on my arm. "We've both been so busy, I wasn't sure when would be a good time to mention it, but I spoke to Lance the other day."

I clenched my jaw, and my wolf's hackles raised. "What did he want?"

She took a deep breath. "He knew about the council no longer wanting me to be alpha, he knew about the challenge getting moved up, and…and he knows about the baby."

I stiffened. "Did he threaten you?" I asked, my voice low.

"At the time, it felt like a threat, but all he did was tell me things we already knew or suspected: the pack is sexist, it was dangerous for me to be alone, and there would be opposition to your rule. I just don't know what his endgame is, and I can't figure out how he found out I'm pregnant."

Rage flared through me so hard, my hand shook as I reached for the bottle of cider. What Bryn had just told me was more than concerning—it pissed me the fuck off. I had the urge to find Lance and kill him—after I found out where he'd gotten his information.

But that would be jumping the gun. He and I would have our day in the ring during the alpha challenge. I forced myself to calm down. The last thing I wanted to do was ruin this time with Bryn by getting angry.

"I'm sorry I didn't tell you sooner," she said.

"Thanks for telling me at all," I said, nuzzling the top of her head. Her scent and her presence did so much to settle my nerves. "You're right—we've both had our own things going on, and it hasn't been easy to find time to talk about everything…but let's focus on us for now." I lowered my lips to her ear. "Shift with me. Run with me."

She brightened, and all trace of her earlier worry vanished. She started pulling off her clothes, more eager than I'd ever seen her.

"Wow, you never get naked this quickly when we have sex," I said as I pulled my shirt over my head.

"Hush, you." The last article of clothing she removed was her panties, which she dropped on the ground, grinning from ear to ear. "We never get to go on runs together. We have sex almost every night."

I laughed and kicked off my pants. "Hopefully, we'll be able to rectify that when things settle down—"

She'd started to shift before I finished speaking. Standing on all fours, she shook out her rich brown fur. Her tongue lolled out, and she cocked one ear slightly toward me. She danced on her toes and lowered herself on her front legs, her tail swishing in the air, ready to go. My heart just about burst with love for her, my wolf whining desperately.

I shifted, and we sprinted into the forest. I'd just set my wolf loose the day before when I was training with Dom, but this was special. Different. The joy of running and playing with my mate trumped everything else. Few things felt as wonderful as her teeth nipping playfully at my ear or her excited keening.

I don't know how many hours passed with us playing and running together, but the moon was out and high above us when we rolled down a hill together into a patch of soft grass. Laughing, we shifted back into our human forms. My heart raced against my ribs as goosebumps rose on my chest. Bryn nestled against my side, and I held her tight. We looked up at the sky as we settled down again.

"I love you, Night," she murmured.

"I love you, too—hey," I said as she threw a leg over my hip and moved on top of me. Her eyes glowed silver in the dark, the waxing moon above framing her wild hair. "Hey," I said again, a smile curling on my lips. "What are you doing up there?"

"You have to ask?" She leaned over me and pressed her lips to mine. I brushed a hand across her face, holding her there as I caressed her thigh. Her tongue snaked out to battle with mine, and I felt myself getting hard. The soft weight of her warm body against mine, the slight vibration of her heartbeat against mine…these were the things I craved when we were apart.

Bryn kissed her way down my chin and my neck, her hands pressed against my chest. She shifted her hips downward until her ass rubbed against my erection, wriggling back and forth. I groaned, gripping her hips.

She raised herself just enough, then wrapped her hand around my cock before sinking down on me. I hissed as she took in every inch of me. With a moan, she sat back, giving me a full view of her stomach to her neck. My hands traced her skin, over the slight firmness of her muscles beneath her stomach and up her breasts to her neck.

Her hair shifted over her shoulders as she looked down at me, eyes still glowing. She bounced on top of me, her eyes locked on mine, and pleasure radiated through my blood. Her hands were flat against my chest, and her nails were claws, piercing slightly. The slight sting elevated my pleasure, and she increased her rhythm, thighs slapping against mine.

The scent of blood and sweat and pussy was in the air. She leaned forward again to kiss me, pulling my lower lip into her mouth and between her sharp fangs. I growled low in my throat, and she answered with a growl of her own. Gripping the back of her neck, I held her mouth to mine. Her pulse beat powerfully under my palm. I moved my hips to meet each rolling bounce of hers. Her soft breasts jiggled and pressed against my chest.

Bryn groaned as she came, her pussy tightening around my cock. While she was still feeling the ecstasy of her orgasm, I rolled on top of her and took control. I took her hands, holding them above her head. My toes dug into the earth for purchase, and she screamed out loud, her voice echoing between the trees as I drove into her. Her legs locked around my waist, her back arching up off the ground to press firmly into my chest.

The pressure built and built until I felt her second orgasm roll through her body. My mate trembled beneath me, her muscles locked around me. Bathed in the soft, silvery rays of moonlight, I came inside her hard enough to leave me breathless.

Chapter 30 - Bryn

The day before the alpha challenge, I found it almost impossible to concentrate on anything. When I tried to read something, the words blurred together and stopped making sense. I read the same sentences over and over, but I still felt so lost.

I only trusted myself to sign rote documents, things I was familiar with and had signed before. But other than those documents, the day was a wash. I couldn't do anything useful.

Finally, I couldn't take it anymore. I left my office and went for a walk. It was my last full day as alpha, and I wanted to stroll through the compound while I still had the authority to do so. I thought about asking Tavi to walk with me, but a sudden burst of nausea sent me stumbling to the trees.

I straightened and swiped the back of my hand across my mouth. Great. My last day as alpha included me throwing up into a bush. How typical. At least this time, it wasn't as violent or noisy.

"Thanks for meeting me out here, Tavi."

My ears perked at the mention of my beta's name and the familiar voice who'd spoken it. I looked up, and sure enough, I spotted Dom's wheat-blond hair through the foliage. I knew I ought to mind my business and give them the privacy they deserved, but my curiosity got the better of me. I crept slowly toward where they stood, moving just close enough to see their faces through the leaves.

"It was no trouble," she replied with a slight smile. "What did you want to talk about?"

"Well…" He rubbed the back of his head with his hand, tussling his silky hair. "I wanted to talk about you, actually."

"M-me?" She touched her chest, her fingers jostling the zipper of her sweatshirt. "Why?"

"I don't want you to think I'm trying to pressure you into spending more time with me, or I don't respect your need for space," he said. "I care about you a lot, Tav, and I would do anything to make sure you're safe and happy."

I held my breath, waiting for Dom to confess his feelings for her. I felt sure Tavi was also holding her breath.

"I need to be honest with you about the way you make me feel. I used to think my feelings for you were what a brother feels for his sister, but they're different than that. I—"

Tavi raised her hand, and Dom's mouth shut immediately. My eyes widened; not even Night could shut Dom up so quickly.

"I…" she hesitated, rethought what she wanted to say, and began again, "Dom, I'm not sure what you're about to say, but if you're going to tell me what I think you're going to tell me, I want you to know that I don't think I'm ready."

He gazed at her as her words sunk in. "What do you think I'm going to say?"

"I-I think you're about to tell me that you, uh—" Her face went bright red, and she busied herself by gathering her dark hair over her shoulder.

"That I like you," he finished gently. "That I care about you. That I'm ready to be more than friends with you…whenever you're ready to let me in."

My heart raced hard against my sternum. Each second I waited for her response was a second that seemed to stretch for eons.

"You have to understand," she finally replied, "I can't make you wait until I'm ready to be the woman you need, Dom. It could take months. Years, even. You are such a wonderful man—" Her voice broke, and she cleared her throat. "You could have any woman you want. There are so many beautiful women out there who can take care of you. I'm just not…I don't know if I can be a normal mate for you. I can't ask that of you. You deserve someone *more*…" She struggled for words, and then her shoulders fell as she gave up, sighing. "Someone more."

"I feel that way, too," he said gently. "Even now, I'm worried that all I'm doing is putting more strain on you by telling you this. It drives me wild that I can't tell if this is hurting you or helping you. If I were a better man—a stronger man—maybe I could be more patient. Maybe I'd know exactly what you need."

She shook her head. "You're the most amazing person I know."

"And you're the most incredible person *I* know," he said with a chuckle.

I could see how badly they wanted to touch as they leaned toward each other. But they held back, as though going that far would somehow ruin the progress they'd made. It made my chest ache for them.

"I'm willing to wait however long, Tav. Even if that means we're tired and gray and reminding each other about the good days of our youth."

"If you change your mind—"

"I won't."

The interruption made the corners of her mouth quirk into a smile. "*If* you change your mind, I won't hold it against you."

"That won't happen," he said again. "But thanks for that."

Her smile widened, and then she hesitated, her lips pursed. After a few seconds, she stood on her tiptoes and gently kissed his cheek. And after a second, she pressed another kiss to his lips.

I nearly gasped. *OhmygoshTavi!* My thoughts went wild as Dom's arms gently—so, *so* gently!—wrapped around her waist.

I needed to get out of there. I had no idea how far things were about to go, but I didn't want to eavesdrop further. I inched backward, trying to go as silently as I'd come, but a twig snapped under my foot, making me gasp. I froze, waited a few beats, and tried to move more carefully out of the forest.

I returned to the cabin as quickly as I could without raising suspicion. I rinsed the lingering bitterness of vomit out of my mouth and went to the office. What I wanted to do now was lay low and throw myself full force into my work. I'd seen something between Tavi and Dom, but they had been too busy with each other to notice my quick exit.

That's what I'd thought, but Tavi walked into the office minutes later.

"H-hi, Tavi." I cursed myself for stuttering. If it wasn't obvious that I'd been eavesdropping, it was now.

"How much did you hear?"

After a few moments of hesitation, I replied, "All of it, I think."

"Oh."

It felt like Tavi was saying a lot with that response, but I couldn't tell if the emotion conveyed was negative or positive.

"I'm sorry, Tavi, I didn't mean to overhear or to stay as long as I did. Yes, I was eavesdropping, but I've been so worried about you, and I wanted to make sure…" I trailed off when tears started pouring down Tavi's cheeks and off the end of her chin.

"Do you think I made a mistake?" she sobbed.

"Oh, Tavi, no…" I went to her and wrapped her up in a hug. Her shoulders were trembling, and the shoulder of my dress became soaked the moment her face hit it. Her arms wrapped around my waist as she clung to me.

"H-he told me that he likes me—maybe even loves me," she whispered through short, hiccupping gasps. "And

I kissed him, but I couldn't…I mean, I shouldn't have done it. Not when I know I'm not ready to be that for him."

"I know, Tavi, I know." I rubbed and patted her back. "You haven't done anything wrong, and you haven't messed anything up. You told him you feel the same way, didn't you?"

She sniffled and nodded. "But I shouldn't have said that. I should have told him I couldn't see him as anything more than a brother. He deserves someone who can give him what he needs and be there for him in all the ways he needs her to be. And I don't know if I'll ever feel right enough to let a man get close to me like that."

"Tavi…"

"I'm not good enough for him."

"Don't." I pushed her back so I could look into her dark, doleful eyes. "You can't think that way, Tavi. You are so strong and intelligent and beautiful. Any man worth his fur would be lucky if you even looked his way."

"That's the old me," she spat bitterly. "The one who hadn't been ruined—"

Dread held me fast with its icy claws. Suddenly, the question that had always lingered at the back of my mind when I thought of Octavia rushed to the forefront. I had to ask, to confirm the terrible fear I'd been too terrified to think about. "Tavi, what did those wolves do to you?"

She closed her eyes briefly, and a bone-deep shudder traveled through her body and into mine. When she opened them again, I had my answer.

I pulled her against me again, hugging her even more fiercely. My wolf was growling, her rage just as complete as mine. "I'm sorry, Octavia." My voice was a rasping whisper. "I should have had them locked up with Troy. Or killed."

"I know you would've. If I'd asked that from you, or if I'd told you the truth sooner, maybe they would still be in prison. Maybe they wouldn't have been able to break Troy out."

"No." I gave a vehement shake of my head. "That is not your fault. There's no time limit on when you feel comfortable telling someone about this. You have done nothing wrong. Do you hear me?" Tears burned behind my eyes. "You've done nothing wrong."

She wept against my shoulder, and we sank to the floor, clinging to each other. I didn't know how long we stayed locked together on the floor, but eventually, the tears slowed, and Tavi's breathing no longer came in such quick, desperate pants.

"Don't tell Dom or Night," she whispered. "Please. You're the only one I've talked to about this. I think Violet has a pretty good idea, but I haven't...you know..."

Now that she was calmer, I risked pulling back a second time so I could look at her. "Of course. I understand. This doesn't leave this room. I swear on my life."

She nodded and let me go so she could run the backs of her hands over her wet eyes. We were sitting close to the desk, so I reached up to grab one of the tissue boxes. My legs ached from being on the floor, but I could endure much more than slight discomfort for Tavi.

She blew her nose. "I can't ask Dom to wait for me," she murmured. "What if I'm never ready to be his mate?"

"Then you and he can stay friends." I pushed her hair behind her ear. "But he did say that he's willing to wait for you. I believe he meant it."

"But he could change his mind. He could find another woman he wants to be with. His soulmate could be out there waiting for him."

"I think it's safe to put a little faith in him, isn't it?"

She shivered, then nodded almost imperceptibly.

"There's so much going on right now. All you can do is take things one day at a time," I told her. "That's all anyone can ask of you. It's okay not to have an answer for this."

She nodded, took a deep breath, and then nodded again. "Okay." She sighed. "Okay." She blew her nose again, then wiped her face. "Thanks, Bryn."

"You don't have to thank me." I smiled. "This is the least I can do for you."

She returned my smile, then pulled me in for another hug. I didn't know what the future held for Dom and Tavi, but something told me I should follow my own advice and not worry too much about it. Things would work out the way they were meant to, and as long as they were happy, I would be, too.

But now I was even more desperate to find Troy, Samson, and Harlon. I wanted them to pay dearly for what they'd done. I wanted to make sure they spent every day of their lives cursing the day they touched my best friend.

Chapter 31 - Night

The morning of the alpha challenge, I was pumped and ready to take on the day. Bryn, however, was a nervous wreck. She'd already thrown up twice, and her hands trembled. Worry for me was written all over her face. Even when I held her and kissed her and assured her everything would be fine, it was impossible for her to relax.

"Don't worry about me," she said when I asked her a third time whether she wanted me to make her some peppermint tea. "I know that this will pass once all this is over. When you're in the ring, don't even think about me. Just focus on winning and making it out in one piece."

I kissed her temple. "I could never stop worrying about you, love." I kissed her forehead. "Just like you can't help tearing yourself up about me." I kissed her lips. "I know you'll be like this until it's over, but I promise I'll be okay. I promise."

It pained me to see her so upset, but nothing I could say would make it easier on her. My actions would be much better at convincing her she had nothing to worry about. The only thing I could do was go and prove to her that her worries were unnecessary. After today, I would make this broken pack a safe place for Bryn and our baby.

I kissed her again. "Hey, do you mind cutting my hair before we go out?" I ran a hand through it. It was still a bit damp from the shower I'd taken the night before. "It hasn't been this long in years."

As I'd hoped, that distracted her a bit. "That's funny."

"What is?"

"The idea of you taking a shower hours before you'll inevitably get dirtier than I've ever seen you."

I smirked. "To be honest, Bryn, the shower was for your benefit more than mine. It's not a bad tactic to not bathe for days or weeks before a battle. That way, you distract or even confuse your opponent with your smell."

She made a horrified expression.

I laughed. "I don't need to rely on those sorts of techniques, but I figured you'd want me as clean as possible while we shared a bed."

"You figured right." She smacked me on her way to her vanity and patted the stool. "Sit, sit."

I took the seat and combed my hair back before she grabbed her scissors. My wolf purred, and I blinked slowly from the soothing feeling. This was the first time she played with my hair like this, and it was so relaxing I could almost fall asleep.

But all too soon, it was over.

"What do you think?" she asked. "I know you like the sides shaved, but I don't have clippers."

I ran my fingers through my hair, mussing it a bit. She was right that it wasn't quite my preferred style, but it was far from bad. In fact, it looked great. For my purposes, which was to keep my hair out of my eyes, she'd gone above and beyond. Now I'd not only claim the alpha spot in front of every King who'd ever doubted us, but I'd also look good doing it.

In the mirror, I saw her chewing her lip as if waiting for me to say it was the worst hairstyle ever. I pulled her into my lap and kissed her. "I love it. Thank you."

She let out a breath of relief. "I'm glad. I've never cut a man's hair before."

"That's good to hear. Because from this point on, I'm the only man who gets to feel your fingers running through it."

She giggled. "What about Dom?"

"Fuck, no," I said, nuzzling her ear.

She giggled harder. "But he's my own flesh and blood."

"So what?" I maneuvered her so she was straddling me. "You're my mate, and I'll fight the next man you do this for. I don't care if it's my beta."

Her laughs turned into little moans as I kissed her neck. We didn't have much time before the challenge, but I didn't care. I wanted her, and I wanted her now.

She leaned back across the countertop, her back pressed to the mirror. I spread her legs and kissed up her thighs toward the prize between them... and paused.

"No panties?" I asked, grinning up at her.

She panted as she looked down at me, her eyes the color of dark smoke with the haze of her lust. "I forgot to put them on..."

"Mmhm." I pushed her skirt further up so I could see her. Her pink slit was wet and glistening. I ran my thumb up and down, getting it slick before I pushed it inside her soft warmth. "Are you sure you weren't anticipating that something like this would happen?"

"N-no," she moaned, her hand gripping the top of her mirror.

"Are you absolutely sure?"

She looked at me and flashed a small smile, the tip of her tongue running along her upper lip. My cock throbbed for her—my mate, the seductress.

I stood, leaning over her as I caught her lips with mine, pushing my thumb slowly in and out. Bryn shivered, arching her back to press more of herself against me.

I left her moaning for me and went down again, this time to taste her. I removed my thumb but replaced it with my mouth. The vanity bumped against the wall as I pulled her legs over my shoulders. She shivered, her thighs pressing against the sides of my head, muffling her gasps and groans. My tongue dipped inside her and then out, lapping at her clit. She throbbed against my tongue. Each lick made her twitch and squeeze against me.

I felt the vibrations of her scream through her legs, and she gripped my hair, tugging, urging me to press harder, to lick more. I knew she was close, but I edged her closer. I sucked her clit, and she jerked once. At the same moment, I slipped a finger inside her again. She shuddered, and the vanity rocked against the wall again. Bryn was dripping for me, so wet that my tongue could hardly keep up.

When she came, her thighs locked around my head, holding me in place while the orgasm shook through her. I'd only intended to give her a little something to hold her over while I fought, but *fuck*, she made it impossible for me to be satisfied with just that.

When the muscles in her thighs stopped jerking, I stood and pressed against her. Digging my fingers into her hips, I pulled her to the edge of the vanity. My teeth were against her throat at the spot where I'd claimed her.

"N-Night," she whimpered.

I growled in response, tearing my pants along the seam so I could be inside her as quickly as possible. My nails sharpened to claws as I gripped her ass and entered her. She cried out, gripping my shoulders.

"Yeeesss," she breathed, raking her nails across my back.

I fucked her, feeling the rush of her blood under my tongue and lips. I could have drawn blood, and I kind of wanted to. She screamed. Anything that remained on top of the vanity slid to the ground as it beat rhythmically against the wall.

I bit her as I came and smelled her blood and mine in the air, just the way it ought to be. When I finally eased my desperate grip, I gazed down at her and found her sleepily satisfied. She ran her fingers through her hair, showing the teeth marks I'd left on her throat.

My heart pounded, and I yearned to sink into her again, but duty called. I'd never been more ready to head into battle.

I tugged on a new pair of pants, then Bryn and I set out for the training ring. By the time we arrived, the marks from our lovemaking had mostly disappeared.

Once we arrived, we separated so I could be at the ring and she could be with Dom, Glenda, Tavi, and Mom. They would keep her calm and protect her if anything crazy happened. Just in case, I had men appointed at key locations around the ring. I wasn't sure how the crowd would handle the challenges, and if their favorite fell, there was no guarantee a few of them wouldn't try something stupid.

Bryn had to be there to announce the new alpha. Had it been up to me, I'd have preferred she not be there at all. She would worry every time I got a scratch or someone landed a punch. I wasn't planning on letting that happen often, but I knew my mate, and even minor injuries would bother her. Not to mention that she wasn't one for violence—at all. It wouldn't be easy for her to watch.

I glanced around me and tried to assess some of the men I'd be competing against. It was obvious who the competitors were because they, like me, were shirtless. I spotted Xavier right away, standing still as a statue, surveying the wolves in attendance like he was already their alpha. I smirked. He was in for a rude awakening.

I tried to find Lance but couldn't see him in the crowd. *"Dom, do you see Lance anywhere?"*

It was a couple of moments before Dom responded. *"I don't."*

Of course. It shouldn't have mattered, but it annoyed me that I didn't know Lance's exact location. It seemed that asshole could pop up and dip out without detection, which was beyond aggravating.

"I'm sure he'll make an appearance soon enough," Dom said.

I took a few deep breaths and nodded to myself. Dom was right, and it wouldn't do me any good to get pissed off before the fight even started.

The elders and the council members arrived, and a few other challengers showed up. Lance wasn't among them. I frowned, meeting Dom's eyes through the crowd. His face mirrored my surprise. After talking all that shit and acting weird around Bryn, Lance wasn't even participating? Why not?

No need to lose your head, Night, I told myself. *This just makes for an easier win.* There were only ten fighters, including myself, with Xavier the biggest threat. It was the best-case scenario, but I couldn't shake the feeling that I'd been denied a real challenge.

"Will the fighters please line up along the west side of the arena?" Bryn's voice, clear as the sweetest bell, sounded over the crowd.

We did. And again, I wasn't too impressed with my competition. Xavier stood with his arms crossed, already assured of his win.

Councilman Grant stepped forward and announced, "We nominate Xavier Chase for the alpha challenge."

Xavier stepped into the center of the ring, and the crowd went wild, screaming and chanting his name. He raised his fist, eliciting even more cheers from the crowd. It was obvious he wasn't just the council's pick; most of the pack was rooting for him. Some undoubtedly liked him for his strength and violence, but it was likely that the majority feared him and didn't want to oppose him when his supporters were around.

I sneered. We'd see how well he fared.

The first challenger went up, ready to fight. The battle began, and within a minute, Xavier had him face-down on the ground, blood spurting into the dirt from the pulp that his face had become.

A pair of wolves dragged the body out of the ring. The next challenger didn't hesitate; he sprinted at Xavier, obviously relying on the fact that he was smaller and more agile than the older wolf. He got in a couple of jabs, but when he went in for his big punch, Xavier caught him by the neck. A revolting crack reached my ears as Xavier crushed the man's neck. He dropped the corpse, and it fell to the ground like a broken toy.

The next challenger came, more hesitant, which worked against him. Xavier went on the offense so quickly that the wolf could do nothing as he tackled him to the ground. The wolf raised his hands to protect his face and head, but it didn't matter. Xavier brought his fists down over and over again, sickening crunch after sickening crunch.

There were those in the crowd who couldn't hide their disgust at the overt, unnecessary violence. This body was dragged away, too. Blood coated the ground and splattered across the ring. Xavier stared openly at me, then raised his bloody hand and pointed.

"Shepherd," he growled.

My wolf's menacing growl had a bloodthirsty grin forming on my face. Neither of us was intimidated in the least.

I stepped into the ring and readied myself for whatever Xavier had planned. This was an ideal situation: he had easily dispatched those poor wolves ahead of me, which got the crowd geared up for his win. All the while, he remained in top form. By the end of this, no one could say I'd cheated or taken advantage of the fact that he was tired because he'd made a show of how healthy and fit he was.

The crowd was chanting his name and screaming for my death. I would have laughed if I didn't think that would be overdoing it. Now was my chance to bring everything crashing down on him.

We approached each other, fists raised. There was nothing fancy about it—we traded a few punches, testing each other's strength. That was how it was at first—until out of the corner of my eye, I saw his bloody fist headed right for my head. *This is their champion?* Slapping it away, I enjoyed watching his eyes widen in shock as the momentum carried him toward me. *What a fucking joke!* I raised my knee, and he drilled himself onto it. I felt the air leave his lungs.

Xavier fell to his knees, gasping and coughing as spittle flew from his mouth. The crowd quieted somewhat, people glancing at each other, eyebrows knitted. The only opportunity they'd had to see me fight was with Troy. They must have expected me to be just as weak as I was then.

I glanced down as Xavier screamed. He ripped through his clothes as he shifted, angrier now than I'd ever seen him, his hackles raised. Xavier tackled me, his claws digging into my chest, but I'd shifted by the time we hit the ground. My wolf let out a guttural roar and kicked him away. I hopped to my feet, sprinting for him.

His sharp teeth gleamed in the sunlight. Xavier was strong and bulky, but when we met in the middle of the ring, he couldn't push me back. Bellowing his frustration, he nipped at my throat, desperate to get my fur in his jaws. Ducking those snapping jowls, I took a page from my mate's fighting playbook and got my head under his belly.

I bucked, and he flew through the air with a surprised yelp. He crashed to the ground with a thud. The tide shifted in the crowd. Those who were screaming for Xavier to kill me were drowned out by my pack's cheers. My blood thrummed powerfully through my body, and I'd never felt stronger in my life.

Xavier struggled to his feet, his breath so hot that it fogged at his salivating mouth. He'd landed on his right leg. He couldn't put any weight on it. Time to stop playing with him and end this.

I rushed him, no longer in the mood to drag this out. Claws out, he pawed at me, scratching my shoulder as I tackled him. I barely felt it. I opened my mouth and slammed my jaws over his throat. His yelp of pain and surprise cut off when I thrashed my head once, breaking his neck. His head thumped lifelessly to the ground when I released him.

A deafening silence fell over the crowd. I threw my head back, and my howl echoed over the arena and spread to every corner of the King compound. I lowered my head and glared at the five remaining challengers. I stepped forward, growling as Xavier's coppery blood dripped from my teeth. The intent was clear: *Come at me if you fucking dare!*

They raised their hands and backed slowly away from the side of the ring. I turned my gaze to the rest of the crowd, laying the same offer at their feet. The slightly sour scent of fear tinged the air. That was all the answer I needed.

I shifted back into my human form, turning slowly to look over the crowd. Finally, I spotted Lance standing at the tree line. Our eyes met for a few seconds, and he turned away. He was declining my invitation to meet in the ring. Not because he was afraid; no, whatever his plans were, fighting with me wasn't part of it. At least, not for the position of alpha. I was reminded of that seething disappointment I'd felt at the beginning of the alpha challenge. I stared after him until I couldn't see him anymore. Whatever it took, I would figure out what his deal was—even if it killed him.

With no one to challenge me, Bryn spoke again. "Kings pack," she announced, "Witness your new alpha: Night Shepherd!"

My wolves and my family swarmed the arena, their words of congratulations drowned by their tears and whoops of victory.

A grinning Dom handed me my pants. "Never doubted you for a minute, Night."

I smirked and pulled on the pants milliseconds before Bryn threw herself at me. Stumbling back, I managed to catch her, laughing as she peppered my face with kisses. Her relief—as well as her dizzying waves of joy and pride—washed over me.

A lot needed to be done from this point forward, but I was looking forward to building the pack my wolves deserved. The Kings the world had known had died with Xavier, and in its place, I would build an empire that would prosper.

The future was here, and I couldn't wait to get started.

Printed in Great Britain
by Amazon